W9-AHB-953

Dear Reader,

I've been editing and reading erotic romance for a decade and have long been a fan of the authors who can create stories that are both romantic and sizzling hot. I have a few key requirements for erotic romance: the sexual tension has to be off the charts, the relationship consensual and the ending mutually satisfying (for both the characters and me!). I want to believe in the strength of the characters' relationship long after I've read the last page. If an author also adds in BDSM elements to their story...well, then you have the perfect erotic romance!

So I'm thrilled that we're able to bring three of my favorite BDSM novellas from the Carina Press erotic romance collection together in this one print anthology. The authors of these novellas have all combined the elements I'm looking for in each of their respective stories to create steamy, romantic, wonderful tales that will help leave you with that good-book feeling.

Our title story, *The Theory of Attraction* by Delphine Dryden, is perhaps the first self-described erotic "nerd-mance" and has received astounding rave reviews, including the July 2012 *RT Book Reviews* Seal of Excellence. In this novella, Cami discovers there can be more pleasure than she ever imagined in submitting... *A Shot in the Dark* is part of Christine d'Abo's successful erotic romance Long Shots series. Firefighter by day, Dom by night, sexy Carter longs to convince Paige to submit to happiness. In *Forbidden Fantasies* by Jodie Griffin, a married couple learns that the spark doesn't need to die after fifteen years of marriage. Their fantasies are brought to life during a special weekend at a unique B and B—Bondage and Breakfast.

Three very different stories, but all three deliver the heat and then bring it up a notch! I hope you enjoy these stories as much as I have, and that you'll visit www.carinapress.com to check out more of our erotic romance and BDSM offerings.

We love to hear from readers, and you can email us your thoughts, comments and questions to generalinquiries@carinapress.com. You can also interact with Carina Press staff and authors on our blog, Twitter stream and Facebook fan page.

Happy reading!

~Angela James

Executive Editor, Carina Press

www.carinapress.com
www.twitter.com/carinapress
www.facebook.com/carinapress

DELPHINE DRYDEN

After earning two graduate degrees, practicing law awhile, then working for the public school system for more than ten years, Delphine finally got a clue. She tossed all that aside and started doing what she should have been doing all along—writing steamy novels!

When not writing or doing "mommy stuff," Del reads voraciously, noodles around designing websites and plays computer games with her darling (and very romantic) husband. She is fortunate enough to have two absurdly precocious children and two delightful mutts. Del and her family are all Texas natives, and reside near Houston in unapologetic suburban bliss.

CHRISTINE D'ABO

Multipublished author Christine d'Abo loves exploring the human condition through a romantic lens. A self-professed optimist, romantic and sci-fi junkie, Christine can often be found chatting about her favorite shows and movies. When she's not writing, she's chasing after her children, dogs or husband.

Christine is published with Carina Press, Ellora's Cave, Samhain Publishing, Cleis Press and Berkley Books. Please visit her at her website, www.christinedabo.com, and come chat with her on Twitter @Christine_dAbo.

Also by Christine d'Abo:
Double Shot
Pulled Long
Calling the Shots

JODIE GRIFFIN

Jodie has always been a reader, but she didn't always want to be a writer. She'd spend hours reading, but school papers were written one painful word at a time, and *never* over required word count. Then, one ordinary day, something changed. A story idea came, demanding to be put on paper. She resisted at first, but the wicked muse refused to leave her alone. After several years of practice, she took the leap and submitted her first story—and hasn't looked back since.

Jodie's own happily-ever-after includes one incredibly supportive husband, one future heroine and two kitties who keep her company as she writes. She works a full-time technical job and does her writing late in the evenings, on weekends and sometimes even in the office cafeteria during her lunch hour—which can be interesting if she's working on a love scene. *Forbidden Fantasies* is her first published work.

Also by Jodie Griffin:
Forbidden Desires

the

theory

of

attraction

DELPHINE DRYDEN

with stories from

CHRISTINE D'ABO

JODIE GRIFFIN

CARINA
PRESS™

If you purchased this book without a cover you should be aware
that this book is stolen property. It was reported as "unsold and
destroyed" to the publisher, and neither the author nor the
publisher has received any payment for this "stripped book."

CARINA
PRESS™

Recycling programs
for this product may
not exist in your area.

ISBN-13: 978-0-373-00204-7

THE THEORY OF ATTRACTION

Copyright © 2012 by Carina Press

The publisher acknowledges the copyright holders of the individual works as follows:

THE THEORY OF ATTRACTION
Copyright © 2012 by Delphine Dryden

A SHOT IN THE DARK
Copyright © 2011 by Christine d'Abo

FORBIDDEN FANTASIES
Copyright © 2012 by Jodie Griffin

All rights reserved. Except for use in any review, the reproduction or
utilization of this work in whole or in part in any form by any electronic,
mechanical or other means, now known or hereafter invented, including
xerography, photocopying and recording, or in any information storage
or retrieval system, is forbidden without the written permission of the
publisher, Harlequin Enterprises Limited, 225 Duncan Mill Road,
Don Mills, Ontario M3B 3K9, Canada.

This is a work of fiction. Names, characters, places and incidents are
either the product of the author's imagination or are used fictitiously, and any
resemblance to actual persons, living or dead, business establishments, events or
locales is entirely coincidental.

This edition published by arrangement with Harlequin Books S.A.

® and TM are trademarks of the publisher. Trademarks indicated with
® are registered in the United States Patent and Trademark Office, the Canadian
Trade Marks Office and in other countries.

www.CarinaPress.com

Printed in U.S.A.

contents

the theory of attraction

Delphine Dryden

acknowledgments

Fervent thanks to Christine for the unflagging enthusiasm, and to Ruthie whose critique came with extra heaping helpings of love for this particular hero.

Chapter One

The weather forecast called for a high of ninety-nine degrees. Again.

Still two digits, though, no big deal for Houston in August. It felt like melting when you stepped outside, but you were just supposed to pretend like it was not all *that* hot. People would assure you they'd known much, much worse.

It wasn't all bad. Hot enough to wilt the lettuce I'd attempted to grow in the backyard, but at least the roses were thriving. I could see them from my computer desk, nodding their pink and crimson heads in a stray breeze. And then a shadow crossed them, blocking their light. Standing up for a better view, I saw my neighbor Ivan heading out for his run.

This told me it was six-thirty, and I needed to stop checking work email from home and get dressed, so I could go into work and continue to check email from there.

I didn't bother to check the clock, because Ivan was better than a clock. Over the past two years I'd learned his routines until I thought I could probably tell you his location at just about any moment of any day. Not that I'm a stalker. But Ivan loves routine the way some guys love football.

He glanced up at my window and gave a nod and wave, which I returned as I did every weekday morning. I wasn't awake that early on weekend mornings, although I knew Ivan still went for his run at the same time. Six-thirty in the morning, out for a run each and every day. He took one of three routes, which I knew because I drove past him most mornings on my way to work. One path was for Mondays through Thursdays. He ran a different route on Fridays, and another still on the weekends, to account for differing traffic patterns so his time stayed consistent.

One week, that's all any good stalker would need to get the entire scoop on Dr. Ivan Reynolds, rocket scientist. But I doubt anyone would ever want to stalk Ivan. Well, maybe if he won a Nobel Prize or something. He's very much an acquired taste, and it took me a good year at least to realize I'd acquired it.

The first time I realized Ivan was sexy, he was being an asshole and then a hero.

We were in my apartment, where Ivan seemed to spend an awful lot of time for somebody who claimed not to like being around people. But I liked to cook, and there were a lot of hungry geeks in the complex, so my apartment had become kind of a social hub. Even Ivan seemed to appreciate the food, although in this instance he was more focused on wondering why the astrophysics department had to have a start-of-the-school-year party.

"It's supposed to help you get to know your colleagues better," I said. I had my head under the sink, looking for the scrubbing cleanser, so I had to listen hard for his answer.

"But I already know my colleagues. And anybody new, I'll meet soon enough. They're people I work with every day. Why am I expected to spend my valuable free time with them as well? And expend social energy on what should just be a crowd of work-related acquaintances?" He asked me these types of questions because my degree was in social anthropology, although I spent my days now writing computer scripts. Ivan's idea of a good party involved bringing your own computer gaming equipment and Cheetos, then staying up all night virtually shooting your friends.

"Because it's fun?" I suggested. "You get to loosen up a little, just for one night. Besides, most people don't really consider social energy to be a finite resource. Partying is not a zero-sum equation."

I hadn't always sounded like these guys. But after a year or so living in a townhouse complex populated almost entirely by astrophysicists and computer scientists, you started to pick up the terminology whether you liked it or not. The demographic was due to the fact that most of us worked at the nearby university, and our complex was close to the science buildings. Generally I liked it, because the guys showed me all the cheat codes for computer games, and at least I always knew I had a bunch of willing protectors if my apartment ever got robbed or anything.

"I don't consider it finite," Ivan said. "But it's certainly not infinite. And there's already enough social obligation surrounding holidays without adding it in at other times. What's that smell?"

"I have no idea, I can only smell the ant spray from yesterday. Damn. Where's that new can of cleaner?"

"It's in your bathroom. Under the left-hand side of the

counter, behind the trash can. It shouldn't be stored so close to the ammonia-based cleaners."

I narrowly missed cracking my skull as I pulled out of the cabinet. "You moved it?"

"Yes. You always leave the top open instead of sealing it up. There's chlorine-based powder everywhere. The ammonia cleaner is in a glass bottle. One wrong move and you could have a cloud of toxic gas."

"Oh, for—don't move my cleaning products anymore, all right? I'll take my chances on the chlorine gas. Jeez. You're right. Is that smoke?"

"It's the bacon."

Fuck.

I turned right when he said it to see the first flames flickering up toward the vent hood. It flared out in a big eyebrow-searing fluff, and all I could think for one second was that the noise sounded exactly like in the movies, sort of a ruffling tearing sound.

"Dammit! Um, baking soda, right?" In the fridge. I had some in the fridge. Right on the other side of the stove, next to the searing flames. So, the pantry was a safer bet and there was probably an old box in there somewhere. I yanked the door to the tiny pantry open, nearly clobbering Ivan with my elbow as he scooted past me on his way to the stove and braved the heat to turn the burner off.

His movements were precise, economical. Without even pausing, he swept the pots-and-pans cabinet open, grabbed the correct lid first time, and slammed the thing down on the flaming skillet with an ear-jarring clang, sliding it off the hot burner at the same time.

And just like that, the flames were contained. Only the

smoke pouring downward from the rattling lid indicated the blaze that had threatened my kitchen moments before.

The smoke, and the quiet but vehement cursing from Ivan as he stood at my sink, running cold water over his reddened wrist.

"Fuck, fuck, fuck," he muttered, bouncing slightly on his toes.

"Oh, shit!" I cried, any more articulate response failing me as I abandoned my search for baking soda and concentrated on my singed hero. "How bad is it? What do you need me to do?"

He held up his free hand as if fending me off. "Nothing. It's fine, I'm fine. It's a first-degree burn at worst. Are you all right?"

"I think I can see a blister." I pointed at the offending patch of skin, and Ivan looked down at his arm as though it belonged to somebody else. Somebody he wasn't thrilled with at the moment.

"It's fine," he said with a bit less certainty. "Are you all right, Camilla?"

"I'm fine, it just scared me. Let me get the first aid kit," I said, relieved to remember I had one in the bathroom, on a shelf in the linen closet, right where it should be.

"Get yourself a tissue while you're back there," he suggested as I ran to fetch the kit.

Until he said it, I didn't even realize I was crying. Most likely from the smoke, I assured myself.

It didn't take long to realize the first aid kit was only going to offer a temporary solution. So I drove Ivan to the emergency room and sat with him for three hours until they got around to treating the burn. Then I brought him home and fixed him dinner at his place as his pain pills began to take effect. He didn't make a single snide remark about trusting me not to burn down his kitchen—not that night, anyway. I refrained from pointing out that if somebody hadn't moved my cleaning supplies without telling me, I wouldn't have been distracted from the bacon for so long in the first place.

It was a really nice dinner. Pork chops, rice and zucchini. And maybe it was the drugs that made Ivan slow down enough to taste the food, but he actually seemed to enjoy it. I'd never seen him so much as tipsy before, so seeing him lose even a fraction of his usual control to the pain medication was fascinating. A kinder, gentler Ivan. An Ivan who said my pork chops were delicious, and who asked if I would stay to watch *Doctor Who* with him. I did; he fell asleep about five minutes into the show.

But I was still thinking back to the Ivan who had marched into my kitchen earlier in the day and calmly, brilliantly, handled the crisis. He didn't like breaks in his routine, but he could apparently be counted on in an emergency. And he'd really been pretty stoic during the hospital visit.

My reclusive, geeky neighbor had just morphed into the strong, silent type. It was a stunning revelation.

The fact that a spell of record high temperatures meant Ivan had spent the previous week jogging with his shirt off certainly had no influence on my perception of him. Even if I had just discovered that he was my own personal piece of secret eye candy, it was the quiet heroism that really made me view him in a new light.

The problem with Ivan was that he didn't seem aware I was female. Much less an available, interested female. He treated me pretty much like he treated everybody else—with exacting, rigid standards, a demand for clinical precision and hardly any manners at all. He was patient in some ways, like teaching people how to do things, whether in the classroom, on the computer or in the lab. But he was horribly impatient in others, like waiting for the group to finish deciding on a restaurant and get in the damn car already. And he did not take criticism well, no matter how constructive.

So I was less than thrilled with his proposition, when he first made it.

"I need you to help socialize me."

"Say what?"

He frowned at the slang. "To help socialize me. Make me more…social. I need you to show me how to do that."

It was out of the blue, and almost a year after that fateful bacon fire incident. We were silently, innocently gardening in our adjacent plots in the common backyard our four duplex buildings shared. Me working on my dead lettuce and flourishing roses, and Ivan fiddling with his tomato plants. Because it was a weekend day, at nine to nine-thirty in the morning, when gardening chores took place in the world of Ivan.

"I think I need more information here." I thrust the trowel into the dirt near a lettuce with a satisfying crunch and levered the dead bunch out by the roots.

Ivan sighed in exasperation and dumped the rest of a measuring cup of water on one of the tomato plants that was hanging upside-down from a wooden stand he'd constructed for that purpose. Each of his four plants was planted differently, because he was conducting some kind of experiment on them. Whatever he was doing, the tomatoes looked obscenely healthy.

"I need to be able to go to a party where there are other professionals in my field and other potential donors, talk to them and make them want to give substantial amounts of money to the university to fund my research. Well," he corrected himself, "the department's research. But my own motivation is obviously selfish, as I really only care about my own project being funded."

"O…kay." I stalled for a few seconds before responding, and uprooted another doomed head of lettuce. "You might want to start with not saying what you just said out loud, about your motivation. Only a thought."

He frowned again. He was only twenty-nine, one year older than me, but he already had a semi-permanent frown line between his eyes. It ran vertically, an exclamation point punctuating his annoyed glare.

"Well, it's true."

"But it's not very nice. And you admit that it's selfish."

"Lies of omission are still lies. I'll never understand why people do that." He checked his watch. It was probably time for him to go inside, have a high-protein snack and spend two hours and fifteen minutes in front of the computer playing first-person shooter games.

We were getting off the topic a bit too rapidly.

"So you want lessons in how to act at a fundraiser, basically?"

Ivan cocked his head and then nodded. "That's essentially it."

It was a chance to spend an awful lot of time with him. In a masochistic way, that sounded intriguing to me. I was hot for him, for whatever reason, and this would certainly put me in a position to gain his attention.

On the other hand, it would be time spent giving him instruction and constructive criticism in an area I myself probably didn't excel in, and one that was also his bête noir. I wasn't sure I was quite *that* masochistic.

Ivan lifted the hem of his shirt to his face, mopping the

sweat from his decidedly elegant brow and revealing his six-pack abs in the process. His khaki cargo shorts were low-slung enough to frame his hips nicely. About an inch below his belly button, a dark trail of hair began a journey down to—

"So will you do it?" He was mumbling through the fabric, still wiping his face.

"Huh?"

He dropped the shirt back into place, cutting off the distraction. "Will you do it? Teach me how to…whatever?"

"Oh. Um, when is this shindig?"

"In three weeks. Right before the students get back."

Three weeks. I could work with that. Maybe.

"I'd have carte blanche? And you won't get mad at me for telling you to do stuff you think is stupid?"

Stupid was me, believing he could follow through on a promise like that. But for all his rough points, he was still a hero. A tomato-growing, fire-fighting, shirtless-jogging hero. And all that could blind a girl.

He promised not to get mad, and I promised to meet with him for daily sessions in fundraiser etiquette starting that night.

"Oh, and can I also have a few tomatoes? As an advance?" I figured it didn't hurt to ask. They looked so delicious, even the ones that were not quite ripe. And I loved fried green tomatoes.

"You can have all you want. Just tell me how many you take and from which plant. I won't eat them, I don't like tomatoes."

I blinked at him, and then eyed the four lush plants with their juicy, curvaceous, ready and nearly ready fruit weighing down the slender green branches. Enough for pots and pots of sauce, for salads and fried green tomatoes and bruschetta and *pico de gallo* made with the garlic and cilantro I'd managed to keep alive long enough to harvest.

"Then why—"

"It's just an experiment."

Interruptions would have to be on the list of social nice-ties to address. "All right, then. You don't get mad and I get all the tomatoes I can eat. And we start at dinner tonight?"

He thrust his slightly grubby hand forward. "Deal."

I slipped my even grimier hand into his and we shook, then stood there for a moment with hands still clasped. Ivan was taller than I was by almost a head, and he was backlit by the morning sun so I couldn't see his expression. But I could feel the warmth of his earthy grip, the strength in his long fingers, and a shiver raced down my spine with even that small contact.

"Deal."

Chapter Two

My friend Athena had a theory about Ivan. It was the latest in a series of theories she'd had about him.

The first one had been simply "Gay."

She usually assumed this about any man who didn't seem interested in her boobs. Giving credit where it was due, she had a fabulous rack, but I didn't think that was the issue in this particular instance.

"Maybe he's just not a breast man."

"He doesn't check out my ass, either," she countered.

"Could you love yourself a little more, please? Maybe he's into eyes. Or a sense of humor or something. Foot fetish. I don't know. He doesn't seem to look at any of the guys that way, either. And some of them are really pretty hot when they're not talking."

"Mmm," she agreed. "Dinesh."

"Indeed."

"Those eyes. Those lips!"

I nodded. "If Ivan were gay he'd be all over that. I mean, wouldn't you be?"

Dinesh lived in the duplex at the far end of the row. He and his wife, Julia, were both quite beautiful, and both did some sort of work analyzing rodent genomes. I found them spectacular but almost unnerving, like they were actually a slightly more evolved species that was simply prettier and smarter than humans. Julia was the only other woman in the complex. Athena lived a few blocks away.

"Maybe," Athena posited, swirling her wine around in its glass as we sat in front of my computer that afternoon, "he simply prefers porn. I mean, think about it, Cami. He spends all his time on the computer, and we all know what guys do on there most of the time. Maybe he's addicted to that and the real thing doesn't measure up."

I couldn't even picture Ivan surfing for porn. If anything, I suspected his browser history at home looked exactly like his browser history at work. With the likely exceptions of sites featuring in-depth mathematical discussions of Halo strategies and the technical details of people's creations in Minecraft.

"If he does look at porn, he does it on a schedule. And I don't know of any unaccounted-for chunks of time that he spends at home. Unless it's weekly or monthly, and it's at a time when I'm not at home but he is." I was only half paying attention to Athena, because most of my attention was focused on the monitor. I was researching etiquette, about which I knew precious little myself. And trying to come up with some sort of plan for that night's "lesson," not to mention the next three weeks' worth. But I noticed her protracted silence after a bit and looked away from the screen to find her giving me a *look*. "What?"

"Stalker."

"Neighbor."

We'd had that talk before.

"I still do not see the attraction. I mean yes, he's hot, but only in the abstract because he's not actually a human being. And you only like him because you think he's Mr. Darcy."

I took offense. Not only was Athena disparaging one of my favorite books, she was knocking my comparison of Ivan to a young, slender Colin Firth. Another talk we'd had before.

"How can somebody be hot in the abstract? And I don't think he's Mr. Darcy, because Mr. Darcy was not a scientist. Completely different personality. But it doesn't matter. I just want to do the guy. Does there have to be a reason?"

The truth was, I did liken Ivan to Mr. Darcy. But only to Darcy before his transformation to a kinder, more considerate self. It was the cool, disdainful yet commanding Darcy that floated my boat. And Darcy was indeed a scientist in his way, studying human nature while being at times every bit as baffled by it as Ivan was. Because so much about human nature didn't lend itself to methodical study.

"I loaned you the ho-ho-ho dress last Christmas. If that didn't turn his head I'm out of ideas. That thing is pretty much the nuclear option."

"I don't look as much like a ho in it as all that." We wore the same size, but I was a bit taller than Athena, and flat in all the places she was curvy. The dress had looked okay and had turned more than one head. Sadly, none of those heads were attached to the body of the aloof and indifferent Dr. Reynolds.

"So is this like a date, tonight?"

"I don't think anything could possibly be further from a date than whatever we're doing tonight."

At least I was right about one thing. It was nothing like a date.

If it had been a date, it would have had to rank with the all-time lame dates in history. Beginning with the way Ivan looked when I answered the door to his ring, promptly at seven.

He was wearing the shorts he'd been gardening in and a pair of boat shoes so decrepit I didn't know how they stayed on his feet. He'd changed into a polo shirt of a particularly hideous neon aqua, and it was threadbare not only at the collar but around the little logo on the chest.

His hair wasn't combed.

On the plus side, the shirt made his eyes look fantastic, somehow playing up warmer, softer highlights in the dark chocolate brown of his irises.

Then he frowned, which shouldn't have surprised me at that point. He was holding out a bottle of wine, and I hadn't even noticed because I was too busy mooning over his eyes.

"Thanks! Come on in."

"Don't thank me," Ivan said, breezing past me. "It's Ed's wine, I was just carrying it for him."

Sure enough, our neighbor Ed was right behind Ivan, his hands full of computer equipment.

"Ivan said you guys were watching *Young Frankenstein* tonight. I love that flick."

Ed was already in the apartment, settling in on my couch next to Ivan with his laptop on the coffee table in front of him. I closed the door and joined them, trying to hide my pique. My big chance to get Ivan alone and talking to me about human interaction over a cozy dinner, and *that* was the moment Ed happened by? Ivan rolled his eyes when I threw him a questioning glance.

"And the computer is also here because...?"

"I'm at work," Ed explained. He was already arranging cables, pulling the power cord from the pile and looking for the closest outlet. "I'm monitoring something."

"Oh. Do you need to use my wireless, or can you get yours this far away from your place?"

"I can get mine. But Ivan already gave me the key to yours."

Another eye roll and a shrug from Mr. Inscrutable on the far end of the couch.

Lesson One: when invited to a person's home, don't bring along an unexpected plus one.

If Ivan even knew what a *plus one* was. Probably not. I couldn't picture him at a wedding. Or a formal dinner. Honestly, had he been raised by wolves? Erudite, scientifically inclined wolves? I pictured a cave littered with test tubes and beakers, computers and model rockets. And little baby Ivan, toddling around in a diaper while the wolves conducted their experiments. This, despite the fact that I'd actually met the man's parents on more than one occasion.

Focus, Cami.

I didn't really see any way out of it. Ed was only doing what most of the guys in the complex did from time to time. They worked together, they played together, they hung out with one another as though their homes were interchangeable. And up until tonight, my place had always been another one of those hangouts. Besides, I suspected Ivan would rather not broadcast his real reason for coming over. Which was probably why he hadn't sent Ed packing in the first place.

"I made lasagna. Who's in?"

Both guys raised their hands. Ivan got up to start the movie. I'd pulled out the DVD already, because I'd planned for us to watch it as part of the lesson.

"Hey," Ed called as I walked into the kitchen, "could I maybe get a glass for my wine? I'm drinking one glass every night. It's an experiment."

He didn't want to share the bottle, though. Because then,

Ed explained, he would have to go back to the liquor store a day sooner than he'd planned. It was not on his way home from work, and of course it was a brand not carried by the local grocery store.

Yes, the evening was off to a rip-roaring start.

By the time the monster came to life on screen, we'd picked up an additional viewer. Lin, another astrophysicist post-doc, had happened by looking for Ivan and stayed to watch the rest of the movie. And to help finish the lasagna, of course.

I'd taught zero lessons in socialization. Ivan hadn't said a word the whole evening, aside from thanking me for dinner. When the movie ended, I got the impression he was willing Ed and Lin to leave just as hard as I was. But our combined psychic abilities were no match for the cluelessness of these two particular geeks, who remained on my couch arguing about Mel Brooks and Ed's wine experiment until well after ten.

I tried dropping polite hints, but nothing worked. After several tense moments, I realized I felt tense partly because I had that you're-being-watched feeling.

Ivan was watching me. I wasn't even sure he realized he was doing it. His eyes followed me around the room as I tidied up and tried to convey that general "let's wrap this party up" feeling. Maybe because it was after ten (time to brush teeth), so he was out of his routine, or maybe because he really didn't know what to do, since participating in the conversation would obviously not serve the purpose of getting the other two to leave. But he seemed a little lost, isolated. And he was watching me as intently as though his line of sight were a lifeline. I'd wanted that for months, but getting it made me so self-conscious I wasn't sure what to do with my hands.

Then it passed. Lin finally said something so egregious it pulled Ivan into the argument, and the talk quickly passed over my level of understanding as I'm a computer programmer, a script monkey, not a rocket scientist. I only knew that once they'd reached this stage, any pretense at civility was pointless and if I didn't kick them out they'd be there all night. Two arguing geeks were stoppable. Three arguing geeks created an infinite argument vortex of doom that sucked time down like a black hole.

"Okay, that's it for tonight. Thanks for coming over, but I'm fixing to head for bed."

Three heads snapped my way. Lin had the grace to look a little chagrined. He made a nice apology and headed out, with Ed close on his tail. Before he was all the way out the door, Ed asked Ivan to carry his wine bottle for him.

But perhaps the evening wasn't a complete loss. Ivan turned at the door and, to my astonishment, smiled. A sheepish, crooked smile, but I still counted it. He did it so rarely, it was like seeing a rose that only blooms once a year in the spring.

"Sorry."

I didn't think I'd ever heard him apologize for something before.

"No problem. There was plenty of lasagna. Oh, and the salad was great with all those fresh tomatoes. You can take my word for that."

He hadn't eaten the tomatoes, of course.

"So the lesson for tonight is…I should have lied more?"

"What, to Ed?" I considered this a moment. "Not lied. I wouldn't call it that. There are times when the other person doesn't need all the information you may have to give. I don't think that's really even a lie of omission. It simply isn't their business. You can keep some things to yourself."

"Like only caring about my project being funded?"

"Exactly."

He smiled again. I realized he had a slight dimple on the right side. Charming. He leaned against the jamb of the open door, as though he was a little reluctant to go. The muggy night air was creeping in, probably bringing mosquitos with it. I didn't care.

"If I'd told him the truth and said why I was coming over here, and that I didn't want anybody else here with us, that would have been more effective."

"But he would have known something you didn't want him to know. And knowing Ed, he would have teased you pretty mercilessly about it. He might have also assumed you were lying to get him out of the way."

"Why would I do that?"

I wanted to beat my head against the door. Ivan was either as genuinely clueless as he appeared, or he was simply in no rush to spend time alone with the horny nerd-girl next door. "To get more lasagna for yourself, of course."

"I see. So, same time tomorrow night?"

"A little earlier," I suggested. "If we go out to eat somewhere the guys don't typically go, we'll stand a much better chance of actually accomplishing something."

Ivan answered slowly, and I had to resist reading more meaning into it than he probably meant there to be. "I wouldn't say we accomplished nothing this evening. I wouldn't say that at all." He gave me that intense, concentrated look again, exactly like when he was watching me clean up earlier. A creeping tendril of desire swirled through my belly.

And then he strolled off into the thick, hot night.

At work the next day, it was almost as hot inside as out. Though the temperature had cooled to a mild ninety-four, the ancient and put-upon air conditioning unit in the refurbished hundred-year-old house where I worked had finally conked out for good that weekend, so we'd arrived for the morning to find the house already hot, stuffy and smelling slightly of mildew. There was a slight breeze through the windows we'd all had to pry open, but not enough to help much. Only enough to ruffle the papers I had stacked so neatly on my desk moments before.

No small feat, either, stacking paper neatly when it was that humid. The pages wanted to stick and rub instead of sliding tidily against one another to get in line. Everything felt damp, even the stapler and the surface of my desk. I was covered in sweat. I had shut my computer down around ten, when the heat in the building rose above eighty-five. When my boss, Agatha, finally told us all to give it up and go home for the day, I was too drained to even cheer. We all offered up a feeble mumble of thanks and cleared the building within two minutes flat.

It was only eleven-thirty, and I hadn't eaten. On a whim, I picked up some burgers and headed for the astrophysics lab. Not entirely a whim, actually. The building was notorious for being overcooled, and right now that arctic blast seemed like the perfect antidote to the heat.

Ivan's mother sometimes called me when her worries about her son got the best of her. This had started about six months after I moved into the complex, after Ivan's parents came for a holiday visit and we got to know each other a little. As his nearest neighbor, good friend and the only relatively normal-seeming person in his small social circle, I guess I seemed the likeliest candidate for surrogate mother. That and the whole female thing.

Her concern was not entirely misplaced, because Ivan often forgot to eat when he was involved in a big project, and he'd been known to let himself get to an almost delusional state of hunger before he realized the problem and remedied it. I liked feeding people, and Mrs. Reynolds made it up to me when she came to visit every few months by providing me gourmet treats I couldn't afford to buy all the time on my worker-bee salary. Imported olives, smoked oysters, organic chocolate with a high percentage on the label. And she told me things about Ivan's childhood that I was sure he would rather not have people know. He was a very smart, very poorly adjusted little boy, and she still saw him that way. It wasn't wholly inaccurate, I guess.

Although I wondered if she'd be quite so willing with the information if she knew what I had in mind for her delicate, maladjusted baby. I had a very active imagination and was working on a dry spell of over two years. I'd thought up things I didn't even know the names for.

She'd called me that morning, and I was able to report that Ivan had eaten at least one meal that I knew of (lasagna) and even vegetables (green salad, hold the tomatoes), within the previous twenty-four hours.

The first thing I did when I walked into the lab was disclose that conversation to Ivan. I might be willing to pass along information about the man's eating habits, but no way would I go behind his back to do it.

Ivan, however, never seemed bothered by his mother's behavior. I would have been incensed if my mother called my friends to check up on me. Ivan seemed to take it as a normal part of her parenting style. "She just remembers the time I had to be hospitalized for dehydration and malnourishment during the run-up to a state science fair. Ever since then she gets worried if she thinks I'm working too hard."

"How long ago was that?"

"Twenty-one years."

"Wait…you were *eight?* And she's *still* checking up on you because of this?"

He'd nodded and gone back to staring into his computer monitor like it held the secret to the universe.

It was pretty evident the apple didn't fall far from the tree. However, that knowledge was now completely supplanted by the vision of Ivan running down the street all sweaty and shirtless. These things overrode my concerns about his genetic stability and turned me into a veritable nurturing machine.

So I brought him lunch (which he had indeed skipped that day) and stayed while he ate. He kept working as he munched, and I didn't even know if he tasted the food. I didn't even know if he knew I was alive.

Well, obviously he knew I was alive, in a literal sense. He could see that I was a human being on the planet, he knew all about my physiology, he even knew that I lived in the townhouse next to his. In fact he frequently pointed that out, because he felt my footsteps when I was upstairs were unaccountably loud given my relatively small size for a fully grown human.

He actually stated it that way, "fully grown human." I sometimes wondered if he thought of himself as something other than human. Lord knows I occasionally thought he might well be some sort of alien.

Some sort of weirdly hot, incredibly brilliant alien.

Hopefully not a gay alien, though. Or an alien who was too jaded by porn to be interested in real girls. He had such nice hands. And something about the way he typed, so fast and automatic, struck me as deeply sexy. Or maybe that was the way he had rolled his shirt sleeves up, exposing the lean forearms that I now knew led to surprisingly firm biceps, toned shoulders and beyond. In the summer I was so used to seeing him in shorts and scruffy T-shirts. The button-down made him look like a grownup. A grownup with hands that looked as though they knew their way around more than a keyboard…

"I thought we could try Mark's on Westheimer for dinner."

"Hmm?"

Dragging my eyes from his hands back to his profile, I thought I saw the tail end of a little smirk. But he hadn't been looking my way, so he couldn't have noticed my ogling, could he?

"Mark's. Over near the Montrose?"

"Oh! Um, okay. Isn't that expensive, though?"

"It'll be on me. The least I can do is feed you, especially after last night and considering you also brought me lunch. And I feel pretty safe in thinking that nobody we know will be eating there on a Monday night."

Nobody we knew would be eating there on any night, as far as I knew. Maybe Dinesh and Julia on a major anniversary or something, but that was about it.

"Great. Well, I should be going." To figure out what the hell to wear.

"I'll pick you up at six. The reservation is for six-thirty." He still hadn't looked away from his monitor. I was kind of grateful for that. He didn't see me standing there gaping like an idiot. Nor did he appear to notice as I left. Totally engrossed in work again, all that intense energy directed straight into the theoretical world where his brain spent most of its time.

It wasn't that I hadn't *wanted* to go on dates. In fact, I would have been thrilled to do so. But before I'd lived at the duplex, I'd spent four years living with my last boyfriend. I'd moved out when we split up—because I found out his "business trips" to Dallas were really booty calls, the asshole—and unfortunately he'd gotten most of our friends in the separation of assets. I had come away with most of the books, so I figured I'd really gotten the better end of the deal.

Which probably explained a lot about why, two years later, I was down to scheming to try and get the nearest guy into bed. Literally the nearest. I really didn't know that many people. I'd grown up near Houston, but it was a big town and a lot of my college friends had moved away. It was down to Athena after I moved, and I was lucky to find a new home that came with a ready-made cadre of *Star Trek* and role-playing game enthusiasts, or I'd have been all on my own.

But Ivan was the only one of the bunch I found remotely interesting in a physical way, and I had to wonder if it was primarily because my standards had shifted from so much time out of play. After all, I hadn't even noticed him at first. Except to find him irritating, and rigid, and difficult to converse with. Funny, I could recall feeling that way, but I couldn't remember the last time I'd found him hard to talk to. Though I definitely still found him irritating and rigid at times.

"When did that change?" I mused aloud.

"When did what change?" Athena mumbled from the depths of my closet.

"Have you found anything yet?"

It was five, and Athena was dressing me. She'd insisted, coming straight from work to do so despite my reassurance that I'd been dressing myself for years.

"Maybe. When did what change?"

"Nothing. It's dumb. I was thinking about how I used to find it really hard to talk to Ivan. Because he's, you know—"

"Borderline autistic?"

"—not good with people."

She emerged, flourishing a piece of midnight-blue silki-
ness on a hanger. "Aha! And maybe that changed when he
offered to take you out to one of the most expensive restau-
rants in town?"

"It isn't like that."

"Pfft. For him, maybe. It's obviously like that for you. Although he's the one who asked, so maybe I really have just
been reading him wrong all this time."

"It's not a date," I reminded her. "He only wanted to make
sure we weren't interrupted again. This is important to him."

"Yeah. Why haven't I seen this on you before? This is actually pretty nice." She was holding the dress up against herself,
checking her angles in the full-length mirror on the back of
my closet door. It was something I'd bought a few years ago
on sale but never quite had the nerve or the right lingerie to
wear. Still had the tags on and everything.

"I don't have a bra for it." It had a halter back and was
low-cut enough in front to actually show a little cleavage. I
didn't really do cleavage. What very little I had of it was usually well hidden.

"Put it on."

After fifteen years of friendship I knew better than to argue.
I started taking off my clothes.

A few minutes later, standing in front of the mirror, I had
to agree with Athena. The dress was perfect. It made my
dishwater-blond hair look lighter, my dark gray eyes look almost blue, and didn't even wash out the little bit of tan I still
had from my last trip to Galveston. She'd made me put on
some strappy silver sandals left over from being a bridesmaid
at my cousin Linda's wedding earlier in the year, and now she
was staring critically at my toes.

"We don't have time to get you a pedi. Unfortunately."

"Ivan isn't going to care what my feet look like."

"We haven't established that. You yourself said he might be a foot fetishist. But I'm afraid that a quick coat of polish will have to do. And none of that sparkle crap."

"But what about the bra?" I wasn't wearing one. And I might not have much on top, but I still wasn't going out in public without a bra on. I did have standards.

"Really? The way the fabric is gathered in the front, it's not like you'll have a nipple problem."

"My sternum is showing."

She shook her head in disgust. "Do you want to get laid or not?"

I *did* want to get laid. I wanted that very much.

And so after I had showered and shaved and lotioned and deodorized, I let Athena mess with my hair until it was almost straight but a tiny bit messy in a fashionable way. Then she painted my toenails a deep red, assuring me I would not, in fact, look like a slutty American flag in the dark blue dress with the silver sandals. I even allowed makeup, which I never wear because I always forget to take it off, so I wake up the next morning looking like a hungover raccoon clown.

"You're sure I don't look like a hooker?"

It was nearly six. And Ivan was usually prompt, so I expected his knock at any moment. We were running down to the wire.

"If so, you're a really expensive one. That's a good thing," she insisted. "It's a nice place. You wouldn't want to go on a date there looking like a cheap hooker."

"I don't want to look like any kind of hooker. And it's not a date," I reminded her, wondering why I thought I could kid Athena when I could no longer even kid myself. "It's a social anthropology lesson."

Chapter Three

"What was the moral of the story supposed to be last night?"

"Excuse me?"

He'd done it again, waylaid me with a non sequitur after several minutes of stifling silence in the car. Why had I thought conversations with Ivan were easier now?

"*Young Frankenstein*. You were planning to talk about something to do with social interaction, and that was meant to illustrate your first lesson, I believe."

"Yes. I was going to talk about context and expectations. How certain behaviors, even certain types of language, are perfectly okay in one setting but not in another."

"Am I the monster in this analogy?"

Was that a little smile I saw? Surely not.

"*Anyway*…during the musical number, when the doctor is trying to prove the monster is sophisticated, what do you think makes it funny?"

He pondered for a moment. "Not the monster singing and dancing. That's funny, but really the joke is that for the doctor, the problem isn't this monster who's scared of fire. It's that the monster is screwing up the number."

The boy was quick as hell, I had to give him that. "So if you're the monster in this analogy, what's your take-away?"

Definitely a smile.

"That Doctor Frankenstein is a douchebag?"

I laughed. "Well, yeah. But no, it's that you don't have to be a great singer or dancer. The performance can suck, actually. You only have to conquer your irrational fear of fire for a short time. If he'd managed to do that, if he'd been forewarned and forearmed, he'd have been applauded by all and sundry and the audience would have been amazed."

We pulled up to the restaurant then, and the valet ushered me out of the car, so it was a few minutes before we were able to pick up the thread of the conversation. By that time we'd been seated, and were looking at menus, so my mind was on gourmet cuisine and wine pairings when Ivan spoke again.

"So my social skills can be the bare minimum, as long as I don't freak out because somebody whips out a lighter, is that what you're saying?"

"Remind me to get to lesson two tonight." I peered over the menu, but he was looking studiously at his own and didn't meet my eyes. "I'm saying the fire is a metaphor for the party itself. Or at least I suspect that's the case."

He frowned again, almost a pout. "I'm not good at metaphors, either."

"You do know I wasn't talking about being scared of fire, right?"

"Yes, because I'm not an idiot. It's not that I don't *understand* the metaphors. But why don't you just say what you're talking about?" It was obviously not the first time he'd been frustrated over this. I had to wonder how he'd ever managed his college English courses.

"In this case I'm saying that the whole idea of the party itself is what scares you. Talking to strangers, pretending to be interested in what they're saying, trying to get them to like you. It's the thing you're worst at. Although I do have some thoughts about how to work around it. But part of the thing you have to get over is getting snippy when people don't say exactly what they mean."

"I wasn't getting snippy. I was merely attempting to point out that it's foolish and inefficient to say things you don't mean all the time. It doesn't accomplish the goal of communication."

The waiter arrived, taking our orders with an ease that spoke of years of practice. Smooth, like the atmosphere. I could see the framework of the original architecture, the vaulted ceiling of the chapel and the elegant Gothic windows. Swathed in warm red and gold, the whole interior looked candlelit and romantic. It was the type of place I would love to go on a date some day. If only this were that day.

"I'm sorry."

He seemed contrite, though the frown line was still there. I sipped at my cabernet and tried to think how best to respond.

"I'm at a nice restaurant with a beautiful woman," he went on. "The minimum expectation is that I not get snippy. And use good table manners."

I nearly spit my wine out, I laughed so hard. After I'd swallowed and stifled my snort in my napkin, I nodded. "That's a bare minimum, I'd say. Although throwing in the 'beautiful' was a nice touch. I didn't plan to get flattery out of you for another week or so at least."

"It's not flattery." He looked, if anything, a little confused.

And like he might be heading toward snippy again. "I'm describing the context."

"Never mind," I said quickly. "That was sweet of you to say. Thank you. Apology accepted."

"I was being sweet?" He raised one eyebrow and gave me that intense look again, resting on his elbows so he could lean closer over the intimate little table. His eyes had gone dark, his mouth curved in that little smile again. I suddenly felt some sympathy with his computer monitor, for having to bear up under that kind of scrutiny all day. It was an improvement. Usually I was a little jealous of his computer monitor for getting all his attention. But now I felt like the problem he was bent on solving.

"You know you were." My palms were sweaty, and I rubbed them across my thighs, hoping the dress wouldn't suffer from the treatment. "There was another part of the movie I meant to use as—"

"What else would I need to do, to be sweet? I've never been accused of that before, now you've got me curious. Maybe I've been doing it accidentally and never realized."

I wanted to believe he was flirting with me. But despite the romantic setting, I couldn't quite bring myself to think it would be that easy. He was doing it accidentally, like he'd said. Trying to follow up on it would probably only confuse and frighten him.

"That's the perfect segue to lesson three, which is about not interrupting people in the middle of their sentences. That's often perceived as very hostile. If you interrupt people," I clarified, "they will not want to give you their money."

"Should I apologize again?"

"Yes." No sense beating around the bush, since that seemed to get me nowhere with Ivan. Literal and straightforward, clearly those should be my watchwords. Maybe I should come right out with it. I tried to think how I would phrase that. *Hey, I don't know why exactly, because you can be a jerk sometimes, but I think your heart is in the right place and your jerkiness seems to arouse me. Let's have sex.*

Nope. That was definitely not going to be said by me any time soon.

"I'm sorry for interrupting you." He leaned back and pulled his wineglass with him, the lanky lines of his body granting him all the natural elegance of an old movie star. Or maybe that was just the setting, and my imagination running wild. "You skipped lesson two."

He sipped at his wine, his eyes never leaving mine, and I grabbed my own glass to gulp a bit of the fortifying liquid before I pressed on. "You have a tendency to break a long silence by jumping into the middle of a subject. It's startling. It takes people a second to figure out what you're talking about, so it's sort of awkward."

The elegant movie-star jaw clenched again, and his fingers tightened dangerously on his wineglass for a moment. I wished I could think of a nicer way to say it, but he didn't seem to get it when I tried.

Literal and straightforward.

"Maybe you need a strategy. Like, something you can memorize, and say to sort of ease back into the conversation."

"A script?"

The idea made me laugh. "That's not the kind of script I write, usually. But yeah, I guess so. Not for life, maybe, but at least for the party. A few stock phrases. Like…I don't know, you could clear your throat and then say, 'Hey, remember earlier when we were talking about whatever?' Or maybe 'So

I've been thinking...' You know, to give people a chance to catch up."

"This is stuff my mother used to tell me all the time."

This was *so* not a date.

"Well, she's a smart lady. Maybe you should have listened."

"But she would never tell me *why*. You're better at telling me why. She always said 'just because.' It was frustrating."

Privately, I wondered if his mother even knew why, herself. Or if she had learned the hard way, and was doing her best to pass those lessons along to her son. Or possibly if growing up in a small town, and staying there most of her adult life, too, had created a better environment for learning these particular life lessons.

I had a certain amount of sympathy for Ivan. Part of the reason social anthropology appealed to me in college was that I often felt puzzled by human interaction. Knowing the reasons behind the rules was comforting.

The food was fantastic, the conversation waxed and waned over the course of the meal. We did better when we veered off topic and started talking about movies and books and video games, worse when we tried to re-engage on the topic of humans and their strange social practices.

But then, on the way out the door, Ivan put his hand on the back of my waist, leaving it there for a moment as we stepped toward the valet stand and waited for the car. And he didn't merely brush against me, either, he actually pressed his hand into the curve at the small of my back like it belonged there.

And then, *then,* he grazed his fingers back and forth across the fabric, sending fireworks down my legs and up my spine, so that I nearly swooned into him. It was the first time in my life I had truly grasped the concept of swooning, but no other term seemed to fit what I was feeling.

I could have sworn I felt reluctance from him when he finally, slowly, dragged his hand away. He let the valet hand me into the car, and he got in and didn't say another word until we were parking the car at home.

"I'll walk you to your…wait. No." He held up a hand and made a little backing-up motion with his finger. "Rewind. Okay, *so I was thinking…*" He looked at me for approval, grinning like a kid, and I couldn't help but grin back. I gave him a thumbs-up, and he continued. "I'll walk you to your door."

"You're a quick study." I started to open my door, but he stopped me.

"No, I'm supposed to get that for you. My mother would kill me. I do know that much."

Chuckling, I waited while he rounded the back of his little hybrid car and opened the door for me. He offered his hand and I took it, then had to stifle a gasp at the renewal of that swooning sensation. It outlasted the touch, which was fleeting.

The night was sultry, typical for Houston in July. But the swampy heat was sweetened with an undercurrent of lush flowers in bloom, my roses and the neighbor's jasmine. Cicadas creaked and trilled, masking some of the traffic noise, and the short walk to our back doors was soft and quiet and so much like a date that I had to bite down on my disappointment when Ivan made no move to follow me in after I'd unlocked my door and flicked on the kitchen light.

He waved and then disappeared into his own half of the duplex, and when I closed the door it felt like there was a world between us instead of a thin wall.

The next day at work I remembered the other point I'd meant to make with the movie, about context and expectations. I was getting ready to fire off an email to Ivan to that effect when I saw that he'd beaten me to the punch. His email jumped right in, as it always did, with no small talk or even a salutation.

You said you had ideas for a way around my difficulty talking to ~~idiots~~ strangers. Perhaps that should be lesson four?
   To recap what we've covered so far:
 ? It isn't a lie of omission if the listener has no need to know.
 1. Different expectations for different contexts (I gather I'm to focus on learning the relevant expectations for this sort of occasion as opposed to, say, how to behave with drunken same-sex peers at a sporting event); determine and meet the minimum expectations for the setting.
 2. Provide segue when breaking a long silence. Use stock phrases if necessary.
 3. If I interrupt people, they will not want to give me their money.

At least he'd gotten the gist of what we'd covered so far. Although I was a little worried about stock phrases. I'd need to make sure he didn't wander around the party, approaching random people and saying "I've been thinking…" all night. I might have to start keeping some sort of list of these ideas, actually, beyond the Post-it I'd originally assigned to the task. It was turning into a lot of lessons.

I was trying to bang out a reply when I saw another message pop up in my inbox. This one, too, was from Ivan.

If you arrive at my house between six-fifteen and six-thirty, using the back door rather than the front, the odds of your being seen are considerably reduced. Most of the occupants in the other three buildings park on the curb rather than in the carport if they are planning to leave again for the evening, meaning they will use their front doors to enter and exit. If they park in the carport, they may leave but will most likely do so on foot, again using their front doors. Nobody is likely to begin cooking outdoors until at least six forty-five or seven, which should give you ample opportunity to arrive unseen.

I will provide dinner. You will provide the instruction.

If I weren't used to this sort of thing, I would be baffled and quite possibly offended. As it was…it was just Ivan.

I wasn't too surprised that he was trying to control things. He hated things being out of control, out of the boundaries of his own expectations. But that didn't mean he couldn't widen those expectations a little. I firmly believed that a good deal of it was practice and willingness. And if I needed any motivation to continue believing that, I need think back no further than the previous evening, the quick smile and piercing gaze, the almost-caress on my back that made my knees wobbly.

So tonight, I decided, I would provide a lesson that gave him plenty of control.

"I *do* know what your project is. The point is to pretend I don't. To pretend I'm from Mars or something—"

"There's no evidence of intelligent life on Mars. And how would you have learned to speak the language?"

"Focus, Ivan. Focus." I picked up a slice of pizza, gesturing with it as I spoke. "It's an exercise. A hypothetical situation. You like hypotheticals, right?"

He shrugged. "They can be useful. I assume you don't mean hypothetical in the scientific sense."

"No, I do not. But that's not important. The point is, you're going to practice on me, as if I didn't know anything about it. Bear with me, okay?"

"Okay."

I munched on my pizza as he settled into teaching mode, describing the stationary laser beam that would one day be aimed at a spacecraft to heat a solid fuel, allowing the craft to move much more quickly and efficiently. It could be much smaller, too, without having to carry its own power source. A pocket rocket, he joked. At least compared to the current size of spacecraft. It was the wave of the future, except for the complicating issue of the international space treaty that made use of lasers in space like that a bit of a problem. And it was actually pretty cool stuff.

He started to lose me, though, when he got into the "laser broom" and how laser ablation would one day be used to clear particles from the path of...blah...something...blah...

"Camilla, can you repeat back my last point?"

I jerked my head up, eyes wide, hoping I hadn't really nodded off. "No. Man, do you really do that to kids who fall asleep in your lecture? That's so cruel."

On the other hand, he was standing right in front of my chair, arms folded, looking very stern and professorial. And a wee bit like an evil genius, a look I'm the first to admit I have a weakness for.

"I don't do that in my classes, no. But I know you already know all this, so there's no excuse."

"Maybe I zoned out *because* I already know this," I pointed out.

"No." He seemed quite firm on this point. "In class, the kids who fall asleep are rarely the ones who already know the material. The kids who already know it bring other things to look at. They're the ones who are surfing the internet instead of taking notes on their laptops, or who have a crossword stuck in their textbook where they think I can't see it. The ones who fall asleep are typically the ones who can't make sense of what they're hearing. Nobody gets bored faster than the ignorant."

Wow. I was amazed that he'd picked all that up. He seemed so oblivious to people most of the time.

"That's pretty astute. So let's work with that," I suggested. "Can you figure out why I wanted you to try teaching me something? What was my point there?"

He was still standing there in front of me. He was in his work clothes, hole-free jeans and a buttoned shirt, sleeves once again rolled up. Today's shirt was a very nice blue chambray with a white pinstripe. He'd untucked it, so it was rumpled at the waist. My fingers itched to smooth out those wrinkles, toy with the last few buttons and the more interesting stuff hiding beneath. Other parts of me itched, too, as I played the mini-fantasy out in my mind. And now he was staring, silent and impassive, as he considered my question. By the time he finally spoke, I was practically squirming in the cheap wicker armchair.

"When I'm teaching, I'm *usually* more patient. And because I've made a study of it in that particular setting, I'm more aware of people's physical cues that can tell me how they're responding to the information. So I can adjust accordingly."

"You don't have to worry about charming them," I added. "You just have to educate them. Is there a reason you've never made a study of people's reactions in general conversations? I'm only asking." It seemed to me it would have saved him a lot of trouble and earned him a lot more goodwill with friends.

He shrugged and moved away, finally, taking a seat on the closest end of the couch to my chair and putting his feet up on the coffee table. "It doesn't come naturally to me. It's work. I don't want to work that hard all the time. I do that in certain specific settings, and I even enjoy the challenge of it in those settings. But I want my friends to be smart enough to understand what I'm getting at. If people are dumb, it's not my job to educate them all the time."

"That's another one of those things you really shouldn't say out loud, you know. About people being dumb. Something to keep in mind. I think you maybe need to treat this fundraiser as a series of mini-workshops. Hear me out." This, because he was already opening his mouth to interrupt. "That's a strength of yours, that teaching mode. And in that context, you already know what to do. So bring that context to the party. Just decide what your lesson is going to be. Keep it short. Narrow it down. It's an introductory lesson, they don't need all the details. You're much...softer, typically, when you're teaching, than when you're in other situations where you're dealing with a lot of people. More relaxed, more accessible. When you were explaining Minecraft to me for the first time, for instance, you were very patient and handled my questions very well."

"But you're not dumb," he countered. Which was big of him, since I was pretty dumb when it came to Minecraft, a computer game I'd never really gotten the point of.

"Thank you. But I think you need to get over this idea that there are all these dumb people. They may not be smart in the same way you are, but on the other hand, they're all able to do things like go to parties without having panic attacks or boring people to tears. That's a different kind of smart."

"I have never bored anybody to tears. Not literally, anyway," he added, before I could pounce on his response.

"Your assignment for tomorrow is to come up with your mini-lesson, so you can practice that on me. And if that goes well, later in the week we can try a field trip."

Ivan swallowed his bite of pizza and raised an eyebrow

at me. "For somebody who doesn't teach on a regular basis, you're doing very well, Camilla."

Nobody else used my full name. Ivan had never used it much before, but seemed to be doing it all the time lately. I decided to like it when he said it. "Thank you."

"Tomorrow is Wednesday, so we may want to skip it and meet Thursday. On Wednesday evenings I have a class, so I'm usually not home until—"

"Seven-thirty. Or seven forty-five if you have to stop for gas."

He blinked, then scowled in what was clearly mock anger. "An interruption, Camilla? Some might perceive that as hostile."

"Well played, Professor. Well played."

"My schedule is really that predictable?"

For about a millisecond, I considered lying. But then I realized that with him, there would really be no point in it. He'd probably know I was lying, and it would only serve to bother him. "Yes."

"Am *I* that predictable?"

And I nearly said yes again, until I caught some hint of an expression in his eyes, a tiny flicker of amusement and heat. Quickly suppressed, but for a moment it had thrown me off balance as much as his casual touch seemed to do these days. Could he possibly be…flirting? Did he even know how? "I used to think so, but now I'm not so sure."

"It's quite possible there are parts of my schedule with which you're not familiar at all," he said cryptically.

"Deep, dark secrets, Professor? That does sound intriguing." It was hard to do sultry and pouty when I was wiping pizza grease off my chin, but I gave it the old college try and was rewarded with another of those spring-rose smiles. They seemed to be getting more frequent lately.

"If the secrets are deep and dark enough, they stop being intriguing and become unnerving. Take my word for it. And on that note, I think we probably need to finish up. My predictable schedule demands I iron a shirt for tomorrow and then brush my teeth."

He seemed genuinely regretful as he rose and offered a hand to pull me up from my chair. This time I knew enough to brace myself for the hot shock of desire, the thrilling enervation from such a little touch. My overreaction would do any Regency romance's maiden heroine proud, but I knew it was probably more a function of anticipation and imagination than any deeper chemistry or mystical bond between us. Still. It was hot, even if it only lasted for a second or two. Even if his momentary flirtation had vanished into the usual chilly, hard-to-read expression I knew so well.

In the fantasy I spun for myself that night before falling asleep, those deep dark secrets were revealed. That simple touch became a violent embrace, worthy of any bodice-ripper. There were a certain number of gleeful perversions committed on Ivan's battered leather sofa. And at some point in the fantasy, Ivan was a vampire, because I was sort of weird that way. He was a real, Gothic-style, Bram Stoker sort of vampire who bit people as a metaphor for having dubious-consent, alpha-male sex with them, I should point out. None of your modern, sensitive vampires for me. I appreciated the classics.

Chapter Four

Flirting for Evil Geniuses 101.

I had decided that would be a better name for my individual course than How to Win Donors and Influence Patrons of
the Sciences. Even though the flirting was so sporadic I still
wasn't sure whether he meant it or not, I was really looking
forward to seeing if I could elicit more of it when we went
on our field trip.

First, of course, I had to convince Ivan that the field trip
was a good idea. He was none too keen on the idea of going
out to dinner and a movie with a group of people he didn't
know. He did know Athena, who would be there, but he also
knew she didn't like him much so it wasn't really a plus. And
her date, and the other couple, were strangers to both of us.

That was exactly the way I wanted it. I thought it was a
great chance for Ivan to start fresh with people and sort of
re-invent himself. He would be there as my date, no history.
Athena had agreed, reluctantly, not to tell the others anything
about him. She had done so only on the condition that she
could tease me mercilessly about the event after it was over.

But she would have probably done that anyway, so really I had gotten the better end of the deal.

"It's always the same, with stuff like this. The same information." I wanted to reassure him that his preparation had been sufficient. "They'll want to know what you do, and you know a short version to tell them, right?"

"I'm a post-doc at the university. I'm in astrophysics. I do research and teach a few classes."

"Great. Stop there. If they ask more, give them just a little bit. Like the first tier of information on your lesson plan, okay? The intro."

"Right." He shuffled through a small stack of index cards until he found the one he wanted, took a few seconds to glance over the information, then nodded. I hoped he would follow my advice and leave the cards out of sight once we got to the theater.

"In no case should you give more in-depth information unless one of the others turns out to be in a related field or something, okay? They may want to know where you went to school, where you grew up. Keep the answers short and informative. Then—this is important—you say..."

"How about *you?*"

"Very good. Don't forget you need to change it up a little. Don't say it exactly the same way each time, you know?"

"Are you mocking me, Camilla?"

I tried not to look at the index cards when I answered. "I wouldn't dream of it. Now let's get moving, or we're going to be late."

"Wait. Wait. What's my lesson plan, here? What am I trying to teach them?"

He had given me an actual, literal lesson plan the previous evening, with all the details relevant to his fundraising event. Tonight was not meant to be a formal outing, the stakes weren't nearly as high. Still, I should have considered that he'd want to treat it with the same over-preparation that he always did.

"That you're a normal, nice guy?"

"I need something more realistic than that."

I wondered if he was objecting to the "normal" part or the "nice" part.

"Okay, how about that you're a brilliant rocket scientist who is pretty reserved socially but pleasant when he has to be?"

"I hate this shit." Ivan was already jingling his car keys, though, and we headed for the car with the question of his objective still hanging. As I was getting buckled in, inspiration struck.

"You're already pretending to be my date. So focus on that part. Are you going to be a boyfriend? Or are you going to be some guy who's hoping to get...um, get me to go out a second time?"

The Friday evening traffic occupied his attention for a few minutes before he finally answered. "Were you going to say 'laid' and then changed your mind?"

Crap, so much for subtle. "Yep."

"That one. I'll be that one."

"All righty." Seriously? Potentially good, but also potentially disastrous. "So what's your plan going to be for that?"

He smiled without looking at me. He kept his eyes on the road when he drove, checking his mirrors frequently at such regular intervals that I'd always wondered if he had some OCD issues. "Remember how I said there are large chunks of my time you have no idea about?"

"Yeah."

"Let's just say I can do that role. Of a guy who plans to get you into bed. However, I will almost certainly not do it the way you're used to."

I had absolutely no doubt of that. "Is this going to be creepy?"

We pulled up to a red light, and I got the full force of the evil grin. "Keep an open mind and follow my lead. And re-member, if you let me be in control of it, my comfort level will be higher. But I will also make it worth your while."

I had a sudden sense that he meant that in far more ways than I had previously considered. And an equally sudden im-pulse to tell him to turn the car around, take me back to his place, and tell me more about how he got girls into bed. But I'd promised Athena, and this outing was meant to benefit Ivan, after all.

"So you're saying you've been going out with girls all this time and nobody knew about it?" I'd lived next door to the guy for two years, and thought I knew as much about him as a stalker. This would have been a big detail to miss.

"No, and I'm not really going to say much more about it right now. If you want me to play that role, I can do that. But I do it a certain way, and usually only with people who are... another certain way. They're looking for a particular type."

Tragically gorgeous uber-nerd scientists with zero social skills?

"Astrophysicists?"

He chuckled. "People who prefer to be in control of their variables."

I could tell there was something he was leaving out, some critical element. But we were almost at the theater, and I didn't have time to get into the details with him. I decided to roll with it. "Okay. You're in control. Consider me your variable."

He seemed amused by the whole thing. This was good,

as it took the edge off his tension and made him smile more than he usually did. Not the tight, polite smile he used around strangers, but the sly, private little smirk that had driven me crazy since the first time I saw it.

Things started off simply enough. Waiting in line, getting the tickets and soft drinks, locating Athena and friends who were already in the theater. We'd arrived in time for previews, so there wasn't really much time for interaction before the movie anyway. Athena and I had agreed to do it this way, movie first and then dinner, so there would be a built-in topic of conversation during the meal. We thought it might help Ivan to have at least one subject at hand, although I was leery of how he might react if he had strong feelings about the movie.

It was a good date flick, a horror film with an improbable serial-killer plot designed to maximize the potential for shock visuals that tended to make a girl squeak and grab her date for safety. And it fulfilled that potential quite well, as it turned out. Not that I paid much attention to the movie. As soon as the lights dimmed, Ivan had leaned in toward me, just close enough to encroach on my seat a little. The armrests were the flip-down kind, so nothing prevented his thigh from pressing against mine from the knee halfway to the hip. The first five minutes or so of the movie were completely lost on me as I processed this. By "processed," I mean, of course, tried to slow my breathing and control the rampant hormones that made me aware of body parts I usually tried not to think about in public.

On my left Athena was ignoring me, because she was pretty into her date and they were giggling about the movie. So I chanced a little gambit, nudging my knee against Ivan's under the guise of getting more comfortable. I ended up with my right knee cocked and resting ever so lightly along the top of his thigh. Like it had arrived there by accident.

He saw that bid and raised it, sliding his hand over my bent knee and holding it there. No accident. I stared straight ahead, and if I'd had laser vision I would've burned a hole straight through the center of the screen. I had no idea what was being projected there. Ivan's hand was only twelve inches of thigh away from my girly parts, and whether or not it was all a façade designed to fool the crowd, the whole arrangement was doing very strange things to my rational thinking process.

Jeez, I *really* needed to get laid.

"Careful," Ivan whispered in my ear. I sucked in a breath and held it as the brush of his lips raised every tiny hair on my body. "You probably don't want to play that kind of game with me."

I might be needy, but I wasn't desperate enough to fool myself into thinking there was any point in pursuing a guy who just wasn't into me. Been there, done that, no interest whatsoever in reliving the experience.

I started to slide my leg away, trying to keep up the casual appearance—darn, these seats weren't all that comfy, what a shame—but Ivan's long fingers wrapped around my knee, keeping me from moving. Startled, I looked his way, but couldn't read his face in the flickering light of the dimly lit scene in front of us.

"Watch the movie," he whispered. And when I turned back to the screen, puzzled and embarrassed, his lips brushed my ear again with predictable results. "You gave me control, remember?"

I nodded, flicking a glance Athena's way to see if she had noticed anything amiss. Her head was on the guy's shoulder now. I wished I could remember his name, since it seemed likely to come up later. Jacob? Jason? Something with a *J*, anyway.

"Watch the movie. I may give you a pop quiz later to see if you were paying attention." Something in his tone and the touch of his lips against the shell of my ear turned my entire right side to liquid heat, and I shivered before I could stop myself. His fingers tightened against my leg in a slow, deliberate squeeze that made me want to whimper.

What the hell was his deal? He really was going to have to come clean about his big secret at some point.

A nudge at my left elbow shocked me from my musings, and I turned that way to see Athena glaring daggers first at my face, and then at Ivan's hand on my leg. Then back at my face, her expression one big silent "What the fuck?"

I whispered, "Tell you later," and tried to settle back down to watch the movie just in case Ivan was serious about the whole pop quiz thing. But between his hand on my leg and the occasional whispered remarks in my ear, I was pretty much a libidinous basket case by the time the film was over, and damned if I had any remote idea what the thing had been about. Some attractive young people had been lured to an old house, and all but one had died horribly after being mindfucked in every possibly way. Beyond that I was clueless.

If there was to be a pop quiz, I knew I would fail it miserably. And I found myself wondering whether that might not have been the goal.

The heat outside the theater assailed me, moist and grasping, the second I walked out. Like walking into a steam room, particularly since I was wearing a three-quarter-length sleeve and had traded my shorts for denim capri pants. The movie theater we'd gone to was notoriously chilly, so I'd dressed for that. The shirt was on loan from Athena, so it was lower-cut by far than my usual, but the extra cooling from all the bare skin on my chest could only accomplish so much against the oppressive heat of the summer night. I hoped the restaurant wasn't too warm, or I'd be miserable.

We gathered outside before dispersing to cars, and more lengthy introductions were made, with Athena staring pointedly at me all the while. And then, fortunately, Ivan turned his phone ringer back on and noticed a missed voicemail from work. He apologized and stepped away to listen to it, and this occupied him while we engaged in the restaurant negotiations that typically so enraged him.

We'd decided on sushi by the time he rejoined the group, so we split up into couples to drive to the restaurant.

"I have to stop by the lab after we eat," Ivan said. Not apologetically, I noticed. Nor did he say that it wouldn't take long, or any of the other usual things one says. "Did I hear correctly? Sushi?"

"Yep."

He smiled. "You could always try 'Yes, Professor.'"

"Huh?"

"Nothing." He opened the car door and gestured me in. "Don't forget to buckle up."

When we'd been driving for a few minutes, he cleared his throat. "So what do you normally order at a sushi bar?"

"Sashimi. Sometimes a roll. It depends, why?"

"No allergies I should be aware of? Shellfish, anything like that? Any very strong dislikes?"

"Nope."

He bit his lower lip and shook his head. "No, Professor."

"Seriously?"

"No, it's all right. I'll humor you for now. As long as you let me order for both of us."

"All right. Control. I get it."

"No, I really don't think you do. But that's okay. This is still helpful. It's helping me to see how to translate this behavior from one setting to another. With new expectations."

At the next red light, he gave me a head-to-toe appraisal then seemed to be searching his memory for the right phrase. "You look very nice tonight."

"Thanks. So do you. You remembered to comb your hair and everything." And he'd come straight from work, so he was wearing decent jeans and a nice enough navy blue dress shirt. "Usually you'd tell your date that before the movie, though. So are you ever going to explain it to me, so that I do get it? The control issue, I mean."

We were pulling into the parking lot next to the restaurant and were lucky enough to catch a space somebody was just vacating. Ivan parked, jerked the emergency brake more forcefully than was perhaps necessary and shook his head. Not a negation, a shake like he wasn't sure how to respond. "That would probably be a bad idea, Cami."

"Camilla," I said automatically, then bit my tongue. If he wasn't allowed to make me call him Professor, I shouldn't be demanding he call me Camilla. "Sorry."

"You're not doing a very consistent job of letting me be in control, *Camilla*."

And the look he gave me then made me understand how the gazelle feels when it realizes that the rustling it hears isn't a stray breeze in the tall grass but a lion about to pounce. Only difference was, I wouldn't have tried to run. I wasn't sure my legs would even work.

"I'll try harder, *Professor*."

Ivan looked fascinated by me. It was heady, that feeling of being the center of his attention. He started to lift a hand, as though he might touch my cheek, but he pulled it away at the last minute.

"See that you do."

Dinner was a study in the surreal.

Ivan was polite and didn't talk much. So that right there was a little bizarre. He said his prepared things about work and remembered to follow up with, "And you?" He remained noncommittal about the movie, and while he may not have charmed anybody he didn't piss anybody off. But mostly he focused on me. Ordering for me, as he'd said he would. Nigiri, and we shared a fried banana dessert that was actually much better than I'd expected. I let him be in control, because I was curious to see what he'd do.

When he offered me the last bite of our dessert on his fork, Athena kicked me under the table. But by that point I was too enthralled to even think about responding to her. Or allowing her to pull me into the bathroom for a conversation, as she seemed bent on doing. I wallowed instead in the glow of Ivan's regard, fake though it might be. I took the last bite of fried banana, wishing it meant more than it did.

The trouble was, Ivan still hadn't given any definitive sign that he was interested in something other than playing a role to practice his social skills. He'd even warned me off. Sort of. And he hadn't batted an eye at the cleavage on display in the borrowed shirt. Or at my ass. Or even at my feet, though I'd gotten a real nail salon pedicure for once and was wearing extremely cute sandals.

Of course, it was perverse in the first place that I wanted him looking at my boobs, ass or other body parts. Mostly I hated it when guys did that. Maybe it was just that Ivan never did it, so that was what I ended up adopting as the objective standard for whether or not he was interested. Because I knew I had nice enough assets in those areas, if not quite Athena-standard, and I wasn't that cynical about using them to good advantage on occasion.

But he wasn't looking. And after we left the restaurant and the company of the others, he'd said very little else to me on the ride to his office. Aloof, that was Ivan. And damned if that didn't make me all the more determined to get under his skin. Or at least into his pants.

"So, was the call about some big breakthrough or anything?" I asked, kicking my heels idly against the leg of the table on which I'd perched to watch him work.

"Kind of," he said, to my surprise. He even smiled a little bit, though his eyes never left the image on the computer monitor in front of him. "We finished our planning and preliminary scale-model testing for the station-mounted parabolic reflector, and that means we can move on to designing the full-size prototype. Paulo wanted me to double-check an equation before he sends the grant reporting in."

"Wow. You mean you actually finished a project stage?" I knew enough about his field to know how rare an occurrence that was in the constantly evolving design process of all things space-related. "Closure?"

"Closure," Ivan confirmed. "At least of this phase."

"Well. Congratulations."

"Thank you."

He typed in a few more things, stared at a few more incomprehensible images on the screen, and then started closing it all down again, apparently satisfied with what he'd seen.

"Is it always this cold in here? My office is so hot all the time." Even in my cold-theater clothes, I felt a distinct chill in the darkened lab.

"Yes. But just like in the movie theater, it would be comfortably warm if you were more appropriately dressed."

"I beg your pardon?"

"Your shirt doesn't make sense," he said, sounding annoyed. "It covers your elbows, but it leaves your forearms and most of your sternum completely bare. It must have extremely poor heat-retention properties." He started toward the door and I followed, then had to wait as he went back to turn his desk lamp off. The room was still bathed in the eerie glow of dozens of LEDs, and the steady red glare of the exit sign.

I took a few moments to process what he'd said about the shirt. I wasn't even sure how to classify it. Nobody could possibly be that obtuse. Could they?

"But it looks good," I pointed out.

Even in the faint light I could spot the tension in his face, the way his upper lip flexed as he geared up to his full problem-solving mode.

"It's impractical."

I shrugged, failing to stifle a tiny defeated sigh. "It's extremely practical. It does exactly what it's designed to do, Ivan. Which any normal human guy with normal human guy needs would know has absolutely nothing to do with keeping me warm."

Then I turned and half whispered as I reached for the doorknob, "Any straight guy, at least."

Before I could open the door, a pair of hands slapped against the wall on either side of me, trapping me between two lean arms. My world constricted in a heartbeat to the cinderblock wall in front of me, cold and gray with layers of glossy institutional paint...and the body behind me, hot and firm and undeniably male.

"Camilla," he growled, "I want to make some things perfectly clear to you, and you are going to listen to me. Do you understand?"

Unable to speak because my heart was threatening to pound its way out of my chest, I nodded. Then I whimpered as he leaned closer still and his breath tickled over the fine hairs behind my ear.

"First thing. I am not stupid."

"I never said—"

"Quiet! You started this, but I'm going to finish it. I am not stupid. I may not like people, I may have asked for help getting through this fundraiser, but that doesn't make me an idiot about all human interaction. And I don't appreciate being teased."

Miserable, excited, I held my tongue and tried to think about anything but the shivering, melting sensation that was beginning to course through my veins. The slight draft near the door could never account for the goose bumps prickling over me. And nothing but Ivan's proximity could possibly explain the effervescent heat between my legs.

"Second thing. I am not blind. If you flash your cleavage enough times, eventually I will not be able to avoid getting an eyeful. That shirt ups those odds considerably. So unless you really want to be ogled, I can't imagine why you would go around wearing such a thing. It's nothing like your usual style. You don't need to wear something trashy to get noticed."

He noticed my usual style? It was news to me. Also news that he knew the difference between trashy and not, and knew I normally chose the latter. Not that this shirt was trashy, although I had to admit it skirted the line pretty closely.

"And third," Ivan continued, leaning in closer, "I want to stress that I am a completely normal human male in a lot of respects. And since I am most decidedly *not* gay," he added, pressing his hips forward into my ass so I couldn't possibly mistake his prominent hard-on, "you're playing a pretty dangerous game. I can only take so much teasing, Camilla. Sooner or later, if you keep it up, I am going to assume you want me to follow through. That would come with some additional requirements you probably aren't prepared for."

Offering a silent prayer to any love gods who might be listening, I arched my back a little so my backside pressed more firmly against that delicious, hot length of barely restrained need.

"Why would you ever assume anything else?"

He hissed through clenched teeth, pulling away for a second and then pressing forward with a groan to pin me to the wall. His hips ground against me, and I shivered as his hands left the wall and circled my upper arms.

"I don't play these games out in the real world, Cami." His voice was rough, almost resentful. Torn, he sounded torn. I felt a surge of raw hope and need, even as he said everything he could to deter me. "I know how to fuck. I like to fuck. I just don't do well with people, and I have very particular tastes." He had worked his hands forward between me and the wall now, and he cupped my breasts and plucked sharply at my nipples through the infamous shirt. "I can't be nice about it. I'm tempted by you, I'd be lying if I said I wasn't, but I'm not like the men you're used to. I don't do sweet. This isn't what you're looking for."

"If you don't know people," I gasped, biting my lower lip as his fingers tugged and tweaked the already pebbled peaks, "you shouldn't make assumptions about what they're looking for. I want this. I want you."

I curled my hands over his in encouragement, and he responded by pulling his hands away only long enough to slip them under the shirt and then back up to resume his previous torture.

"You don't even know what *this* is."

"Then *tell* me. What are you, into cross-dressing? A furry? What is the big deal?"

Ivan yanked his hands from under my shirt, grabbed my shoulders and spun me around to face him. His expression was grim, his eyes stern and ominous in the scarlet glow. He said he was tempted, but he seemed to be looking for something from me, and I felt frustrated beyond words that I didn't know what it was. I wanted to give it to him. Short of putting on a fur suit, in that moment I would have agreed to about anything. Maybe that was what he needed to see.

"I like to be in control."

"I think I got that part."

"No." He squeezed his eyes shut, gripping my shoulders at the same time as though he was trying to force the understanding into me. "Camilla, I like to be *in control*. And for my partner to give up her control to me."

Slowly, very slowly, a picture was beginning to form in my mind. "You mean like tying people up and stuff?"

That earned a smile. "Sometimes. But there's more to it than that."

"Like ordering people's food for them? And quizzing them on the movie?" And why did that suddenly seem like the sexiest of all possible things?

"You didn't pay attention to the movie at all, did you?"

I shook my head, unable to speak in the face of the intensity in his eyes as he leaned closer.

"Bad girl."

Oh, holy fuck.

In the National Geographic movie of my twisted mind, the

lion had just leaped on the gazelle, pinned it to the ground and mounted it from behind. Apparently, the devouring could wait. I should point out that these little flights of fancy on my part often involved extremely improbable animal pairings. I blamed cartoons.

"Ivan…" I wasn't sure what else I planned to say, but I felt I should say something to distract myself from the creeping wetness between my legs, the wobble in my knees and the mad thrill in my stomach.

He shook his head. "Professor. Or Sir."

"Oh. I get it now."

"Do you?"

"Not really but I think I want to," I half moaned. "I really, really want to." With every lust-soaked fiber of my being, I wanted to. But I had absolutely no idea how to proceed.

Ivan, however, did know how to proceed. It took him a few seconds of deliberation, during which he stroked my shoulders and trailed his fingertips over my collarbones in a deliciously enticing way. I could feel my nipples tightening in response, wanting to be touched again by those evil-scientist hands. But I sensed that I had to wait, to let it be his decision whether to take it further. To let him be in control.

"Maintenance has already come and gone," he said at last, "and I don't think anybody else will be in tonight. We'll hear their key first if they try to get in, anyway." He sounded as though he was talking himself into it, as much as he was re-assuring me. "If you want this, then prove it. Right here and now."

Underneath his brusqueness I heard the lashing of doubt, and I decided to quell that doubt. Who knew if I would get another chance, if I turned this one down?

"What do you want me to do?"

"I want you to strip. Then I want you to get on your knees and wait for further instructions."

Okay. I hadn't really predicted he'd come right out and demand something like that. But I'd gotten a taste of his touch, I wanted more, and I was determined to follow through. Gulping, I started to reach for the hem of my shirt, only to experience a moment of stage fright that froze me with only my stomach exposed.

He was standing there, watching. Not saying anything. Not helping. Just watching. He still had one hand on my hip, and his fingers were tracking along my waistband, but other than that he was a blank.

And right then I decided that my new goal was to replace that blank with something. Anything. Any expression. I wanted to see him feeling things. I wanted to see him have feelings so strong he couldn't hide from them. Couldn't control his reactions. I wanted to make Ivan Reynolds completely lose his shit. Barring that, I would settle for Ivan making me completely lose my shit, which seemed a lot more likely.

I think he was maybe a little startled when I pushed his hand out of the way and moved a few steps toward the center of the room. He let his arm fall to the side as my shirt and bra dropped to the floor, followed within seconds by my shoes and pants. I was able to scoop off my undies, too, getting the whole thing in one go. Not the most graceful undressing I'd ever done, to be sure, but it was practical. And I was naked. In the middle of the astrophysics data lab, kneeling in front of a still fully clothed Ivan.

Of all the possible outcomes I might have predicted for our little field trip, this was not one of them. Not in my wildest dreams. But I was beginning to think my dreams had not been nearly wild enough.

Chapter Five

If Ivan was surprised that I'd not only agreed but shucked all my clothes off in the middle of his deserted workplace, he hid it well. The impassive mask stayed in place, and as the cold of the room started to seep into my skin I could feel my body flirting with panic.

He took a step back and then circled me slowly, seeming to consider me from all angles. I straightened my spine automatically, pulled in my stomach and forced my hands to unclench from where I was leaving fingernail marks on my bare thighs.

"Have you ever done anything like this before, Camilla?"

He was standing right behind me, but when I turned my head to look at him, he spanned the top of my skull with one hand and gently turned me back to the front. Even that touch, short and efficient and nowhere near an erogenous zone, made me yearn for more.

"No, I haven't, Professor.

It sounded like he was pacing back there, in the narrow space between me and the wall. I kept my eyes straight in front of me, trying to count all the many LEDs in my field of vision.

Green, blue, red, they winked from the bases of monitors and power strips, from the DVD player and TV in one corner of the room, indicating the readiness of all these machines to be turned on and used. I felt a certain kinship.

He cleared his throat very pointedly before speaking again, and I grinned. He was putting his learning into practice, even now. "Have you ever heard of a safeword?"

I shook my head. I had no idea. But that was all right, because he explained it.

"A safeword is what you say if you want to stop. If something is too much for you to handle. It's a get-out-of-jail-free card, and if you use it, everything stops. If we're going to do this, you'll need to choose one. Something you aren't likely to say accidentally in the, ah, throes of passion."

"Are there going to be throes of passion?"

"Oh, yes, Camilla. You can count on that. If you can't think of a word, for now you can just say red. Or red light. Red means stop. You understand?"

His pleasant baritone voice had grown even deeper, almost hypnotic. He spoke slowly and carefully, enunciating very clearly, sounding very patient but very much as though he had a clear destination and meant to get there on schedule. It was like listening to the hottest lecture ever.

"I understand, Professor," I said after a moment. "Does that mean you're into S and M?"

"I'm not a sadist, no. But there are other reasons to mix pain and pleasure. Have you ever been beaten in an erotic context?"

Was this a real conversation I was having? Surely it had to be an especially odd dream. "No, I can't say as I have, Professor. It doesn't sound all that erotic."

But when he crouched down behind me, his trousers and shirt brushing against my naked back, his hand pulling my hair to one side so he could murmur in my ear, now *that* was erotic. I was aware I had a personal wetness issue of possibly embarrassing proportions going on. Somehow I couldn't bring myself to move, or to stop him.

His lips brushed the tiny hairs along the ridge of my ear as he spoke, and I shivered in a way that had little to do with the chill in the air. "Don't knock it 'til you've tried it." Then he went on, though I was having trouble attending to what he said, given the proximity of his mouth to first my ear, then my neck right where it was most sensitive. "The position you're in right now is 'kneeling down.' Your knees need to be wider apart."

Widening meant that squirming would be less useful to ease the growing tension between my legs, but I decided to play along. I'd come this far, I might as well see where the path led. And I was already sitting there naked, so I'd pretty much already crossed the Rubicon as far as sane decisions went. I could always use the safeword, I reminded myself, as I scooted my knees outward. *Red means stop.*

"Better. If I tell you to kneel down, this is what I want to see." He stroked down my flanks on both sides, letting his hands come to rest at the creases where hips met thighs, and delicious heat followed his touch. "Say 'yes, Professor.'"

"Yes, Professor." Was that my voice? I sounded so needy. He had barely touched me. He hadn't even kissed me yet.

"Now I want you to kneel up." He pressed up on my hips, coaxing me to rise until I was upright on my knees. "This is 'kneeling up.' It's a useful position, particularly for fellatio."

I gasped and tried to mask it with a cough. Lame. Transparent. Why did it sound so much filthier to hear Ivan say "fellatio" than it did to hear most people say "blow job"? I heard him laugh gently behind me, and it relaxed me a little. Made me feel less freaked out. Which was short-lived, because what he asked me to do next freaked me out even more.

Shifting one hand up between my shoulder blades, he pushed very gently and said, "Now, bend over until your head and shoulders are on the floor. But leave your hips high, like they are right now."

"Okay, wait, hold up. Wait. You haven't even *kissed* me yet. Can we do that?"

He had seen me naked and molested my breasts, so why this missed step seemed so significant I wasn't sure. But it was. It was something I needed. And at twenty-eight I'd learned that sometimes you had to ask in order to get what you needed.

He eased up but left his hand there on my back, making soothing circles with his fingertips. Then he shifted his grip to my neck, cupping it firmly and tipping my head back as he leaned over my shoulder. I caught his smug, intent expression for a fraction of a second before his mouth closed over mine and my eyes closed to savor the kiss.

Like drowning, that kiss. Like taking in water and giving back a piece of my life in return. Ivan tasted like bananas and secret surprises. His tongue seemed to know mine already, seemed to know precisely how to stroke and flex and play and assault my mouth until all I could do was cling to the arm he'd thrown around me at some point in the misty dawn of the kiss.

"Now," he said once he'd pulled away, while I was still trying to catch my breath and figure out which direction the ceiling was, "bend over and put your head and shoulders on the floor for me." This time, his push was a little firmer and against my neck. It didn't need to be. I went over, not really caring for the moment how exposed the position made me feel. The kiss had somehow really brought home to me that Ivan knew things I didn't. They were things I wanted to know. If this was what I had to do to learn them, I'd do it.

With my ass in the air and everything exposed, the cold bit more harshly against my very wet pussy, and I felt a tiny flicker of embarrassment about what that must look like. But it was tiny and fleeting. I got the impression he'd seen that sort of thing, and much more. I doubted I could do or say anything to shock this stranger I'd known for two years without really knowing him at all.

Ivan, calm as ever, continued his lesson. "This position is what I want to see when I say, 'Present.' You're presenting your anus and vagina. For inspection, for penetration, discipline, play. Whatever I choose. Are you still following me?"

Oh, and there went my comfort level again. But with the ghost of panic came a fresh wave of arousal, made all the more keen by the knowledge that I couldn't hide it from Ivan.

"Yes, Professor," I moaned. I was more turned on at that moment than I could remember ever being, during four years of being a live-in girlfriend. The actual sex, assuming we ever got there, might give me a heart attack.

"Do you know anything about BDSM, Camilla?"

"No. Is that what this is? Professor," I added hastily. Up until this evening I'd felt pretty sophisticated for knowing what the letters in BDSM stood for. Most of them, anyway. None of the initials stood for anything like this, that I knew of. Ivan ignored my question and continued the sexy lecture.

"In BDSM terms, I'm what's called a Dominant. A Dominant plays with a partner called a submissive, and they engage in what's called a power exchange. The submissive grants power to the Dominant to do whatever he chooses, within boundaries they agree on. In return, the submissive gets freedom from having to make decisions, and usually also pleasure or other intangibles they can't get on their own. But ultimately the submissive has the real power, because the submissive can safeword to stop the proceedings."

"Like a veto."

"Exactly. Everything that's done to the sub happens with the sub's consent."

"Can...can I sit up while we talk about this?"

"No, I don't believe that's necessary." He put his hand on my back again, petting my spine from nape to tailbone and back again in long, soothing strokes. "I like you this way. At my mercy." After a few more strokes, he continued the motion over one buttock and down to my damp, needy sex. I couldn't hold back a whimper when he slid a finger inside me and began to tease in and out. "You like it, too. You're so wet right now. So ready. Do you always get this lubricated so easily?"

"No," I admitted. He pulled his hand back and brought it down on my ass with a smack that sounded loud as a gunshot in the empty room. I yelped and raised my head, staring back at him in shock.

"No, *Professor*," he reminded me. Calm. No expression. Watching. Waiting to see what I would do. The sting was already fading on my butt, leaving only a spreading warmth in its place.

I considered getting up right then, pulling my clothes on and demanding a ride home. But if I said "red," I firmly believed he would stop and never make another move on his own. In the end I lowered my head back into place, let my shoulders settle, and let out a deep breath I hadn't realized I'd been holding, before whispering, "No, Professor."

"Good girl." And the finger was instantly teasing again, slipping between my folds and down to make a hot, slow circle around my clitoris. I groaned and arched my back a little more, but he withdrew again.

"Let's see, that's three lessons for you so far. And I've had what, four? Five? I think maybe we need to keep it even. If you want to continue this. Do you want to continue this, Cami?"

He was walking around as he talked, and I could hear clothing rustling in the background. Was he taking his clothes off?

"Yes, Sir," I answered, keeping my head and shoulders down.

"The next lesson is that you don't get to have an orgasm unless I say so."

"As long as I do eventually get to have them, I'm cool with that, I guess. Um, Professor."

More rustling noises, and then a zipper. It sounded too long for pants, more like a bag being zipped up. Which turned out to be the case.

Ivan appeared in front of me, his shoes right next to my forearm. "Kneel up, Camilla."

It felt strange to be upright, strange not to have my ladyparts on display. How quickly I'd adapted to that exposed position. I suspected that adaptation said things about me I hadn't really considered before. Or at least not chosen to examine in detail.

I was face-to-face with the bulge in Ivan's pants, and although I had never been a tremendous fan of giving head, I found myself half hoping that was next on the menu. If I made him come, I supposed was my frustration-addled reasoning, he would return the favor. Instead, he just held out my capri pants and the shirt that had started us down this trail to insanity.

"Get dressed. We can pick up where we left off at home."

No underwear, no bra. For about three seconds I looked for them, and even got as far as opening my mouth to ask where they were. Then I saw Ivan's mouth twitch at the corner, in-

voking the dimple. And saw that he was now carrying his
laptop bag, one hand resting possessively over the outer flap.
He had confiscated my undies.

"Get dressed."

I had never been in Ivan's bedroom before. It hadn't really occurred to me, but it struck me as I stood in the doorway that
he never invited anybody upstairs. Given that, I was happy not
to see anything appalling, like severed heads of former lovers.
Or half-eaten sandwiches lying around. Or a wall covered with
news clippings, photos and deranged scribblings. The room
was meticulously clean, like the rest of the apartment. Like
everything in Ivan's life, or so I had always thought.

"When we're in this room, you'll be naked unless I tell you
otherwise." He nudged his shoes off his feet and picked them
up to place them in his exceedingly tidy closet.

We'd covered some basics in the car, the stuff that was necessary but annoying to have to talk about. Condoms would be
used. I was not on the Pill. Neither of us was diseased. Neither of us had engaged in any high-risk behaviors like un-
protected sex or sex with gay men. As for other stuff, I took
Ivan at his word that he didn't do anything hard-core, what
he called edge play, or anything that might involve blood or
other vectors for the transmission of disease. He always wore
a condom, he said, and I believed it. He was too finicky and
regimented about stuff not to be consistent with something
that important. And I knew his stance on lying.

But before my clothes came off again, I still needed a bit
more information. Or maybe I could sense he was a little on
edge, too, now that we were finally in his room. This seemed
much more real, somehow, than the incident in the data lab.

"How many other girls have you done this with?"

He took a minute to answer. While he considered, he re-moved his shirt slowly, toying with the buttons as he rumi-nated. "It's hard to say. I go to a club, usually, and I've had a lot of play partners there. About three I've played with more frequently over the past few years. But I've never brought any of them home with me. And you would be the first submis-sive I've trained for myself."

"I'm still not too sure about that," I admitted. "That whole submissive thing."

"The label or the requirements?"

His shirt came off, and my mind flew away for a moment. I really did wish I'd known much sooner what stellar shape Ivan was in. His abs were like something from a magazine.

"Both, I guess? I don't think of myself as submissive, and I don't have rape fantasies. The whole alpha-male thing has never really had that much appeal for me."

"Do I seem like an alpha male to you?"

He had a point. "Well, no. Not really. Not what most peo-ple would think of that way."

"Have I asked you to submit to anything without consent-ing to it first?" Ivan was pacing around behind me again. It seemed a standby mode of sorts for him.

"No."

"I don't have a rape fantasy, either, Camilla. What I do have is a fondness for experiments. To me, all this is just a way to experiment with our own bodies and minds. To test the boundaries of what we can do with ourselves, what we're *willing* to do. A chance to be both observer and subject."

That made sense to me. "And to control your variables."

Another soft chuckle. And then a pair of hands tugging gently up at the hem of the pullover shirt I still wore. "Even I know I can't really control all the variables. But this way…

it's as close as I've been able to get. If you're staying, take your clothes off."

I let him complete his motion, pulling the shirt up and off over my head, stretching my arms up to help. Then I took my pants off for the second time that night and, because it seemed like it might be the right thing to do, I knelt down.

"Good girl." Ivan's fingers tracked across the top of my head as he walked past, heading across the room where he laid my clothes neatly across the back of a barrel chair.

I scanned the room, still not seeing any evidence of Bluebeard activity or anything else ominous. All I saw were a sturdy Mission-style bed with a forest-green duvet, a pair of matching nightstands with drawers and a bureau on the opposite wall. The two tall windows were covered in plain, sheer white curtains, glowing gently with second-hand illumination from a nearby streetlight.

"I'm amazed you're allowing me into your room, Professor," I ventured. "Do you ever let anybody up here?"

"No," he confessed, returning to stand in front of me. "People might move things around and look at my stuff. They're agents of chaos, basically."

"I'm an agent of chaos? Good to know, Sir." I was getting the hang of the whole title thing, I thought.

"Oh, you are. You definitely are. But two things, you want to hear them?"

"Yes, please, Professor."

"Good, I'll tell them to you while you go take the covers off the bed and then get in the middle of it and present for me."

That wording would take some getting used to. I popped up and scampered over to yank the duvet off in one quick motion, before realizing how overeager and extremely uncool I probably looked. Ivan kept talking. "First, you should keep your friends close but your enemies closer, and chaos is the enemy. Fold that, and put it on the chair. So if you're an agent of chaos, maybe I need to keep a closer eye on you."

"I'm the enemy?" I gave up trying to fold the slippery down-filled coverlet neatly and wrapped it up into a semi-tidy lump on the chair before proceeding back to the bed.

He gave me a cockeyed grin, dimpling all over the place, and nodded his head. "Chaos personified. I have to keep you closest of all, obviously. Second, I may not let just anybody up to my bedroom—you'll never see Ed up here, for instance—but popular opinion notwithstanding, I'm not actually a *total* freak, and I am a guy. I'll let somebody up here if I think there's a good chance the end result will be sex."

Since I was currently in his bed, rear end in the air and ready for action, I guess he had good reason to feel assured of that outcome. It was much more comfortable to assume that position on the bed than it had been on the hard, coarse-carpeted floor of the astro lab.

Ivan made a slow circuit from one side of the bed to the other, finally ending near where he'd started, up near my head. "Beautiful," he murmured, and out of everything that had already happened, *that* was the first thing to make me blush.

"One of the intangible benefits people often say they get from submission is a sense of having permission to do things they wouldn't normally do. You've given the choice of activity to the other person, so the responsibility is on that person if he or she exercises their power to make you do something you'd otherwise be too ashamed or shy to do. It's also why some people like to be bound. They can't blame themselves for their responses then. They can allow themselves to react freely in a way that regular, vanilla sex wouldn't provide."

I nodded, thinking about this. It sounded like a lot of rationalization, but I knew that human brains were brilliant at rationalizing, and that tricking yourself as Ivan described was actually pretty easy to do. That capacity was kind of a feature of our brains, more than a bug.

"Have you really never been spanked? In bed, I mean. I have no interest in learning about your childhood at this time." Ivan sat on the bed, one leg dangling over the side, the other tucked up under him. Casual. Relaxed. Very at odds with the way I was feeling.

I laughed. "No, I haven't. And don't worry, my childhood is the furthest thing from my mind right now."

He smiled and started to caress my back in those long, slow, measured movements, ending each stroke with a trip down to the crease at the bottom of my buttocks. Nerve endings fired and sparkled, as if they remembered good things from his last visit and were eagerly anticipating more.

It was a long few seconds of silent petting, and I had relaxed a little when Ivan said, "I'd like to put you over my knee and spank you, Camilla. But I won't do it tonight if it will scare you off."

The way he said "tonight" made it sound as though he expected there to be subsequent nights, and I found that reassuring. "You'll stop if I say to stop?"

"I'll stop if you say *red,*" he clarified. "If you say anything else—*no,* or *stop,* or *please don't*—I'll keep going and probably spank you harder for it. I'll spank you harder for struggling or trying to block my hand or get away. I'll only stop for the safeword. But if you say it, I stop, that instant. Red for stop."

"But why—"

"Some people like to struggle and be prevented from escaping. Some people like to plead but be forced to submit to it anyway. That's why your safeword should never be something you're liable to blurt out accidentally. But I really wasn't planning anything that drastic, my little newbie. Come over here and assume the position, and try to keep an open mind. Science experiment, remember?"

"Right," I said, though I harbored grave doubts about the validity of any of this as a scientific endeavor. Still, I crawled over and lowered myself over Ivan's lap, feeling awkward and foolish and wildly aroused all at the same time.

He petted first, exploring every contour of my ass and dipping between my cheeks to play with my pussy. "Even your external labia are wet, Camilla. Are you craving penetration by now?"

"Oh, God, yes, please," I moaned as his fingers acted out his words. He slid two of them deep inside me with one quick thrust, and then withdrew almost as quickly. I didn't feel the first smack coming, and when it did, it jolted me out of my sexual daze.

"You didn't address me properly." He slapped his hand down again on the same spot, bringing fire and heat to the surface of that buttock.

"Professor. Please, Professor," I corrected myself, breathing through the sudden pain.

He rewarded me with another caress, this time teasing along my slit until he found my clitoris. "Name four characters from the movie we saw tonight, Camilla."

I got two of them, but drew a blank when I tried to think of any others. A series of quick whacks this time, connecting with the zone where my ass and upper thighs merged. His hand was flat, firm, inescapable. And then his fingers were inside me again, pumping slowly in and out. I moaned and started to writhe back into his hand as all the punished nerve endings tingled with a new kind of sensation, nothing remotely like pain. It was like sex magic.

"Remember the science?" Ivan said, obviously amused at my sudden transformation from reluctant victim to enthusiastic participant. "You just learned something about what endorphins do. Let's see, what else have you been a bad girl about lately? Hmm..."

"Cleavage?" I suggested.

"Cleavage, *Professor.*" The hand wreaked its havoc again, harder this time, but when I tried to squirm away as the pain intensified, Ivan tightened the grip of his non-spanking hand around my waist. "No, Camilla. Stay right there. You've been teasing me all week, first with that dress at the restaurant, then today with the shirt. You've been bad, and you'll take your punishment."

More whacks, until I was near tears, and a breath away from saying the safeword. The only thing that prevented me was the hope that at any second he would relent and—

Oh, my God. The softest touch imaginable against my clit and pussy, as Ivan cupped his hand against me. I was so sensitive from the spanking that I could swear I felt every tread in every fingerprint, each crease on the palm of his hand. Suddenly I was throbbing, nearly panting with want. I lifted my bottom, trying to push into the touch, but he wouldn't allow it. Only when I settled back into his lap did he press his hand closer, toying with me only enough to tease, not to get me off.

"Have you learned your lesson, Camilla?"

I nodded. I had certainly learned *a* lesson. "Yes, Sir." I hoped I sounded suitably repentant, as I wasn't really up on the appropriate etiquette for this situation. Strangely, it really hadn't arisen in my research on how to conduct oneself at a fundraiser or similar event.

"And will you let me spank you again if the occasion calls for it?"

"Yes, Professor." I planned to make the occasion myself, as soon as possible, if need be.

"Hmm. Down to the floor, then. Kneel up between my knees."

I was confused for a second, then realized what he wanted when I recognized the hot, firm lump that had been pressing into my hip. Scooting off his lap, I swung my legs around and under me and slid to the floor, waiting for his next move.

It was a surprisingly cozy place, that spot on the carpet at Ivan's feet. I was close enough to him that, had I wanted to, I could have rested my head on one of his thighs. His hands were already busy unfastening his jeans, working them down his hips and his long runner's legs along with his boxer briefs, and finally kicking the whole mess aside. He left the discarded clothes on the floor, my first clue that he wasn't quite as calm and in control as he seemed.

Apparently Ivan had been hiding more than just a nice set of abs under his clothes all this time. He took his cock in hand and pumped it a few times, but even with his hand obscuring the view I could see he was more than adequately equipped for whatever happened next.

"Hands behind your back, Camilla. Only use your mouth."

I could do that.

"Yes, Professor."

He slipped his free hand behind my head to pull me closer, and I licked at the tip of his cock as soon as I could reach it. Then I sucked the smooth, mushroom-shaped head between my lips, rolling my tongue over the surface until it was slick and hot, and Ivan was making noises of approval and encouragement.

I liked his smell, musky and genuine, and the salty tang of evening and arousal on his skin. He was rock-hard, and seemed as ready as I felt. When I dipped my head and took as much of his cock in as possible, then slid my mouth up and down his length, he cursed once, very softly. It was one of the few times I'd ever heard him use a bad word. I tried the trick again, flexing my tongue up to rub against the sensitive bundle of nerves right behind the head of his penis.

"Enough."

Ivan didn't give me a chance to push any further. He stood and moved to the closest nightstand, pulling the top drawer open and scrabbling inside for a few seconds before coming up with a condom.

"Bed," he snapped, as he smoothed the sheath down on himself with quick, practiced movements. "Present."

I did what he asked and waited. Knowing how turned on he was, I expected penetration and was startled to feel his hands on the back of my thighs, his thumbs parting my labia. And then his tongue, unexpected and warm, slicking inside me as his clever fingers found my clitoris. I would have thought it might take me some time to work myself back up, but after a few seconds of Ivan's attentions I was the same wriggling, eager bundle of overtaxed nerves I had become on his lap.

"Don't come," he reminded me. Which was good, because I'd forgotten I wasn't supposed to, and I was damn close. I wanted him inside me, too, though, almost more than I wanted to come. So I exhaled one, two, three long, deep breaths, and willed my body to be patient. But he kept going, working my clit in a steady, inescapable rhythm that I couldn't resist for long.

"Please, Ivan," I finally cried out, desperate for release.

The mouth of delightful wet wonderment went away. "Professor," he said patiently, and for a moment I thought he was going to start spanking me again.

Instead he positioned his cock at my entrance and pushed halfway in on a single thrust, seating himself fully with the second. A little rough, and faster than I'd expected. And perfect.

I was made for this man to fuck.

It was the kind of thought I would toss aside later, treating it as a byproduct of hormones and delayed gratification. But that future dismissal made it no less true in the moment. I opened myself up, and Ivan claimed me like I'd been his all along. Claimed me for science, perhaps. For himself, certainly. I wasn't sure I could bear it, the sweet bliss of him inside me, his hands steadying my hips. And then he started to thrust, and I could feel my legs shake and my stomach clench with the effort to hold off, hold back.

Might as well try to keep the tide back with a plastic bucket and shovel from the dollar store. The orgasm seemed to gather from all over my body, traveling slowly but inexorably toward the place where my body and Ivan's were joined. He had reached around me to keep stroking the hypersensitive nub of my clit, and after a few beats I was done for.

He could feel it, or maybe I was more vocal than I thought, because even as the pleasure crested and started to suck me under, I heard him laugh. "We'll need to work on that, then."

And then I was drowning, swamped with delight from my head to my toes, thrilled to the core of my soul by the possessive thrumming of this man's cock inside my body and his skilled hand against my clit. Ivan cursed again and sped up, finally giving up his words in favor of a sweet, inarticulate cry of triumph as he lost himself in me for the first time.

Chapter Six

When I felt fully conscious again, I opened my eyes to see Ivan lying on his side watching me. I was flat on my stomach, head still pillowed on my arms, body still pleasantly humming with delight.

He didn't say anything at first but reached out a hand very slowly as though he thought I might pull away. He brushed a few hairs out of my face, tucking them carefully behind my ear, and then ran his fingertips down the contour of my cheek to my chin. Proving my shape to all of his senses, perhaps, finding a new way to see me. With his hesitance came a vulnerability, and I could read more than I usually did in his expression. The boy he had once been, the man he had become, the one still shaping the other day by day whether he acknowledged it or not.

"I've never done this," he whispered, seeming concerned.

"Done what?"

"Post-coital demonstrations of affection."

Turning my head a little, I caught one of his fingertips between my teeth for a second, then let it slide free from my lips with a pop. "You're doing fine."

I resisted the impulse to tell him to do what came naturally. I wasn't sure that any part of human interaction came naturally to Ivan. Instead, I enjoyed the attention for a few moments before taking the conversation in a different direction.

"How did you start this? Not tonight, I mean this whole thing. Kinkiness or whatever you call it."

Ivan's hand stilled for a moment, then continued its exploration of my chin and throat. "My college roommate, a random assignment. He was very into the leather scene. He was convinced I was gay, too, since I hadn't ever done anything with a girl, so he was always trying to introduce me to single guys. One of them was somebody he knew from a BDSM club. A Dominant, Marco. He wasn't thrilled with Kevin's attempt to set him up by luring him to a bar and then pretending to casually run into me there. Kevin got embarrassed and fled the scene, but Marco stayed to talk. I found him strangely easy to talk to."

"That would be strange." I didn't know that Ivan ever talked to *anybody* easily. "He didn't try to pick you up?"

"No, we just talked. In his day job he's a therapist. I wound up telling him some things about myself I hadn't ever articulated before. About why I hadn't dated, or done anything else. He suggested I try a venue where people were more open-minded and communicative about sex, and the roles might be a little easier to understand. I tried it, because I was desperate. And it turned out to be right for me."

He had dragged his fingers down to my shoulder, and now he gently pressed me up and over until I was lying on my back.

"Because you get to be the one in control?"

"That's part of it. But the expectations are also clearer to me. People at the club usually negotiate what they want and don't want in plain language. There's rarely a hidden agenda. Sometimes people even flag their preferences with different colors so you know what they're into before you even talk to them. And the science of it also appeals to me, like I said."

To punctuate that point, he gave my nipple a sharp unexpected tweak and then, before my squeak of surprise could fade, leaned in and swiped his tongue gently over and around the offended area. The pain faded but the sensitized nerve endings soaked in that contact and translated the wet heat to pure ecstasy, a thrill that traveled down my torso to nudge at my clit. More sex magic. He was right, it was appealing. Fascinating, in fact, to see what my own body could do given the right stimulus.

"Do you like having that stuff done to you, too?"

"I've tried it, but no," he said flatly. "Not at all."

"Good, because I don't think I could be a Dominatrix. That's the word, right?"

He shrugged. "Or just Domme. And no, I can't really see you in that role, either. Cami, what are we supposed to do now? Do we go to sleep? Do you go home?"

I would have preferred a passionate insistence that I stay, but I couldn't help smiling at Ivan's cluelessness. "Do you want me to go home?"

"I'm not sure," he admitted. "I want you here. And it would be more convenient if we wanted to have sex again later. But I don't know if I can sleep with another person in the bed."

Fortunately I knew Ivan well enough not to be hurt by this. "Let's think of it this way. Because really, I could go either way. If you were over at my place right now, would you go home at this point?"

A little smile played around the corners of his mouth. "If I were at your place right now and trying to do this, I'd probably be in the middle of a panic attack."

Ouch. "Ivan, it's not really the done thing to tell a woman you've just slept with that sex with her would bring on a panic attack."

"Oh. Sorry. I meant because the setting would be so strange for me, to be doing that activity. I think I'd feel too uneasy. Here at least I've fantasized about those things, and all my equipment is here. So it's not quite so hard to equate this setting with sex."

"There's equipment?"

He chuckled. "Out of all that weirdness I said, *that* was what you ask about?"

"Honestly, I'm mostly only staring at your mouth while you talk. I'm too blissed out to really comprehend much of anything right now." I rolled to face him and patted his cheek softly, then ran my fingers into his hair. It was thick and silky, and slightly wavy from the humidity. Good hair for running fingers through. The dark brown looked almost black in the filtered streetlight glow. "That was a joke, by the way. Not the bliss part, the comprehension part. I was paying attention, but I wasn't sure what to say."

"I got that one. But thanks."

"Do you want to do this again sometime?"

He nodded solemnly. "I want to do this again all the time. We should quit our jobs and stay home and do this until we can't move."

"Tempting. For now I think I'll head back to my place so you can sleep, and I can take a shower. We can see each other tomorrow, because, you know, we're next-door neighbors. Plus we'll both be in the backyard at nine, gardening."

He walked me to my door and kissed me goodnight, like a

regular date. Only the kiss went on for a lot longer than that, and involved some naughty suggestions murmured in my ear, many of them including fancy Latin terms.

I'd turned the ringer off on my cell phone during the car ride home the previous evening, because I knew Athena would be calling to hound me for details about why Ivan had been so affectionate at dinner. When I looked at my phone in the morning, I decided I'd been smart to do so. She'd called twice and texted about five times since then, although the last few looked like drunk texts so those really didn't count. I called her back once I'd poured myself a cup of coffee.

"Details" was all she said when she picked up the phone.

"Do you want gory particulars or do you want a sketch?"

"You have gory particulars? Oh, congratulations, sweetie! You broke the dry spell!"

"Oh, yes." I blew over the surface of my coffee, but it was still too hot to drink.

"So did the dress from the other night have a delayed reaction?"

I could hear her banging around the kitchen, or at least it sounded like the clatter of pots and pans. "Actually, yeah, it kind of did. Apparently he found it very distracting indeed."

"So? How was it? I can't believe you did it with Ivan. I mean I know you've wanted to jump him for months, but still. Eh, different strokes, I guess. I shouldn't judge."

"It was…" How to even begin to describe last night? I had more lurid details than I would ever share with Athena. I couldn't even imagine her reaction if I gave her the full story of what had happened. For all her talk, she was basically a wholesome sort. Not that I thought of what Ivan and I had done as *un*wholesome. But it was certainly... "Interesting. It was interesting."

"Oooh. Oh, Cami. I'm so sorry. Ugh, and you have him right next door, too. Are you—"

"No, no, not interesting like code word for *bad*. Actually interesting. It was very good. Very. Very, very good. Let's be clear on that. Did I mention good? Because you have no idea."

Athena took a few seconds to digest that. "Okay. So interesting how, exactly?"

She sounded as dubious about asking as I did about telling. "Well, you know how I was assuming he had no experience with sex?"

"Yyyyesss..." Dubiouser and dubiouser.

"I could not have been more wrong about that. And last night I learned a thing or two. Or five. Dozen. Because he schooled me. He schooled me *good*. And any more detailed than that would be way too much information. Sorry."

"Holy shit."

I sipped my beverage, imagining I could feel the caffeine going to work in my system. "Athena, I could not agree more."

Often in a new relationship there was that "Lost Weekend" period, the time when you first started having sex and couldn't get enough of one another. Time seemed to disappear when you were rolling around in bed, and there was a lot of falling asleep on the job after too many late nights of not being able to say goodbye without hopping right back in the sack. Or at least that was what had happened to me with the only two semi-serious long-term relationships I'd had.

I wasn't expecting that sort of a weekend with Ivan. In truth, I wasn't sure what the hell to expect. I only knew I was in trouble because I'd found his awkward attempts at afterglow cuddling to be very sweet and endearing. Either he was genuinely lost in the woods or he had the best clueless-guy con in the world going on. So I approached the backyard at gardening time with a little trepidation.

What I got was a reprieve. Dinesh and Julia were down there, too, trying to assemble a new barbecue grill. A few of us had the small, cheap kind of grill you tend to have when you live in apartments. This was the real thing, a big black monster of a barbecue. It had a lot of pieces.

"We're planning to cook for anyone who wants it tonight," Dinesh informed me cheerfully, "if we can just figure out how to put the damn thing together."

Julia gave me a wave, then frowned back down at the parts strewn in front of them, wiping her forearm over her face. It was already heating up. Her dark auburn hair, skimmed back into a pony tail, was frizzing a little around her face where a few wisps had stolen free. I resented the fact that she looked no less beautiful with the frizz. "I still need to go to the grocery store."

"I can get this," her husband assured her. "Go. It'll be done when you get back, babe."

They kissed, a light brush of the lips as she bent down for a moment. "Text me if you think of anything else we need, okay?" I felt a pang of envy at the casual exchange. Ivan, tending his tomatoes, seemed oblivious to the whole thing. And, aside from a nod when I'd first stepped outside, oblivious to me as well.

Once Julia was gone, Dinesh growled and shook a socket wrench at the sky. "Why do I get myself into these things? Why, why?"

"I did wonder." I took the wrench from him, before Dinesh could damage anything with it. He had his strengths, but it was generally conceded that being handy was not one of them. He could have rendered a beautiful three-dimensional model of the grill on his computer in no time, but the odds were slim he could assemble the real thing well enough for it to be useable for cooking. Neither of us was all that surprised when Ivan, brushing soil off his hands, reached out calmly for the tool and scooped up the instruction sheet.

Without saying a word he spent a few seconds perusing the instructions, a few more seconds scanning all the tools and parts, and then set to work. Within ten or fifteen minutes, the completed grill stood before us, ready for its debut that evening. After the initial glance, he'd set the instructions aside and never looked at them again.

"Country boy skill set," he said by way of explanation, when he had tightened the final bolt and put the last tool back in the box Dinesh had brought out.

Dinesh nodded and shrugged philosophically. "You'll get the first burger. Thanks, man."

"You're welcome," Ivan said gravely, then smiled just a bit. "If you need any tomatoes, let me know. I have a few ripe ones." He made a stiff gesture over his shoulder at his plants, each of which sported at least a couple of fat, gorgeous fruits that practically begged to be picked.

"Yeah, what are you doing with all of the tomatoes, anyway?" Dinesh asked. "Julia said you don't eat them."

"It's an experiment. I'm gathering empirical data to demonstrate that my father's method of growing tomatoes is less effective than it could be."

I hadn't heard the actual nature of the experiment before. "But why? I mean, if you don't like them, why do you care?"

Ivan looked at me like he didn't quite understand the question. "Because I think his reasoning is flawed. Or clouded, more accurately, by his insistence on adhering to traditional methods when the upside-down method is demonstrably superior on several key indicators including water usage, insect management, fertilizer requirements and—"

"Hey, thanks for the help, bro, but I need to get upstairs and start working on this shindig. See you later!" Dinesh vacated the patio like a man running from a burning building, leaving me and Ivan alone between the barbecue and the tomato plants.

"I thought he'd never leave," Ivan said, and took my face in his hands. I was expecting him to kiss me but he didn't. Instead, he stood and stared at my face like he was drinking me in. His eyes had golden flecks in the iris near his pupils, I noticed for the first time. His nostrils were flaring. He traced my cheekbones with his thumbs, seeming fascinated by the texture. "Camilla."

"Professor. What were you planning to do with all the tomatoes after the experiment, by the way? Before I claimed them, that is."

"Take them to a soup kitchen. I know somebody who volunteers at one. One of my old roommates."

"Not the same roommate who—"

"Yes, that one. Will you come upstairs with me?" He seemed not just hesitant about asking, but actively uneasy, and I wasn't sure what answer he wanted to hear. I was pretty sure about the answer I wanted to give, however.

"Of course."

His eyes shifted over to his plants. But then his fingers moved over my skin again, weaving into my hair, and he turned back to me, looking perplexed and frustrated. And like a light bulb going on over my head, I realized both the problem and the solution.

"But, Ivan, you should probably finish taking care of your tomatoes first. And I need to deadhead a few roses. And then we can go up, okay?"

The sheer relief on his face was equally gratifying and worrisome. Gratifying to know I'd gotten it right in one shot. Worrisome to know that he was really that bound by his routine, and by all the compartmentalizing he did to minimize his exposure to the unknown. Almost as though his entire life was one big coping strategy. I really wasn't quite sure how to feel about that.

I'm shallow and easily distracted by novelty, so all my concerns about Ivan's elaborate coping mechanisms vanished within sixty seconds of entering his bedroom. His transformation when we entered that room was dramatic. From slightly disheveled fellow gardener to the Professor in one easy step. Not the astrophysics-lecturing Professor, but the one I'd met the night before. The one who could lecture me about kinky stuff any time.

"Strip," he said curtly when the door was closed behind us. "That was your last reminder. The next time you neglect to remove your clothes upon entering this room there will be consequences, Camilla." He moved past me to the bed, sweeping the duvet off and bundling it into the chair before returning to stand in front of me.

"Is that right, Professor?" I couldn't shift gears as quickly as Ivan could. Possibly because this was still all new to me. My hands shook a little as I pulled my T-shirt off and started on my bra.

"Yes." His smile was made entirely of wickedness. "Swift and unpleasant consequences."

A shiver ran down my spine, half lust and half the kind of

fear a horror movie generated. You knew it was coming, you knew it wouldn't hurt you, but it scared you a little anyway and that was exactly what you were there for.

When my clothes were shucked off into a pile by my feet, Ivan stepped in closer and once again framed my face with his hands. "I think I'd like to keep you here all day, Camilla. Do you have any pressing obligations?"

He was close enough that my nipples brushed against his shirt, making me even more aware that he was still wearing all his clothes while I was naked as a jaybird. Or *nekkid,* as we said in Texas, which meant you were naked and up to no good.

"No, Professor. Except to please you."

"Somebody's been reading up. Did you go on the internet last night when you got home?" He didn't sound too perturbed about that.

"I might have done a little light reading, Sir."

He tugged his T-shirt off, but left his shorts on. "I may assign you some reading, too. I'll have to think of a few selections. But that will be later. For now, I have other priorities."

After brushing a faint promise of a kiss against my lips, he stepped away and disappeared into his closet for a few moments, returning with one hand full of black webbed nylon strapping. He must have seen my eyes widen in alarm, because he grinned and shook his head.

"If you're scared of tethers and Velcro cuffs, remind me to wait a long time before I take you to the club."

"What are you planning to do with those?"

"About what you might expect." He slung the straps onto the bed and patted the sheet encouragingly. "Come here."

When I hesitated, biting my lip, his eyes grew stern and he approached me bearing a set of the cuffs. "Camilla, go to the bed now or you're going over my knee."

That didn't really help me with my decision. But after a few seconds I flipped a mental coin and complied. "Yes, Professor."

He put me on all fours in the middle of the bed, cuffing my wrists and ankles and tethering me to the head and footboard with some slack. I could see the versatility, because there was still enough play in the tethers to allow me to lie face up or down, or in any number of positions. But not quite enough for me to wriggle completely off the bed, or use one hand to free the other. When I was all secured there, trembling a little from nerves and excitement, Ivan knelt on the bed beside me and slipped a mask over my head, carefully shifting my hair to accommodate the strap as he settled the black silk blind on my nose. It was heavy and blocked the light completely. I swallowed hard and tried to focus on breathing slowly, calmly.

"The lesson for today," Ivan murmured in my ear, "is about trust."

"Okay. I trust you, Professor." I meant to sound a little less anxious as I said it.

"It goes both ways, Camilla." He started touching me, hands running over my shoulders and back, reaching under me to cup a breast or tweak a nipple. Those hands kept busy as he spoke, and I never knew where to expect them next. "You trust me not to hurt you while you're tied up, at least not in a way we haven't agreed on. I trust you to give me everything you can, everything I ask for, and be honest about your limits. And of course you also trust me to reward you if you comply. If you're good." One hand slipped between my legs, tracing up and down one inner thigh in a slow, torturous tease. "If you're bad, on the other hand, you trust me to rein you in. Which are you going to be today, Camilla? A bad girl, or a good girl?"

"I'll be good if you'll move your hand up about another

two inches, Professor," I tried to joke. He pulled his hand away so fast I could almost hear a swish in the air as it moved. But his voice remained calm, smooth. In control. I felt him get up from the bed, and then footsteps as he walked around.

"No. It isn't a negotiation. Once we're in a scene, once we're doing…this, the time for negotiation and bargaining is over. Which means that now, trying to talk me into giving you pleasure any sooner than I intended to makes you a bad girl, and a little slut. Do you know what happens to little sluts?"

"S-spankings, Professor?" *Woohoo!*

"No. No, I think this is more serious than that. I think this calls for flogging."

Something smooth and soft flapped over my ass and dragged up my back, tickling along my spine. It took me a second to identify it, even after what Ivan had said. Flogging. It was a flogger. A whip. He was talking about *literally* whipping my ass.

"Since this is your first time," he went on before I could form a protest, "we'll begin very slowly."

It was very slow indeed. So soft it was almost a caress, those first few slaps against my butt. The wide leather strips were surprisingly gentle, almost a tease, and before long I found my-self almost wishing for more contact. That wish was granted only in tiny increments, with Ivan always waiting for me to show signs of acceptance before he ramped up the strength of the blows another notch.

Later, when I knew more about it, I would consider the utter mastery of his performance with something like awe. He led me, in the space of a few minutes, from fear of the flogger to craving more of it. By his slow, measured tactics, he guided me through that same change of mind a dozen or more times, until I was tugging on my tethers and leaning hard into each sharp, biting snap of the tails against my ass and thighs. When he stopped I cried out in frustration, only to yelp when the whip snapped up sharply against my drenched pussy.

Then it was over, and I felt the bed dip under Ivan's weight again. "That's better. You seem a little more compliant now. Are you going to behave, and stop trying to make deals?"

"Yes, Professor." I turned my head, even though I couldn't see him, but he was already moving away down the bed. I wanted him back, wanted him to touch me some more. But I knew what would happen if I asked. Maybe I could be sneaky about it.

Moaning softly, as though still overcome by the flogging and the general lustiness, I slowly lowered my shoulders down until I was in that same humiliating but oddly compelling position he'd put me in last night. Presenting myself. Offering myself. I felt the caveman appeal of it, the mindless and ancient allure in such a blatant display of arousal and willingness.

"Bad girl. Back on all fours."

He didn't even raise his voice. If anything, he sounded amused. With a sigh, I pushed against the bed to lift myself again and was startled by a cold touch against one nipple.

"This will hurt a bit, but it will make your nipple very sensitive, both during and after the time that it's on. The pain will generate arousal in the same places as if you were fondled there. More, possibly."

He clipped something onto my left nipple and I tried to pull away. With soothing touches and a low, calm voice he convinced me to remain still long enough to allow the sensation to settle in. The initial pinch was sharp but receded to an ache. As Ivan brushed his fingers around the tightening skin and over the plump tag of tender flesh caught in the clamp, I was blindsided by a wave of searing pleasure-pain. The heat spread through my body like a blush and intensified when he affixed the second clamp.

I felt hot and cold and sore and tingly, all at once. My body was as confused as my brain, and only the strong undercurrent of pleasure kept me from trying to bolt. The clamps were heavy enough to drag down slightly, stimulating my nipples continuously, swaying and causing chills to race through me with each ragged breath I took. I couldn't resist the dark glow of pleasure that had started its slow burn between my legs. Whimpering, I tried to no avail to pull my thighs together, to squeeze the needy ache into something manageable.

Ivan stroked my back, rubbed my neck with one gentle hand. He sounded so considerate, so concerned, as he was doing these deliciously awful things to me. "Easy. It's a lot to take, isn't it?"

Gulping, I gasped out an affirmative, only to receive a swift and sharp pop on the tush.

"Yes, what?"

"Professor! Oh, God..."

"Shh." The warm hand on my neck again, massaging tenderly, and then another hand slipping beneath me to slide down my abdomen. I tried to buck toward it, craving his touch, but the tethers kept me from moving as far as I would have liked. "Be still. I'll take care of you, Camilla. Trust me."

When I stopped moving, he began stroking me, petting, dipping in and out of me. He was thorough and methodical, as though he were attempting to learn the geography of my pussy by feel. And always he talked, reassuring me.

In the absolute darkness, I clutched at his words like a lifeline. I reminded myself I'd chosen to try this, that I could stop if I wanted to. Only then did I realize it might well be an addiction in the making, because although I told myself I could stop, I knew I didn't want to get to that point. I would let it continue because now I wanted to see what came next. Whether it was the science, or the sex, or simply the sheer weirdness of it all, I was hooked. It was something I had needed, without knowing it.

As Ivan's questing fingers placed another clamp, sweet pain lanced through my clit. He chuckled when I gasped, and patted my butt. "And just think, these clamps don't even have weights on them. This time. Now let's warm that ass back up."

I groaned as the flogger snapped against my skin, a deep guttural noise I didn't even recognize as coming from myself. My whole body throbbed with the need for release, and the hot lash of leather served only to heighten that need. It was only a few strokes, though, and then it stopped. Ivan ran his hands over the marks, raking his fingernails delicately against my hypersensitive skin and murmuring in approval when I shuddered. When he flicked the clamp on my clit, I almost came, an instant rush of sensation that waned only a bit when the little charm I could feel swinging around finally stopped moving.

Hands, parting my labia, holding me wide open. I wanted to beg, to scream at Ivan to do it, just fuck me, make me come. I had never said such a thing in my life, never known I could be that person. But with wanting came the knowledge that he would only "punish" me, prolonging my sweet agony, if I did that. So I bit my lip and strained to be still as he did what he liked.

One finger, one long finger, dipped inside my pussy. I couldn't stop a shiver, and the quick clench of my body around that welcome intruder. Then it was out again, traveling upward. Ivan teased his slick fingertip into my ass, and then flicked the clit clamp again. Crying out, I pushed back toward him, wedging his finger a tiny bit deeper in the process.

My orgasm hovered like a shimmering entity, surrounding my clit and pussy but not quite connecting. The added pressure in my ass sent a new batch of sensations romping up my spine, but got me no closer to coming.

"Not until I say so, Camilla. Or it will be your last one for the day."

"Oh, God. Please!" I couldn't help myself.

"No. Not yet. I want to be inside you, so I can feel you come on my cock."

But he had some mercy after all, because the next thing I knew he was there, sliding into me in one hot, thick rush. I could feel the blood thumping through my body, pounding across every overheated inch of me. The friction was almost unbearably good, and I gasped with each slow slide of his cock in and out. So slow. Too slow. I pounded the mattress, tears of frustration soaking the bottom of the mask.

Ivan slid deep and then stopped, leaning his spare frame over mine and reaching under my chest with one hand. "This will hurt for a few seconds," he warned, and released the clip from one nipple.

Many, many profanities came out of my mouth that I didn't even know I knew. And many more when he repeated the strange reverse-torture on the other side. The pain was so sharp, and lingered longer than a few seconds. Far worse than when the clamps had been applied, which I didn't understand. But when I said so, Ivan grunted and then gave a terse, "Explain it to you later."

Right before his hand moved again I realized where he had to be headed next, and I couldn't restrain my protest. "No, not that one. No, *no no no,* don't do that yet. Please, no—"

"Shh. It's okay. It isn't coming off right this second. But you might not be able to come if it's still on. And I know you want to come, don't you, Camilla?"

"Why wouldn't I be able to?"

He resumed his slow, even push and pull, coaxing my arousal back to the fever pitch I'd been at earlier. "Blood flow. Nerve pressure. Some people can, some can't. It also depends on the clamp style and other things. But I don't want to chance it, because I want you to come while I'm in you. I want you to come *for me*."

I was still catching my breath from the nipple clamps coming off, and the insistent tug of the remaining clamp as Ivan worked his cock inside me was already pulling me back toward the edge. But he was right, and I could feel it now. Primed though I was, the little metal clip would keep me from getting there, to where I had to go. And he could tell.

"You're close, aren't you, Camilla? You're starting to tighten around me, but you need that clamp off in order to come, I think. Do you want me to take it off?"

Defeated, in an anguish of want, I finally nodded only to hear his evil chuckle.

"If you want it off, Camilla, you're going to have to ask more nicely than that."

"Please? Please, Professor?" Was that my shrill little voice? I was practically shrieking.

"No, that won't do. I need to hear you say, 'Please take the clamp off my clit, so I can come for you, Professor.'"

My head shook back and forth violently. There was no way. Tremors racked my body, my brain was soaring, and there was no way I could form all those words.

Then he started stroking my clit, teasing around the clamp as he pistoned in and out of my swollen pussy. I felt like things were on fire. Like things might fall off. Like I didn't know what was pleasure and what was pain anymore, and didn't care as long as I got to come. And somehow I shaped the words, blurting them out on a single wailing breath.

"PleasepleasetaketheclampoffmyclitsoIcancomeforyouProfessorfuckfuckfuck!"

Silently, he slipped his fingers around the tiny metal wings and pressed, releasing the pressure, and for a second or so I thought I'd been reprieved. The relief was so great, the building pleasure heightened to a breathtaking intensity by the returning sensation. I started to come, feeling the inexorable wave hit just as the searing pain did. Bound, defenseless, beaten, my body no longer knew what to accept, what to deny. The filter was gone, it was all sensation to me, and it was all as terrible as it was exquisite. On and on, seemingly forever, the throbbing finally subsiding into a dull, rhythmic ache as the last filaments of excruciating pleasure trailed through me, drawing my energy out with them as they went.

I could feel Ivan tensing, growing even fuller inside me, and he growled like a wild thing as he came. Animals together, we gasped out the end of our pleasures in unison before collapsing, utterly spent, onto the cool and welcoming sheets.

Chapter Seven

Before my foray into etiquette instruction, I considered myself an expert on searching the internet. But try as I might, I was unable to find a web page or other resource that covered how to teach your kinky lover who lived next door how to get people to give him money so he could build a better rocket.

Not that I didn't find a host of interesting stuff along the way. The public domain is filled with etiquette manuals from the late eighteenth through early twentieth centuries, and I now knew where to look should I ever need to know when and how a gentleman uses a formal or informal bow, or whose box one may visit during the entr'acte at the opera, or in which order to place the salad, meat and fish forks for a multi-course dinner.

Sadly, bowing was out of fashion in Houston these days, and there would probably only be hors d'oeuvres at the fund-raiser. So I'd decided to take a different approach and narrow down my focus to a few simple concepts for Ivan to remember throughout the evening. Guiding principles, instead of too many specific rules.

"Okay, first thing. You need a pause button."

"Do I get to stop time for everybody else, while I can still move around? I've wanted one of those for a long time."

"Focus, please." I gestured with my hamburger and a tomato slice threatened to slip out the side. "Before you even open your mouth to talk, you need to say 'pause' in your head, and apply a quick test to whatever answer you've thought up."

"Usually I'm thinking about my answer before the other person is through talking. So I'm ready to speak once they've stopped."

In the flickering light of the tiki torch, Ivan's handsome face took on a slightly demonic cast. I thought back to how we'd spent most of the day and shivered. Maybe I could get him to light a few candles later when we went back upstairs.

"Maybe that's part of the problem. Let's do an experiment. I'm talking now, and you're already formulating what you're going to say. So what part of what I just said are you going to—"

"I don't think the problem is on *my* end. I'm only responding rationally to whatever's being said."

"Aha!" This time, the tomato squirted out to land with a wet plop on my paper plate. I picked it up and carefully reinserted it. "That's exactly it. This explains so much. You're not listening to the whole thing. You latch on to the first thing being said and don't even pay attention to the rest. You interrupt because you want to stop all that noise and respond to what *you're* thinking about."

"Yes. Exactly. Isn't that what I said?" He took a bite of his own burger, looking a little grumpy and defensive. But not nearly as grumpy as he would have been a day ago.

"That's the problem, don't you see? You have to listen to

the whole thing. Not just listen, understand it. All of what the other person is saying. Before you decide how to answer."

He shook his head. "That would take forever. Nobody would ever be done talking if we did it like that."

I bit back a smile. "Honey, it doesn't take forever. It takes practice. And it takes a willingness to see something from another person's point of view. Maybe you should try it right now. Get some practice in."

I nodded toward the little group clustered in lawn chairs near the grill. Dinesh and Julia of course, along with Ed, Lin and two other tenants. One of them, I saw, had brought his girlfriend along. This was surprising as we had all suspected the girlfriend was fictional. But there she was in the flesh, a nice-enough-looking young woman who seemed to be getting along with everybody.

From where we sat on the low wall at the edge of the patio, Ivan and I had a good view of everything without having to participate. I knew that was his preference, but he needed to practice, and this was a particularly good opportunity as there was a stranger in the group.

"Remember, listen first to all of what they're saying before you think up your answer. I think the pause button goes on your brain, more than your mouth. The second thing is, run everything through a filter before you say it. Is it true, is it necessary, is it kind? If it isn't at least two of those, don't say it, and cruel-to-be-kind doesn't count."

"Is that a Buddhist thing?"

"I think maybe it's a Catholic thing. Really not sure. It was something from the internet. And now it's your second rule."

"I thought my second rule was to transition out of a long silence."

Sighing, I downed the last of my burger before answering.

"These are the rules for tonight. I'm trying to simplify so you don't feel like you need to whip out the index cards. Pause button. True, necessary, kind. Try those two things, and we'll see how that works out."

Grumbling, Ivan reached for my plate and took our trash to the big garbage can next to the carport. Then he swung by the group as if he were just stopping on his way back to me. I wandered over to my roses and fiddled with them, surreptitiously watching as Ivan lingered to work his way into the conversation.

At first, I saw a lot of false starts. His mouth would flap open then clamp shut so quickly I could practically hear the snap of his teeth. But after a few minutes, he got a thoughtful look on his long, lean face as he leaned in to hear our neighbor Ben's girlfriend discuss her recent trip to Costa Rica.

If I hadn't known better, I might have been jealous. Because Ivan wasn't merely paying attention. He was devoting his attention, bestowing it all on the speaker, taking in not only her words but her gestures and body language as well. And when she paused, he said something that startled her.

"You didn't actually like it there."

"I…didn't say that. It was a great opportunity. And I'd always wanted to go."

He ignored the slightly frantic slashing gesture I was making across my throat, and pressed her further in a soft, insistent voice I recognized from earlier, in his bedroom. It was hypnotic, that tone. "Tell me what you didn't like about it."

Like a bird seduced by a cobra's hypnotic swaying, the girl started describing not flowers and colorful birds, but oppressive heat and insects large and small. And disappointment. When she finally stopped, Ivan nodded thoughtfully but said nothing, and a lull fell over the group until Dinesh broke it by offering another round of burgers.

Clearly we still needed some work on defining "necessary" and "kind." But at least he had listened. And watched. And apparently had an epiphany, because when we went back to his place after the crowd had dispersed, he was practically cackling with glee.

"I got it. I get it now. I know what to do. This is awesome!" He swung me around his tiny living room before tugging me up the stairs after him.

"Are you going to tell me what this amazing insight was?"

"Maybe once you're naked."

He actually started telling me before I had shed the last of my clothes. "I decided to just focus on one person, and then I pretended I was at the club and she was a sub I was meeting for the first time. Trying to figure out what she was really interested in."

"What?" That sounded like a tactic with potential for disaster, if ever I'd heard one.

"No, no, it's because of what you said. About listening and understanding before I try to answer. At the club, I'm usually trying to figure out what the sub needs. Not so much from what they say, but from how they say it and their physical cues. We should shower and wash off this mosquito repellent."

He had covered us both with bug spray before we walked out the door, citing statistics about the incidence of West Nile virus and various fun facts about encephalitis. Evidently, he was equally concerned about the potential neurological or other systemic effects of leaving toxins on the skin for too long. I had known this about him before, of course, but I had never participated in the washing-off portion of the obsession. He cleaned me off and was very thorough.

"The problem is, you kind of brought the mood down," I pointed out, a little breathlessly, as he worked on me with a soapy washcloth. "She wanted to talk about her trip, and you made her talk about how she didn't like it."

"She wanted to talk about that," Ivan insisted. "You could tell from her word choices and the way her mouth moved when she spoke that she hadn't enjoyed the trip, despite what she was saying. Yet she raised the topic, so obviously she wanted to talk about it."

It was difficult to explain the concept of a party pooper to somebody who didn't really get the concept of a party. "We all recognized that, but it brings everybody down. Even if you sense that she wanted to vent or something, you don't do it when you're the center of attention at a small gathering. Not if it's negative like that."

"Fine. Obviously I will never get this. Spread your legs for me, Camilla."

Oh. He had used *that* voice, the one that somehow seemed to be plugged directly into my libido. In one sentence, the frisky playfulness of the shower turned into something full of dark promise.

He was still being thorough. Very, very thorough. I leaned into the shower wall in front of me for support, gasping as Ivan's fingers slipped through each fold. And then a sharper gasp as he plucked a single hair.

"Ow," I complained, but he was already soothing the sting with gentle pressure.

"I want to shave all this off. I want to see all of you. And it will make you even more sensitive."

Could I stand to be any more sensitive down there? I really wasn't sure.

"Can we take a rain check on that? I'm not too sure about—"

"No. I want to do it now." He sounded calm but decided. As if we were talking about something mundane, like paying a bill or scheduling a dentist appointment.

"What if I said no?"

"Hmm. Well, that depends. Are you saying this is a hard limit? Is it no, never, under any circumstances?"

It was getting hard to think with his fingers stealing back and forth along my slit, taking little detours to toy with the hair in question. "No. Not a hard limit."

"In that case, saying no would mean that I restrained you, shaved your pussy while you were tied up and then punished you for refusing in the first place." He reached around me to turn the water off, and had handed me a towel by the time I finally responded without looking back at him.

"And if I say yes?"

He snickered into my neck before nipping there delicately. "I'll shave your pussy first, *then* restrain you and punish you for arguing with me."

As I dried off I pondered those two options, and the curious mindset that made both seem highly attractive. I wondered what struggling might accomplish, and thought of that delicious horror-movie fear. Neither of us had a rape fantasy, perhaps. But at the same time I felt an urge to press the limits. To see how far he really would go. Or maybe to see how far I would go.

"The safeword's still red, right?" I whispered, hoping not to break the tension building between us.

"Yes, Camilla, the safeword is red until you change it," Ivan confirmed, sliding his arms around me from behind and pressing a kiss to the top of my head. "That's the other side of the trust thing, remember?"

"What do you mean?"

"I trust you to be honest about your limits. Not to let me push you somewhere you don't want to go, then resent me for it afterward. I need that, because I don't really...I don't always understand..."

I didn't want that. Didn't want his insecurity triggered now, here, popping the bubble of idyllic sex euphoria we'd created over the past twenty-four hours. Squeezing his arms, I wrapped him around me a little more tightly. "I know. But you get this part, right? And I'll tell you if it's too much. You can trust me."

Ivan rested his chin on my head, reminding me how much taller he was. After a moment or two of silence, he seemed to pull his mindset back to where it had been. "Professor," he murmured.

"Professor," I acknowledged, with a quiver of anticipation. "Please don't do it, Professor. I don't want to be shaved down there, I'd be so embarrassed for you to see me like that." This was true, actually, but not normally something I would have admitted. Not that any of this was normal anymore. I was heading in an entirely new direction, and God help me if Ivan didn't take over the lead again soon because my nerve wouldn't last for much longer.

But I had no cause to worry any longer. He was there instantly. "I want to see you, Camilla. Every bit of you. See you and taste you with nothing in the way. No hiding anything from me. Your embarrassment makes your gift of submission more meaningful."

I tried a little tug, as though I might walk myself forward

out of his embrace. His arms were firm as steel, and didn't budge. "Let me go!"

"No, Camilla." He slid his arms more firmly around me, and then scooped me up as though I weighed nothing, which was at the very least quite flattering. He carried me into the bedroom and plunked me on the bed. Before I could even rebound, he had cuffs strapped around my wrists and was securing them to the headboard. I struggled to twist my hands around, to pull myself free, but before I could manage that, he had pinned one of my legs by straddling it while he strapped the other ankle and thigh with more cuffs. Cleverly designed little fuckers, too. They clipped together, hobbling me on that side. I lost my leverage, and could only kick ineffectually as he secured the other leg.

And then I couldn't kick at all. I brought my knees together and he chuckled. "Enjoy that range of motion while you can."

He shifted my hands one at a time, clipping those cuffs to my thighs as well. Finally he secured tethers from the clustered cuffs down the sides of the bed to attachment points I couldn't see. He tightened them to open me up again, preventing me from pulling my arms and legs any closer together. Then he stood back and surveyed the handiwork his superior strength and my admittedly halfhearted struggling had wrought. I was well and truly immobilized, splayed on my back with bent knees like a frog in a biology lab. When I tried a little harder to free myself and realized I truly couldn't, my heart started to thump double-time.

"Shh. Easy. I'll be right back." Ivan went back to the bathroom, and as I watched him go, I realized he'd pulled his shorts back on. After a few seconds he returned bearing some small scissors, an electric shaver and a towel.

"This won't be a very close shave, but there's less chance

of injury this way since you're being uncooperative," he explained as he folded the towel in half and slid it under my hips. "Later, when you've learned to be a good girl and be still while I shave you, I can use a real razor and get much closer. Or you can have it waxed. Up to you, as long as that pussy is kept bare for me."

Pinned open as I was, I wouldn't have thought I could feel any more naked. But by the time Ivan had finished clipping and then buzzing the hair away—doing a fair amount of teasing in the process with the smooth, flat, vibrating back of the electric shaver—I felt exposed in a whole new way. Possibly because the newly revealed skin was so sensitive and still cool after the sudden loss of its insulation. I wanted to feel it for myself, but Ivan left me in the restraints while he put away the shaving gear.

When he returned, he had a dollop of some clear gel on his fingers, and he proceeded to smooth the cold stuff into the shaved skin. Clearly this was not meant solely as skin care, though he assured me it was just aloe.

"Mostly I know it'll soothe the burn but still not taste too bad."

"Am I going to be tasting—*ooh*."

His tongue was scorching hot, licking a sizzling path from my perineum up to my already tingling clit. With nothing in the way, I could feel every subtle touch, every press and flex and flick, and each nibble of his lips. And with no way to move, either to pull away or to get closer, I was utterly at his mercy. And he knew it.

"This time," he said between licks, in a tone of casual cruelty, "I'm going to try something new. For your punishment, I mean."

"Oh." It was about all I could muster. My brain was already

soaring, my body burning with the need for more. Coherence had failed me during the shaving.

"Yes, Professor," he reminded, and nipped sharply on one of my outer labia, making me yelp.

"Yes, Professor!"

"It's not all about whips and paddles and cuffs, you know."

"Whips and paddles and cuffs, oh, my!" I couldn't help but answer, and then giggled like an idiot. "Professor."

He looked puzzled for a second, then his handsome face broke out in a grin that would have shamed a movie star. "Cute. You're very cute. Don't go anywhere."

And then he was back in his closet, rummaging around. I wiggled my hands and feet, surprised at how comfortable the position was. Once past the initial chagrin of forced exposure, at least.

Some day I would have to explore Ivan's closet. I wasn't sure where he hid it all, but he seemed to have a broad inventory of kinky goods stored on those tidy shelves. This time he came forth with a back massager, one of the big industrial-strength corded kinds with a blunt, rounded head. I tried not to look too puzzled when he pulled a condom over it. Was a back massage part of the punishment? My shoulders *had* been a little tense lately…

Consider it a mark of my sheltered life that it honestly did not occur to me, until immediately before he did it, what Ivan planned to do with the massager. Up 'til then, the only vibrator I'd ever seen had been pink with sparkles and looked like a deformed bunny rabbit.

After plugging the machine into the wall, he flipped it on and smiled a deeply wicked smile as he looked from it to me. "You don't look worried enough, Camilla. I suspect this will be quite a learning experience for you."

He turned the massager off, tossed it casually to one side on the bed and teased me with his fingers at first. He slid one long digit inside me, then two, twisting to press at the most sensitive spots he could find. He bent down every so often to lick or suck at my clit for a few seconds at a time, always leaving me wanting. Within a few minutes I was hanging on a knife edge, so close to coming he could have pushed me over with five seconds of effort.

"Please, Professor," I begged without thinking. "Want to come, please?" Within the constraints of the cuffs and lines, I was wriggling with needy impatience.

"Oh, you'll get to come. Right now, actually."

He turned the Vibrator of Doom back on and pressed it straight to my clit.

For a few seconds it was just too much, buzzing over too large an area for me to even process. Then it started, deep and hard, a climax that grew and grew until I was desperate for it to peak, one that felt like dying when it finally burst into full bloom. It consumed me, stealing my breath and racing through my veins like smokeless fire, and as it ebbed I could hear Ivan's chuckle over the buzzing vibrator and my own harsh panting.

And then...he *kept* it there. Despite my begging, my frantic attempts to get away, the eventual tears, he kept the vibrator in place, only adjusting the speed down and lessening the pressure for a few seconds of almost-relief as the first orgasm abated. Then he cranked it right back up again, slipping his fingers roughly inside me to pump in a steady, brutal beat, ignoring my pained insistence that I couldn't come again. I did just that within a few seconds. Even higher and sharper than the first time, reaching a point where I saw stars, where my thighs jerked in violent spasms as the pleasure shrieked through me. And that state went on and on, never lessening and never quite going over the top to get to the other side, an endless paroxysm of ecstasy that I could neither escape nor deny.

Ivan seemed to know what I would need, that after he finally relented and took the vibrator away what I would crave was to be filled and held. I heard myself whimpering and begging and scarcely recognized the sound of my own voice, except to note I knew how that girl felt because she was pleading to be fucked, and it seemed I would expire on the spot if I wasn't fucked within the next five seconds.

He got there in the nick of time, sliding smoothly into me and pressing his hands to my face as I screamed my relief. "Shh. It's all over now. I've got you."

When he kissed me, it was the sweetest thing I'd ever known. Me, cuffed in an obscene display and tied down to the bed, still shaking through the end of a climax I didn't even know how to categorize, and Ivan, the author of my current condition. But with his mouth pressed gently over mine, his tongue slipping in to flirt with mine, I felt not only desired but appreciated. Cared for. Needed, even, because I had no doubt Ivan needed all this as badly as I seemed to, if not more. That kiss was a rare moment of perfect understanding.

A few minutes later, when he came to his own shuddering conclusion, the look on Ivan's face made me cry all over again…even though I couldn't yet put words to what I was starting to feel.

Chapter Eight

That Monday was like being thrown into ice-cold water after spending the entire weekend in a sauna. Not merely unpleasant, possibly aneurism-inducing.

I'd spent two days cocooning with Ivan, even literally sleeping with him after our exhaustion got the better of us Saturday night and he found he actually could sleep with somebody else in the bed. Even if the sex hadn't been...different, it would have been hard to go back to the daily reality of tedious work, bad coffee and wearing clothes.

Monday brought me back into the real world on multiple fronts, none of them fun. First of all, the repaired air conditioning in my office was not really repaired. It operated at a noisy fifty percent efficiency or so, and only achieved enough cooling to make the office officially habitable. It was still miserable and sweaty hanging out there all day with the temperature in the low eighties and a funky smell oozing from the ducts. But it wasn't quite hot enough to send us all home again.

My boss, usually a mild-mannered and levelheaded researcher, was in the final stages of freak-out that always occurred near the end of writing a grant. And since my work related directly to many of the statistics she was using in her proposal—my scripts found the patterns in the data her research generated—I was one of the first in the crosshairs. She would send me to compile one set of figures, and then by the time I brought her that report, she'd decide she wanted the numbers presented a slightly different way. And by the time I brought her *that,* she was on to wanting another set of numbers entirely. And so on.

That was on top of my usual day-to-day work, of course. And answering the phone if there was overflow. There was always overflow.

And worst of all, my mind was not on any of it. Mentally I was still back in Ivan's apartment, in his bedroom, tied to his bed or kneeling on his floor or getting a paddling and liking it very, very much indeed. My bottom was still a little tender from the unaccustomed treatment, but it was the sweetest reminder of the weekend.

I wanted to email or message him, something subtle but sexy, breezy and cute. None of my thoughts were anywhere close to subtle or breezy. Borderline cute, maybe. It was pretty much all about the sexy, and the opposite of work-appropriate. So I really couldn't figure out what to say, despite wanting the connection so badly. I was almost giddy with relief when I returned from an especially trying session with my boss, Agatha, to see that Ivan had emailed me first. No subject, no salutation. One paragraph.

It was more than enough.

Sense memories of you persist and do not seem to abate as the day progresses. It's disconcerting, Camilla. I don't like it when my mind plays tricks on me. I would much rather simply have you here in the flesh, to feel and taste and smell with my actual senses. Instead my mind keeps conjuring this false perception of your presence. I think it means I miss you.

I read it three times before closing it. Then I opened it up and read it once more for good measure. It was so purely Ivan. The most convoluted yet precise way possible to tell me he was thinking about me. For some reason I found it almost painfully beautiful, and actually started to choke up a little before I got myself under control and fired back a quick response. Quick, because I couldn't say a fraction of what I wanted to say, not from work.

Professor,
Me, too.
~C.

The rest would have to keep until that night. But somehow, though the end of the day couldn't come soon enough, the wait now seemed a tiny bit more bearable.

I wish I could say we were discreet and tasteful about our reunion that evening. Sadly, as it happened, we were neither. Ivan greeted me on my back doorstep when I came home, and pinned me to the door in a liplock before I could even turn the key. We were still there, necking and panting and generally acting like teenagers in a hormone frenzy, when Ed, Ben and Ben's girlfriend came strolling by on their way out somewhere.

The gasp and somebody's cry of "Whoa!" broke us apart, and then there was much throat-clearing, waving awkwardly and avoiding eye contact among us. For four of us, that meant glancing to the side or up or down or anywhere that seemed safe. For Ivan, it meant a very obvious eyeroll followed by a grumpy glare that finally got the little group of friends moving along again. As soon as they were safely past, he spun around, turned the key in my lock and shuffled me through the door before closing it firmly behind us. Then we repeated the mutual attack from the other side of the door, with no onlookers and a lot more groping.

I don't know how he got my shirt and bra off in that process, but I'm fairly certain wizardry was involved. By the time we finally came up for air, I was in slacks and heels, and feeling overdressed in even that much.

Ivan trailed his fingertips inside my waistband. Then he slipped one hand all the way down to tug at the top of my panties, stoking the heat that had been smoldering all day.

"Have you been a good girl today, Camilla?"

"Define good, Professor," I purred. Did he want a good girl or a bad girl right now? Did it make any more difference to him than it did to me?

Ivan looked thoughtful. "I'll have to start thinking up some responsibilities for you, for when we're apart. For when you're at work, especially. And some restrictions. No orgasms, for one thing. Unless I've approved them."

I couldn't help but laugh. "It's not like I'm in the habit of doing *that* at work anyway, Professor. I wish I had that kind of time."

He cocked his head. "Maybe you should make the time, in that case. That can be your first task. Sneak an orgasm in at work tomorrow. Think of me when you're doing it. And when you've finished, email me to let me know. You can be discreet in the email. But I'll want a full accounting afterward. With a lot more descriptive language than 'doing *that*.'"

"You're joking. Right?"

"No. I'm quite serious." And he looked it.

"I can't do…I can't masturbate at work. It's not conducive."

Ivan shrugged. "Not my problem. I want you to make the time and do what it takes to get into the right frame of mind. I believe it will help you relax, help get your mind off the tension of work for a short time. And it will also help keep you sensitive and primed to respond to me later."

How could something that patently self-serving sound so damn sexy? I had to wonder about my own wiring sometimes.

"And if I don't do it? How would you know, anyway?"

"I'll know," he assured me cryptically. "And if you don't do it, then you won't be permitted to come later that night, either. Now take your pants off."

I was already on it.

The week went along that way, for the most part. Frantic, kinky after-work sex, hurried dinners over which we attempted to discuss the fast-approaching fundraiser, followed by more mind-blowing lewdness until we both keeled over from exhaustion.

Ivan approached having sex like conducting an experiment. He was knowledgeable. He was thorough. He used all the resources at his disposal and was determined to get his result or know the reason why not. He aimed the full force of his attention at me, and it was so intense it almost scared me.

But as the days passed, something else started to take root. Fragile, tender at first. Neither of us addressed it head-on. But we spent more and more time together just…being together. With me naked, typically, and Ivan at least nominally clothed. The dynamic, skewed as it might seem, felt unquestionably right to me. Ivan seemed soothed by it as well. He seemed to relax into that role of confident, quiet dominance as if he was putting on a favorite pair of slippers at the end of a rough work day.

Wednesday I capitulated and managed a coffee-break climax in the bathroom at work, and Ivan greeted me that night with barely restrained triumph. And praise, and petting, and allowing me to climb all over his naked body, exploring as I hadn't had a chance to do before. I wallowed in it, a completely sensual beast for those few magical hours.

Afterward, we talked about nothing much at all.

"How about pets? Any pets growing up?" I wound my fingers through his springy chest hair and stroked the smooth skin beneath, enjoying the interplay of textures. "Country boy, you must have had pets."

"Of course." Ivan was staring up at the ceiling but his eyes were half-closed. He looked as sated and drowsy as I felt. "We always had dogs, for one thing. And there was usually at least one cat around the house. More in the horse barn, of course."

"Horses? Your family lives on some acreage?"

"Mmm. A hay farm. My father's family has owned the land forever. Mom was a dressage rider when she was younger. The horses are mostly hers, and one of the dogs at any given time."

"One house dog, the rest for hunting?"

"Yeah."

It was a common enough arrangement in our neck of the woods. A pair of highly trained but goofy retrievers or hounds in a kennel out back, and something smaller and cuter for the lady of the house. At least ostensibly. In my experience, the cutesie little house dog usually ended up attaching itself to the biggest, least likely male, who would then pretend not to dote on it while sneaking it table scraps.

"So whose was the cat?"

"Mine, I suppose. Cats do what they like, though. They

don't really belong to people. I prefer the cat to Brodie. That's my mother's current dog. The last one was Pumpkin. They're always apricot toy poodles."

"Okay, so…how about school? Tell me about your academic career, Professor Reynolds."

He chuckled and tightened his arm around my shoulders, stroking my upper arm in an absent-minded way. Half draped across his body as I was, I could see his face darken a little as he considered the question.

"In elementary school, they wanted to put me in a special class at first. I kept biting the other students and screaming at the teachers whenever they got things wrong. Sometimes I stood up and started explaining things to the whole class. I would pitch a fit if they tried to make me stop before I was done."

"Shit. Seriously?" Maybe it shouldn't have surprised me. A mind like Ivan's didn't come free, and as tough as he found social situations now, he must have been completely in the dark about it as a kid.

Ivan nodded. "But since I had been reading from the age of two or so, and was already doing calculus by the time I was kindergarten age, my parents suspected something was up other than ordinary brattiness. They took me into Houston, and then to Dallas, and had me tested eight ways from Sunday. They never would tell me what all they found out, but I spent the next year or so being tutored at home and seeing a 'special doctor' a few times a week. That was when I was six, seven years old. When I finally went back to school, it was a private school."

"For…for kids with behavior issues?"

"No, no. Just a private school. I was on a special track. I basically tested out of all the grade school information that year, but my parents drew the line at my skipping the school experience completely. When I was nine, they made me go into the seventh-grade class and then move up with that group. They wouldn't let me move on to college. By the time I graduated from high school I was fourteen, but the graduation was still basically for form. I had also been taking college classes for a few years by that point under a special arrangement, so the next year I finished my undergraduate degree and was able to start working more seriously on my thesis."

"Your life almost sounds like an astrophysics version of—"

"Please. *Please* do not reference any television characters from the late eighties right now."

"—Mozart," I offered. "Have you ever had a time in your life when you were just doing the standard thing like everybody else? No special arrangements?"

"Not really, no. I didn't think about it much growing up, though. I was too insulated. I didn't even move out of my parents' house until after I'd started working on my PhD, and then it was only to the graduate student dorm for a year."

"Oh." It made more sense now. The odd sophistication of his kinky roommate wouldn't be quite so odd for a grad student. I altered my image of two eighteen-year-olds braving the club scene together to the very different picture of an eighteen-year-old Ivan and a twenty-something leather aficionado. The older guy who was sure the young Ivan was gay, taking him to bars, trying to fix him up. It made me mad, all of a sudden, angry enough to want to punch something.

Always perceptive in the ways I least expected, Ivan picked up on the tension in my body. "What is it?"

"Nothing." I shook my head as if that could clear the pictures away. "It occurs to me that your old roommate was kind of skeezy."

Ivan shrugged. "He saw a confused kid, and thought he knew the answer because he saw something of himself in me. He was right, we did have something in common. It just wasn't the thing he thought it was. But it's okay. Besides, I've gotten my own back, since then." He pressed a kiss to my forehead and smiled. "We've played together at the club a few times. On more than one occasion I've tied him to the St. Andrew's cross and whipped his ass until he had welts on his welts."

"But he's a guy," I protested. And almost immediately realized how incredibly dumb I must sound.

"I don't have sex with him," Ivan clarified. "Although he always makes it a point to remind me he's available if I change my mind. But it's only been friendly beatings between us."

We both laughed, and I buried my face in his shoulder to hide what I suspected might be a slightly manic grin. All the strangeness, all the joy of the last several days, had formed a shimmering bubble of delicate tension in my chest. I knew the bubble had to pop, and soon, because that's what always happened. But for the moment I was able to shelter it in the protective half circle of Ivan's arm around my body.

Cheap soap and white tile
Contrast sharply with pleasure
Work bathroom of bliss

Why haiku? Because by Friday I was already running out of ways to be discreet when I emailed Ivan regarding my new break-time hobby. I thought maybe haiku would be an interesting challenge for Ivan, requiring him to use his strength with rigid structure to help overcome his weakness at metaphorical thinking.

I should have considered how quick a study he could be at

some things. His answer had me blushing so hard I was afraid my coworkers would notice.

Delicate petals
Flow open to receive me
Sweetest kiss of all

Holy crap, the boy had game. Did he even realize that? I still wasn't sure. Or maybe I was that easily impressed. Probably if my coworkers had read that, they'd have thought it was all about actual flowers and regular old mouth kissing.

I was puzzled to see a fresh email from Ivan come in a few minutes later. Written from his phone, I saw, which also surprised me since I knew he preferred the regular keyboard to thumb-typing.

Need to change dinner plans and stay in. Heard something distressing. Can only discuss it at home. Be upstairs when I get there.

Distressing? What could he possibly have heard in the five or ten minutes since he emailed last? I was too busy to think about it much, because Agatha dumped a fresh load of work in my inbox.

The brusque tone of the email didn't tip me off to the level of Ivan's anxiety, because he was usually brusque. By the time he arrived at his bedroom door, though, he was so tense I could see the veins standing out on his neck.

I was already naked, already kneeling down. Ivan stormed into the room and started to pace, running his hands through hair that was already badly rumpled. He seemed to be struggling for words, and I wanted badly to get up and soothe him, calm him down enough to tell me what was wrong.

But I sensed it wouldn't be welcome. He had to get there on his own.

"I was in the break room on the second floor," he finally blurted out, "and I'd dropped a quarter. It rolled under one of the machines so I crouched down to try to reach it. You know how there's a half wall?"

"Yes, Professor." I was picturing the room in question, the little vending machine nook separated from half a dozen wobbly tables by a somewhat pointless waist-high wall where the stained carpet gave way to dull linoleum.

"They were getting coffee from the coffeemaker by the sink, so they didn't come back there to the machines. They thought the room was empty."

"They?"

"Dr. Donovan and his crony, Dr. Yu. Discussing my position. *My* position. And how well they thought Dr. Lance Leandro would do in it. What a great 'rainmaker' he would be at the fundraisers. They were looking *forward* to it."

"Wait. Lance Leandro, the hunk from *Science Street?* How could he do your job?"

Ivan snorted. "Not very well at all. But his background is actually in astrophysics. And," he added grudgingly, "he did some of the seminal research in this area at Caltech before he landed his current gig on television. Pretty boy."

I had to stifle a laugh at that. Ivan might not have charm, but he had looks in abundance. It wasn't surprising he didn't know that, but it was still a bit rich to hear him accusing anybody else of looking too pretty. But the impact of what else he'd said was finally sinking in, quelling any thought of laughter.

"Oh, sweetie. And you're sure they were talking about your position?"

Ivan, still pacing back and forth across the stretch of room next to the bed, nodded with a look of disgust. "They named the position. I'm not tenured, I have very little security if they really want to replace me. What am I going to do? I'm terrible at finding work. Nobody else in Texas is doing this right now. I'd have to go to California or Florida. And I don't know people there. I don't have *family* there."

His support system. For somebody who was rotten with people, Ivan sure relied heavily on them. He couldn't move. I couldn't even imagine that. Him living thousands of miles from his hometown, all his tentative friendships, the system of routes between safe, known places he'd spent so much time establishing.

Him living thousands of miles from me.

But we had been together a week, if one could even call this temporary insanity we'd hopped into "being together." I really didn't know what it was. What it might be. So his proximity to me shouldn't—couldn't—be a factor. I tried to put it out of my mind as I shifted to ease my knees.

"What do you need me to do? How can I help?"

He shook his head and slowed to a stop in front of me. "You probably can't. Just help me get through this party without making too big an idiot of myself. But I don't suppose it matters much."

"Maybe it matters more," I suggested, tipping my head back to look him in the eye. He cupped my cheek with one hand, an unexpected gesture of fond regard that stole my concentration for a moment.

"What do you mean?"

I tried to remember what I meant, while I pushed my head into his caress like a greedy kitten. "Um...oh, I mean if you charm enough big donors at the party, maybe they'll reconsider. Because it isn't all about the fundraising, right? And when it comes to the science part you still have more credibility."

He mulled it over for a few moments, rubbing his fingers into my hair and stroking with a steady rhythm that seemed to soothe him as much as it soothed me. "What other suggestions do you have for me?" he asked at last.

It took me a moment to pry my mind away from the most immediate suggestions that sprang to mind. "I thought we could consider some literary examples. Characters who become more relatable, and what they do to accomplish that. We probably don't have time to read the book, though, only to watch the movie."

That was how we ended up watching *Pride and Prejudice* that night. Because whose transformation could possibly be more instructive than Mr. Darcy's, despite my own decided preference for the Darcy of the story's first half? And what sexier way to watch it could there possibly be than sitting naked between Ivan's knees, my head on his thigh, while he stroked my hair and gave me sips of wine from his glass?

My being there with him like that seemed to calm him. He gave the movie due consideration, although he didn't see what was wrong with Darcy to begin with. He agreed with me that a sound spanking or two definitely could have fit nicely into the narrative.

"But her mother really is awful," he objected near the end of the film. "Why shouldn't Darcy point out her shortcomings when even Elizabeth would agree Mrs. Bennet is clearly doing things wrong? Wrong by the standards of the time, I mean, when social niceties were so significant as indicators of standing?"

"Because it would be an even worse shortcoming to point

all that out. By being a snot about it before, he was actually being much less classy." Privately, I added, *though a hell of a lot sexier.*

"His first proposal makes sense, though. He's absolutely correct about the damage the marriage will probably do to him socially. It's a significant challenge they'll have to overcome."

"True," I conceded, "but it's not really the sort of thing a girl wants to hear during a proposal. It's not like she wouldn't have been aware of all that. He'd have done much better to stick to telling her he was in love with her, and leave discussing the obstacles for later. He made it all about him."

"Of course the actual speech he makes isn't in the book, so we have no way to know what he really said. Only that he dwelt on the consequences too warmly," Ivan mused.

It took me a moment to absorb what he'd said. "Wait. You've read this, and remember it that well? I didn't even remember the way the thing was worded in the book. Why didn't you tell me?" I turned around and caught him smiling at me with what I could only characterize as extremely fond tolerance.

"Watch the end of the movie," he said softly, gesturing to the screen.

I turned around, but my mind was far from Hertfordshire. This wasn't the first time I'd had cause to wonder how much Ivan really wanted or needed the help I was giving him. But it was the first time I'd wondered whether the whole thing had been an elaborate ruse to get me to go out with him. So silly, if that was the case. I would have said yes if he'd asked. Apparently he was exactly as dumb as most guys in that respect. They rarely thought to just ask. Or they over-thought, and scared themselves out of it.

"So what's my lesson? Since I think it's pretty obvious we

both think Darcy had a certain amount going for him in the first place," Ivan clarified. "What makes the transformed Darcy more desirable?"

I lifted my head from his lap and thought about it. "Well, for one thing, the early Darcy was a serious drag at parties. Too busy looking for things to condemn, instead of considering ways to enjoy himself."

"I always find ways to enjoy myself," Ivan protested. "I usually bring a book or my computer. If I have to attend a party at all, I mean."

He didn't seem too put out when I laughed at that.

"But that approach isn't going to win hearts or donations. So what did Darcy do differently, how did he change?" I stood and stretched my legs as I spoke, having honestly forgotten I was nude until I felt Ivan's hand cupping my butt, stroking down the back of one thigh.

"Did I tell you to get up and distract me, Camilla?"

Grinning, I took a longer stretch to see what would happen. "Sorry, Professor."

"You might be later. Darcy traded his external and internal motivations."

"He what?" I'd been looking for an answer about being nice or paying attention to people. Ivan's summary forced me to actually think again, when I'd already started shutting the thinking parts of my mind down for the evening.

"Turn around." Patiently, Ivan turned me to face him, his hands on my hips, his legs sliding between mine to part them until I was practically straddling his lap. "To begin with, Darcy's internal motivation was all for himself. How would things work to his advantage, how would things reflect on him? And he had an external locus of control. He viewed the dictates of society as forces that controlled him. If he acted a certain way, it was because society demanded that. Lace your fingers behind your neck, Camilla."

"Huh? Oh…" I put my hands to my neck, trying to focus on Ivan's discourse about Darcy while at the same time battling sudden, overwhelming arousal. The sexy professor voice was like an aphrodisiac to me now, I realized. God help me if I ever tried to audit one of Ivan's classes.

"Very good. Have I mentioned that your breasts are almost perfectly symmetrical? Today at work, I couldn't stop thinking about the feel of your nipple on my tongue, hardening as I sucked. It was very distracting. As was the thought of ejaculating all over your breasts. I like that idea very much. Would you like that?"

Guh.

"Y-yes, Professor."

"Of course what really matters is that I'd like it. But it's good to know what you find rewarding. Do you like the idea of being marked that way? Like territory, or property?"

"Oh, God, yes."

"It makes you wet just to think about it."

He wasn't making an assumption, he was testing a theory, pressing one long finger between my legs and sliding it between folds that were already slick and throbbing in anticipation of that touch. My legs were getting wobbly. I bit my lip and tried to slow my breathing.

"After he realizes his approach is ineffective, Darcy begins to see the constraints of class and social expectations as matters of choice, and he realizes that he is a free agent who must take responsibility not only for his choices but their consequences."

"Wow. That's a really good analysis." How was he thinking so calmly about character development at the same time he was driving me crazy doing *that* with his hands?

"I don't buy it, though," Ivan said firmly, thrusting another finger inside my clenching channel. "I think he was just putting up a good front because it was the only way to get Elizabeth to marry him, so he could get her into bed."

His lips grazed my belly and I swayed toward him, nearly falling into his lap but snatching myself upright at the last second.

"There's another possible explanation," I gasped, trying to act like I had the same control, the same degree of cool, as the man currently driving me to sweet distraction. "Darcy was shy and insecure, but when he realized he didn't have to impress everybody and he could be himself with Lizzie, he turned out to be okay. Oh, *God,* do that again."

"No."

"Please?"

"No. What's the lesson for tonight? Wrap it up. You tell me mine, and I'll tell you yours."

It was hard to think with my body melting, much less talk. How I managed, I really don't know. "What you did at the barbecue. Focus on one person at a time, get into that one person's head. That works for you. Now, *please?*"

"Upstairs."

Chapter Nine

Ivan's bed was taller than mine, because he had it up on risers. I found out why that night when he bent me over the edge of it. It was the perfect height to support my upper body but allow me to plant my feet comfortably on the floor. This was fortunate, as I was to spend quite a bit of time in that position. As soon as I was situated, Ivan set about securing me into place with cuffs and tethers. Not very tight, as I could move my arms quite a bit and bring my legs all the way together. But I couldn't get away, which was the main point.

"Comfortable? You'll be there quite some time," he said, resting one hand on my lower back.

"Yes, Professor."

I wasn't merely comfortable, I still had that melting sensation, like I was sinking into the bed. Boneless and accepting, but at the same time coursing with eagerness.

"On with the lesson, then."

As he spoke, he rubbed my back gently, relaxing me even further. Then he slid his hands down, spreading my ass with one palm on each cheek and kneading until I was aching for him to shift his attention to my pussy or clit.

"Beautiful," he murmured. It never ceased to amaze me, the things he suddenly chose to give opinions about. "Have you ever had anal sex?"

My brain made a record-scratch noise and I lifted my head like an antelope sniffing for predators. "No! Have you?"

Ivan snickered at my entry in the stupid-question-of-the-day contest. After a second, I joined him. It really was pretty stupid. Obviously he had, as if it mattered.

"Yes. And I'd like to have it tonight."

"Oh, holy cow. Wait, is that my lesson?"

He leaned over my back, still fondling my butt, pressing his semi-hard cock against the cleft and nibbling on my neck. "Your lesson for tonight is that you're mine, Camilla, and I can take you whenever and however I like." He slid his tongue around my earlobe, pulling a chill from me, chuckling when I pushed my hips back into his. "I can have you on your knees, servicing me with your mouth. I can spread your legs and fuck your pussy whenever the mood strikes me. But tonight..."

He paused, nipping harder against the taut muscle that led from my jaw to my shoulder. The hint of pain made a delicious contrast with the unexpected dirty language Ivan was indulging in. When I groaned, charmed beyond sense at the combination, his lips curled against my skin. "Tonight I want to teach you to take my cock in your ass like a good little slut. Because I'm in the mood, and it's time you learned that your ass is mine to fuck, just like your pussy and your mouth."

Evil. Pure unadulterated evil, this man was. His voice and hands were clearly agents of some dark, seductive force that caused me to do things I would normally never have considered. Because when he said all that, it sounded like the best idea in the world. Really, I could hardly wait. Except that I was still a bit—

"Scared," I confessed, despite the fact that I was grinding my hips back into his body in a steady, needy beat. "It'll hurt."

"So does paddling," he reminded me. He moved his hands down a bit and used his thumbs, stroking my slick lower lips apart and dipping between them. "This doesn't really have to hurt as much as you'd think. Not if it's done right. I assure you I will do it right, because I want you to enjoy it so you'll let me do it again. I'll go slowly, and I'll do a lot of prep work."

"'Kay," I mumbled into my arm, resisting the urge to beg so early in the evening. "Prep work?"

He stood and pushed away from the bed, leaving me chilly again from the loss of his heat. I heard fabric rustling, and the drawer to the bedside table being opened, and some other noises I couldn't identify. I knew better than to try to turn around and look, however.

What was more, I didn't want to look. I didn't need to. I wanted the surprise, the shock and apprehension dissolving into pain and pleasure. I wanted to accept whatever Ivan chose to do. To submit to it, absorb it. Not mindlessly, either, despite how brainless with pleasure he often made me feel.

He called it taking, but I felt as though he were *giving* me these things, these actions, like pieces of himself. Challenging me to receive these odd gifts, because they were all he had to give. His attention, his regard. His respect, which was the strangest thing of all, because I had expected to feel degraded at some point in all this and instead I felt valued beyond measure. Cherished. Strong.

"Professor?" I couldn't hear him, but I sensed he was still there in the room behind me.

"Yes, Camilla?"

"I need you," I whispered. A last-minute alteration from what my mind had first supplied for me to say. It was way too soon to say that other thing, to even think that.

"You'll have me soon enough." His voice was calm, reassuring. I basked in it. "Do you want me to tell you the plan for the evening, so you'll know what to expect?"

"No." I was vaguely bewildered to hear myself sounding so insistent. "I don't. I trust you."

I could hear him approach, feet padding softly on the carpet. Then the warmth of his thighs against mine, his stomach leaning in over my lower back again. Skin to skin, against my back—he had taken off his shirt, but his jeans and the warmed metal of his belt buckle scuffed against my legs and ass.

"I know you trust me, but you said it was scary, too. Are you saying you want to be surprised?" He sounded a little dubious.

"I'm saying…" I struggled to frame it in words, this incoherent jumble of feelings and desires. "I trust you. And I want to just be here and accept whatever you choose to do to me. I want to—to give that to you."

A moment of thick silence followed my words, enough time for panic to knock on the door. Then I heard Ivan sigh, a long, shaky exhale, and the next thing I knew he was leaning over me again, first kissing my shoulder and then biting there as though the kiss weren't enough.

"Camilla, you…my God," he whispered against my skin, his voice sounding oddly strained. "Sweetheart, do you even know? You're so perfect and you don't even realize."

The endearment seeped into me like a touch, warming me as much as his body did. "Did I say a good thing, Professor?"

"Oh, you said an amazing thing. Tonight I'm going to make very, very sure you know how much it means to me."

Words left me as Ivan's hands started wandering, his mouth not far behind. He covered me with touches and kisses, always teasing away from the most sensitive areas, chuckling cruelly when I protested. Soon I was the opposite of relaxed, every nerve ending alive, every muscle taut with anticipation. I was already wound up so tightly, I felt I might climax from a single touch or word.

When he dropped to the floor behind me, nipping and licking the tender backs of my thighs, I spread my legs shamelessly and tried to wriggle closer to him. He laughed and pressed my hips to the bed, pinning me easily. Soon his knees were nudging my stance wider still and I felt his breath, scorching hot against my pussy as he tightened the straps at my ankles to keep me from closing my legs.

My next attempt to move earned me a sharp pop on the back of one leg. "Be still."

I obeyed, biting back a moan of frustration. It felt too good, I wanted to argue. Nobody could possibly be still for that. Instead I breathed out slowly, forcing myself to settle into the bed once more.

He rewarded that effort with a lick, then another, and then a muscular curl of his tongue into my slit and out again. That wasn't his destination, though. He slipped a finger into my pussy like a placeholder and slid his tongue higher, skating over my perineum before executing a lazy circle around the tightly puckered opening that was his objective for the evening.

Whatever I might have expected, the reality was something entirely new. He had played a little there with his fingers before, but this time Ivan licked and teased at my ass, awakening nerve endings I hadn't even been aware of. He flicked his tongue over the opening, a shocking delight, then brought his conveniently slick finger into play. When he started to work it into the tiny, resistant hole, slow heat shimmered over my back until I felt like a bed of living coals, waiting for a single breeze to fan me into flame.

It dawned on me at a certain point that Ivan clearly knew more about that part of my anatomy than I did. He seemed to know exactly where to push and where to stop. The first tight band of resistance yielded when he kept his finger inside the rim and licked around the perimeter, pressing with his tongue until my muscles submitted and relaxed to allow the intrusion. Then that finger pulsed in and out, in and out, a fraction of an inch deeper each stroke, as his clever tongue meandered down to tickle my clit.

By the time Ivan's finger was buried to the last knuckle, I was so close to an orgasm that my pussy was clenching in tiny spasms of want. For a moment, I thought he might even let me come. And then he pulled his finger out, prompting another hot rush of sensation over my back and legs, and backed away again. I heard a click and a squirt, then Ivan spoke again.

"You're very tight, Camilla. I'm glad I picked this up the other day, I thought it might come in handy."

Something cold, slippery and much larger than a finger pressed against my rear. Ivan used the fingers of one hand to spread me and add more lube, as he gently but insistently pushed into my ass again.

"This plug isn't quite as big around as my cock, so it'll be a good intermediate step. No, sweetheart. Be still."

I had started to grind mindlessly against the edge of the mattress, my need beginning to crowd out any other considerations. At Ivan's words I stopped, trembling with the effort it took. He nudged the plug a little deeper, straining the snug ring to the edge of pain before retreating a little. And then another nudge, insistent and steady, gaining a little ground.

Apparently recalling my positive reaction to his earlier unprecedented display of skill at talking dirty, Ivan began to narrate. "Your ass is starting to stretch. It's opening up to take the plug, just like it'll take my cock later when I'm ready to fuck you. I've imagined this, you know. So many times. Tying you down so you can't get away, getting you so excited your pussy is soaked. Flogging that butt until it's hot and pink and you're begging for an orgasm. Begging for my cock. And then only letting you come when I'm finally fucking your tight little ass."

I groaned, and then gasped as the plug finally popped past the tightness and seated itself inside me. It burned a little, but that subsided quickly into a naughty, buzzing heat as Ivan continued to pet and praise me.

I could have wallowed in that state indefinitely, but he had other plans. This time, after he left me, he told me to watch him. I turned my head, craning my neck until I could see him over my shoulder in the semi-darkness. When he was sure he had my attention, he unbuckled his belt with seductive deliberation, pulling it from his belt loops one at a time and then doubling it over in his fist.

Sweet Jesus.

I closed my eyes, unable to watch anymore as he brought his arm back for the first swing. The leather whistled a little in the air, and the blow cracked like gunfire, louder than I was expecting but not hurting quite as much as I'd feared. A deep thud, leaving a sting in its wake. And then another, and another, until my entire rear end was burning like hellfire over a deeper, restless ache.

Until Ivan pressed his hands to my hips and told me to settle down, I hadn't realized I was moving. To get closer to the belt or to retreat from it, I honestly couldn't have said. I had lost track of the swings, the smack of the leather against my skin, as the individual blows were lost in the greater picture of pain and anticipation. Wet, I felt so wet, throbbing between my legs with the need to be filled, fucked, taken. The first brush of the Professor's fingers over my mound brought me right to the edge of orgasm and stranded me there, crying literal tears of frustration, as he took his time removing his pants and donning a condom.

Was it mercy or cruelty that he slid into my waiting pussy and thrust deep, balls slapping against my clit, once again taking me so close to climax I could taste it? Cruelty, I decided when he stopped moving after only a few thrusts. Definitely cruelty.

"*Please...*" I wailed, yanking against the wrist restraints.

"Shh."

More cruelty. He began to manipulate the plug inside my ass, twisting it, pushing it in and out to stretch me even further, until I stopped straining against it each time it entered me again.

He pulled it and his cock out at the same time, and I was too far gone even to struggle or protest the loss. And then he pressed the head of his cock against the still-tight clasp of my ass, slicking more lubricant onto himself before snapping the bottle shut and lobbing it onto the bed where it bounced in front of my face, an unexpected focal point.

Slowly, so slowly, with excruciating care, he worked his way inside me. First the fat head of his cock, sliding past the tightest point with a snap of sudden, brief pain that drew a sharp cry from me. He stopped but didn't pull out, waited and spoke soothing nonsense until my body adjusted to his girth before resuming his slow, deep push.

There was burning, but it paled in comparison to the shivering pleasure that crept over me, beginning where his cock was entering me and overtaking my whole body in the span of moments. The thrill was dark, primitive and frightening but also too dazzling to resist. When I started to try, the restraints at my legs snapped tight, keeping me spread and defenseless against Ivan's incursion.

"Shh. No, Camilla." His voice sounded as controlled as ever. "You can't fight this. You can't get out of the cuffs. I'm going to fuck your ass, and you're going to take it. Oh, that's it," he muttered as I shuddered and then relaxed a fraction more. "That's it. Good girl. Just open up for me and take it, take my cock. Tell me how it feels to have me inside your ass."

"Good," I moaned. "Full. Hot." I seemed to have been reduced to single syllables, but the Professor didn't seem bothered by that. And even his calm was slipping away now, a tremor beginning in his voice to match the one I could feel in his thighs where they pressed so close against the backs of mine. Losing his shit. That knowledge was arousing in itself.

"All the way inside you now. Feels so hot and tight. Your butt is still red and warm from my belt. So good." He eased out a little and pushed back in, deeper still, with a little grunt that echoed my own. "Oh, *yessss*..."

He started thrusting, keeping his strokes short and careful. Each push of his cock inside me sent chills racing up my spine and down to my neglected pussy. My brain seemed stuck, unable to quite grasp the reality of what I was doing, what I was letting Ivan do. It felt amazing, no longer painful at all but like sorcery, a dark magic spell of arousal that had me in its thrall.

I was suspended, floating, skating along the thin boundary between pain and pleasure, frustration and orgasm, insanity and sheer bliss. When Ivan pushed a hand beneath my hip to find my clit, I forgot how to breathe.

"Come for me now, Camilla. I want to feel you."

It took pathetically little time and effort for him to tip me off that cliff. A few strokes, a few cries of pained and ravenous need from me, and I was plunged into an ocean of electric ecstasy, a whole-body orgasm that ripped through me in crest after exquisite crest.

Ivan, his reserves of restraint exhausted, gripped my hips firmly with both hands and began to pump quickly, his rock-hard erection conjuring up aftershocks of pleasure. I could feel another orgasm start to build, responding to the dual stimulation of Ivan's cock inside me and the mattress edge beneath my pelvis. It shot through me, claiming the last of my breath and awareness, just as Ivan shouted out his climax and slammed deeper still, emptying himself in hot, shuddering bursts.

Chapter Ten

The next evening, as I took my clothes off in what had become our ritual, I studied Ivan whenever I thought he wasn't looking. His appeal, I decided, was the same thing that made him different from other people. His focus, that ability to attend to something with every bit of his mind, dedicating every powerful brain wave to whatever it was. At the lab, he was tuned to his work with as much narrow intensity as one of the lasers he was building. In a conversation with more than one person, he struggled because there were too many threads to focus on. When he chose one, he did far better.

And in his apartment, when it was just the two of us, all that attention was directed at me. I began to suspect that his real motivation wasn't to dominate, so much as to ensure that his partner was as focused on him as he was on her. On me.

He'd certainly accomplished that.

"What are you thinking about, Camilla?" Ivan's question drew me out of my reverie and back to the present.

"You, Professor," I answered instantly and honestly. I think the answer startled him a little. But he seemed pleased.

"We did something last night that you were scared to try. Tonight I'd like to try something that scares me."

I couldn't even begin to imagine what might scare Ivan. I didn't have time to ponder it, however, because Ivan was gesturing for me to follow him into the bathroom. That setting did nothing to ease my mind, but all he did to begin with was turn the shower on.

"Not too hot," he said softly, almost as if he was saying it to himself. "Or I'll never be able to finish."

"Finish what, Professor?"

Without answering, he took his clothes off quickly while I stood by the sink waiting. Then he pulled me into the shower enclosure, shutting the door behind us.

It was warm, and close. The sight of Ivan's wet skin made me want to lick him, taste him. But I wasn't sure if that fit into his plan or not, so I stood where he put me and watched him for further instructions.

"Wash me off." He handed me a washcloth and nodded at the bar of soap. It wasn't as fun as licking him, but it definitely still seemed like fun. I grinned as I lathered up the cloth. Starting at the neck, I worked my way down, being careful not to miss any spots. The soap was the glycerin kind, with a musky scent and creamy lather. I recognized the smell and enjoyed knowing that after the shower I would smell of the soap, too. A little reminder of Ivan to carry throughout my day.

When I would have lingered over Ivan's more entertaining bits, he admonished me to keep my mind on my work. Chagrined, I continued down one leg and then finished with the other, finally standing and handing back the cloth. He pressed it back toward me as he stepped into the full stream of the shower's spray to wash his hair.

"Scrub up."

This was getting disappointing, and he still hadn't told me what his scary thing was. But I complied, scrubbing off quickly. Ivan had short hair, it didn't take long to wash, and then he turned his attention to my hair, making me lean back while he shampooed and conditioned it meticulously. The massage of his fingertips on my scalp as he rinsed the conditioner away lulled me, so I wasn't expecting the abrupt change of mode when he finished with the cleaning tasks and turned me back around to face him.

He didn't say anything, just pressed down on my shoulders until I went to my knees. Then, contrary to my expectation, he took his half-erect penis in hand and stroked himself, spreading his legs a little for a sturdier stance. Within a few seconds he was hard and ready, and I licked my lips in anticipation of tasting him.

But he didn't let me, didn't bring his cock to my lips as I was expecting and even hoping he would. Instead he kept jacking himself, harder and faster than I would have thought comfortable, and right when I could see the telltale quivers and hear that little about-to-come catch in his breathing, he leaned down and brushed the underside of one of my breasts.

"Hold them up," he said in a hoarse voice.

I scooped a hand under each boob, lifting them up a little, not sure if that was what he wanted.

And then with a gasp, he was shooting hot jets of come all over my breasts, working himself more and more carefully until he was done. Still panting, he lowered one hand again, swiping his fingers through the stuff on my chest and spreading it over one nipple. Little circles, ringing the already hard bud, drawing my notice to the fact that I was ravenously aroused.

Ivan lifted the goo-covered fingers to my mouth next,

watching as I licked them clean. He pushed them in a few times, fucking my mouth with them, and I saw his cock twitch at the same time a sharp thrill of need made me squirm in frustration.

"I didn't even slip and crack my head open," Ivan murmured, looking pleased but amused with himself.

"No. Why? Was that a possibility?"

He helped me to my feet and we shared the task of rinsing off. "It's always a possibility. Most accidents happen in the home. Bathrooms are the most dangerous room of all. You should always be alert and cautious, which is why I never masturbate in the shower. Until today."

"Wait. This was the first time you ever did that? Seriously?" I could tell the scene was over, and I didn't even bother with calling him Professor. I was starting to get better at reading his mood about that.

Ivan nodded as he shut the water off and opened the door, handing me a towel. "It's always scared the crap outta me. I live alone. If I fell and got badly hurt I'd be screwed."

"*That* was your scary thing?" I still couldn't quite wrap my mind around that one.

"Are you…judging?"

"No," I assured him quickly. "Everybody has different things that bother them. It's cool."

But as we ventured back downstairs to watch a movie, I couldn't help but wonder about Ivan's ability to cope in the real world, and how reliant he was on the few people to whom he was close. If I hadn't come along, would he have *ever* gotten up the nerve to jerk off in the shower? Surely that was standard behavior for guys.

Ivan, of course, was far from a standard guy. And I reasoned with myself that jerking off in the shower was not exactly a social coping behavior. Not something he'd ever be called on to do out in the big, scary, real world. Or at least I certainly hoped not.

We were in our usual places Thursday night, watching television, when Ivan popped the question.

"Will you come with me tomorrow night?"

I hadn't expected him to ask, and it took me a second to respond. "Um...like as your coach, or a date, or—"

"In whatever capacity."

"Sure. How dressy is it?"

"I have no idea, for a girl. I'm wearing a suit and tie, if that helps."

It did. I was already thinking of my options. Buying something new was out, but I could make do.

"We kind of got off track. Me helping you, I mean." It wasn't an apology, but I did feel a little bad. The sex had sidetracked us, and although we'd tried to keep covering social interaction, we usually seemed to cut it short in favor of studying our own interaction. Which was more fun, naturally, but probably not helping Ivan get through his party obligation any more successfully.

"No. I think this has helped, in a way," he said. "I've done more spontaneous things these last few weeks than I ever have in my life. Plus I'm definitely more relaxed."

That part wasn't too difficult to understand. We were screwing like bunnies, no matter what other bells and whistles we added, and that tends to ease anybody's tension.

"So what have you learned, then? Do you have your index cards handy?"

Ivan chuckled. "No, I've memorized them. Little white lies, know the context, use transitions and don't interrupt.

Pretend I'm interviewing a new sub at the club, but don't try to make them talk about something that's a downer. Since you'll be there, are you going to give me some kind of signal about that, by the way?"

"I'll fiddle with my earring or something. It sounds like you've got it all down. In theory, at least. The main thing to do is stay calm. And when in doubt, shut up. People like talking about themselves. So let them do that whenever possible."

Ivan frowned. "I hate talking about myself."

"Well, I'm still not convinced you're actually people, honey."

"I'm a superior mutation?" He seemed eager to embrace the possibility.

"I was thinking more like an alien or a pod person. But sure."

"Superman was an alien. I could live with that."

I shrugged. "I always preferred Clark Kent."

He waggled his eyebrows at me. "I always suspected that Clark Kent was the real personality, and—"

"Superman was the disguise," I chimed in. "Exactly. Lois was such a fool."

"Maybe not. Superman was duplicitous, so you can't blame her for falling for his lies. But at least she knew what she wanted." Ivan shrugged. "She wanted the hero."

Chapter Eleven

Friday was surreal, as my day was a mixture of preparing for the fundraising event and preparing for a tropical storm. The thing was winding up in the Gulf, supposed to make landfall Saturday night, but the weather was already getting strange and the tension in town was running high—ever since Hurricane Ike, Houstonians had been particularly edgy about big windstorms. The local news was full of warnings and retrospectives. I had already secured two five-gallon water jugs earlier in the summer, which meant my main preparation consisted of double-checking the first aid kit and camping gear, and stocking up on some canned goods on my way home from work that afternoon.

At home I watched footage of people reminiscing about the hurricane, while I painted my toenails a soft pink. The constant drone of the news and weather reports served as background noise while I ironed the dress I'd picked out. A white and hot-pink floral sleeveless, with a modern flair that somehow saved the pink from looking too girly-girl.

It bordered on too casual but had the tremendous benefit

of being a cotton-linen blend, and therefore much cooler than any of my other options. The air felt heavy and sodden, weighing like a damp, hot blanket over the entire city. As soon as I walked outside I knew I'd be covered with sweat that had nowhere to evaporate in the saturated air.

Still, I was happy with my appearance overall. The dress fit nicely and didn't tend to wrinkle too badly. I'd curled my hair a little at the ends, knowing it would be futile to straighten it, given the humidity. It draped in soft, dark blond waves that swept past my shoulders. Silver sandals, pearl earrings, and I was all set.

I critiqued my look in the full-length mirror and decided I looked the part…whatever part I was supposed to be playing at this function. I still wasn't really sure. Doting girlfriend, social coach, sex slave? Probably not that last one. Future faculty wife?

Where the hell did that come from?

I didn't have time to analyze it. Giving myself a last once-over and pronouncing myself as ready as I'd ever be, I grabbed my purse and headed out the door.

Ivan cleaned up well. He looked so good in his suit and tie, I found myself wondering what he'd look like in a tux.

"White lies, context, don't interrupt. Use transitions, when in doubt shut up," Ivan muttered as we abandoned his car to the valet and walked to the department chair's front door.

"It rhymes," I realized. "Kind of, anyway."

"You interrupted me," he admonished. "Now I have to start over. White lies, context, don't interrupt. Use transitions, when in doubt shut up. Interview a new sub, but don't bring down the whole club. Pause because you can't rewind; true, necessary, kind."

I squeezed his hand. "You'll be fine."

The party was already in full swing when we walked in. In this case, full swing involved soft Latin jazz in the background, a sophisticated babble of conversation, and a sea of nearly identical dark suits broken up by dresses like colorful tropical islands.

"Oh, and remember to smile," I threw out at Ivan as he steered me toward a tight cluster of suits accented by a peacock-blue dress. "But not too much."

He shot me an exasperated look, but at least I'd distracted him from the extreme tension I'd sensed as he neared the group, which included his boss.

"Dr. Reynolds," the older man said as we approached, "I'm pleased you could make it. And who is this?" I caught the flicker of surprise when he realized I was actually there *with* Ivan.

"Dr. Donovan, Mrs. Donovan, this is my friend Camilla Novak."

I shook hands and exchanged meaningless pleasantries with the Donovans—she was the peacock-blue dress, and she seemed to view Ivan with new interest since he'd arrived with a girl on his arm—and with the three other suits they were talking to. The names went in one ear and out the other, but I gathered that two of them were alumni, so I did my best to be charming in hopes it would set a good example for Ivan.

He did very well, better than I'd expected. Other than a few too many repeats of "So I was thinking…" he managed to converse at least as well as anybody else in the decidedly nerd-heavy crowd. He remembered his manners, introducing me as he went along— "My neighbor, Camilla…My friend, Camilla…This is Camilla, she works for Dr. Agatha Spiers…"

Never "my girlfriend, Camilla." Never "my date, Camilla."

I wasn't aware I'd expected to hear anything like that, until I *didn't* hear it and felt disappointed. The party kept me too busy to think too much about it, though.

Over the course of the evening, I decided that Ivan wasn't nearly as unusual as I'd thought. It seemed at least half of the astrophysicists there were as hyper-focused and introverted as he was, and most of them didn't even have the looks to compensate for the lack of social ability. I couldn't help thinking of a bunch of subterranean dwellers, reluctantly emerging into the open-air world to participate in this bizarre ritual, prickling like a bunch of hedgehogs whenever anybody got too close.

That thought led to giggling, which led to Ivan looking at me like I'd gone nuts, but I decided against sharing it with him. Some things were better left unsaid, and I suspected that "hostile astrophysicist hedgehogs in suits" was probably one of those things.

An hour or so into the event, Ivan started to loosen up. I left him for a few minutes to find the restroom, and when I returned he was engaged in a lively conversation with Dr. Yu and two potential donors about the laser ablation "broom" and the many potential practical applications for miniaturized rocket components. I gave him a minute before catching his eye and tugging on my earring. One of the donors was starting to look bored.

Ivan faltered then shut it down, let Yu finish what he was saying then waved at me as if he'd just seen me.

"Camilla! Gentlemen, this is my friend Camilla." He worked it so smoothly I was flabbergasted, spinning the introduction and changing the subject as though it was for my benefit.

My baby's walking on his own!

That was another one of those thoughts I planned never

to share with Ivan, but I really was proud of his progress. Heightened awareness and sufficient motivation, I suspected, had made the difference for him where previous efforts had failed. Still, I felt I'd played a part in it, and was thrilled with his success. Even Yu seemed pleasantly surprised by this sudden social adroitness on Ivan's part.

A sudden commotion from the front room drew our attention, and as the buzz filtered through the crowd, my sense of vicarious achievement ebbed, replaced by a sick foreshadowing of doom.

A special guest had arrived at the party, and after a minute the excited crowd parted to reveal the famous face of Dr. Lance Leandro, science hunk.

The man was handsome, it couldn't be denied. His looks were the modern version of clean-cut, wholesome but with a deliberate hint of scruff maintained to keep him accessible. His golden-brown hair was a little long, as if he needed a cut but hadn't had time. His golden-brown skin had none of the orange glow that gave away fake tanning, but instead appeared to be a natural result of good fortune, genetics and time spent outside doing adorably rigorous field work. I could have sworn at one point I saw light sparkle off one of his teeth.

He was also smart, of course, and seemed as nice and amiable in person as he did on television. For close to half an hour he let Donovan introduce him to people, and his cheerful energy and brilliant smile never seemed to flag.

In short, he was the anti-Ivan, and accordingly Ivan seemed unable to remain long in Leandro's presence. The whole focus of the party had shifted to the science hunk, however, so there was practically no getting away from Leandro without leaving.

"I don't know why we're still here," Ivan said. Yu had abandoned us after a few minutes to meet the celebrity scientist, as had most of the other people at the party. They were all trying to look cool about it, though. Leandro was talking to Yu and Donovan, while several of the women in the crowd edged closer while trying not to look at him. They planned to back into the man, I supposed, then feign surprise and introduce themselves.

Whatever worked. But I'd also noticed something more interesting than the science hunk, and wasn't about to let Ivan go out this way, as though Leandro had chased him out. What I saw gave me hope that there was one last shot at making a good impression, and I crossed my fingers as I stood on tiptoe to whisper in Ivan's ear.

"Stop trying to walk out, and listen. You see Mrs. Donovan? She's sitting over there on the end of that couch." Ivan started to turn his head and I cleared my throat loudly. He caught himself and just flicked his gaze that way, finding the well-preserved blonde in peacock-blue, then nodding. "The lady she's talking to is Adele Streetford. Mrs. Bubba Streetford. You know who that is, right?"

Any Texan would know. Streetford was one of the best-known alumni of all time, and his own huge company had only grown bigger when he'd married the heiress to an oil and gas fortune. The couple had their name on buildings all over town.

Ivan nodded. "So what?"

"They aren't looking at Leandro."

He risked another glance at the two attractive forty-somethings, then at his Adonis of a rival. "Okay, so they aren't into Leandro. Still, so what?"

I wondered why there was never a handy wall to beat my head against when I needed one. "Mrs. Donovan isn't looking at Leandro, but she's been looking at *you* all night, dork.

I think she has the hots for you. This could be a golden opportunity."

"You want me to peddle my flesh to Mrs. Donovan?" He sounded like the idea was more unappealing than unthinkable.

"I want you to schmooze. Subs at the club," I prompted. "She's the department chair's wife. Her friend is a gazillionaire, married to another gazillionaire. Neither of them wants the science hunk. They're subs at the club. They want a threesome. Your job is to figure out who will be on top, who wants what, whether there are any special—"

"Oh, *I'll* be on top," he said firmly, in *that* voice. A tiny smile was forming at the corners of his mouth and eyes. Steely. Perfect. Ivan was back in the game.

"Remember to steer the conversation around to your short lesson on rocket science," I reminded him.

"Wait for me by the bar, Camilla."

I blinked up at him. For a moment, his eyes were the only thing in my world. "Yes, Professor."

Even as he walked across the room, I could tell he had this one nailed. Within thirty seconds both ladies in question were eyeing him with interest, and by the time he sat on the coffee table facing them and the conversation really kicked off, both of them looked enthralled.

I hoped he didn't forget what he was doing and really organize a threesome.

The crowd around the handsome and charming Dr. Lance Leandro ebbed and flowed. I considered going over to introduce myself but decided I'd better wait by the bar.

Ivan returned in fifteen minutes with a manic gleam in his eye. "We can go now."

"It went well?"

"It went better than well. I'll tell you in the car."

★ ★ ★

Quite possibly, I'm a bad person. I knew I should have been overjoyed for Ivan, but on the way home I only felt tired and let down, and I wasn't sure why.

"I think Mrs. Streetford is a closet Domme," Ivan said, startling me up from my sour mood.

"I beg your pardon?"

He shrugged. "Just a feeling. It still worked, though. Thank you, Camilla, that was a brilliant idea. Streetford is thinking of endowing a chair."

"Nice. And Mrs. Donovan will know you helped convince Mrs. Streetford to encourage the endowment. I told you it would work. Subs at the club."

"There's more," he said. "Donovan and Yu may want to replace me, but they won't be doing it with Leandro."

His smug expression roused my interest. "Do tell."

"Lady Donovan was pissed about it, and she was also pissed that he had the nerve to show up at the fundraiser. He's been using the rumor of a job offer from the university to leverage his contract negotiations, she thinks. In any case, the negotiation is over and he's signed up for another two seasons of his show, to the tune of close to a million bucks. He's not going anywhere."

"Shit! Did Donovan know?"

Ivan shook his head. "Apparently not until tonight. He was happy to see Leandro anyway because he brought a big check."

"So your job is safe. Congratulations!"

"Safe from Leandro. Safer than it was, anyway." He turned into the driveway and slipped the car into his parking spot, turning it off then relaxing his head against the seatrest for a minute. "God, I'm glad that's over with. These past few weeks have been crazy. Now I can go back to doing all my normal stuff again."

He sounded so happy, for a moment I smiled with him, then with a dizzy rush I grasped what it was that had me so down.

He'd introduced me to his entire department tonight. He'd called me his friend, his neighbor, the girl next door. But not once had he introduced me as his girlfriend.

We'd never talked about the future. Now he said he wanted to go back to the way things were before. All his "normal stuff," he'd said. Nobody knew Ivan's normal stuff like me, his almost-stalker. I knew I wasn't a part of that routine, and I felt a sickening lurch in my stomach as I realized I never would be.

Stupid. I'd been so stupid, not to see that in dealing with me, he'd adapted exactly the same strategy I'd told him to use at the party. Pretend it was the club. With me the pretense had gone a little further, maybe, but it was still only his coping mechanism. I couldn't even blame him, because he'd warned me before we started. He told me he didn't play out in the real world, and the whole thing was a science experiment to him. I should have listened.

I let Ivan open my car door as usual, took his hand and let him help me out of the car and walk me to my door. It was ten o'clock, time for Ivan to brush his teeth and go to sleep. We'd missed television time.

The kiss he gave me at my door was affectionate and brief, and then he was gone.

Chapter Twelve

Saturday, nine o'clock in the morning. A weekend day.

I looked out my kitchen window, knowing what I would see—Ivan with a measuring cup, watering his tomatoes. Although he was back in his beloved routine, he didn't look especially happy. I wondered what that was all about. I scanned the garden and noticed that the last of my lettuces had finally crossed the line from struggling to dead. I had forgotten to water it yesterday, and now it was a shriveled, brownish hunk of rot.

Then the sky caught my attention, and I craned my neck for a better look. Although the storm wasn't due until late afternoon or early evening, the sky already had a dull, gray quality. It looked too windless, flat and eerie, and I backtracked to the living room to find a weather report.

While I slept, the storm had evidently picked up speed and was now due to make landfall in another six hours or so. It was right on the cusp of being upgraded to a Category One hurricane. Lovely.

I double-checked my supplies, then started cooking things

in case the power went out for long enough that the stuff in the fridge started to turn. Outside, the smell of barbecue indicated that somebody else had the same idea. Dinesh, I saw. Julia was bringing him a large rack of ribs to put on the grill.

Leaning out the door, I waved at them. "Can I throw some chicken on there, too?"

"Sure, go for it," Julia said cheerfully. "Ivan, you got anything?"

He looked up from his tomatoes. "No, I'm good. I have some extra bags of ice in my freezer and I think I can fit everything in there if I need to." He glanced my way, puzzled.

"What's the matter?" I asked, finally mustering the fortitude to venture out and talk to him.

"I bought extras of almost all my supplies. More than I usually would, I mean. In case you need anything."

I shrugged, looking away. "I think I have everything I need, thanks."

"Are you...angry with me?"

Was I? I had to think about it for a bit. "No," I said at last, taking a step back. "I'm annoyed at myself, but I'm not angry with you. I'd better go get that chicken while Dinesh still has room on the grill."

I walked off before he could say anything else. When next I looked, he was carrying the last of his tomatoes inside to shelter them from the oncoming storm.

He looked forlorn, which made me sad, too.

We all lunched like kings in the gathering gloom, enjoying the last few minutes outside despite the occasionally wicked gusts of wind that broke the deathly stillness to swipe at our napkins and paper plates. The sky was a grim purple-gray with a sickly tint of green by the time we finished securing the last of the outside furniture and the grill in the shed next to the carport.

Ivan was right behind me as I opened my kitchen door. I turned, lifting my eyebrows in a silent question, and he took a step back, looking confused.

"I really think you're angry with me, Camilla," he said earnestly, as though he was trying to talk me into the idea. "I've been watching your facial expressions. Did I do something wrong?"

I reminded myself that this was Ivan. He didn't do subtext or innuendo. He said what he meant, and I would probably have the most luck if I did the same, no matter how odd it felt to lay my feelings out in the open that way.

"At the party, you introduced me to everybody as your friend."

"Was that wrong?"

"Ivan, you called me your friend, your neighbor. Somebody who worked in another department at the university. You never... I was disappointed, I guess. You never introduced me as anything *more* than that. Like your girlfriend. And then you said you wanted to go back to the way things—"

"But you're *not* my girlfriend. Why would I introduce you that way? You're my submissive." His brow was wrinkled, and it was evident he was trying very hard to understand me.

I wanted to give him credit for that, I really did. But I was so tired of finding reasons to give Ivan extra credit, and it hurt so much to hear him come right out and say it like that.

"You interrupted me," I pointed out. "You said you wanted to go back to the way things were before, to your old routine. I'm still not sure when you managed to fit trips to a bondage club into your old routine, but I know I wasn't in there."

He stared at my mouth for a few seconds after I was done

talking, waiting to make sure I was through. "I went twice a month on the first and third Saturdays, but I left the house at ten-thirty in the evening. You were usually either still out or already inside watching television."

"That's late for you to be up," I said skeptically.

"I kind of thought of it as a substitute for dreaming. Something apart from my real life."

I was reminding myself that he didn't mean that in a poetic way, or as a metaphor, when a flash of lightning split the darkening sky, with a thunderclap of brain-rattling magnitude hard on its heels.

"I need to get inside."

"I never meant to disappoint you, Camilla. I just thought you understood."

If he kept talking, I was going to cry, and I didn't want to do that in front of him because he would be confused, and I'd have to deal with the confusion, and it would all be about Ivan instead of about the twisting pain of loss threatening to choke me.

"You should go," I told him. "It's time to get inside."

"Come over to my place. I have plenty of supplies." He took my hand, but I just squeezed his fingers then dropped them. A burst of wind whipped his hair from one side to the other and he flicked the strands impatiently from his eyes.

"I'm good right here," I insisted. "I need to go in, make sure my cell phone's all charged up and everything. I'll talk to you later, okay?"

Reluctantly, Ivan stepped back and let me close the kitchen door, shutting him out along with the weather.

I cried and cried and ate all the ice cream in the freezer, because if the power went out, it would have to go anyway. By the time the rain started to fall, my tears had started to dry. I felt arid, empty, and the torrential downpour seemed bitterly ironic. It was about five o'clock, the storm was pushing Category Two strength, and I realized I was out of ibuprofen at the exact moment the power zapped out with a boom.

Nobody was there to hear me scream, for which I was grateful as that would've been embarrassing. The explosive sound had scared the hell out of me, and my thumping heart supercharged the headache as I ventured from the relative safety of my dining nook to the much more exposed kitchen window. The percussive thud had rattled the windows and doors, even vibrating the ground under the chair I'd been sitting in. I feared that something big had hit the house, though it was more likely a blown transformer.

From the window I saw rain, and lots of it. Fitful wind, still whipping in multiple directions, not yet bending the trees sideways as it would when the full strength of the storm swept past. I couldn't see any fallen trees, or anything else out of the ordinary. In the storm-darkness, something caught my eye in the direction of the carport and I stood on tiptoe, trying to make out the looming black shape.

I screamed again at the pounding sound by my ear, then realized it was somebody knocking on the door.

"Cami!"

I could make out Ivan's voice through the rising wind and rushed to unlatch and open the door. It slammed open, dragging him in with it, and we struggled together to close it against the wind, the rain-drenched floor giving us little traction.

When it finally clicked shut, I slammed the bolt home again and rested my head against the wood, trying to catch my breath. Once I regained a modicum of composure, I turned around, eyes wide, to stare at my bedraggled neighbor.

"What the *fuck?*"

"There's a utility pole in the front yard. Are you all right? You should be in your closet."

"I'm fine. I know there's a utility pole in the front yard, it's always been there. You came over here in the rain to tell me that?"

"Not *next* to the yard, Cami. *In* the yard. It hit the corner of my roof before it finished falling, I think. I was worried it might have rolled this way, toward your front windows."

After a stunned moment, I processed what he'd said. "Oh, my God! Are you okay? Were you up there?"

"I'm okay. And no, I wasn't up there. We need to get in your closet now."

He was already headed upstairs, and I followed from habit, even as I protested. "The dining room should be fine. It doesn't have any windows."

"But the living room does, and there's no door between the two like there is at my place."

For the first time I realized he was wearing a backpack. It was dripping, leaving a trail behind him as he made his way to my room and into the closet.

"Leave that outside, it's soaked. Your shoes, too. What's in there, anyway?"

"Survival stuff. All of me is soaked," Ivan pointed out. "May I borrow a towel?"

This day was getting so strange. I ducked into the bathroom, grabbed all three clean towels from their shelf and returned to the closet to find Ivan standing inside it, stark naked, standing a big flashlight up in one of my boots so it pointed toward the ceiling. The reflected light was more than bright enough. A little pile of other junk was on the floor near my shoes. I recognized a hand-cranked weather radio, a multi-tool and a few other useful items.

"You stopped to pack this up after the pole hit your roof?"

"No," he said, as if it should be obvious, "I packed this before the storm hit. For emergencies." Like most geeks, Ivan was probably more taken with the idea of preparing for the imminent zombie apocalypse than for an actual emergency; still, I was impressed at his foresight.

I tossed Ivan a towel and he dried off quickly while I tried to look elsewhere. "I probably have some sweats or something that'll fit you." When I started to leave the closet, however, he grabbed my arm to stop me.

"Camilla, *please* tell me what I've done. You know I'll never figure it out on my own."

That was certainly true.

I turned slowly, letting Ivan close the door behind me. He seemed to relax, at least fractionally, once it was closed. At least it was a big walk-in, easily six feet by ten. We'd have plenty of room to wait for the zombies.

"You didn't do anything wrong, honey. I did. Could you put a towel on, or something, at least? It's a little hard to have a conversation with you when you're naked."

He shrugged and took one of the dry towels I was still holding, wrapping it around his hips. He opened the closet door only long enough to toss the wet towel out—I noted that his sodden backpack, clothes and shoes were already out there—before closing it again and turning to face me. Even in the towel, he still looked pretty damn good.

"What could you have done wrong?"

Sighing, I tried to figure out how to say it without embarrassing myself completely. There wasn't a way, though. I supposed with Ivan it didn't really matter anyway. He wouldn't understand what was embarrassing about admitting such a thing.

"I let myself forget that this was just a science experiment to you, even though you were absolutely clear on that right from the start. I started expecting something long-term, and last night when I realized you didn't feel the same way, I was disappointed. For future reference, though, when you're sleeping with somebody, it's kind of bad form to be blunt like that and *say* 'You're not my girlfriend.' Maybe learn to sugarcoat it a little, like say you're not interested in a commitment, or…"

He had opened and closed his mouth several times while I spoke, as though he was struggling not to interrupt. Once I stopped, though, he bit his lip and waited.

"I'm done talking," I finally prompted him.

"I know. I'm trying to figure out what to say." He pursed his lips and stared at the far wall for a bit, then nodded. "Okay. I did say that the sex was *like* a science experiment. I never said it was *just* a science experiment."

"Let's not argue about—"

"Don't interrupt, Camilla," he reprimanded gently. The dark burr in his voice sent a shiver down my spine. "It never occurred to me to introduce you as my girlfriend because I don't consider you my girlfriend. You're my friend. You're also my submissive."

"I get that. You said that already. And the BDSM stuff isn't real life." My voice was cracking. *Fuck*. I was trapped in this stupid fucking closet with Ivan now, about to start crying again, and I wanted to punch him right in the solar plexus for being himself. "You've been as clear as it's possible to be, and I should have known better than to let myself get...get all...*dammit!*"

I turned my back to him, pressing my hands over my eyes and trying to breathe slowly through my nose to stop the tears. When I felt his hands on my shoulders I flinched, but he held on tighter and turned me back around. He offered me a travel pack of tissue, which I guess he'd had in his magic emergency backpack.

"I'm doing something wrong," he said as I snuffled into a tissue. "You shouldn't be crying. Do you...? I don't understand. Do you want to *stop* being my submissive?"

Oh, for the love of—

"I'm going back to the dining room."

"No!" he insisted. "It isn't safe down there. And we can figure this out, Cami. We can *do* this."

"Do *what,* Ivan? Be friends with kinky benefits? Fuckbuddies? I thought we had more than that, I thought...oh, hell, I obviously wasn't thinking at all. Okay, I know you don't get this stuff. But I thought I was your girlfriend, and I was happy about that because I really like you. I thought you felt the same way, although it's hard to tell with you. You seemed so interested. I wanted there to be more, and I guess I just imagined more, and that was dumb of me. But no, I don't want to be your submissive anymore. And now I really, really wish we could get out of this fucking closet."

"It's a windowless room on an interior wall," he reminded me, almost gently. "Camilla, I think I've figured it out. The problem, I mean."

"You're going to go back to your dining room? Or hey, maybe I could fit in my pantry."

Ivan smiled. "You'd be well-provisioned but far less comfortable. I meant our communication problem. *Girlfriend* doesn't seem like the right word for what you mean to me. Probably that's what I should be calling you to other people, since I can't introduce you at parties as my submissive. But to me, saying you're just my girlfriend would be...it would feel like I was saying I wasn't pleased with you, or proud of you. And I *am*. I've never had a submissive of my own before, because I've never met anybody I felt a connection with until now. On the other hand, I've also never had a girlfriend, so I don't have a basis for comparison."

"Oh," I whispered. I hadn't planned to whisper, that was just what came out.

We were standing closer together now, and I wasn't quite sure how that had happened. I could smell Ivan, the damp and sweat layered over soap and deodorant, with a lingering whiff of barbecue smoke. If I leaned forward a few inches I could reach out my tongue and taste the salt of his skin.

"The thing is," Ivan went on, his voice soft and soothing over the counterpoint of the howling wind outside, the insistent thrumming of the rain on the rooftop, "I think this is love. But I've never been in love before, either, so I don't know."

"No basis for comparison," I concurred.

He nodded solemnly. "Nevertheless, it's my working hypothesis."

"You can never prove a hypothesis, though."

"True," Ivan agreed. The towel slipped off his hips, but he ignored it. "As long as it's not proven false, though, we're in good shape."

His fingers slid through the hair behind my ears, shaping themselves to my skull.

"I hypothesize I love you, too."

Ivan smiled. The uplighting from the flashlight gave his

face a sinister cast as he leaned over me, making him look for all the world like a sexy old-school vampire as he murmured, "Professor."

"Professor," I amended dutifully.

"This is all out of order, Camilla," Ivan pointed out. "We're in *your* room instead of mine, I'm naked and you're dressed. We need to straighten things out, I think. Correct some imbalances."

"That sounds like it could take some time, Professor."

"Then we'd better get started."

It had felt stifling, just a few minutes ago. Now it felt cozy, almost romantic, stuck in the closet with the storm howling with eerie insistence outside. Ivan undressed me slowly, teasing as he went, and by the time I was naked we were both starting to breathe more heavily.

The emergency backpack contained an emergency box of condoms, which Ivan said he always packed just in case. I found that a little too convenient, until he showed me the laminated checklist he used for packing and I saw that it did, indeed, include condoms. I guess it never hurts to plan ahead for safe sex, even in the face of hurricanes or raging hordes of the re-animated undead. Go figure.

What we didn't have was props. No cuffs or ropes, whips or paddles or anything else. Just Ivan, who kissed me sweetly like the best prom date ever until I melted into a puddle of limp willingness at his feet.

Instead of orders, he gave me himself, kneeling down to face me and kissing me again as we tumbled to the floor together. The rushing scream of the wind outside almost masked our sighs, but not the groan he made when he rolled me underneath him and pressed my hands to the carpet over my shoulders. I could feel his sheathed cock, hard and hot between my thighs, and I rubbed against it instinctively, half expecting him to tell me to stop. He didn't, though. I worked myself into a sweat under him, until I was slick and swollen and so ready I was almost crying again, before he finally made a move.

Ivan skimmed his lips over mine and angled his hips, pushing inside me slowly until he was as deep as he could go and then stopping there. I arched up into him, wanting to get even closer, feeling as though I could never be close enough. He let one of my hands go so he could work his fingers under me, gripping my ass to pull himself into me with more force until we were both writhing and crying out at the blissful pressure.

His face was beautiful in the dim light, sheened with sweat and stern with intensity. Ivan looked down at me and pulled out almost all the way, then slid back into me one slow inch at a time, watching my face as avidly as I watched his. Out and in, over and over. It was an agony of delight. I came before I was quite ready for it, gasping in surprise and bucking my hips up. He never changed his tempo, even as I quaked and begged.

My eyes closed at some point, and when I opened them again Ivan was smiling down at me, looking amused and a tiny bit smug. Then a shiver passed through him and his face tightened. His hips snapped against mine sharply the next time he thrust inside. I didn't know if it was cause or effect, but his pace changed then, and he drove into me with increasing urgency until his cries and taut muscles in his face and shoulders signaled he was close.

Raising my free hand to his face, I stroked his cheek before letting my fingers curl around the back of his neck, pulling him down for another kiss. He plundered my mouth until he came with a shuddering cry.

The storm was still blowing when we started to notice our surroundings again. The closet, large though it might be, was still growing stuffy and slightly dank as the lack of air conditioning started to sink in. The wind's screaming tapered off to an even more ominous silence, as the eye of the hurricane passed.

I pulled my sleeping bag down from a shelf and spread it out for us to sleep on. We covered up with the remaining dry towels and were asleep well before the wind started picking up again.

Seventy-six degrees. It was almost chilly that morning, even though the power was still out so the air conditioning hadn't been running all night. The storm had cooled things down, a small recompense for the destruction it had wrought.

I looked out the bedroom window and saw Ivan down on the patio, wearing his running clothes with—alas—a T-shirt. They were the clothes he'd had on last night, and he'd thrown them on this morning not minding the damp. When he looked up at the window and waved at me, I realized I was breaking his routine—he didn't usually see me there on Saturdays or Sundays.

It was already after seven o'clock. Ivan was starting his day off-schedule, anyway. To my pleasant surprise, he hadn't seemed too perturbed by that. Nor had he displayed any signs of panic from sleeping in my closet all night. When I pointed this out, he'd just grinned and kissed the tip of my nose. He still insisted on going for the run, though.

It wasn't my usual time to be up on a weekend, but I was curious to see the damage, so I pulled on some clothes and ventured outside. Everything looked fine in the backyard, aside from the debris everywhere. Little twigs and a liberal amount of shredded leaves coated the surfaces like bizarre confetti, plastered to the walls of the houses and the cars by the sheer force of the wind. According to the radio, the storm hadn't even hit the city full on, and I could only imagine what the area in its direct path must look like.

I wandered down the row and around the side of the building, only to stop in horror at the sight of the utility pole leaning from the fence line straight into Ivan's front bedroom window. The wires hadn't snapped, and I was fairly certain it was a telephone pole rather than electric, but I still got a little lightheaded thinking of it. Ivan could have been in that room. We could have been in there together.

Things happened for a reason. I grinned like an idiot, thinking about the improbable things that had happened in my closet last night as the storm raged outside. Hot, sweaty, decidedly naughty things, even more creative than usual because we were stuck in there for hours with nothing else to do. Strangely, I woke up more than ready to do further naughty, sweaty things. Preferably in a bed, however.

In half an hour or so, Ivan would be back from his run, and if the water was back on—it had gone out at some point in the wee hours of the morning—he would take a shower. I planned to wreak further havoc with his schedule by joining him. Then breakfast, then checking email if we could get an internet connection. And later—far later than the usual time of 9:00 a.m., I suspected—we would most likely do some gardening. Today that would probably consist of picking up storm leavings from all over the yard.

After that, barring any other errands, we might well do something spontaneous and deliciously deviant. Or we might

a shot in the dark

Christine d'Abo

dedication

For Mark.

acknowledgments

A writer never works in a vacuum.
I'd like to thank my wonderful editor, Deb,
whose sharp eyes make my stories so much better. The fun is just starting.

Chapter One

Paige stood in the doorway of the kitchen and knew her mouth was hanging open. There wasn't anything about sex that could startle her. She'd been around the block and back more than once. So it was odd that catching two of her employees fucking on the island in the kitchen threw her completely off-guard.

Granted, it had been an awfully long time since she'd seen any action herself. Her tastes tended to run a bit darker than the vanilla—although public—sex she was witnessing. Mitch and Beth still hadn't been alerted to her presence, which was understandable given they were groaning and moaning loud enough to wake the dead. Mitch hadn't fully removed his pants, and Paige only caught the occasional glimpse of his white ass as he thrust into Beth.

Paige disengaged from the scene unfolding in front of her. It was missing the spark she craved—all surface and no substance. Like watching a porn movie with the sound turned off.

Knowing she couldn't let this go on much longer, yet hating to ruin their fun before she had to ruin their lives, Paige stepped back out of the kitchen and leaned up against the counter. It gave her a moment to get her head straight and her temper under control. Things would only be worse if she lost it and started yelling at the pair.

God, she hated playing everyone's mom all the time. Every situation had her being the heavy, and damn she was getting tired of it.

Ian was forever picking fights with her, pushing her on every decision she made in regard to the business. She loved her brother and would be forever grateful to the little shit for encouraging them to start the store, but he wasn't the one with the business degree. He always questioned why she'd want to do things a particular way. Sure, occasionally he was right. He had solid instincts when it came to what his customers wanted. Ian was also a jerk half the time.

At least Sadie wasn't giving her any trouble. After their mom's death and the mess with their dad, Paige had worried about her sister. Not that Paige didn't still keep an eye on her, but Sadie was now happily settled in a relationship.

A moan from the kitchen was followed by a high-pitched squeak—and wasn't *that* an embarrassing sex noise—and finally the soft muttering of voices and laughter. Closing her eyes, Paige tried to slip into that place in her mind that gave her strength. It was getting harder and harder to find her center these days, almost to the point where she didn't think she'd be able to get there at all anymore.

Not without help.

Which she would never ask for again.

The sound of approaching footsteps had Paige straightening up and flicking her long ponytail over her shoulder. She knew the image she'd be projecting. Ian would have called it her schoolteacher-from-hell glare, and it was something she'd learned to do at a young age. People didn't bully you if they were scared to death.

When Mitch and Beth finally spilled out of the kitchen, their clothing mostly where it should be, they didn't see her immediately. She waited, perversely enjoying the way Beth tensed and Mitch frowned before they both turned to her.

"Shit," Mitch muttered.

"I hope you didn't do *that* in the kitchen." Paige braced her hands on her hips. "Because it would get us shut down for at least a few days with the cleanup."

Beth sputtered for a moment before stepping between Paige and Mitch. "Paige, oh, my God, we're sorry. It was a onetime thing and I promise it will never happen again."

"That's right, it won't. You're both fired." And once again, Paige was forced to be the bitch. "I'm sorry but this is something I can't turn a blind eye to. Beth, I'm disappointed in you. You've been with us since the beginning and know how much something like this could screw up the store. The health factors alone…"

It hurt knowing that the young woman was trying to pay her way through university and needed the job. That Paige was now in a position of being forced to choose between what was right for the store—and therefore her family—and someone she considered a friend. It sucked big time. But at the end of the day, she was still the boss and had to act like it, even when the task was far from pleasant.

"Paige, this wasn't Beth's fault." Mitch stepped up and put his arm around Beth's waist. "She didn't want to do that in there but I kept pushing. If you need to let me go, that's fine, but please keep her on."

"Admirable, but I can't. As they say, it takes two." Paige pinched the bridge of her nose and this time let the sigh slip through. "Please leave your aprons on the counter. I'll do up your final checks and have them ready for you on Friday."

"Paige, I'm—" Beth started, only to be tugged away by Mitch.

"Let's go, babe."

"No, she needs to understand—"

"She understands. Come on, I'll take you home."

The silence of the shop pressed down on Paige once the door had closed behind Beth's sobs. She'd only intended to grab her bank files to work on at home. It was a rare night when all three Long siblings were off and Beth was holding down the fort. Wednesdays were normally quiet enough that Ian could be convinced to take a break. She knew he'd only be upstairs—her baby brother's social life was as destitute as her own these days—but she didn't want to call him down to cover the last half hour of store hours. God, he'd be pissed when he found out about Beth, and if Paige could put that encounter off a bit longer, it would be best for everyone.

That would teach her to be proactive.

Paige slipped on an apron, slapped her file folder onto the counter and flicked it open. With luck there wouldn't be any customers, or at least, no customers with expectations beyond a simple coffee. She would have to call Ian if someone insisted on a fancy mug of something or other. Why the hell they needed a menu for coffee was still beyond her realm of understanding.

Coffee. Mug. Done.

There was little traffic this time of night, the occasional set of headlights casting wide shadows on the walls of the empty shop. The words on the page blurred as she stared too long at one spot. She should be feeling angry, furious if she gave it much thought. But all she could muster was a strong sense of disappointment and the regret at knowing she'd have to tell Ian they'd all have to work longer shifts again.

More work, less chance at a social life.

At least Sadie was getting some.

The smell of coffee couldn't cover up the scent of sex in the room. Paige was strangely affected by it, and found herself more than a little disturbed by this. Why the hell did they have to do something so stupid in the store?

The muted sounds of chatting and laughter grew louder as a group of people pushed their way through the front door. Paige set the folder aside and plastered a smile on her face.

"Welcome to Pulled Long. What can I get for you?"

The group continued to chat as they considered their options. Most wore leather and silk, and several of them had attractive piercings. While there were many clubs in Toronto they could be heading to, if they were on foot and in this part of the neighborhood, there was little doubt they'd be on their way to Mavericks.

One man stood behind the rest, and by behind she meant towered over. His blond hair was cut close to the scalp on the sides and long enough on top to project the image of a model rather than an army grunt. Paige did her best to ignore the way he stared at her, even as she tried to sneak glances at him. Black leather pants and what had to be a navy blue T-shirt. It was hard to tell given the length of his leather jacket.

Finally, they threw orders Paige's way. Fucking three cappuccinos, an Americano and two lattes. Paige smiled her way through their list and quickly promised herself she'd re-read Ian's coffee guide at the next possible opportunity. Making coffee shouldn't be this painful.

It took her longer than the other baristas to get the drinks ready, but thankfully the group didn't seem to mind. They filtered over to the tables, enjoying the empty store as they waited.

Everyone except for him.

"You seem pretty quiet here tonight." His voice had a smoky quality to it, like he'd spent most of the day talking. "Business is good I hope?"

"We're doing well, thanks. Wednesday nights never seem to have much of a rush. Which is a bit of a blessing sometimes. It gives me a chance to get caught up on my paperwork." *Not that I'm doing anything else.* "What can I get for you? Cappuccino or a latte?"

He smiled and tipped his head to the side. "This may seem like an odd request, but do you have a plain, strong coffee? Nothing fancy?"

Paige couldn't hold back her smile. "You sound like me. Let me get you a cup."

"You don't like fancy things?"

My God, is he flirting? Paige filled one of the to-go cups and slid it over to him. "Not in my coffee."

"I promise I won't tell your boss you said that."

"Thankfully, I am the boss." She grinned. "One of them at least. But if you can keep it from my brother I would appreciate it. He's the coffee snob of the three of us."

The man took a sip. His lips twitched and he almost lost some of the seriousness of his expression. "Ah, you're one of the Long sisters then. If I had to guess, I'd say you were Paige and not Sadie. Am I right?"

Paige flinched before forcing her body to relax. It was hard not to be freaked out when a stranger knew who she was. "How do you know that?"

"Josh from Mavericks. He's done nothing but sing the praises of this place since the anniversary party a few months ago. Tells people the owners are open to a variety of lifestyles and we should try and support you."

It didn't hurt that Josh was half in love with her sister *and* her sister's boyfriend. "He's been supportive."

The man flicked the tail of his jacket up and slid onto the stool in front of Paige. The rest of the group came up one by one to get their drinks, each one casting him a strange look before wandering back to their table. The feeling of unease grew inside her as she finished the last drink and handed it over to a young woman whose outfit was more hooker than fetish. With nothing left to keep her busy, she was forced to focus her attention on the man.

He took another sip, his gaze slipping down her body. Paige had never been so thankful for her black barista's apron.

"You never answered my question."

She grabbed the cloth and began to wipe down the counter. "Which one?"

"If you're Paige?"

She knew he wasn't going to let this go until she relented. "Yes."

"You're the oldest, right?"

"I am indeed." The next time she saw Josh, she was going to kick his ass. "I feel like I'm at a bit of a disadvantage."

He took another large gulp of coffee before holding out his hand. "Carter."

"Nice to meet you."

Carter's hand was huge as he wrapped his fingers around hers. Paige wasn't a small woman, but she felt downright tiny compared to this man. His grip was firm and his hands were rough. He didn't strike her as an office rat, but if he was she could tell he didn't shy away from manual work. He projected strength and confidence, even as he sat there.

The beginnings of something tingled low in her gut. Paige pulled her hand away, the smile on her face feeling strained. "Nice to meet you," she repeated lamely.

She turned her back on him and ducked down to check the inventory levels. It was something she would normally do after close, but there was no way she could continue to be the focus of Carter's visual inspection. With luck, he'd take the hint and leave her in peace.

The group's noise levels increased as they scraped the chairs along the floor. The bell above the door sounded as the group laughed and chatted their way out.

"Carter, you coming, man? Should be lots of people there now."

"I'm not done with my coffee. I'll catch up with you soon." *Shit.*

The silence that descended on the store wasn't as all-encompassing as it had been before. Carter said nothing, the sounds of his sipping and the weight of his stare on her back the only indications of his presence.

Paige closed her eyes and got her annoyance under control. Other than knowing her name, Carter hadn't done anything to warrant her reaction. She'd been tense before finding Beth and Mitch, and now with the rest of her evening shot, Paige knew she'd be less than pleasant company.

Taking a breath, she stood up and faced him once more. "How's the coffee? Can I get you anything else?"

"It's amazing and no, thanks." Another sip. "Trying to get rid of me?"

"Not at all. I figured you'd want to catch up to your friends. I know Mavericks starts to get busy this time of night."

Carter nodded, but instead of moving to get up, he leaned on the counter. "It's the same crew there as always. Josh needs to do a membership drive. Get some fresh blood into the place."

Paige wasn't sure why, but her pussy was starting to take notice of Carter's intense hazel eyes. Every time she met his gaze directly, a tingle would make her clit pulse and she'd drop her gaze. Shit, she didn't even know if he was into that. Her unconscious reaction to the powerful and in-control man annoyed her as much as it aroused.

She'd made a promise to herself she wouldn't let herself get into the scene again, no matter how much she needed it.

"Have you been to Mavericks?"

His question caught her up short. "Yes." She went back to counting the cup lids. "But that was years ago. I don't do that scene anymore."

Carter hummed. "Don't do Mavericks, or *the scene* any-more?"

Okay, screw you, buddy.

"I'm sorry. I know you're a friend of Josh and we certainly appreciate your business here, but I don't know you and I'm not about to discuss my personal life with a stranger. If you can finish your drink and head off to your party, I need to close the store now."

Paige stared into Carter's eyes, ignoring the way they sparkled. It was hard to maintain the gaze, but she knew he wouldn't leave her alone otherwise. The cocky bastard was a Dom. She should have clued in the moment he walked in the door, but she was understandably rusty.

With luck he would actually listen to what she wanted and leave, but there was always a chance he wouldn't. Paige put her right hand on the handle of the scissors under the counter in case he wanted to push her too far.

The fear building in her chest loosened as he took a final

sip of his coffee and got up from the stool, smiling. Before she had time to react, Carter lifted her left hand to his mouth, turned it over and pressed a kiss to the inside of her wrist.

"Thank you for the coffee, Miss Long." He let her go, turned and marched out of the store.

Paige let out a shaky breath and slowly released the scissors.

It had been fine. He had been nothing but gentlemanly toward her, leaving when it was clear she was uncomfortable. Carter was a handsome man, almost certainly a Dom, and hadn't done anything to her.

She was fine.

She wiped away the moisture threatening to spill from her eyes and closed up the store for the night.

Chapter Two

"They were doing *what* in the kitchen?"

Paige had wanted to wait until at least midmorning to let Sadie and Ian know about her evening's adventures, but it wasn't to be. Beth was supposed to have worked that afternoon and Paige figured she was safe to try and get a bit of extra sleep. However, Beth had taken it upon herself to try and win back her job with a call to Ian.

As a result, she now had an angry brother in her living room, while she sat curled up on the couch trying to pull her brain to the land of the living after a crappy night's sleep.

"They were fucking on the kitchen island. How many other ways do you want me to say it?"

"You fired them? On the spot?"

"You're not honestly standing there trying to convince me I should have kept them on?" Paige had more than enough guilt over what she'd been forced to do without needing Ian adding to it.

Ian pressed the heels of his hands to his eyes and sat on the opposite end of the couch. "No, I'm not." Resting his hands in his lap, he leaned back and closed his eyes. "I was looking forward to having a few nights off to rest."

"I know."

Truth be told, Paige had been more than a little worried about Ian over the past few months. He was more often than not working eighteen-hour shifts, always hovering around in case someone needed something or there was a problem with the equipment. He'd lost weight, and his skin was paler than normal.

But with them now down two employees, Paige knew it would be Ian who would be picking up the extra shifts. *Yeah, no guilt there.*

Reaching out, she squeezed his thigh. "We'll hire a few more people. I'm sure I can find more students to cover the shifts without much effort."

Ian didn't say anything. If Paige hadn't known better, she would have assumed he'd fallen asleep. After a few minutes of letting her concern start to creep up into the danger zone, he pushed himself to his feet like a shot and bolted to the door.

"Ian?"

"I'll let Sadie know what's going on. You take your morning off and rest up. You look like shit." He kept his back to her as he moved, pausing at the door. "Don't worry. You did the right thing."

It was stupid, but the tension in her body lessened with his blessing. "I feel like crap about it though."

"As you said, they didn't give you much of a choice. It would have been better if it had been Sadie and Paul, then we could have yelled at them."

"You okay?"

He pressed his head to the doorframe, a soft chuckle slipping from him. "Yeah. Get some rest and we'll see you at lunch?"

"I'm not going to take the morning off. Don't argue either. Do you want me to call Beth?"

"No, I'll do it."

The soft click of the door as he left was unnerving. While Paige and Ian had their moments, she hated seeing him dejected. Ian was their driving force, the glue that kept them together and moving forward when things threatened to pull them apart. If he was wearing down, the rest of them were screwed.

Paige pulled herself together faster than she would have normally and bolted for the bus. It couldn't hurt to have all hands on deck today until they figured out next steps. Maybe she could call a temp agency to see if they had anyone looking for some flexible hours.

Out of the three of them, she lived the farthest away from the store. Paige had bought her small home years ago, right after she'd kicked Rick out. She'd saved enough to afford a modest down payment and had stayed there ever since. When they'd found the location for the store, she'd considered selling and getting someplace closer for all of ten seconds. It was her refuge, her pride and joy, the one place she could go to clear her head.

If she couldn't find her internal peace the way she preferred, the last thing she could afford to do was give up her home.

Stepping off the bus, Paige had her head down as she walked to the shop. Unusually distracted, she didn't notice the men coming her way until she was almost on top of them. Startled, with her hand on the doorknob, she was shocked to see a familiar pair of hazel eyes.

Gone were Carter's leather pants and shit-kicker boots. This morning he had on a pair of blue uniform pants and a uniform shirt with the Toronto Fire Rescue Services logo on the left breast.

Firefighter. Nice.

Carter didn't exactly smile at her, but his gaze brightened and the corners of his lips twitched. "Hello again."

"Hi." She found it hard to keep her eyes locked on his. "I'm surprised to see you."

Carter nodded to his considerably older friend. "When I came on shift this morning, I was telling Garry here about the awesome coffee I'd had. He wanted to try it."

The man in question was standing behind Carter. Garry smiled and took the door from Paige, pulling it the rest of the way open. "And it better be worth it. He dragged me halfway across town for this."

She let Garry go in and could only follow when Carter bowed slightly. "After you."

"Thanks."

Unlike the previous night, the store was buzzing with activity. The line was long, but Ian and Sadie were flying behind the counter, taking orders and making drinks as quickly as they could manage.

"I need to get back there and help out." Paige started to move past Carter when his hand wrapped around her arm. Her stomach somersaulted when she recognized the glint of interest shining back at her.

"I got the feeling last night we might have a lot in common." His voice still had that same smoky quality and Paige found herself swaying closer to him, wanting to be pulled into his hard chest and held there.

She stepped back. "I'm not sure about that."

"I'm just about to work my next twenty-four hour shift and then I have a few days off. While I don't normally drink anything but coffee when I'm getting close to working, I do go out to the clubs. Maybe I could convince you to come out with me sometime. Friday night? Nothing serious. Someplace neutral if that would make you more comfortable."

Carter's intense gaze traveled over her face, and for the first time in a long while Paige wanted to say yes.

"Carter, what do you want to drink, man?" Garry's voice cut through the din of the shop.

"Plain black." He didn't back down from Paige's stare. "You didn't seem to be shocked by our appearances last night."

"We have lots of customers from Mavericks in here. I'd be in a constant state of freak-out if I reacted that way every time a customer walked in wearing leather and a collar."

Someone bumped into Paige as they scurried past on their way out the door. Carter led her to the side wall and turned his back to the rest of the shop. The illusion that they were once again alone, surrounded by the scents of coffee and sex, had Paige's nipples beading inside her bra and her panties growing damp.

"You noticed Tina's collar?"

Shit. She shrugged in what she hoped was a close approximation to something relaxed and uncaring. "It was hard to miss it."

"Actually, it would have been easy to miss it. Ryan is protective of her and didn't want Tina wearing something that would draw a lot of attention. Most people who see it think it's nothing more than an elaborate necklace."

Paige had to concentrate to keep her breathing even. Without breaking eye contact, she licked her lips and slipped her hands into her pockets. "I guess I know what to look for."

Carter nodded, cast a glance at Garry placing their order

and ran his hand down Paige's arm. "Meet me at Mavericks Friday night. For a drink."

"I don't think—"

"Simply a drink. I can offer Josh as a reference if that will make you feel better. I'm curious." The lopsided smirk he gave her softened the intensity of his face.

"Curious about what?"

"You."

"Carter, we need to go, buddy." Garry was at their side, two coffees in hand. "It will take us forever to get back through traffic."

"I'm coming. I'll meet you at the truck."

"Too hard to get parking, he says. He leaves his truck at the station and makes me drive."

Carter stared at Garry for a moment before the other man chuckled and walked away. "I'm going."

When Carter turned his focus back to Paige, something in his face changed, hopeful. "Take this."

The business card was warm from his body heat. Paige didn't look at it before she tucked it away into her back pocket. "I haven't said yes."

"When you've had a chance to consider, call me and let me know either way."

When he left, Paige had to give her head a shake. *Did that happen?* Ignoring the pounding of her heart, she slipped behind the counter and threw on an apron. "Can I help the next person?"

The hour that followed was frantic as they dealt with the late-morning rush, which quickly bled into the lunch-hour crew. Sadie was in back making extra sandwiches and another batch of her tarts while Paige and Ian handled the front. She ignored the sidelong glances Ian threw her way and focused on helping the next person in line. After an eternity, the line finally dissipated, leaving the siblings with the chance to catch their collective breaths.

Ian ran his hand through his hair and let loose a tired chuckle. "I'm trying to decide if our newfound popularity is the result of the ad in the student newspaper, or if Josh has been telling all new members at Mavericks to come here."

"It's probably both." Sadie bit down on a sandwich, her brown bob tucked neatly behind her ears. "Either way, we're going to have to hire a ton more staff if we're going to keep up."

Paige sighed. "That's going to be my job for today. I think we'll start with a Help Wanted sign in the door. I was going to call some of the placement agencies to give them a heads up. Students will be our best bet."

Ian groaned but for once didn't argue with her. "I'm going to take a quick walk. If I'm going to be here all day then I need some fresh air for a bit."

Paige watched him leave, not liking the way his shoulders slumped forward. She turned to Sadie, but before she could even ask, her sister held up her hand.

"I don't know. It could be that the reality of being a business owner is finally hitting home with him. I think he's tired."

"If he wasn't so stubborn and would back off for a bit, then maybe he wouldn't be stressed out." Paige loved Ian with every fiber of her being. He was hardworking and would do anything for either of them. But when he got fixated on something, he let that thing consume him.

"He's a bit like you that way." Sadie tried to hide her smile by taking a sip of coffee.

"I know when to take a step back and reevaluate. Ian doesn't let go. Ever."

"I *meant* he doesn't have much of a personal life because he's forever working."

Paige rolled her eyes and threw a towel at her sister. "I have a social life." It was simply on temporary hiatus.

"Apparently. Who's the cutie firefighter?"

"No one." Grabbing a piece of paper from the file folder she'd left behind the counter, Paige held it up. "Do we have any markers? I want to put up a sign."

Sadie crossed her arms and stared at her. "That's evasion if I ever saw it. Who is he? Did you meet him at a club?"

"Just because you and Paul are all happy-family now doesn't mean you can interrogate the rest of us. He's some guy and I'd appreciate it if you'd stop meddling in my life."

Sadie's arms dropped to her side. "I've never meddled."

Shit. "Sade, I'm—"

"No. Stop right there." Sadie took a step back, her eyes brighter than they should be. "I have never once *meddled* in your life. In fact, I've suffered at the hands of your *meddling* for years now."

Paige stood still, the words for once not coming. It was a common enough accusation from Ian, but never Sadie. Not once.

"I don't know what's happened to you, but you've gotten worse over the past few months. You hardly smile anymore, and when you do seem to be in a good mood it hardly ever lasts." Sadie cleared her throat and moved toward the kitchen. "I think you need to take a closer look at your life and what you have going on before you continue to pick on the rest of us. I'm going to get some baking done. Call me if things get busy." Without another look, meek and mild Sadie stormed off.

Paige's hands shook as she reached for a mug, needing the

caffeine jolt to help right her world. Had she sunk to the point where she was pushing away Sadie, one of the few people still important to her? She didn't have a lot of friends, not anymore. She'd left them behind when she walked away from Rick. The result had been her leaning on Sadie and Ian, and, from the sound of things, driving them both nuts.

The last thing she wanted to do was force them away. While they didn't know the reasons for her breakup with Rick, or why she'd stopped going out and doing a lot of the things that had been a part of her life, they still tried to be there for her. She'd made a deal with herself the night she left Rick that she wouldn't tell them any of the details.

Neither of her siblings needed that level of shit in their lives.

The bell above the door announced the arrival of Customer 1645, or Blue Eyes as Sadie called him. Ian had been trying for months now to figure out his name, and he played along by not giving Ian any hints. Ian was head-over-heels-in-lust with the man, and for once Paige had to agree with her brother's tastes. A bit of the darkness that had settled on her lifted when Blue Eyes smiled her way.

"Hello, beautiful. How is the coffee business today?"

"Much better now that our favorite customer has shown up."

Blue Eyes scanned the store without appearing obvious. Paige pulled out a large cup and tried to keep her face as impassive as possible. "He's gone for a walk."

"Who?"

Like you don't know. "Ian. Sorry, no one to bug you about your name today."

Blue Eyes chuckled. "That's okay. I'll have to come back later to make up for it. I don't know if I could survive without my dose of the third degree."

"I'm glad. He'll be sorry if he misses you."

"The boy works too much." Blue Eyes took the mug and slid a toonie across the counter. "He needs to have a few nights off. Go out with a few friends. His girlfriend maybe?"

Subtle as a sledgehammer, fella. "I think Ian would develop hives if we even *suggested* he date a woman."

"Ah." Blue Eyes couldn't cover up his grin. "His boyfriend, then?"

"If Ian had one, he'd spend a lot less time here." Paige held out his change which he, of course, refused. She threw it in the tip jar. "It would be wonderful if that situation changed."

"I'm sure it would do him some good." Blue Eyes took a sip of the coffee and hummed pleasantly. "Perfect. Make sure to say hi for me."

"Will do."

It was a solid forty-five minutes later before Ian came back, his hair messy from the wind. "It's getting bad out there. Feels like rain." He stopped and frowned. "Shit. I missed him, didn't I?"

Paige wasn't sure how Ian could possibly know, but it probably had to do with the smirk on her face. "Yeah, sorry."

"Fuck." He marched over to the sink and washed his hands. "I'm never leaving for a walk again."

"Don't be such a baby. Plus, I think it was a good thing."

"What? Why?"

"He was asking about you." Paige relaxed, enjoying the easy conversation for once. "Wanted to know if you had a boyfriend."

Ian dropped the milk frothing cup, spun around and stared at her. "You're kidding."

"Nope. I think he might be slightly insane because it appears he likes you."

Ian tried to fight his grin but lost the battle miserably. "That's...that's good. Yeah."

"He said he'd try and come back later."

"I'll be here, unless you've managed to find a few fully trained baristas in desperate need of a job in the last half hour?"

"No. Sorry."

Ian shrugged. "A boy can dream."

The rattle of something being thrown into the sink in the kitchen had them both jump. Paige cringed, knowing the only reason Sadie was taking out her frustrations on her cooking instruments was because Paige was a complete bitch.

"What's wrong with Sade?" Ian's eyes grew impossibly wide. "Paul hasn't fucked up already, has he?"

"That would be me holding the honor."

"Oh." Ian set his towel down and moved beside her. "Dare I ask?"

Paige knew things were bad when Ian was playing the peacemaker. "I might have implied that she was trying to meddle in my personal life."

"Christ, Paige."

"I know! I'm a bitch."

"What brought that on?"

Without saying anything else, she hauled the business card out of her pocket and handed it over.

"Who's Carter West?"

"Someone who came into the store last night."

"Firefighter. Sexy."

"He came back this morning and gave me his card. He wants to go for coffee."

"What's wrong with—?"

"At Mavericks."

"Oh." Ian said it in such a way that it sounded like he fully understood Paige's reservations and general bitchiness.

"She was only teasing me and I overreacted."

"Because you've never done *that* before."

Paige punched his shoulder. "Not helping."

"Sorry." He held the card up again, examining the text as if it held the mysteries of life. "Are you going?"

The mental image of Carter fully dressed in his leather, shirt off and a leather paddle in his hand made her stomach flip. "I don't know."

"It's only Mavericks. If you're worried about the guy being a creep, talk to Josh. He'll keep an eye open for you."

"Actually, Carter said he knew Josh."

"There you go." He held out the card and Paige took it back, not wanting to put it back in her pocket. "You know how strict he is about members. If the guy was a douche he wouldn't be allowed within ten miles of the place."

Arguments and roadblocks popped into her mind, none of which had anything to do with Carter himself. He'd given her no reason to doubt his intentions that the offer would be anything beyond coffee…at a sex club.

Ian stood in front of her and held her shoulders. "You're always running around worrying about me and Sade, but I think you need to start with yourself. You haven't been out with anyone since Rick, right?"

Paige shuddered at the sound of Rick's name, but thankfully Ian didn't notice. "No, I haven't."

"Then do this. Go for drinks. See where it leads. You never know, it might turn out to be awesome."

It was as though Paige saw Ian for the first time. He'd long lost his baby face, fine lines starting to appear around his eyes and mouth. In a few years they would be more prominent, and he'd start to look like their dad even more than he did now. Not that she'd ever make the comparison within earshot of Ian.

"When did you grow up to be so smart?" She leaned in and kissed his cheek.

"About ten minutes ago." Ian pulled her in for a hug, squeezing her tight before pushing her away. "Now go call him. I can cover the front."

"Should I suck up to Sade now or later?"

Another loud bang from the kitchen gave her all the answer she needed. Ian rolled his eyes and jerked his head in the direction of the back. "I'll talk to her in a few minutes. Why don't you use my cell for now?"

The nerves Paige had expected to feel didn't show up as she finally made up her mind to act on her desires. "Thanks. I'll sneak around to the alley and suck up after."

Outside it was warm despite the strong breeze. The air was refreshing after the heat of the shop and the saturated coffee-scented air. Paige slipped into the alley between the buildings and pressed her back to the wall. She was close enough to the street to still feel the buzz of energy around her, but far enough away that anyone coming by wouldn't be able to hear her.

With Ian's phone in one hand and Carter's card in the other, Paige found herself at the moment when she knew her life would change one way or the other. Even if Carter turned out to be a jerk and she never went near him again, it would start her back on the path to a social life.

That wasn't necessarily a bad thing.

Paige flipped the phone side-over-side, trying to will her body to cooperate with what her head knew she wanted. She would be fine. History wouldn't necessarily repeat itself because she was putting herself out there once more.

Right?

Taking a deep breath, she punched in the phone number and waited for an answer. The sound of Carter's recorded bass over his voice mail relaxed her enough so she could speak.

"Ten p.m. Friday at Mavericks."

She ended the call and prayed she hadn't made a mistake.

Chapter Three

The music was as loud as Paige remembered and no less annoying. She sat at the table closest to the bar and did her best not to watch the Domme going to work on the male sub strapped to the St. Andrew's Cross. The moans that undercut the music practically screamed out to Paige, making her skin tingle with every crack of the riding crop against his ass.

It had been far too long for her.

The damp glass in her hand was slowly growing warm. The rye and ginger burned down her throat, her current buzz more the result of her nerves than the alcohol. Carter's return message had been nearly as brief as her own. He had to do something special at the station, needed at least an hour to go home and change before he would meet her at Mavericks.

"Make sure you wear something nice. And don't put any panties on," he'd said off-handedly before hanging up.

It would have been easy to dismiss his comment as a smart-assed remark, something he threw out there to try and ease the tension. Paige knew better. Because if there was one thing she'd learned early on, it was that Doms didn't say anything they didn't mean.

It was a test, one Paige had to think long and hard about while she was getting dressed.

The table, while giving her an excellent view of the cross, was also in a direct eye-line with the main entry. Refusing to check her watch, she kept her gaze down and did her best to ignore the men and women who approached her. Only when Josh slid into the seat next to her did Paige acknowledge him.

Josh pushed her unbound hair off her shoulder, the strands kissing the middle of her bare back. "I didn't think I'd see you in here again."

She snorted, ignoring the way he cocked his eyebrow. "It hasn't been that long."

"Three years."

"I've been…" She couldn't find the right word. Shrugging, she took a sip of her drink. "Preoccupied."

"I'm glad you made the time." Josh trailed his fingers down her shoulder and along the line of her biceps. "Who are you meeting?"

"What makes you think I'm meeting anyone? Maybe I decided I wanted to have a night out on the town."

Josh chuckled. "I've known you too long to believe that. Plus Paul might have mentioned that Sadie said something about you meeting someone here tonight and hoping you'd get laid so you wouldn't implode."

Paige did her best to relax her clenched jaw. "I'm going to kill her."

"She didn't mean anything by it. I think it was her way of asking if I'd come check up to make sure everything is okay." He stood and righted his black silk dress shirt. "But I can see you're fine."

The music quieted as the DJ switched beats, letting the un-restrained cries of the sub on the cross fill the space between. Paige's gaze was drawn to where he was spread out and help-less, exposed for the entire club to see. The Domme twisted the nipple clamps, wrenching another cry from him.

Josh started to walk away when Paige grabbed his hand. "Do you know Carter West?"

A sly smile crossed his face. "Yes, been coming here for a couple of years now."

"Is he…" She licked her lips. "Do you trust him?"

"Yes." Josh didn't miss a beat. "He's one of the best Doms I've seen in here. Doesn't mind-trip on anyone, and the women he does play with always leave satisfied."

That was something at least. "Thanks."

Josh squatted in front of her and placed a hand on each of her knees. "If I had any suspicions of a potential problem, I would say something. If you've caught Carter's eye, then I know you'll be fine. He'll treat you right."

"If he ever shows up." Paige hated feeling like an insecure twelve-year-old. Hell, she hadn't felt like this even when she *was* twelve. "He's twenty minutes late."

All Paige could picture was Carter sitting at the coffee shop having a drink with his friends while she sat here alone like a dumbass. It would be a shitty way to start her return to so-cial circles.

"He could have had a late call. I assume he was working today."

"Yeah, he said they asked him to come in for a special event. I didn't think about there being a fire."

"I can check if you want?" Josh took Paige's hand and pressed a kiss to her wrist.

Heat spiraled its way through her body. She had to be hard

up if a chaste kiss from a friend could get her worked up. "I'll give him a bit longer."

"Okay. Come find me if there's a problem."

Paige didn't watch Josh disappear back into the crowd. Her eyes might have been fixed on the table, but she was aware of every person who walked inside. It was hard to relax her body, her mind refusing to go to that place she desperately wanted it to be. There had been a time before Rick when she'd needed more than a break. Wanted someplace where she could melt into the background and let every compounding concern dissipate.

Closing her eyes, Paige took a shallow breath through her nose and let it out through her mouth. The music rose louder, surrounding her as she breathed in and out. She ignored the sounds, the moans and laughter—the only thing that was a concern was how big a breath she could manage. In and out.

Time began to melt away as she waited, breathing. The knots in her shoulders and neck screamed out. Paige acknowledged the pain, relaxed into it and let it go.

In and out.

"Now isn't that an attractive image."

Paige opened her eyes slowly to see Carter standing over her, his hands clasped behind his back.

"Attractive?" She squeezed her hands together.

It was odd how everything slotted into place, Paige sitting here waiting for Carter and the way his gaze took in everything about her the moment he arrived. There was none of the agitation she'd experienced with Rick, the shame and embarrassment at being turned on for wanting a spanking. She knew what she needed now, what she craved from a man.

Carter lacked the edge that was apparent in Rick. She had no misgivings that he would be easy on her, but she didn't think he'd be cruel. Paige didn't have an urge to be abused, simply controlled.

Her tongue darted out and wet her lips. "I wasn't sure if you were going to come."

"We had a school visit that ran a bit long. We were late starting because of a call. Hard to show them the truck when it's not there." He pulled out the chair Josh had vacated earlier, spun it around and straddled the seat. The sleeves pulled up, revealing his firm forearms, and Paige wanted to push the material up higher. "Can I get you anything?"

She held up her still mostly full glass. "I'm fine. Thanks."

One of the waitresses came by and tried to flirt with Carter. He smiled but barely acknowledged her beyond a simple, "Water, please."

Paige waited until the woman was gone before meeting his gaze. "It's been a while since I've done this."

"Had a drink? You need to get out more."

She didn't want to smile but couldn't help it. "No, do a scene."

"I got that impression. I also suspect you haven't taken a lot of time for yourself recently."

It wasn't much of a stretch as far as assumptions went, but Paige found herself stiffening. "I don't have time for luxuries these days. Our business is in a critical stage and I need to make sure I'm there doing what I can."

Carter shifted forward until his hands hung in the space over the table. They were large hands, with long thick fingers that would cover half her face if he cupped her cheek. "Taking time for yourself isn't a luxury. What will your business do if you've burned out and refuse to get out of bed one morning?"

"I would never—"

He held up his hand and Paige snapped her mouth shut

without thinking. "You're wound so tight, I'm surprised you haven't exploded yet. Relax."

The muscles in the small of her back protested as Paige tensed. Her stomach churned, and the tightness in her chest returned once more. She knew he was right, knew if she didn't do something soon everything she'd worked to rebuild would fall apart. "I can't." Somehow her whisper reached him over the noise in the room.

"Yes, you can."

"I *can't*." The tightness in her chest crept upward to strangle her throat. "I've tried hard to be what everyone needs. It's like my head spins and spins and I can't figure out a way to slow things down so I can breathe."

There were tears in her eyes, yet she couldn't make herself care enough about what Carter would think of her to stop. He was right—the world had been pressing down on her for ages and she needed it to stop.

Carter continued to stare at her for a few minutes. The silence between them should have been awkward, seeing as she hardly knew him. But it wasn't. Rising to his feet in a single, fluid motion, he held out his hand for her to take.

"I think you know exactly what it will take to make things better. I'm not sure what happened to stop you from getting what you need, but I'm offering to help."

Paige bit the inside of her cheek and stared hard at his hand. Josh trusted this man. She was attracted to him, which was a bonus. Things didn't have to be about sex and if she said no, she got the impression Carter wouldn't push things.

Safe, sane and consensual.

A relief.

Paige put her hand in his. "I have rules."

"I would imagine you do. Let's go somewhere to discuss them."

She gave his hand a squeeze and tried not to think too much about what the hell she was about to do. The contact of skin on skin brought a rush of noise. She hadn't even realized the absence until the sounds descended on her awareness again.

People around them laughed, the sound punctuated by the continued slaps of leather on skin. Paige shivered, her body craving the thing that terrified her the most, needing to give in to it. Carter didn't release her, keeping her hand close to his side as they threaded through the crowds to the metal staircase that led to the upstairs rooms. It had been years since she'd walked this path, each step one farther away from the woman she no longer wanted to be.

When they'd reached the top, Paige caught sight of Josh waiting by the hall. He'd obviously been watching their ascent, waiting for their arrival. He nodded their way. "Carter, I assume you'd like one of the equipped rooms tonight?"

"If that's what Paige would like."

It was odd having a Dom ask her opinion, but since they hadn't worked out any of the basics, she appreciated that he was taking things slow. Nodding, she stepped closer to Carter. "Thanks, Josh."

"I'm happy to help." Reaching into his pocket, he pulled out a black key and tossed it to Carter. "Third on the left. No two-way."

Thank God for that. The last thing she wanted tonight was to be the main attraction for a bunch of voyeurs. Her feet took a bit of convincing to move once Josh walked past them. She was going to do this? Voluntarily going into a room with a Dom, one she barely knew?

Carter glanced her way and gave her fingers a gentle

squeeze. "Anytime you change your mind, you say the word and we're back to coffee."

This time the nod she gave him was a bit shakier. "Let's go where it's quiet."

Walking was much like breathing. Once step at a time. In and out. Her boots pinched her feet, and her ankles ached as she moved quickly to keep pace with Carter. People moved out of their way, but several cast curious looks in their direction. There was no one she recognized, even though many of the people she'd hung out and played with still came to Mavericks. As long as she kept her head down, she should be able to avoid drawing attention to herself.

The key slid easily into the lock, giving way with a soft click. Carter held the door open for her and stayed where he was, giving Paige the freedom to explore. Things weren't too different from how she remembered.

On a table along the side wall was a long, low chest. Paige walked the length of it, touching the various instruments laid out for inspection. A paddle, riding crop, soft leather cuffs and lengths of nylon rope, all there waiting to be used. The polished silver knobs on a series of drawers shone out from the black wood. Paige let her hand drop to the closest one, circling the cool metal with her fingertip.

She cast a quick glance over to Carter, who remained still by the door. Taking a breath, she pulled the drawer open. The dull shine of the red butt plug seemed ethereal against the black cloth. It wasn't too intimidating in size, though it had been a while since she'd used one. Closing the drawer, she went to the next and found a glass dildo. The blue and green cascading swirls could have belonged in an art show, not trapped in something that would hide them from sight.

"See something you like?"

Paige jumped when she realized Carter had shut the door and finally joined her in the room. "Yes."

"Show me."

She held it up without hesitation, her body relaxing as she let the power of his command wash over her. Carter walked over, reached out and held her wrist. It would have been easy enough to pull away from his grip, but surprisingly she didn't even have the urge. Instead, she found herself watching as he pulled her hand in to better examine the dildo.

"This could be fun." He fingered the smooth surface. "I approve."

The air in her lungs grew heavy and it was suddenly hard to swallow. "Rules."

If her sudden change in conversation bothered him, Carter didn't show it. "Tell me."

Shifting her gaze to his hand once more, Paige tried to remember all the feelings that had exploded inside her years earlier. She didn't need the same things now that she had back then. Her emotions ran deeper than they had when she was twenty-five and discovering these things about herself.

"No scat, golden showers, blood or breath play. Orgasm denial is fine. Pain is fine. I prefer to be bound, blindfolds are fine, but gags are hard for me. If there is sex, condoms are a must."

He nodded. "Any limitations on toys?"

"No."

"I expect to be referred to as Sir while we're in this room."

Paige sighed, unanticipated relief flowing free. "Yes, Sir."

"Safe word?"

"Let's stick with basics, Sir. *Red* stop, *yellow* slow."

Another nod. "I want you to get on your knees in the middle of the room."

Paige had to let the breath she'd been holding go before she could move. Her steps grew even more uncertain as she moved to the place he'd indicated. The rational part of her brain couldn't believe she was doing this. She knew nothing about the man. They were only supposed to be here for coffee, not bondage.

Bullshit.

It was hard to still her body and fight off the urge to squirm as she lowered herself to her knees. Not sure what to do with her hands, Paige laced them behind her back and did her best to clear her head.

Minutes silently ticked off and she knew Carter was letting her mind do its thing. He was far quieter than Rick ever was. While Rick would boss and yell from the moment they started a scene, Carter hardly twitched. It made Paige nervous, anxious and excited all at once.

Carter finally moved to stand behind her, depriving Paige of even her cursory glances. When he finally spoke, his voice seemed to seep beneath her skin, calming her.

"I think it's time we got to know each other a bit."

The impulse to respond nearly won over her common sense. She wasn't being asked to become an active participant in the conversation. Not yet.

"I have a bit of a confession to make. The reason we came into the store the other night was because I'd seen you before."

Paige sucked a breath in and squeezed her fingers together hard to keep from moving.

"It was after a call we had down the street last month. At Wilson's Jewelers. I'd come out of the back, stinking of smoke and plastic, wet from head to toe, looked up and you were there. You went back into the coffee shop shortly after that."

She remembered watching the aftermath of the small fire,

finding the scurrying of the firefighters almost hypnotic. After a few moments, she'd lost interest and went back inside where business had picked up as a result of the extra pedestrian traffic.

"I'd figured you might've been a customer and that I'd have to ask around before I'd figure out who you were. Imagine my surprise when I showed up at the shop and there you were, bursting with indignation and wearing a prickly shell."

Carter's footsteps echoed in the small room as he approached her from behind. When he pushed her unbound hair to the side, exposing her neck to him, Paige shivered but didn't try to stop him.

"You looked tired and lonely that night."

"I wasn't—"

He quickly drove his fingers into her hair and tipped her head back at an awkward angle. Paige snapped her mouth shut.

"Not yet," Carter whispered. "I get the impression you do an awful lot of talking and not as much listening as you should." He rubbed his thumb across her cheek and eased up on his grip.

Paige sighed, hating how her body responded to his firm hold. Heat was building up low in her pussy. Her clit tingled from wanting to be touched. Still, she didn't move to relieve herself of the pressure.

"Do you have any idea how beautiful you are?" Carter released her hair, letting his fingers comb through the strands. "As I was saying, you looked lonely when we came in. You covered it up pretty quickly with that smile of yours and a little eye roll. But I still saw it."

Because he hadn't said she couldn't, Paige watched Carter walk over to the corner of the room and grab the sturdy chair sitting there. The heat from her pussy rose up through her torso to make her nipples hard. When he placed the chair about half a foot away from her and sat down, legs spread wide, Paige thought her world would explode.

"Stand up."

Paige got to her feet, the rush of blood sending painful prickles through her legs. The long leather skirt she'd put on hung heavy on her hips, hugging her ass and making her feel like she was overdressed. The hunter green corset was looser than it had been three years ago, but still did the job of thrusting the tops of her breasts up for Carter's inspection. He made a spinning motion with his finger and she had to fight a sigh as she complied with the request.

"Stop." The second she had, Carter's hands were on her ass, squeezing. "This is a sight I could charge admission for."

This time Paige couldn't stop her dismissive snort and was rewarded with a sharp slap to her ass. The contact wasn't muted by the leather and had her gasping in surprise.

"Behave." Carter resumed his inspection. "I bet you would be stunning in PVC. It would cling to you and I'd be able to see every curve of your body." Another slap, but this time with less force. "Now, I want to see if you listened to me. Bend over and touch your toes."

Her pussy clenched in anticipation. This was what she'd been thinking about all evening while she'd waited. God, she wished she could see his face, but it would be impossible with her skirt. Still, as Paige leaned over and wrapped her hands around her ankles, keeping her legs as straight as she could manage, she tried to catch a glimpse of Carter.

"Eyes on the floor," he snapped.

Dammit. "Yes, Sir."

His hands never left her body as he slowly pulled up the leather. "Your legs are shaking. It must be hard for you to stand there like that in those boots. I noticed you were a bit unsteady walking on them. Maybe I should make you walk around in nothing but them until you're more comfortable. Then I'd be able to fully appreciate your legs."

He stroked his fingers down the backs of her thighs. Paige had to hold her breath to keep from moaning out loud. This was too much, too gentle. She needed more than this, and if he wasn't going to act soon, she'd walk away.

Liar.

There was a brief pause when he got her skirt to the edge of her ass. "Sweet Paige, did you do what I asked? Will I be pleased with what I see when I lift this up?" He teased her, jiggling the fabric until the edge tickled her sensitive skin.

Not bothering to wait for her response, Carter finally flipped up the skirt to reveal her bare ass. His low moan was all the response Paige had hoped for.

Running a finger first down one cheek, then the other, Carter leaned forward so his breath ghosted across her skin. His second hand began to explore the sensitive dip above her ass, teasing but not going any further.

"Thank you for this, Paige. I promise I will be good to you." A single kiss placed to the small of her back was followed by a two-hand squeeze. "Now whatever will I do with you?"

Chapter Four

Paige wasn't expecting the slap. The force drove her forward, sending her stumbling as she fought to regain her balance. Carter's big hand cupped her hip and pulled her back into position. The muscles in her back were protesting the stretch, and sweat was collecting beneath her hands where she held her boots.

Slowly, the turmoil in her mind began to recede and all Paige was able to concentrate on were the physical sensations playing havoc through her body. Carter never once released his hold on her, keeping her locked in the moment.

The second spank was as forceful, but she was better able to relax into the sting of flesh on flesh. Her pussy was soaked and if Carter were to reach between her legs, his fingers would come out drenched.

She tried to push that image from her mind.

"You like a spanking." The statement didn't seem like much of a revelation to him. "I think that is as good a place as any to start. I want you to lie across my lap. Make sure to brace yourself."

The little streak of shame came on as strongly as ever, right after the rush of desire. Paige kept her eyes lowered as she stood, temporarily relieving the pressure on her back, and moved to Carter's side. Without a word, she shuffled as close as she could and tried to stretch across him with at least a tiny bit of dignity and grace, but failing as she lost her balance and dropped her chest hard across his thighs.

Rick would have yelled at her and, back then, Paige would have accepted the humiliation as part of the deal. Carter helped steady her, shifting his legs and pressing a hand to the small of her back as she slid forward to brace her hands on the floor. The heels of her boots made it possible to keep her feet touching.

"Good girl. I know that must have been hard for you. It's been a long time, hasn't it?"

Paige squeezed her eyes shut tight, not wanting the interrogation to continue. She didn't want to think, talk or do anything else other than be spanked. "Yes, Sir."

"Yes, Sir, what? How long, Paige? I want an exact time period for the last time you were stretched out, offered up and waiting for someone to turn your ass a nice shade of red."

It had been more black and blue than red, but she didn't think Carter needed to know that.

"Three years."

The slap that time was with the full force of his hand, which he didn't cup. The sudden sting had her crying out and pressing her face to the side of his calf. "Three years, two months and a few days. Sir."

"See, I knew you would have the exact time. You're a precise person, aren't you, Paige?"

"Yes, Sir."

"How about we play a little game? I'm going to pick a

number between one and thirty. You have to guess what the number is. If you guess correctly, then I'll do something you want. If you guess incorrectly, I'll spank you the difference between the two numbers. Understand?"

Paige squirmed and thrust her ass in the air. "Yes, Sir."

Carter continued to circle her ass with his fingers, humming as if he were considering the answer to a serious problem. "I have my number. Now it's your turn. I want you to think about what number I could possibly choose for you. What's an acceptable number for beautifully tense Paige, who needs someone to help her let it all go?"

Paige's mind went blank. Even the concept of numbers themselves seemed overly complicated. Her brain wanted to focus on his fingers and the heat seeping into her body from his.

"I'm waiting, Paige."

God, why couldn't she do what he wanted? "Ten, Sir."

"Oh, Paige, that wasn't close at all. I chose thirty. That means you'll be spanked twenty times. That's a lot for my poor hand." He almost sounded contrite. "I have to tell you that I wasn't planning on working that hard tonight. It's been a long, tiring week for me. How about I make you a deal? Would you like that, Paige?"

Every time he said her name, more tension bled away from her body. The twitching muscles of her back and arms started to give way as she sank deeper into the moment. The slap reminded her that she was supposed to be answering him.

"Yes, Sir. Thank you."

"I will spank you ten times with my hand. For the remaining ten I will let you choose either a flogger or a paddle. Isn't that nice of me?"

She groaned. "Yes, Sir. Thank you, Sir."

"Fuck." His mutter was barely a whisper. Carter cleared his throat and adjusted his stance again. "I want you to count each one. I'm not into that thanking shit, so you don't have to bother with it. I only want you to count and feel."

Slap!

The contact this time wasn't like his previous swats. Paige cried out and had to force in a breath to say what he'd wanted. "One."

Carter's thighs tensed and for a second she anticipated another quick spank. Instead, he shifted her closer to his stomach, until the hard line of his cock pressed against her side.

Slap!

"Two!"

Tears welled in her eyes and she could feel her nose start to fill with the unshed tears. Paige couldn't keep her mouth closed anymore. Letting it fall open, she breathed in the scented air of the room, enjoying the buzz it gave. The tang of the leather seeped onto the tip of her tongue as she dipped it out to brush Carter's calf. The rest of her mouth watered and she wanted to get more of her mouth on him. She wanted to drown in him, even as he kept her on the precipice between pleasure and pain.

Slap! Slap!

"Three. Four." The words were choked, fighting to come through the tight muscles in her throat.

Carter had worked a surprisingly large area on her ass, even landing spanks along the tops of her thighs. He stopped to massage the skin, leaning over to coo at her. "Good girl. I'm proud of you for coming this far."

The tears were flowing freely now, but Paige didn't care. Carter was taking care of her in a way she hadn't ever remembered feeling. It hurt, but it was good, exactly what she needed. The tears washed away the pain of the past, giving her a clean slate.

Slap!

"Five."

"We're halfway through the first part. I wish you could see yourself. Your skin is pale, making the red almost glow. Like a fire truck." He chuckled and slapped her even harder.

"Six."

Paige hadn't realized she'd been holding her head up until the muscles refused to cooperate. Gravity pulled her down, the tears breaking free and dripping onto the floor as Carter continued. Bliss.

"Seven. Eight."

"It would be fantastic to spread you out on the cross in the main room. I could take my time with you, work you over until you were begging and screaming for me to release you and let you come." He dipped his finger between her ass cheeks to tease her hole. "I can't believe how wet you are right now."

Without warning, he pushed a finger into her pussy, crooking it to press down against her G-spot. Paige moaned and shuddered, dangerously close to losing her balance along with her mind.

"I figured it had been a while for you, but three years is too much. You need to take better care of yourself."

"Nine." The pain was no longer as sharp as the sting melted into numbness. Her body no longer fought the pain, but welcomed it, used it to fire every inch of her. It was getting hard to count out, mostly because her mouth was dry and her throat scratchy. On some level she knew her face would be splotchy and her eyes and nose red. She mostly didn't care. "Ten!"

Carter reached down and helped her turn to sit up. While

ten slaps was not much of a punishment, not even remotely close to what she'd taken in the past, the spanks were still more than she'd had in years. Her body shook and the damn tears streamed down her face.

"Want to stop?" His voice was soft, as was the kiss he pressed to her temple.

"No, Sir," she said, sniffing. God, she couldn't stop yet. "We're only halfway."

"I wouldn't think any less of you, Paige. It's been a while since you've been here."

By *here,* she knew he wasn't referring to the club. "I can handle it, Sir."

When she tried to sit up, Carter gently pushed her head to his shoulder. "Not yet. Let's do this right first. You're still fighting things and that won't get us anywhere."

Before she could protest Carter stood, taking her up in his arms, and walked them over to the chest.

"Josh usually stocks...there it is." He reached into the bot-tommost drawer and pulled out a bottle of water. He tossed it onto her lap before returning them to the chair. "Open it."

Paige was sluggish but eventually moved to comply. The plastic ring cracked and gave way after a few tries, water slip-ping down the side of the bottle. She lifted it up to Carter's mouth, but he shook his head and took it from her.

"I'm not the one who needs this." He pressed the opening to her lips and waited for her to open her mouth.

The water calmed her as it soothed her throat. She closed her eyes as she drank, not able to handle Carter's intense scru-tiny. It was odd, his being able to read her as easily as he could. Not that Paige imagined herself as overly complicated, but Rick had never managed to figure out what she'd needed out of their relationship, even after having been together for years.

When Carter pulled the bottle away, Paige unconsciously chased it, wanting more. He chuckled and pressed his finger to her lips. "Not too much. I don't want you getting sick."

Paige would have normally protested, bitching at him about how she knew exactly what she needed and could handle. The fight had dissipated along with his spanking, leaving her calmer and relaxed. "No, Sir."

"Are you ready for the next ten? They will be harder."

Hell no, she wasn't ready, but she nodded anyway. This was something that she not only needed, but wanted desperately.

"Good girl. I want you to go over and pick out what you want me to use. Get the thing that will help you get where you need to go."

Paige couldn't keep her gaze from the chest and the toys she knew were within. While this was part of the scene and not at all unexpected, the idea of walking over there to pick out her instrument of doom wasn't as appealing as it had been in the past. Still, she was determined to see this through to the end and wanted it to be Carter on the delivering end. Sliding to her feet, she stumbled back to the chest and carefully considered her options.

Two paddles immediately caught her attention. The first was thick with leather knots covering the surface at irregular intervals. Reaching out, she ran her fingertips over the top, letting the varying texture pick at her skin as she went. It was elaborate, elegant in its design, yet no doubt effective when used properly.

The second paddle was simple in nature, almost as if it didn't belong. The wide head was oak or maple. It had been sanded smooth, any imperfections long removed. Paige ran the palm of her hand across the surface, sighing at the smooth feel. She picked it up and made her way back to where Carter sat. Paige held it up for his inspection, as her nerves began to creep up on her again.

His gaze flicked from her face to the paddle. Holding out his hand, he waited for her to hand it over.

"Easy to swing, yet heavy enough to leave an impression." Carter slapped his open palm with the wide face. "Nice and big too. I'll be able to hit most of your ass with this. I approve."

Paige relaxed and nodded. "Thank you, Sir."

When she stepped closer, intending to climb back on his lap, Carter crossed his legs and leaned back. "Not yet. I want to make sure I do this properly. Need room to move."

"Whatever you want, Sir." It came out harsher than Paige intended, dragging a snort from Carter.

"This has nothing to do with me at all, as you are aware. We are simply getting to know each other, seeing if there is something here we might want to explore further. You can walk out that door anytime you want, I won't move a muscle to stop you. But if you stay, I want you to give yourself over to me completely. That means doing what I ask, without the snark."

Paige let her gaze drop, hating her inadequacies. "I'm sorry, Sir. I didn't think it would be this hard."

"It's not like this is your first time. Which means you've had a nasty experience that stopped you from coming back when it's something you clearly want. Look at me." Leaning forward, Carter braced his arms on his knees, letting the paddle dangle, and waited until she met his gaze. "Answer me truthfully. Do you feel pressured in any way to be here with me?"

"No, Sir."

"And while I know we've only begun, have I done anything, anything at all to have made you feel uncomfortable?"

"No, nothing."

"You can leave, Paige. I hope you don't, but I'd understand. Is that what you want? Think before you answer."

Was it? Despite the emotional hurricane raging inside her, Paige knew the center of the storm was approaching. If she could hold on a bit longer, she'd sink into that place where her mind would find comfort.

Paige met Carter's gaze and relaxed. "No, Sir. I don't want to leave. I've been running away from this for a long time and I need to get my head straight. If you're willing to help me, I would appreciate it."

Carter leaned back once more and folded his arms. "Then you know what to do."

With her heart pounding, Paige reached behind her for the zipper. Her fingers were steady as she pulled the tab down, having fully accepted what she was doing. Carter was someone Josh trusted, and she trusted Josh. More important, Paige trusted *herself* to leave if there was a problem.

Holding the skirt together with one hand, she kept her gaze on Carter, making sure that they were both on the same page, before finally dropping it. The air was cool in contrast to the heat coming from her ass and her pussy. Even though she still wore the corset, Paige felt more exposed than had she been completely naked.

Carter's gaze drifted down her body, stopping on her breasts, her stomach, lower. He flexed his grip on the paddle. "Beautiful."

Paige's face heated.

"Now you have another choice. Do you want to do this over my lap again, or would you prefer to lean over the chest? I can work with either."

Being on his lap would cut the sting down, given the slightly awkward angle, but would let her feel him. The chest would give him room to move, allowing him to make every smack count.

"The chest, Sir."

Carter nodded, indicating she should move. The boots and corset would project an interesting image as she walked over. She made sure to add a little enticing sway to her hips as she went.

Paige cleared her mind and braced her hands on the edge of the chest. She hated when he didn't move right away. Being watched was hard for her, especially when she wasn't in motion. All the noise and activity kept her grounded. It was easier to hide, distract others when she never stopped long enough for others to notice.

Squeezing the edge, she was once again forced to close her eyes and take several deep breaths to calm herself. Everything relaxed into place, as she concentrated on the beats of her heart and the steady in-out of her breathing. She'd gone deep into herself and hadn't realized Carter was standing beside her until he ran a hand down across her ass cheek.

"That's better," he muttered, giving her ass a small pinch. "I want you to keep your eyes closed and concentrate on your breathing. I'm not going to go easy on you, but I will check to make sure you're okay. Understand?"

"Yes."

He slapped her ass hard, and Paige cried out.

"*Sir.* Yes, Sir."

"Good girl. I want you to count like you did before."

The comforting presence of Carter's body beside her disappeared, causing Paige to whimper. Unlike before, he didn't touch her body as he moved into position behind her. Again he waited and Paige knew he was waiting for her to do as he'd asked. She let her head hang and started to count the breaths.

In and out. *One.*

In and out. *Two.*

In and out. *Thr—*

The crack of the wood hitting her ass was almost as loud as the scream she let loose. God dammit, that hurt! Paige let out a small sob and gave her head a shake. "One."

"I want you to think about the reasons why you walked away from this, Paige. You had one, a serious one if I had to guess. I need you to consider if that reason is still valid."

The sting had morphed into a burn, her already sensitive flesh and ragged nerves not ready for the hit or the question. Still, she let her mind wander to Rick. He'd hurt her, hadn't listened to what she'd needed, when she'd needed it. He'd been after his own pleasure, using her as a tool to get off rather than a partner to share a life with.

But not Carter. This was all for her.

The second smack was as hard as the first, but the burn had shifted into a numbness that heated her entire cunt. She was wet as the tingling traveled down her thighs. Fuck, she hadn't been this turned on in years. Light pressure against her clit would be all she'd need to make her come. Not even Rick got her this hot in their time together, and he'd done a whole hell of a lot more than paddle her ass.

After the third smack, Carter stepped in and ran a hand down her back. Paige was sweating beneath the corset, the fabric scratching against her skin as she adjusted her stance. Her legs shook and she wasn't sure if she'd be able to hold herself up much longer.

Carter slipped one hand around her hip to hold her steady, while he dipped the other between her legs. Her clit was swollen and it wouldn't take much to push her over the edge. Fuck, she needed to come badly, or else she might possibly go mad.

Teasing her opening with his finger, Carter hummed in her ear, nipping at the lobe.

"You're standing there taking it. You're listening to me and doing what I want. But we've only started, haven't we?"

"Yes—" she swallowed "—Sir."

"Are you ready?"

Paige couldn't answer verbally. Instead she nodded and pushed her ass back toward him. Carter's soft growl was the only acknowledgement he gave. He pulled back and landed two hard smacks in rapid succession. He didn't hold back, and yet he wasn't trying to break her.

"Four. Five."

"That reason for you not coming here, I want you to think about it again. If it's not an issue for you any longer I want you to say goodbye to it and let it go. Do you understand me?"

She nodded again.

Smack!

"Six."

Rick was long gone. He'd moved to Montreal a few months after she'd kicked him out and changed her phone number. She'd been scared and angry for a long time after that. Scared she'd find herself back in another emotionally abusive relationship, when she needed pain as a release. Angry for having been too blind to appreciate the difference.

Smack!

"No!" The tears were flowing down her face again, but this time it had little to do with the physical pain. Rick had taken this from her. *This* was what she'd wanted, needed, and she wouldn't let the specter of her past relationship control her any longer.

"No what, Paige? Who are you saying no to?"

"Rick. Fucking asshole." She wouldn't let him continue to win.

"That's my girl. Let it go." The kiss to her bare shoulder. "He's not here anymore and you are okay."

"I'm okay," she mumbled, nodding her head. "I'm okay."

"Now, what number was that, Paige? I need you to tell me."

Numbers? Shit, she was supposed to be counting. Five? No, that wasn't right. "Seven."

"That's right. See, you know. And that means we're almost done."

With smack number eight, the blackness of peace slipped over her and Paige was no longer able to find her voice. Somewhere she registered the last two smacks before Carter's arms were around her and her face was pressed to his chest.

"Fucking gorgeous. You're amazing, Paige. I want to taste you. Need to…"

He set her on the table and dropped to his knees. Paige's mind floated as he spread her thighs wide and breathed in her scent. Carter's attention was focused on her cunt and he pushed a finger into her. Paige gasped when he leaned in and licked a swipe up across her lips.

The tingle from the blood rushing through the over-sensitized area ignited to a full-out blaze. Paige moaned, mesmerized by the precision of his licks. He tasted every inch of skin he could get his tongue on. As he increased the pace of the finger pumping into her, her battle was lost. Screwing her eyes shut, she let the orgasm explode, rending apart the remains of her resistance.

She must have blacked out because the next thing she knew she was sitting on the floor, wrapped up in Carter's arms.

"There she is."

Blinking up at him, Paige let the real world filter back in

through the haze of her post-coital bliss. She swallowed down a dry lump.

"Here." Carter held up the water bottle and let her take a few sips. She whimpered when he took it away. "In a second. Let that settle first."

After a few minutes and several more mouthfuls of water, Paige noticed that Carter's hard-as-rock cock was still firm beneath her. Resting her hand on his chest she leaned in and placed a kiss on his cheek.

"Would you like me to take care of that, Sir?"

He smiled, kissed her forehead but gave his head a shake. "I'm okay."

"But—"

"No buts. This wasn't about me. We're getting to know each other tonight, and I'm not ready for that."

"You feel ready to me." Paige let her head fall against his shoulder, trying to ignore her disappointment. "If you're sure?"

"I am. And before you go off thinking that you did something wrong or that I'm not attracted to you, stop." He bucked his hips up. "Clearly that's not the case."

Why she was girlishly pleased by his comment, Paige didn't want to examine too closely. "Why not, then?"

"I don't have sex with someone I've just met, sub or not. Scene or not. It's my one rule."

"Oh."

They sat in the quiet of the room for several long minutes, but Paige didn't feel uncomfortable in the least. Carter was constantly touching her, running his fingers through her hair, twirling the ends and tugging slightly, squeezing her hip. For the first time in ages her mind calmed and she seemed more settled in her skin, ready to face the world. She liked it.

Slipping her fingers between the buttoned fabric of his shirt to touch the warm skin of his chest, Paige turned her face. "Now what?"

"If you're up for it, I suggest we go back downstairs, get ourselves a drink and talk."

"Talk? About what?"

"Date-type things."

A date? A scene wasn't normally the sort of thing she did when she first started dating someone. Then again, there would be no awkward moments of her needing to explain how she loved to be tied up and spanked.

Carter cocked an eyebrow at her, when she sat up and carefully got to her feet. She smiled as she bent down to get her skirt. "I want a rye and ginger."

Chapter Five

"Dear God, the apocalypse must be on its way."

Paige turned to stare blankly at Ian, doing her best to ignore the surprise on his face. "Sorry?"

"You're humming."

Paige opened her mouth to protest, only to shake her head, confused. "What the hell are you talking about?"

"You know, humming. That thing you do when you can't remember the words, are in the shower or generally in a good mood. Lady Gaga, from the sound of it."

"I am *not* humming." Though she did have "Bad Romance" stuck in her head this morning. "You're imagining things."

Her phone chose that moment to buzz, announcing another text message. Her hand slipped into her pocket to curl around it, but she didn't pull it out. No way she'd do *that* in front of Ian.

Ian rolled his eyes and added more beans into the roaster. "I'm not saying it's a bad thing. It's kind of nice actually."

True, she'd been feeling lighter since her night out with Carter, but she hadn't realized others were noticing. They'd spent the rest of the evening down in the bar, talking about the submissive strapped to the cross. Carter had wanted to know her impressions of the Dom's technique, how he wasn't pushing the sub far enough. What her preferences would have been.

That had been a far more difficult conversation.

Still, when he eventually put her in a cab to make sure she got safely home, the care with which he helped her into the truck and gently shut the door, Paige knew she wanted to see him again. The texts had started later that night.

Carter had plans for the weekend, but he didn't let that stop him. At first the texts were a distraction, little updates about what he'd been doing peppered throughout her day. But the more she received, the more she liked it. Carter wasn't chatty face to face, his sly humor usually delivered with a soft chuckle. But through his notes, Paige started to see more of his sarcastic nature slipping through. After a week of messages, Paige found she was looking forward to them. The steady buzz of her phone was a pleasant distraction from her day.

"There it is again! A smile."

Turning her back on her brother, she concentrated on stacking the clean mugs under the counter. "Shut up, Ian."

"This doesn't have anything to do with a certain fireman, does it?"

"No."

"Because you haven't said much since your date with him."

"No, I haven't."

"Does that mean things are going okay? Are you going to see him again?"

"One date, Ian. That's all. If there was something earth-shattering going on, you'd be the second to know."

"You're worse than Sadie with the personal life details."

"For God's sake, Ian, the last time I said anything to you

about my personal life you freaked out." Paige leaned forward and rested her head on the side of the counter door.

He tapped the top of her head, reaching over her to fill the coffee pot with filtered water. "You were talking about your sexual preferences. I don't want to hear anything about that. I only want to know if you're interested in this guy. If there's a chance I might need to hire yet another staff member because you're going to be out half the week."

"We haven't even talked about a second date, and the first one was barely that." She couldn't count it as a date when he'd spanked her soundly before giving her the best orgasm she'd had in years. That was way more intimate than learning about each other's reading preferences or their favorite colors.

The phone in her pocket buzzed again. This time she snuck a peak. Sure enough, Carter's phone number was on her screen.

How bout burgers? Do u like em w/ cheese or r u into veggie?

Smiling, she quickly thumbed. *Meat's yummy. xtra cheese & bacon on mine plz.*

Within seconds of her hitting Send, Carter's reply bounced back. *Then we shld go. I know a place.*

When?

2morrow?

Her stomach did a little flip. *Sounds good. I'll call u 2nite?*

KK.

She was going out on a date. Again.

The bell over the door sounded and Paige turned around as she shoved the phone back into her pocket. "Welcome to Pulled Long. What can I get—?"

Oh, hell no.

Rick stood inside the doorway, his hands on his hips and a grin on his face. "Hello, Paige."

She'd pictured this day a few times after their last phone call three years earlier. None of the scenarios played out positively for her. At least this was public and Ian was here. While Rick might not have understood the line between foreplay and fucked-up, he never did anything outside of a club or their apartment to draw attention to their lifestyle. She hadn't given him any chances after leaving him.

Swallowing down the sick rising in her throat, she plastered on her best fake smile and pretended he was another customer.

"What can I get for you? Our special today is mocha lattes and lemon loaf."

Ian came up to stand beside her, his hands balled into fists below the counter. "Hello, Rick. I'd heard you'd left town?"

"I did, but now I'm back. Not enough interesting work in Montreal to hold my attention. I moved back to Toronto a few months ago."

With every step he took closer to the counter, Paige's chest tightened. She fought to keep her panic from showing, not wanting to give him any reason to think he could still affect her like this.

"What can I get for you?" Her voice was steady, but she found it challenging to keep her gaze locked on his.

The door chime sounded again as Blue Eyes walked in. "Hey, kids." He didn't let Rick's presence stop him from making his way over to the counter and taking up residence on one of the vacant stools. "Can I get a black coffee and one of Sadie's muffins, gorgeous?"

Ian glanced at Blue Eyes before turning to her. "Are you okay?"

"Why wouldn't she be okay?" Rick stepped up flush to the counter and threw a twenty between them. "One coffee. Double, double. You, go talk to your boyfriend."

Paige had always hated the way Rick had treated Ian, and her brother was more than ready to get into a fight with anyone who wanted to push matters. She reached up and took Ian's fist. "Go see to our other customer. I can handle this."

"Are you sure?"

She smiled. "Not like you're far away."

Ian gave Rick one last glare before moving down to talk to Blue Eyes. Paige ignored him to concentrate on the bastard at hand. "Let me get your coffee."

The weight of his stare was like an electrical current running up and down her spine. She wanted to scratch her arms to chase away the feeling of bugs beneath her skin but wouldn't give him the satisfaction of seeing her uncomfortable.

The sugar was swallowed up by the chalk-colored coffee, the best effort she was willing to make for him, letting her know it was done.

"There you go." She slid it across the counter. "Anything else?"

Leaning over to close the distance between them, Rick grinned. "I heard a rumor you'd gone back to the club."

Fuck. "Who the hell told you that?"

"Doesn't matter. Though she did say you were all alone for a long time. Like you didn't know what to do with yourself."

Paige hadn't recognized anyone there that night, certainly not anyone from their old crowd. "I was fine."

"Yeah, the person said that too." There was something in Rick's tone that had Paige paying attention. He lowered his voice and placed his hand over hers. "I heard some asshole took you upstairs. You were gone for a while and when you came back the two of you were smiling and laughing at people. Is that true? You find someone who could pretend to give you what you want?"

"Shut up. That's none of your damn business." She tried to pull her hand away, but he pressed down hard, preventing her escape.

"No, you listen. I left you alone because you told me you weren't into pain anymore. That you didn't need to be spanked and tied up, and 'please, Rick, you don't need to do that anymore. I'm over it.'" His cheeks were red and his eyes were bug wide as he whispered softly enough so no one but Paige would hear. "I don't care what you think. Your ass still belongs to me."

"Let me go."

"No."

Paige jerked on her hand, but he held her fast. "I said let me go."

"I think you better listen to the lady." Blue Eyes was on his feet and beside Rick before either of them realized. "You're getting dangerously close to assault."

"And I'll make sure you won't be using that hand again anytime soon," Ian said with enough venom to make Paige believe every word.

Rick glared at them and for once did the smart thing. Lifting his hand, he grabbed his coffee and took a step back. "We can finish this conversation another time."

Blue Eyes stepped between them, forcing Rick backward. "See, I also think that is a bad idea. You're going to leave now and if this nice lady tells me that you've been bothering her, then my friends over at the police station are going to take a special interest in you. Understand?"

Taking a long sip of his coffee, Rick stepped back again, keeping his gaze on Paige. "Sure thing. I have to meet someone anyway. Thanks for the coffee."

Blue Eyes walked forward, forcing Rick to leave and keeping her view of her ex thankfully blocked.

When the door closed, Ian pulled her into a hug. "You okay?"

The sting of tears was back. Paige burrowed into his arms and tried not to cry. "I will be."

When Blue Eyes came back in, the muscles in his jaw and throat were still tense. "I think he's gone for now. Who the hell was he?"

"Her ex-asshole." Ian kissed her temple. "I don't know why you decided to leave him, but I'd never been happier. What did you ever see in him?"

"I would tell you, but you said you didn't want to hear about my sex life." Paige sniffed as she pulled away.

Blue Eyes laughed. "She told you."

Paige reached across the counter and pulled Blue Eyes in to kiss his cheek. "Thank you."

A grin split his face as he slipped his hands into his pockets. "All in a day's work." He turned to face Ian. "Do I get a kiss from you too?"

"I never kiss on the first date," Ian said casually. The effect was ruined by the dark blush covering his cheeks.

"But we haven't had a date."

"I don't even know your name." Ian smiled, reaching for a mug. "Let me get you some on the house for defending the honor of an employee of Pulled Long."

Blue Eyes kept his gaze on Ian, who turned to make the drink. "I'll keep that in mind for future payments. Nothing better than free coffee. Your pocket's buzzing."

Paige blinked at him. "What?"

"Your pocket. Someone's trying to get in touch with you."

Carter. Pulling out the phone, Paige groaned when she realized she'd missed seven texts from him.

Jason put hemorrhoid cream in Scott's socks. Entertaining party. When will u b home?

Paige?

Customer?

We can do burgers tmrow if u want?

I might make u do naughty things to earn yr supper. Crawl across the floor naked.

I keep thinking about yr red ass and how good yr pussy tasted. Want more.

U there?

Her hands shook as she ran her thumb across the display. "Ian, I'm going out back for a few."

"Go ahead. I've got things covered."

The air in the kitchen still smelled of the cookies Sadie had made early that day. It gave the illusion of warmth and safety, that life was simple and uncomplicated and the man she'd thought loved her wasn't back in her life. Without thinking too hard, Paige pressed Carter's number, nerves making her breathing shaky as the phone rang.

"Hey." His low voice warmed her, chasing away some of the darkness. "You on a break?"

"Hey. Yeah, I needed to get some air."

"What's wrong?" The certainty in his voice left no room for her to argue.

She sat on the stool and tried to find the words. Nothing seemed adequate enough to describe the hell her emotions were churning up. "Remember you asked me why I left the clubs and didn't do scenes anymore? Well, he showed up today."

"Are you at the store?"

"Yes, but—"

"Is Ian or Sadie with you?"

"Ian's here, a customer too."

"Don't move. I'll be there in twenty minutes. Thirty tops."

"Carter, you don't have—"

"Don't finish that sentence. Thirty minutes and I'll be there. Then we can talk."

The dial tone sounded before she had a chance to argue further. Okay, the reason she'd called him was more for the comfort factor than anything, and wasn't that screwed up seeing as she'd only known him for a short time. Still, he was coming, and knowing that helped her ease up on her panic.

The baking smells and the soft laughter of Ian and Blue Eyes helped her spin down enough so she was no longer nauseated. Rick wasn't stupid. He wouldn't do anything to hurt her with the guys around. And while he could probably figure out where she lived, she'd long ago had monitored security installed. She still had her phone unlisted, which would mean he couldn't get to her that way.

Paige pressed her thumb to her wrist until her nail cut into the sensitive skin. The small burst of pain was enough to help center her mind. Closing her eyes and pulling her legs up, she sat precariously on the small stool and let her mind wander as she ran through the meditation techniques she'd learned.

Time melted, and it wasn't until the door to the kitchen was pushed open that she realized she'd slipped out of reality and into her own head. When she opened her eyes, Carter stood there, his hands on his hips, staring at her with an odd expression on his face. He was wearing a T-shirt and jeans despite the coolness in the air.

"Hi." She tried to let her feet fall to the floor, but she'd lost the feeling in her legs. "Mind giving me a hand?"

Carter moved to her side and slipped an arm around her waist. The smell of sun and beer clung to him. "Go slow."

The sting from the pins and needles returning had her sucking in a breath, fighting against the chewing sensation. "God, I hate this."

"Then you shouldn't sit that way."

"It was that or beat my head against a wall. I figured this would be less painful for everyone."

Carter chuckled. "Let me know when you can walk again."

Paige put her hand over his, holding him in place, and leaned into his side. She'd missed the comfort his physical presence offered, even if they were in constant communication via text messaging. With the life coming back to her extremities, she looked up and shrugged.

"I could go for that burger right now."

The scowl on his face told her the distraction wasn't going to work for long, but for the moment he didn't push.

"Can Ian do without you?"

"He's a bit distracted at the moment, but I think he'll be fine."

"The guy at the counter seems pretty taken with him."

"If Ian doesn't ask him out soon I think Blue Eyes will. I don't know why they've been playing this game for as long as they have."

"Probably for the same reason you're not telling me about Mr. Asshole who showed up and freaked you out. They are scared of the consequences."

Paige didn't like to think of herself as being scared of anything, but in this instance she couldn't argue with him. "We can go to my place. Only if you want." While the last thing she would normally do was to bring someone back to her place, knowing Carter was there in case Rick decided to show up was a comfort in itself. "I'll buy the burgers."

"I have beer in the truck."

Paige told Ian she was leaving. "Sadie said she could come in if you need her."

Ian gave Carter the once-over. She knew he didn't know what to make of the fireman yet, but his reaction was already better than it had ever been toward Rick. "No problem. We're pretty quiet here today."

Blue Eyes remained surprisingly silent for once, though he did nod at Carter.

The entire way from the store to his truck, Carter had an arm around her waist or a hand on her shoulder. The constant physical contact was enough to help keep her from frantically looking around to see if Rick was watching. Not that she had any illusions about him coming to find her again, but he would think twice about it with Carter present.

They rode most of the way to the burger joint in silence, and Carter only filled her in on a few of the details about the happy-to-be-a-single-guy party he'd been attending. "It was sad how what we all wanted was a girl to go home to."

"They should go out more."

"That's what I said, but I wasn't about to tell them where." He changed lanes and pulled down the side street leading to her house. "I don't think any of them could handle going to a place like Mavericks."

Paige smiled and twisted her hair around her finger. "They don't know about your preferences?"

"They think I'm an overbearing jerk and they can't figure out why any woman in the world would be interested in me."

"I can name a few reasons."

"Then I might bring you down to the station house and

you can let them know personally. Use inches and diameter if you need to."

That had her laughing. "Next left. Third house on the right."

The burgers were still warm when she tossed the bag on the kitchen counter. Carter followed her right in and didn't even check her place out. It was nice to know he respected her privacy as much as he did her body.

"I can give you the fifty-cent tour later on if you want."

"Food first, tour later. I missed out on the steak."

They slipped into easy conversation as they ate. Paige kept her focus on his face for as much of the conversation as she could. Carter's blond hair was messier today and his clothing more casual than she'd ever seen him in before. He wasn't at all self-conscious about anything, and his easygoing nature wrapped around her and helped her relax.

It was only once they'd cleared the dishes away and they'd opened up their third beer that he pulled her over to the couch and turned her to him. "Are you going to tell me what happened earlier, or am I going to have to make it a command?"

There was no malice. Paige knew he was trying to appeal to all aspects of her nature—the woman and the submissive. He would do whatever she needed to make this easier.

She slipped to the floor by the couch, spread her thighs and bowed her head. "If you don't mind, Sir."

The silence stretched on for several moments before he set the beer bottle on the side table with a soft *thunk*. "Paige, who showed up today?"

She licked her lips. "Rick."

"And who is Rick to you?"

"He is…was my Master."

"Your…what?"

She took a breath. "He told me to refer to him as my Master. He was my first serious partner and Dom when I was young and naïve about the lifestyle. At the time, I didn't understand there was a difference between being submissive and being a slave. Pain for pleasure, instead of pain for..." She shrugged.

Carter's fist tightened where it rested on his thigh. "Did he ever cross the line with you?"

She snapped her head up. "I didn't even know there was a line. I figured being submissive meant I had to take everything he dished out. I liked pain, but he didn't always know when to back down."

"Did you safe-word out a lot with him?"

"I didn't know what that was until over a year of us being together. By then, it didn't seem important. He wouldn't have listened to me anyway."

The muscle in Carter's jaw twitched and his breathing grew shallow. "What happened? You left him?"

She nodded. "I came home late from the office one night. Everything we ever did was normally easy to conceal. The marks from the flogger, the riding crop, his belt, they were all on my back or ass. But when I was late..."

The events of that evening weren't as clear as she would have liked. The nurse at the hospital had told her it wasn't uncommon for head injuries to cause problems with the victim's memory. The woman had tried to get Paige to admit she was being abused, but she couldn't come to terms with it to admit the truth. She'd asked for the pain, got off on it, yet Rick never knew when enough was enough.

She hadn't left him that night. It had taken her two weeks to build up enough nerve to get her things and get safe.

None of this could she adequately put into words to tell Carter. She knew he'd react the way Ian would if she'd ever told him. Shit, the only person who knew the truth was Sadie, and she'd been ready to set fire to Rick in his sleep.

"You were late?" Carter relaxed his hand and laid it flat on his thigh. Paige wasn't fooled into thinking he wasn't still furious.

All she could do was tell him what she remembered as plainly as possible. "I was late and it had ruined Rick's plans. He'd had tickets to something and we weren't going to be able to make it. He punched the back of my head and knocked me out."

Carter somehow stiffened more. "I'll kill him."

"You'll go nowhere near him. Rick has been out of my life for a long time now. I'm a different woman from the girl I was when I was with him. I know more about the lifestyle. I know what my rights are, what I like and what I don't like. I have a voice and I'm not afraid to use it. I'm not weak."

"No, you're not. But you're not over this either." Leaning down, Carter framed her face with his hands and pressed a kiss to her forehead. "If you were, going to Mavericks wouldn't have been as traumatic for you."

"I was scared he would find out I was getting back into it and would show up." She chuckled, the sick feeling in her stomach threatening to come back. "Guess I was right."

"He won't lay a finger on you."

In that moment, Paige believed Carter was capable of doing bad things to a person.

"I swear I'll do everything I can, talk to everyone I know to make sure you can go wherever you want without this fucker bothering you."

Normally, such a statement Paige would either brush off as being optimistic or foolhardy. But by the combination of absolute belief and the quiet steel in his personality, Paige knew Carter could live up to every single promise he made her.

"Thank you," she whispered.

The kiss came out of nowhere. One moment they were staring at each other, and the next he had her pulled against his chest, his mouth devouring hers. Her body ignited as his hands roamed down her back to cup her ass and pull her onto his lap. Carter shifted to kiss a path across her jaw to her throat and down until he reached her collarbone, where he nipped her.

"I swear no one will touch you." He licked the hollow of her throat and cupped her breast. "You can walk out of my life tomorrow and I'll still make sure no one ever hurts you again." He pulled back, brushing his nose against hers. "Let me prove it to you?"

"Okay, okay, yes."

Chapter Six

Paige didn't know what Carter had in mind when he carried her to the bedroom. She couldn't speak, even to give him directions, leaving him to push every door open with his foot until he found the right one. When he dropped her on the bed he pointed at her.

"Stay."

There wasn't the malice she'd grown used to over the years, a simple command and the promise of pleasure. Paige let her head fall back against the mattress as he moved around the room. Scarves she hardly ever wore were scooped up from their home in her closet to be deposited beside her on the bed.

"Safe word?"

Unlike their first time, Paige knew she had to give him a real answer. "Apples."

"No chance you'll be calling that one out mistakenly." He picked up a blue silk scarf and ran it over his palm. "Strip."

The shirt came off with ease, though her jeans caused her grief. She managed to toe off her socks before pulling her underwear down and her bra off. Being naked in front of Carter was easier this time. Whether it was from the expression on his face as his gaze slipped down her body, or the way he relaxed as she spread out on the mattress, arms above her head near the headboard, only to be rewarded with a soft growl, Paige wasn't sure.

"How could anyone…?" Carter snapped his mouth shut and moved to wrap the scarf around her wrists. "Let me know if this gets too tight."

"I will."

"I mean it. I don't want you feeling any discomfort that I'm not expressly giving you. You're in control here, Paige. Never forget that."

Once he'd finished the knot, he placed the ends of the scarf in her hands. She thumbed the binding. The knot was loose given he'd used silk. If she didn't struggle too much, it shouldn't be a problem.

Carter yanked his shirt off and let his pants fall to the floor. He stood there in his boxers, prominent erection tenting the front.

"Someday I would love to gag you. I hope that's not a hard limit for you." He leaned forward and draped the second scarf across her mouth, letting the soft material tease her as he trailed it over her face. "There's something sexy about the moans a woman makes when she's gagged. Begging without words, using your whole body, and I have to figure out exactly what you want. Not today, though. Right now I want to hear every sound. I want you to scream and beg and moan until your throat is raw."

He moved the scarf down to brush the peak of her left nipple. The silk caught on the tip, causing goose bumps to rise down her arm and over her chest. Paige bit down on her bottom lip, not wanting to give in to what he wanted yet.

"I could kill you with kindness if I wanted. Have you ever had someone tease your body to the point where you want to come, but you can't? That orgasm is a hair's breadth out of reach for long enough that you think your body is going to explode or you'll die from the denial? Because when you do come, it's like your whole world has been rewritten."

Paige couldn't stop either the full body shudder or the moan he wrenched from her when he pinched her nipple. She scissored her legs and bucked her hips up, trying to get him to touch her where she knew he wouldn't. Not for some time.

Carter slapped the side of her thigh. "Settle down. I'm not ready for that yet and neither are you."

The sting was like a hot balm on sore muscles after a ten-kilometer run. It helped settle both her body and her mind, pulling her back into herself until she focused on nothing but Carter.

She could tell he was watching her carefully, evaluating every move, moan and sigh she made. Canting her hips, she hoped to encourage him into action. He narrowed his gaze, evaluating what she needed. Paige bucked her hips again, hoping he would understand even when she didn't.

Paige was surprised when he reached in and slipped the silk scarf beneath her leg, to tie it high up her thigh, where the limb met her body. The material was constricting, applying pressure in a way she wasn't used to. Shifting on the bed caused it to pull hard, chafing the skin and putting in her hands all the control over how much or little she wanted the pain to be.

With a sigh, she relaxed into the mattress and let herself float.

He understood.

"There is so much I want to show you." His fingers teased her nipples, pinching and twisting the skin. "Can I, Paige?"

The sting of his forefingers on her nipple was a blessed relief, as was the thrust of his fingers into her cunt. Rick had never done this for her, turned her on until she questioned her sanity. Carter could take her higher if she let go and trusted him.

With a groan, she made sure he knew he had her full attention. "Yes."

Much as he had back at the club, an expression of awe and respect echoed over him, before the control of his Dom self wiped the emotions from his face. "Don't move. I need to get a few things."

He coiled the silk scarf on her stomach, the end slithering over her side to tickle the skin. She didn't have a lot of equipment here at the house, not anymore. Carter would need to be creative. Paige closed her eyes to better focus her hearing, to see if she could figure out what he was doing. The fridge opening and closing and the rattle of cups and cupboard doors echoed in her too-quiet home. His returning footsteps elicited a shiver through her.

Paige opened her eyes when Carter entered the room and tried to see what he'd brought back. She frowned at the sight of the bag of frozen peas.

"I wasn't planning on needing these today." He tossed a handful of condom packages on the bed beside the peas. "But I've been carrying them around since our meeting at the club."

He ripped open the first condom package and began to fill it with the frozen peas. Paige moaned and tried to twist away from him.

"Stop!"

She complied without thinking.

Carter leaned over her body, but didn't touch her skin. "You want me to show you?"

Eyeing the condom, she nodded slowly.

"Then stay still."

"Yes, Sir." She hated that her voice lacked her normal confidence.

Carter went back to ignoring her, to focus on his preparations. When the condom was three-quarters of the way full, he tied it off, resealed the peas and returned them to the kitchen. Paige could feel the cold bleeding off the condom by her leg and shivered at the idea of where exactly he was going to be putting it.

"I'm going to use another condom to make sure we don't have any accidents," he said as he walked back in.

"Where are you going to put that, Sir?"

He chuckled. "Where do you think? Right into your hot little pussy, Paige. It's going to feel amazing to have all those cold little balls rubbing against all those hard-to-reach places. Won't that be fun?"

Can I shove it up your ass? "Yes, Sir."

"I can tell you're excited about it. But I think we're going to start with this first."

The small drinking glass was one of the ones she used for juice in the morning. Paige flexed her fingers around the scarf holding her hands in place as Carter took her cooking oil and poured some into the palm of his hand.

"I can tell from your reaction you've never done anything like this before. Have you?"

"No, Sir."

"Have you ever heard of cupping?"

Paige shook her head, her gaze locked onto the barbeque lighter he'd dug up from her junk drawer.

"Don't worry, I'm not going to burn you. I only need to heat things up a little bit." Igniting the lighter, Carter held the flame just inside the cup. He moved it around without touching the glass, which fascinated Paige.

"It's not going to scar, is it?" Rick had threatened her with a lighter once, but thankfully he'd never followed through.

"Nope. I've seen too much of that shit at work to get off on doing it to someone. No, this is all about heating the air to get a little suction going."

Carter moved over her and, before she had time to realize what he was about to do, he pressed the cup directly down on the top of her breast. Paige cried out at the immediate, intense suction, and the skin inside the cup turned red.

"The ancient Chinese used this as a method to help heal infections, working it alongside acupuncture. Of course, people in the lifestyle soon figured out there was a whole lot more you could do with it."

With care, Carter slid the glass down her breast until he reached her nipple. He stopped shy of the sensitive spot. "Look at me."

Paige found it hard to lift her gaze from the glass, and it took Carter's hand on her chin to break the spell and allow her to comply with his command. She was panting, the air making her lips dry as she tried to fight through the sensations unleashed upon her.

"Keep looking at me, Paige. I need to see your eyes."

She nodded, wanting desperately to see her skin as he reached out once more and slid the glass over her nipple. The suction sent a bolt to her cunt, making her gush as her orgasm threatened to come. The bastard hadn't even touched her yet.

"Too much. Fuck, Carter. *Sir*."

"I have the perfect thing to make it better."

He abandoned the cup and reached for the condom. How

she'd forgotten about it, Paige didn't know. Carter slipped a second condom over the first and tied it off.

"I don't want anything breaking and having to take you to the hospital." Lifting her leg, he slipped between them, placing her left ankle on his shoulder. "Don't you dare move."

Paige's entire body shook as she thrashed her head. "Too much."

"You're doing amazing. This will help."

Carter probed her with his fingers, opening her lips and spreading her wide. At the first touch of the cold condom, Paige cried out and bucked her hips. Carter's large hand on her stomach forced her still as he slipped the ice-cold pea-filled condom deep inside her pussy.

"It's too much. Too much." She moaned and squirmed, trying to get away from the cold rush and hot suction.

"No, it's not, or you'd be safe-wording out. Relax into it. Let the feelings wash over you." He reached up and moved the cup, shifting the suction from her nipple to the side of her breast. At the same time, he pumped the condom in and out of her, rubbing the frozen bumps against her G-spot.

Nonsense words spilled out of her like water from a tap. Everything around her disappeared into nothing, and her entire existence consisted of the pressure and cold.

As quickly as he'd penetrated her, Carter pulled the condom out and set it out of sight. Reaching up, he slid the tip of his finger underneath the lip of the glass and broke the suction. Paige let her head drop back against the bed and tried to slow her breathing.

"Look at you." Carter ran a finger along the now-purple skin, sending another surge of pleasure through her. "I could spend all day marking your body. You're beautiful."

The suction of his mouth on her nipple was completely

different after the pressure from the cup. The skin was more sensitive than she'd ever felt in her life. She tried to pull her hands free, wanting to push his head away, but the silk scarf held her tight. Fuck, she needed to come.

Releasing her with a pop, Carter sat back and reached for the barbeque lighter once again. "Ready for some more?"

He didn't wait, drizzling some of the cooking oil on her stomach before grabbing the cup and heating the air once more. The pressure on her stomach was different from her breasts. The pressure bordered on agony as he got close to her ribs, only to back away before he hit the bone.

It was different from the sharp bite of a flogger across her ass or back. The pain burned and stretched, pushing her to the edge of her limits before Paige found herself relaxing into it. She lost the ability to focus, and the blessed numbness of her brain allowed her to simply let go. There was nothing beyond the sensations. Nothing beyond what Carter would give to her.

"Paige, look at me again," the voice was asking her, but she was slipping away from it. Fingers on her chin and the feeling of her head moving. "Paige, still with me?"

Somewhere in her head she knew she should answer. But it was too perfect, the pain and pleasure all jumbled together in her body.

The pop of the cup being released from her stomach gave her a jolt. She sucked in a deep breath, as if she'd been holding it for hours. Carter rained kisses across her face, muttering words she no longer had the capacity to recognize.

She needed to come. Needed it badly.

"You will, baby. I'm going to make you come now. But I need to know if you can handle this? Can you take more?"

"Please."

"*Look* at me."

She found his beautiful hazel eyes and did her best to hold on to his gaze. The smile on his face shone up into his eyes as he pressed a kiss to her lips. "I want you to come when you can. Understand? Don't hold anything back."

"Y-yes, S-s-sir."

He spread her pussy lips wide, pausing only for a moment to finger her gently, before he pressed the cup with the heated air to her clit.

Paige screamed. In her mind's eye she could see the sensitive skin turning bright red as the blood rushed to the surface. It was stronger than any man's mouth had ever been, creating a glorious pressure she couldn't escape. The press of the cold condom once again into her pussy had her orgasm crashing over her.

Carter fucked her through her release, rubbing the frozen balls in the right spot. Her body convulsed, muscles tightened, and her throat went raw from the unending screams pouring out of her. Finally, the cold was gone and the suction was broken, leaving her completely lifeless on the bed.

She didn't realize she'd been crying until Carter took the orphaned scarf and used it to dry her face. The silk holding her wrists had to be cut off—she'd twisted and turned it tight, and now her hands were getting cool from lack of circulation. Carter moved each of her arms down, massaging her shoulders and biceps, helping the sensation return to them.

Paige wanted to help, wanted to sit up, shift around, anything to move, but her body wouldn't cooperate.

Once he'd fixed her up, freeing her body, Carter stretched out beside her. "Better?"

She nodded. "Fuck me?"

He opened his mouth and she knew he was going to say no. Drawing on strength she didn't know she possessed, Paige rolled onto her stomach and, with agonizing slowness, drew her knees beneath her chest and somehow lifted her ass in the air in offering.

"Fuck me."

"Paige, I—"

"Please, Sir. Carter. I need… I want you to…"

"Shh, shh, shh. It's okay. I wasn't going to. This isn't about me. But you want me to? Honestly?"

With her face pressed into the mattress, she nodded, rubbing her nose against the harsh fabric. Carter ran a hand down her ass, squeezing the flesh.

"Shit. Okay, baby. Don't move. Not a muscle and I'll give you what you want."

The sound of another condom being opened had her heart soaring. Paige waited, listened, trying to picture what he looked like sliding the condom over his cock. Shit, she hadn't even seen him completely naked yet. Still, she could afford to wait for that pleasure if he would only fuck her into the mattress now.

The pressure of his hands on her hips, holding her where he wanted, nearly made Paige jump. But the constant stroke of his thumb against the small of her back helped to settle her nerves. He lined up his cock and nudged the opening of her pussy.

Everything was still on overdrive as he pushed his way into her. Carter sucked in a sharp breath, holding himself still once he was seated deep in her body.

"Christ, I can still feel how cold your pussy is. It must have felt amazing having that frozen cock inside you. Did you like that, Paige? A nice cool cock before having my hot one inside you?"

"Yes. So good."

"Can you squeeze me? I want to feel you."

She found the strength to tighten her vaginal muscles, clenching his cock as he pulled back and thrust in once more.

"I'm not going to last long. I'm going to fuck you hard. Come again if you can."

She didn't think it was possible, but as Carter began to pound into her at a steady pace, the vibrations sent little jolts to her clit.

"C-can I touch myself?" Her tongue wet her bottom lip, and she touched the quilt with the tip.

"No." But he didn't leave her hanging. Instead, Carter leaned over her body, braced himself with one hand and reached between her legs with his other.

He rubbed circles on her clit with this thumb, keeping the same rhythm as his thrusts. Paige widened her legs, giving him better access and helping to drive his cock as far as he could into her. Within a matter of seconds, a second orgasm, every bit as powerful as her first, sucked out every last bit of life from her. When she didn't think she'd be able to hold on any longer, Carter's thrusts lost their rhythm and he cried out.

They collapsed, Carter covering her body with his, his cock still hard and twitching inside her. He moved her hair aside and pressed a kiss to her shoulder. His heavy weight was a reassuring presence as she found herself slipping back into reality from the narrow world of her subspace.

"Hey, you still alive?" he whispered as he pulled her into his arms. "I need to know if I should call the paramedics."

"Still here," she slurred before exhaustion won.

Paige wasn't sure how long she'd slept, but the shadows of the late afternoon stretched long across her bed by the time she could once again open her eyes. She ached all over but wasn't in any pain beyond what she'd normally feel after a hard fuck.

She ran her fingers over the breast where he'd put the cup, letting the ache of the light bruise worm its way through her.

Carter was sleeping. The relaxed expression on his face was a change from his normally intense look. It made him more handsome, if that was even possible. The slight upturn of his lips gave him the appearance of a man pleased with himself.

Hesitantly, Paige lightly rested her hand on his chest, waiting to make sure she hadn't woken him, before playing with the light dusting of hair that covered him. She was sated, a deep sense of peace she'd rarely experienced before running through her. Rick had never done this for her, taken her outside of herself to a place where she could simply exist. No pressure, no expectations, only being.

"God, you think loud." Carter's voice was barely more than a rumble.

Paige snorted softly and rested her chin on his chest. "Sorry."

Cracking one eye open, he smiled at her. "You okay?"

"A bit sore, but nothing I can't handle."

"Was it too much for you?"

Instead of answering, she nipped at his nipple.

"Okay, I'm sorry. You're superwoman."

"And don't you forget it."

He tightened his hold around her. "What are we going to do about Rick?"

"We?" Rolling her head to the side, she dug her chin farther into his chest and ignored his wince. "I don't think it's a good idea for you to even lay eyes on him."

"I know assholes like him. Now that he knows you're trying to get back into the scene, he'll do whatever he can to get to you. You pissed him off by walking away. He's not going to let you forget him while you go off with another Dom."

He shifted, letting his fingers trace down her back. "If you decide that's even what you want to do."

Until she'd run into Carter, Paige hadn't considered dating anyone else. She'd been tempted to try an anonymous club, but the idea of being surrounded by strangers, letting someone tie her up and push her limits, hadn't held an appeal. Then again, Carter had been a stranger until recently, and she felt like she'd known him for years.

Resting her cheek against his chest, Paige was beginning to think she could be happy if she could deal with Rick once and for all.

"If I met the right person, I might be convinced."

"The right person?"

"He would have to be a good listener, but someone who knows when to push my buttons. He also needs to have an active imagination so I can try weird and wonderful new things."

Her head was jostled as he chuckled. "You liked that, huh?"

"Yup." She kissed his chest. "Unexpected too."

"You were too."

"Not a bad thing, I hope."

Weaving his fingers through her hair, he placed a kiss to the top of her head. "Not even a little. In fact, I think it might be one of the better things to have ever happened to me."

The sudden tightness in her throat choked off any response she could verbalize. Silently, she promised herself she would deal with Rick, say goodbye to him once and for all and move on with her life.

Because for the first time in years, Paige had something and someone to look forward to.

Chapter Seven

Mavericks was packed tighter than Paige ever remembered seeing. The throng of people pulsed with the beat of the music, writhing and grinding together on the dance floor. There was a never-ending parade of people to the various stations Josh had set up around the main room. Spanking benches, leather cuffs hanging from chains along the wall, the St. Andrew's Cross, all were being used.

Paige would have preferred to be flogged.

Her call to Rick's cell phone had been the most nerve-racking one of her life, made all the worse by his calm, almost smug reaction. He'd agreed too easily to her suggestion to meet at the club, and the idea of needing to dress the part knowing he'd be here to see her had her skin crawling.

Carter had wanted to come with her when she'd suggested the meeting a few days ago, but she'd said no.

"I need to do this on my own if he's ever going to listen to me."

She could tell by his expression he was less than pleased.

"Paige, you don't know what he'll do once he gets you alone."

"Then I won't let him get me alone." She took his hand and squeezed his fingers hard. "I don't know where we're going yet, but if I don't work this out, I know I'll always have this lingering doubt about our relationship. Let me handle Rick."

"I don't like this."

Carter's intentions were pure, but she needed to do this her way. It was the reason she'd arranged to meet Rick on a night Carter was working at the station. The well-meaning bastard would try and show up otherwise.

Josh kept circling around her table but made no move to approach her. He probably assumed she was meeting Carter and for once wasn't going to interfere. Lucky her.

Paige swallowed down the last of her rye and ginger, scanning the crowd once more for Rick. It was typical, him keeping her waiting like this. It had always made her feel uncomfortable, doubting both the information he'd given her and her own resolve to stay for him. She'd never dared get up and leave when they were in a relationship—tonight she was tempted to see what would happen.

At ten minutes to midnight, she finally caught sight of Rick pushing his way through the crowd toward her. Smoothing her hands down across her leather-clad thighs, Paige sat up straight.

"You're late," she said as soon as he reached the side of the table.

"I was busy." He didn't sit down, instead crossed his arms and looked down at her. "Let's go somewhere private."

"No." There was no way she'd fall for that. "We do this here or we don't do it at all."

Rick stared for several long seconds before grinning. "I see you've grown a backbone over the years."

"I've learned what my rights are and where the line is. Something I don't think you've figured out yet."

Rick fell into the seat beside her and propped his feet up on the table. "Bitchy little Paige. Your bark was always stronger than your bite." He licked his lips as his gaze roamed over her body. "You wanted to talk. I'm here to talk."

Still, after all this time, it was a challenge to meet his gaze directly and speak. The years had been kind to him, his good looks now being augmented by the slightly graying hair at his temples. He was every bit as cool and confident as he'd been when they'd first met.

Taking a breath, Paige steadied herself. "I know you've come back to town to work. I know you are aware that I came here last week and I met someone."

"I heard he took you upstairs too. How did that work out for you, little girl? Did he press all your buttons the way that you liked? Did you keep comparing him to me?"

The memory of Carter, his face buried between her legs, making her scream, only to refuse to fuck her because he wanted to get to know her, sprang to mind. "I can honestly say I didn't think of you once after I got up there."

Rick dropped his feet to the floor with a thud and leaned into her. "You were mine for two years. I know you better than you know yourself. Better than some jackass who followed you home one night and spanked your ass. He did spank you, didn't he, Paige? You always liked that."

"What we did is none of your goddamn business. That's why I wanted to meet you here tonight. We were through the night you punched me. I will never get back with you. You have nothing to offer me. I originally stopped coming here because I didn't want any reminders of you. But no more."

Pushing away from him, Paige rose to her feet. "You don't scare me, Rick. I don't need you to be happy. You don't make me unhappy either. You're no longer a blip in my life that impacts me one way or the other. I've moved on and I suggest you do too."

She tried to step away only to have Rick grab her arm.

"We're not done talking."

"Yes, we are. I plan to continue coming here to play and spend time with my friends. If I'm lucky, I'll be here with someone who I hope will become serious about me. But even if that doesn't happen, he's helped me realize that I'm not going to let you have control over my life anymore. Goodbye, Rick. I hope you have a happy life, but stay the hell out of mine."

Jerking her arm free, Paige managed to keep the smile from her face as she walked past him toward the door. She'd nearly escaped when Josh caught her.

"Everything okay?" He nodded toward Rick. "I'd be more than happy to throw his ass out if he's giving you a hard time."

Paige knew she should have done this ages ago, but admitting the truth was far harder than she ever thought possible. "Remember when I stopped coming?"

Josh nodded.

"Rick punched me in the back of the head. I went to the hospital, but there was no permanent damage. I left him shortly after that."

Josh closed his eyes and for a split second, Paige knew he would kill Rick if she gave her blessing. "Why didn't you say anything?"

"Before I didn't realize he was crossing a line. When he went too far, I was embarrassed. I should have known it wasn't normal, some of the things he was doing to me, but I was too new to the scene and he kept me pretty isolated when it came to talking to other people. I figured it was me, that I had the problem."

"You won't have to worry about him bothering you at Mavericks again. His membership will be revoked tonight and his money returned. If he did that to you, chances are he'll do it to someone else."

Paige knew she shouldn't feel thankful, but she did. "I'm going to head home and call Carter. I know he'll be fuming when he finds out I did this alone."

"I think he would surprise you. Carter cares about you and doesn't want to see you get hurt. He won't care that you did things on your own, only that you're safe. Which you are." Josh glanced behind her, but Paige didn't want to turn and see. Chances were he was glaring at Rick, and he was the last person she wanted to see.

"I'm going to catch a cab. I'm sure we'll see you next week."

"Let me get it for—"

"Josh, I'm fine. It's a cab out front." She rolled her eyes for good measure. "I'm not going to be walking anywhere far dressed like this."

"Only if you're sure?"

"I am. Thanks."

The early autumn air had turned cool, making her shiver as she waited for a cab. It wouldn't be long before one would eventually show. The laughter from people going in and out of the club brought a smile to her face. Finally, after a long time sleepwalking, she was awake and feeling more like herself.

Thoughts of what she and Carter could do together, everything from scenes they could act out, to things she'd like to do with him around the city, filled her head. He had a slightly evil streak too. The other morning he'd threatened to slip in her bullet vibrator with the wireless remote and tease her with it all day long.

The scary thing was she was hoping he would do it.

A cab turned the corner and started toward her when a hand fell heavily on her shoulder. Rick pulled her a step away from the curb and into the shadow of the building.

"What the fuck, Rick? Let me go."

"I wasn't done talking to you." Pressing her to the brick wall, Rick kept his grip tight on her shoulder, cutting off her leverage.

"What you don't seem to understand is that I'm done with you. You can't control my life and there's no way you're getting back into it. Now let me go or else you're going to learn the hard way that I'm not someone you can screw around with anymore."

Paige was shaking, but it wasn't from fear. Anger had her focus narrowed down to Rick, her body growing numb as she tried to get herself under control. Something must have shown on her face because in the next moment, Rick was pulling back from her, frowning.

"What the hell has gotten into you?"

"I've grown up and figured out more than a few things about my life." She pushed his hand away and this time he didn't stop her. "I'm not the fucked-up girl who was dealing with her mom's death and a dad who didn't want much to do with his kids. I figured if I hurt enough on the outside, then the inside wouldn't matter. But I clued in that what you were doing to me and what I was doing to myself wasn't helping."

"You needed it. Everything I did to you."

Paige pushed his shoulder. "No, jackass. I get aroused by someone else being in control. For those moments I get to set the rules, but someone else is taking care of *me* for a change. It wasn't about the pain. Not the way you thought it was." She pushed him again and this time he stepped away. "And it certainly didn't give you the right to punch me in the head!"

Rick shook his head but didn't say anything else. Relief washed through her when she realized he wasn't going to do anything. Taking a breath, she stepped past him out into the streetlight once more.

"I'm going home. I'm tired. You are not invited. You're not invited back to the club or my life, in fact, anyplace near me. There is no *us*. There won't be an *us* again. Please, for once listen to me and leave me alone."

Paige would never be certain if Rick would have agreed with her or not. Before the words barely had a chance to leave her mouth, a shout from behind her had them both spinning.

"Hey!"

The expression of rage on Carter's face was terrifying. He was dressed in an old gray T-shirt and his uniform pants. The loud echo of his boot-clad feet on the sidewalk sent Paige into a panic.

"Carter?" *Shit, shit, shit.*

"Is that your new fucking boyfriend? Yeah, sure you've changed, Paige."

"He was supposed to be working tonight."

Carter reached for her and pulled Paige to his side before she could stop him. "Did he touch you? If you've laid as much as a finger on her—"

"Carter, I'm fine—"

Rick jerked Paige out of Carter's grasp and shoved her aside. "And who the fuck are you to tell me what I can and can't do? We were having a conversation before you showed up to play asshole."

"Boys, stop it—"

"Conversation? It looked like she was trying to get away from you, and you weren't taking no for an answer. Big man picking on a lady. Does that turn you on, asshole?"

"Carter!"

He jerked his head around to start at her. "What?"

"I'm fine. I want to go home."

Every emotion running through her was bound to be on her face. Dammit, this was the reason she'd done this on a night he'd been working. The confrontation wasn't worth the pay-off. Rick would never back down from something like this. Doing her best to silently beg him, Paige held her breath and hoped Carter understood.

Please walk away.

Carter ran a hand across the back of his neck. "I don't like him giving you a hard time."

"He's not and he won't be coming around here anymore. Will you?"

Rick stared at her before letting his gaze shift to Carter. "She's not worth my fucking time."

All the tension from the past three years lifted. "Good. Now, Carter, since you no longer appear to be working, please take me—"

"The little cunt is all used up now anyway."

The next few seconds slowed down to next to nothing. Carter stepped around her, without touching her coat, to slip between her and Rick. He grabbed Rick by the collar of his shirt and pulled back his fist before letting it fly into Rick's face. She could only watch helplessly as Rick crashed to the ground in a heap. He rolled on the ground, moaning and clutching his chin.

Time came rushing back, along with her ability to think. "What the hell, Carter!"

Within a matter of seconds, the bouncers from Mavericks were out on the street with them, bringing Josh not far behind. He scooped Paige and Carter up in his arms and directed them away from the mess that was Rick.

"I suggest the two of you go for a walk. I'll clean this up."

Carter jerked out of his grasp. "I don't need you doing anything, Josh. I'll take care of this asshole once and for all."

"Carter, get yourself under control," Josh said, keeping his distance. "Go for a walk and cool down. I don't want to see you back here tonight."

Paige left the two men behind her and made her way toward the coffee shop.

"Paige!"

"I don't believe you." Paige increased her pace. Who the hell did he think he was, punching Rick and generally stepping in where he wasn't invited? She hadn't asked him to do anything—shit, she wasn't sure Carter was even the man she wanted to date, let alone have him running around defending her honor.

"Paige!"

She stopped dead and spun around to face him, not caring who else was around to witness their impending fight. "What?"

"Will you talk to me?" His face was strangely shadowed in the dim overhead light from the streetlamp. "Are you hurt? Did he do anything?"

"You think it would have been too much trouble for you to have asked that before you knocked him unconscious?"

"He called you a cunt. What the hell did you expect me to do?"

"Maybe trust that I had things under control and was dealing with him in my own way."

"You tell me he punched you in the back of the head and put you in the hospital, and you want me to trust him enough to be around you alone? Everything else aside, does that sound even remotely reasonable to you?"

"Of course it doesn't sound reasonable. If it was Sadie or Ian doing something like that I would have kicked their asses." Paige turned and continued her trek to the shop, acutely aware of Carter's presence half a step behind her. "But I also know myself. It may have taken me a few years to figure it out, but I have. If I hadn't done that on my own, I would never feel like I was free from him."

Carter's hand on her shoulder had her slowing down until she stopped in the middle of the sidewalk, her gaze locked on the store ahead of her.

"Paige, I'm not him."

The seemingly out-from-left-field statement made complete and utter sense to her. "I can't know that. Rick wasn't like that when I first met him either. You're...you do things that make me question myself. Sure it feels amazing at the time, but I could easily find myself going too far and getting hurt again. If I hadn't dealt with Rick once and for all, how could I trust myself to deal with...?" She swallowed hard, suddenly feeling guilty.

"How could you deal with me?" Carter's hand disappeared. "I guess you're right. How could you ever trust yourself with a man who wants to push you to your limits and help you get over them? How could you let yourself go and be happy when you're always second-guessing the other person's motivations?"

"Carter, I—" She turned to face him, but he was already backing away from her.

"It's fine, Paige. I guess we did things a bit on the fast side. I'm glad you've worked things out in your head and dealt with Rick."

"Where are you going?"

"Back to work."

Panic ripped through her, turning her stomach sick. "Look, we can talk this—"

"I don't think so. Sorry."

Carter walked away almost as fast as he'd arrived. Paige couldn't move, stuck fast, watching his retreating back. It wasn't until he turned the corner out of sight that the tears threatened to spill. The last few feet to the shop were painful to walk.

She was about to open the door when Blue Eyes came flying out. They bumped into each other, equally anguished expressions on their faces.

"Sorry," he said in a voice that had none of its normal spark. "Wasn't looking."

Paige smiled weakly. "Neither was I. You okay?"

"Not really. But then again, that would be par these days. Take care of yourself."

"Wait." She caught his arm as he tried to step around her. "That sounds like you're not coming back."

"I won't be." His gaze drifted over her to the store window. "You have a good night."

And with that he was gone.

Paige entered the store to see Ian frantically cleaning the espresso machine. "I just saw Blue Eyes leave. What the hell happened? He looked upset."

"He's married. To a woman."

"What?" Would this night never end?

"Well, they're separated actually. The divorce is almost finalized." Ian jerked the drip tray out of the bottom, sloshing old coffee over the side as he threw it in the sink. "That's not the issue. A woman!"

"Ian, stop cleaning and look at me."

His shoulders slumped forward as he dropped his chin to his chest. "I don't know how I read him wrong."

Paige flipped the lock on the door, turned over the Open sign to Closed and marched toward the back. "I have booze in the office. Come on."

"We can't close up, we still have another hour."

"Booze. Now."

She knew he wouldn't be far behind her and quickly grabbed a few coffee mugs before heading back. It had been a long time since the two of them simply talked, and tonight seemed like the best night for it.

"I take it things didn't go well at Mavericks tonight?" Ian leaned against the doorframe as she filled the two mugs half-way with the rye. "And I'm not drinking that shit straight."

"Then get some ginger ale and come sit down."

Ian snorted and pulled a can out of his apron. "I come prepared. Fill mine higher, will ya."

They sat in silence as they nursed their drinks. Paige couldn't get the image of Carter's pained expression out of her mind. All she'd wanted to do was prove to herself that she wasn't weak for wanting the things she did. That she could handle herself if she let herself go back into the lifestyle. There was nothing wrong with that. Was there?

"So," she said with a frown. "A woman?"

Ian groaned, letting his head fall into his hands, sending his drink sloshing close to the top of his mug. "She called while he was here. They had some sort of fight, I don't re-member what about, and he ended up hanging up on her. In the eight months that he's been coming here to…to get coffee, I never once suspected he wasn't gay. Straight men don't flirt with me."

"Just because he was married doesn't mean he's not interested in men."

Ian downed the contents of his mug in several long swallows and stood up. "I refuse to be some sort of experiment for a straight guy with a broken heart. Fuck him. Fuck…" He pressed the heels of his hands to his eyes. "Shit, I never did learn his name."

"If it makes you feel any better, I think I screwed things up with Carter tonight."

"Jesus, Paige. What happened?"

Getting sympathy from Ian was a bizarre twist in Paige's life, one she wasn't sure she knew how to feel about. She finished half her drink, adding to the alcohol already in her system and making her buzz pick up strength.

"How much do you know about what I did with Rick?"

"As little as possible. I know you're a…you like…" He waved his hand. "Yeah, don't make me say it, okay?"

"I swear to God you stopped maturing at twelve."

"Sadie says the same thing." He smiled softly, almost like his old self. "What happened with Carter that makes you think you screwed things up?"

"I went and talked to Rick tonight when I knew Carter was working."

"You did what? After what that asshole did to you?"

She knew she'd regret telling Ian the truth. "Will you relax? I met him where there were lots of people around. I told him there was no chance of us ever getting back together and if he was smart, he would cut his losses and run."

Ian pulled his chair up beside hers and sat down once more. "Well, that's positive."

"Except Carter showed up when Rick had me up against the wall outside. I had the situation under control but then Rick called me a cunt and things went downhill from there."

"Bastard's lucky I wasn't there. I would have clocked him."

Paige could feel the blush heat her face. "Carter did."

"Good for him."

"Then I ran away. He caught up to me but I bitched him out for interfering."

"Brilliant, Paige."

She punched him on the shoulder. "You don't get it. I had to do it by myself."

"I do get it, but that doesn't mean Carter did the wrong thing. Did he tell you why he showed up tonight? I thought he was working?"

Ignoring the creeping feeling of dread, Paige shook her head. "I never gave him a chance to say."

Ian sighed. "You do seem to enjoy making it hard for anyone to get close to you."

"It's not...I'm not like that."

"Bullshit. You like to play at having this hard shell, but you're too scared to let anyone see that you're as human as the rest of us."

"I'm not scared." But she was and for once, Paige wasn't going to be able to hide this from Ian. "It's...I don't think I can trust myself anymore. I screwed up bad with Rick. I should have been able to see the kind of jerk he was and done something earlier. What if... I mean, what if Carter is exactly like him? I don't think I could handle it if he tried to..."

Ian slipped to his knees in front of her and rested a hand on either of her thighs. "Paige, look at me."

She tried, but when she realized she was crying she shook her head.

"Please?"

It struck Paige as odd every time Ian came across as the man he'd become and not her annoying little brother.

He smiled at her and gave her legs a squeeze. "You're one of the strongest people in my life. And even though I know I don't show it sometimes, I trust your judgment on more things than I'd ever admit to. You're the most stubbornly logical person I know."

She smiled, wiping away her tears. "Thanks."

"Did you ever once feel Carter was a threat? That he would do something that you wouldn't like, or wouldn't stop if you'd asked him to?"

"No." Even when they were together for the first time at Mavericks, she'd never once experienced the pain or fear like she had when she'd been with Rick.

"And you've already proven that you know how to handle yourself if things get bad, right?"

"It's not that easy."

Ian sighed. "I know it's not. But then again, sometimes it is. Sometimes we need to take the chance and put ourselves back out there to see what will happen. If it means anything, the last few weeks that you've been around Carter, you've been the happiest I remember seeing you in a long time."

Paige hated the feeling of dread coiled up in her stomach. "I thought I was."

"You were."

Shit. "I doubt he'll want to talk to me again after tonight."

"Women." Ian got to his feet and kissed the top of her head. "Go to bed and think this over. Then first thing tomorrow morning, go down to the station and find him before he goes home. Talk to him. I think you'll be surprised."

Could she do that? Put herself out there and lay herself bare to Carter like that? With her luck, he'd turn and run the other way the second he laid eyes on her.

"I'll think about it."

"Excellent." Ian grabbed the bottle of rye and tucked it under his arm. "Now if you'll excuse me, I'm going upstairs to my humble abode and get shit-faced. I'll see you tomorrow."

"Ian!"

He poked his head back into the office. "What?"

"For what it's worth, I got the impression Blue Eyes really likes you."

"Thanks." Ian's smile seemed painful. "But sometimes that isn't enough."

Chapter Eight

Paige stood at the edge of the walkway leading to the fire station, staring at the front door and coming up with twenty reasons why she should turn around and never show her face here again. The shift wouldn't have changed yet, which meant unless he went home after going to Mavericks last night, Carter would be inside. The early morning air was cool, making her shiver as she tried to convince her feet to take the last few steps necessary to get herself in there to apologize.

God, she hated this.

"Can I help you?"

She turned to see Garry coming up behind her.

"Hey, you're Carter's girl, right? From the coffee shop?"

"Hi, yes, that's me." It was hard to ignore the shop-girl title, but the last thing she needed now was to get into a pissing match with a friend of the man she currently needed to grovel to.

"He should still be in there if you're hoping to see him. Shift's not over for another hour."

"I know." She was five kinds of fool, but she couldn't back out now. "Mind if I follow you in?"

"Not at all. If you want, we can surprise him a bit. I got a call from the boys earlier to say he was being a right bear last night. It will do him some good to see you."

Paige somehow doubted that. "I'll do my best."

With no way to gracefully retreat now, Paige followed Garry into the station. Heat from the vent chased away the chill on her skin and helped to settle her nerves. Carter wasn't the type of guy to lose it on her, let alone do it in front of his buddies. If anything, she was expecting his reception to be as chilly as the morning air.

"I'll tell you what," Garry said as he hung his coat on a hook in the small office near the lobby. "We can do this right if you're up for a little fun."

In for a penny. She smiled. "I'm game."

There was something slightly evil in Garry's smile. "This is going to be awesome. Follow me."

The echo of distant male laughter grew louder as they made their way through the station until they reached the truck bay, where Garry pointed toward one of the suits.

"I could get into tons of trouble for this, but it'll be worth it. Why don't you slip into one of those and climb up into the truck. I'll send Carter in for something and you can surprise him. How's that sound?"

Like a bad frigging idea. "Is there someplace I can change?" Paige already had her jacket off and her purse in hand.

"Washroom right over there. I'll give you a few minutes before I'll send him along."

"Why do I get the impression you're far too excited about all of this?" she asked as she took the heavy jacket and pants from Garry.

"Let's just say this is payback from my birthday party last year."

"Do I want to know?"

"Nope."

"Okay. Thanks."

"Ten minutes," Garry called back over his shoulder as he jogged from the room.

With no time to think about every way this could spectacularly backfire on her, Paige pulled her shirt off and stepped out of her jeans, leaving herself clad in only her black bra and panties. Then she got into the too-large fire pants and pulled up the braces before slipping her arms into the jacket. Garry hadn't given her boots, which left her with her sneakers. She gathered up her clothing and jogged over to the truck as quietly as she could manage in the heavy gear.

The damn thing was huge. It took some careful maneuvering to get up on the running board and into the front seat, before she could slide her way into the back. It was weird sitting up high. Even as she pressed her body down low in the seat, the feeling of being visible, exposed, was overwhelming. Time slowed and she was left with nothing to do but count her own breaths as she fought to maintain her control.

She ignored the list of *what ifs* racing through her mind and tried to relax her muscles one by one. Her pounding heart slowed and she stretched out to fill most of the small back seat.

"Which truck?" Carter's loud yell echoed in the bay.

"Two," came Garry's answering call.

Paige closed her eyes and listened to Carter's footsteps grow closer. A burst of cool air had her nipples standing on end and her eyes flying open as Carter hauled himself into the driver's seat, muttering under his breath.

"Lose something?" she asked, hoping to sound coy and not freaked out.

To his credit, Carter didn't startle. He turned around, eyed her sprawled out on the back seat and quietly closed the door. "Garry?"

"He mentioned something about a birthday party last year."

Carter's soft sigh was the only clarification she received on the matter. "What are you doing here?"

"I…" She sat up, struggling under the weight of the protective jacket. "I wanted to ask you a question."

He frowned. "Ask away."

"Why did you show up at the club last night? I knew you were working, but you never told me what had brought you there."

Carter seemed lost in thought even as he tapped out an uneven beat on the steering wheel.

"I called your cell phone, but you weren't answering. I tried the store when I was on my break. I got Ian and he told me where you'd gone but didn't say what you were doing."

Paige beat down the urge to kill her brother. He had his own issues to deal with. "I wasn't trying to deceive you."

Carter finally looked at her. "I know. For half a second I figured maybe you wanted to go play without me. But after, I remembered our conversation the other night about you wanting to deal with Rick your way. It was a public place and the type of spot where I figured you'd want to talk to him. And while I'm a domineering prick some days and need to learn when to back the hell off, I also couldn't stand the idea of you being alone with him. I took a supper break and came to check on you. I was concerned."

The guilt of the previous night came back with a vengeance. "I'm sorry. I'm stubborn and stupid sometimes. I've had to be the one to take care of Sadie and Ian for years now. I think I've forgotten how to let someone look after me. I did need to deal with Rick on my own, but what I said to you wasn't fair. You're nothing like him. Not once have I ever been concerned for my safety with you. Just the opposite."

Paige bit down on her bottom lip and let her gaze slip to the floor. "I haven't been this attracted to anyone in a long time. I think I scared myself, and when I get scared I try and put as much space between me and that thing as possible."

"I happened to be that thing?"

She smiled. "No, that would be my own chicken tendencies. I'm sorry you bore the brunt of my stupidity. I hope you can forgive me."

Turning fully around to face her, Carter hesitated for a moment before nodding toward her chest. "What's this about?"

She shrugged. "Make-up present? It was spontaneous and I didn't put any planning into it."

The weight of his stare bored into her skull, making Paige feel as though he could see every thought in her head. It was a challenge not to squirm as she realized the Dom in him was trying hard to come out and play. It was hard not to want that, want *him* when he was like that.

"If I told you to come over here and get on your knees in front of me, that wouldn't be an issue? Because after last night I got the distinct impression you wanted nothing more to do with me in my Dom capacity."

The time for words was officially gone. Paige got to her knees and shuffled as best she could in the confined space and got as close to him as she could. For good measure, she let her gaze fall to his chest and she put her hands behind her head. "No issue, Sir."

He let out a growl, low and animalistic. "We can't do this here."

"I'll go where you want, Sir."

"Get out of the truck. Don't forget your things."

"Sir?"

"I'm not going to fuck you where the others can see, or have my boss walk in and fire me. Get your stuff because I'm going to take you home."

Paige moved like she'd been given a shot of electricity. Grabbing everything she could, she tossed the clothing down to Carter and climbed down the truck to the floor. Before she had a chance to say anything, he picked her up and slung her over his shoulder. Squealing, she struggled for a moment before he landed a slap to her ass. Not that she could feel the contact through the pants.

"Garry, mind covering the last part of my shift for me? I have an emergency at home that requires my immediate attention."

The chuckles that answered announced their audience. At least Paige could blame her red face on being upside down.

"No problem, I've got your back. We'll see you later."

Her head spun as Carter carried her out to his truck and tossed her into the passenger side. "Don't move."

"No, Sir."

Excitement built at the idea of seeing Carter's place. She knew he lived close to the station, but that was the extent of it. She pulled the jacket closed, ensuring no one would be able to see her bra. "Should I get dressed, Sir?"

"I said don't move. That includes getting dressed. I have plans for you." The small, devious smirk took years off his face.

"Oh." This was going to be fun.

"Yes. Oh." Traffic slowed them down as Carter navigated

toward the Gardiner Expressway. "Actually, I've changed my mind. What are you wearing under there?"

"My bra and panties."

"Perfect. I want you to play with your nipples. Tweak and flick them until they are nice and big."

Paige's breath caught. She slipped her hand inside the jacket, letting her thumb graze over the lace-covered nipple.

"Open the jacket. I want to see what you're doing."

With her fear and guilt now gone, it was easy to relax and follow Carter's lead. She arched her back, thrusting her breasts into the air and letting the jacket fall open. Even though he didn't turn his head, Carter watched her using the rearview mirror.

"Pinch it harder, Paige. I want you so worked up you'll be begging me to let you come."

Unsure if she should be vocalizing her pleasure or not, Paige decided to err on the side of caution and let out a soft moan as she canted her hips in time with her pulsing squeezes. The stiff material of the pants rubbed her in the right place, making her pussy clench from want of being filled. Traffic opened up and Carter managed to catch the next three green lights, speeding up their journey.

"Take your other hand and put it down your pants. You're not allowed to come, but I want you to play with your clit. I want those panties nice and wet."

"Fuck," she muttered as she did exactly what he wanted. "I'm already drenched."

"Good girl. That's what I want. Pinch your clit a bit to help take the edge off."

"Hurry."

"Almost there. My place is up here."

They turned down another side street, lined with older

brownstone houses. Carter pulled into a small driveway, shoved the transmission into park and practically kicked the door open. "With me."

Paige let him pull her across the seat to come out his side of the truck. Carter scooped her out of the truck and into his arms. She pressed her nose against the side of his throat to lick his skin.

"I have the bottom apartment. Nice and insulated."

Under normal circumstances, Paige would have admired the nice stonework of the stairway leading down to his front door. She would have loved the simple yet elegant iron grating on the window of the heavy wooden door. Over time she would grow to appreciate the hardwood floors and the way the walls seemed to absorb the noise from the outside.

But right then, in that moment, the only thing she could think about was Carter.

He set her down in the middle of the living room, and she got to her knees without being told. The controlled in-out of his breathing had grown more ragged, and Paige knew it had little to do with any exertion he'd expended while carrying her.

"Take the jacket off."

It fell easily to the floor, pooling over her feet.

"Look at me."

Carter fumbled with the front of his pants, pulling his cock free from the confines of his underwear.

"First, I want you to know that I accept your apology. Second, I'm not even a little sorry for what I did to that asshole. I'll punch him again if he comes within half a city block of you. Third, if we are going to make a go of this I need to know that you trust me. Trust that I won't do anything you're uncomfortable with. And trust yourself to know when to stop me."

"I do."

"It might take some time for us both to believe that, but I'm willing to give it a go if you are." Without releasing his cock, Carter reached over and cupped her cheek. "Because I can't stop thinking about you, and the idea of you not being around would drive me nuts."

A warmth Paige never remembered feeling before spread out from her chest and touched every part of her being. Tears welled up, but she refused to cry, not now. Instead she eyed his cock and licked her lips.

"Please, Sir."

Carter stepped closer to rub the tip of his cock across her bottom lip, growling when she stuck out the tip of her tongue to tease him. "Open up."

The head of his cock breached her lips, and the heady taste of his sweat and skin made her mouth water. Moaning, she lapped at the underside of his cock, teasing the bundle of nerves as he slowly pumped in and out of her.

She went to reach for him, but Carter pulled away. "No hands. Put them behind your back and keep them there until I say."

He didn't move close until she did as he'd asked. The angle of her head and the stretch of her arms behind her made everything that little bit uncomfortable. Her muscles ached and it was hard to swallow but she relaxed her throat as much as she could, giving Carter room to thrust deep.

"All fucking night I wanted to leave the station again and come find you. I haven't been able to get you out of my mind since I walked into your shop."

Paige let her teeth scrape along his shaft. She wanted to tell him she'd been the same way, but she wasn't willing to release her prize. Instead, she pulled back, releasing his cock, only to dive back in and run her tongue from his base to the tip.

"You've been bad, Paige."

She nodded, wishing she could suck his balls. "I should be punished, Sir."

"That's right." He pulled back but left his cock out. "Stand up and follow me."

At some point she'd need to analyze how happy following Carter around made her. Right then, she didn't care.

The size of his bedroom wasn't anything out of the ordinary, but at that moment, it felt monstrous. Carter pulled an armchair from the corner and sat down. "Stand over there and let me see you take those pants off."

Unlike the other times they'd been together, Paige had none of the embarrassment or concern. The unequivocal want reflected in Carter's eyes made her feel like the most beautiful woman in the world.

Slowly, she slid the braces down her arms, one at a time. The waist of the pants was large enough they would have fallen to the floor had she not held them up. Being naked except for her bra and panties, dressed in clothing that clearly wasn't hers, was more of a turn-on than Paige would have expected. She took her time sliding the pants down her legs, letting the scrape of the heavy material tease every inch of her skin. Making sure to keep her ass high in the air, she stepped out of the material and slowly stood again.

"Turn." His voice was little more than a harsh whisper. She did as he asked and waited. "Walk backward toward me."

It was hard not knowing where she was going, but somehow Paige managed to without stumbling. Carter's hands were on her ass cheeks as soon as she got into range, squeezing hard.

"Bad, bad girl." He pinched first one, then the other cheek. "Bend over and touch your toes."

Paige could feel his hot breath on her skin once she'd assumed the position. Carter ran his fingers inside the edge of the lace of her panties, his knuckles rough against her skin. He hooked a finger and pulled the thin fabric hard to the side. Paige shivered as the heat from his mouth got closer, quickly followed by the hot swipe of his tongue over the top of her ass.

"Whatever should I do to punish you? What do you think?"

The press of his thumb against her asshole had Paige crying out, her body swaying forward, trying to escape him. Carter slapped her ass hard, pulling her back into place with her panties. "We're not doing this again."

"Sorry, Sir."

"Have you ever been fucked in the ass, Paige?" He pushed his thumb in a little, stretching the muscles.

"No." It was one of the few things Rick wasn't interested in.

"Want to try it?"

She swallowed and closed her eyes. "Whatever you want, Sir."

Another squeeze before he released her. "I have lube and condoms in the bathroom drawer. Go get them."

Paige didn't remember standing up or finding her way to the small bathroom. She ignored the lotions, combs and creams and grabbed the items she was after. Upon her return, Carter had pulled off his shirt and kicked off his boots. Sitting only in his pants, he watched her walk back.

"Turn around, back into position."

By the time she'd handed over the supplies and bent over, Paige's heart was pounding madly. The jerk of her panties to the side and the returning teasing of his thumb left her head spinning.

"You're tight here. I'm going to have to work you open so I don't hurt you." He slowly pressed a lubed finger into her ass. "Fuck, you're squeezing around me hard. You need to relax, baby. Like that."

Carter pumped his finger in and out of her ass, turning and stretching her. It was odd at first, uncomfortable, but the more he teased her, the faster she relaxed and started to enjoy the sensations. When she started moaning, he added a second finger.

"No, don't tense up on me now. Keep yourself relaxed. This is only two fingers, not big enough, but you're getting there."

He slipped a third finger into her pussy and pumped his hand in steady beats in and out. Paige gasped, and her body shook while she held her position. She wanted to throw herself on the bed and spread her legs wide and beg Carter to fuck her. Of course, he wouldn't do it if she was obvious about the whole thing. Instead she did her best to give him what he asked of her, knowing he would make everything else wonderful.

"Think you can handle another one? Of course you can." He didn't even wait for her reply, removed the finger from her pussy and added it alongside the other two in her ass.

"God, Carter, Sir, it's too much. Please."

"You're not safe-wording out on a few fingers in your ass, are you?" He fanned out those fingers, stretching her open and making her pussy pulse.

"No, no, I'm not. No."

"I want to see you when I make you come from this. Go lie down on the bed on your back."

He slapped her ass, sending her stumbling in the direction of the bed. Paige happily fell onto her stomach on the bed with a giggle.

"What's that? Laughing?"

"No, Sir." She giggled again.

Carter was on her in an instant, pinning her legs down and slapping her ass as hard as he could. The stinging blows came hard and fast, and Paige cried out in pleasure and pain as she tried to escape his unexpected punishment.

As quickly as it had begun, Carter flipped her around until her tender ass was pressed into the not-so-soft cotton comforter. Once upon a time, Rick would have been glaring at her with disdain. Instead Carter's beautiful hazel eyes smiled down as he grabbed her legs and lifted them up to his shoulders. Leaving them in place, he quickly rolled the condom down his shaft.

"Bad, bad girl." The tip of his cock nudged her stretched hole. "Laughing when you're supposed to be getting punished."

"Sorry, Sir." She didn't even attempt to hide her grin.

"I can see that." He slapped her ass and pushed into her with one long, slow stroke.

Paige had no idea who moaned loudest. All she could feel was Carter stretching her wide, her chest tightening and pleasure shimmering through her body the deeper he went. When he couldn't go forward any farther, Carter let her legs slip to his sides and ground his pubic bone against her clit.

"I want to hear you, Paige. Every groan and grunt. I want you crying out, begging me to let you come. Do you understand me?"

She swallowed and nodded frantically. "Yes, Sir."

Paige tried to buck up into Carter's thrusts, but he forced her hips down into the mattress. "Just feel."

Feel she did—every inch of his cock sliding in and out of her body. The pounding of his heart against her chest as he collapsed onto her, driving himself deeper. Her voice grew raw from the force of the cries escaping her. Her fears and reservations melted to nothing as her orgasm stampeded closer.

"Need to come," she managed to whisper.

Carter leaned in and nipped at the tip of her nose. "Beg."

"Please, please, please, *please.*"

With every word, Carter slammed into her ass harder, forcing his body hard against her clit. When she didn't think she could take another second, he slipped his hand between their bodies and pressed against her.

"Now."

Paige screamed until she couldn't take any more, then she bit down on his shoulder. The pleasure was nearly paralyzing, obliterating her sight, leaving her only with her hearing. Carter didn't slow or hold back. He thrust into her a few more times before letting out an answering cry. Panting and sweat-soaked, they fell together.

Sleepiness encouraged her to roll close to Carter's side, tucking her shoulder under his arm and letting her head rest on his chest.

"Am I forgiven?" she asked, playing with his nipple.

"Only if you agree to come to the station holiday party with me in November."

Paige knew things were finally going to be okay. "Yes, Sir."

★ ★ ★ ★ ★

dedication

To N. and E.
Guess what?

acknowledgments

So many people need to be thanked when your first story gets published, and I hope I don't miss any. My husband and daughter, for allowing me to steal some of our family time for myself when I decided I needed to write. Candace Irvin, who read my very first efforts at novel writing and generously walked me through my beginner mistakes—and there were many. Dee and Rae, who challenged me to be a better writer, and encouraged me to keep going even when I thought about giving up. Ditto for Anita, Jeanne and Jenna. My editor, Deborah Nemeth, for her spot-on suggestions and patience with all my newbie questions. And last, but in no way least, the women of The Wicked Muse—Chelle, Ami and Marcy—for the fantastic critiques and moral support. I couldn't have gotten this far without any of you.

Chapter One

God, she hated conflict, especially the kind between her and Alex. And really, if this whole emotionally draining, nerve-twitching situation was anyone's fault, it was his. After all, he'd been the one to give her the gift card she'd used to buy the first book. And the second. And the third.

Jessica Meyers sighed disgustedly as she tested the water of her bubble bath. No, none of this was Alex's doing. It was all hers, and she was going to have to find a way to fix it. Soon, before the confused frustration she saw in her husband's eyes turned into something irreparable.

It was late, but she needed to unwind. The kids were sound asleep, and Alex, a Maryland State Trooper, was still at work. He probably would be all night, unless the MSP caught a break on the case that had been all over the nightly news. It was quiet for once, and maybe now she could figure out what the hell she was going to do to make things right again.

She lit some aromatherapy candles that matched the scent of her bubble bath, turned off the overhead light, and climbed into the claw-foot tub, sighing as the steamy water did its thing on her muscles. She settled back and closed her eyes, breathing deeply, letting the soothing aroma of eucalyptus seep into her pores. Her hands drifted idly over her stomach, back and forth through the thick bubbles.

Alex. She loved that man so much, even more than the day she'd said *I do*. They'd been through a lot together these past fifteen years, but never once had she been sorry she'd married Alex right out of college. She still wasn't sorry. She couldn't imagine *ever* being sorry. And yet, as much as she loved Alex and their life together, she was restless and itchy, and it had all started with a book.

It had been another Friday night, and she'd been alone in the house. Ten-year-old Kara had been sleeping at her best friend's house, and seven-year-old Ben had gone on a camping trip. Alex and Jess had planned a much-needed date night, but then Alex called her to say he'd caught a case and would be working late.

Jess was frustrated, but she'd been a cop's wife long enough to suck it up and not blame Alex for things out of his control. Rather than sit home alone, she drove to the bookstore in Frederick, looking for something new and fun and distracting to read.

She picked up book after book, looking at the covers and reading the backs, but nothing caught her attention. She was kneeling on the floor, surrounded by possible choices, when she found *it* on the bottom shelf.

The cover drew her attention first. It showcased a hazy photograph of a wrought iron four-poster bed with plush white bed linens, rumpled as if someone had just woken and stepped out of the room. A silky black scarf, tied in a knot like a blindfold, lay at the foot of the bed. Men's ties were looped around each of the four posts.

Her mouth went bone dry, her mind whirling with images of what might've happened in that bed. She flipped the book over to read the back cover copy and got sucked right in. The erotic promise in those words flowed over her like warm honey, and she turned to the first page. Exactly what she'd been looking for. She paid for her book and headed home.

As she read, she found herself shockingly aroused by the words on the page. She'd never read anything like it before, but the visual images she got from the words had her hands trembling, her heart pounding, and her core slick with desire. The woman in the story was bound facedown on the bed, helpless to stop what her boyfriend had planned for her, but she was a willing subject. He knelt beside her on the mattress, one hand fisted in her hair as he swatted at her bottom with his other. In between swats, he dipped his fingers into her moist sheath, using her own fluids like gel to ease his way into the snug depths of her anus. The woman struggled on the bed, her orgasm just outside of her control. He held it out of her reach until she was a writhing mass of need, begging him for mercy. Finally, he let her go over.

After Jess finished the book, she lay in bed, restless, unable to sleep for all the thoughts bouncing through her mind. She was aroused and so damn tempted to make herself come. She needed the release but doubted it would be enough by herself.

And then Alex came home. She stripped him of his clothes before their bedroom door even shut all the way. To say he was stunned was an understatement, but he didn't complain in the least. He laughed, low and sexy, as he peeled off her nightgown and backed her up against the bed. He rained kisses across her cheeks, then bent to cover her breast with his mouth. She sucked in a shaky breath and squeezed her eyes shut as images from her imagination took over.

He turned her toward the bed, his body hard and hot behind her. When he finally stroked inside her, she shuddered, coming apart at the seams. But she couldn't let loose, not all the way. She felt frozen, until she pictured herself in one of the scenes she'd read earlier, tied facedown to the bed, at her lover's will. She grabbed at the sheets, forcing herself to be still, pretending to be under Alex's control. It seemed wrong, but her body didn't think so, and as Alex came with a shout, she let go.

It was the most explosive lovemaking they'd had in months, but she turned away from him, curling up on her side, silent, tremors shaking her body as he tried to get her to tell him what was wrong. She didn't even try to explain it to him, because she didn't know if she could. The guilt eating at her gut had only gotten worse when Alex curled up behind her, his warm, sated body spooning hers, his lips against her hair, whispering words of unconditional love.

Jess jerked back to the present with a start when she heard the garage door, her pulse pounding as she withdrew her trembling hand from between her thighs. She hadn't expected it, but Alex was home. *Thank God.* She sighed with relief, the same sigh she breathed each time he came home from a shift, safe and whole.

The door to the bathroom opened. Already clinging to the edge of orgasm from her own touches and vivid memories, Jess picked up a bath pouf and started running it over her raised leg, letting the soap suds slide down to the junction of her thighs. Her breath hitched and she did it several times, pretending not to notice her husband leaning against the door, his arms crossed.

Even though he wore a sexy-as-sin smile on his face, his eyes held a wariness that had grown over the past few months, as if he wasn't sure what kind of reception he'd get. She hated that she'd put that look in his eyes, and vowed to find a way to fix the mess. But tonight was not the night for her personal demons. Alex looked exhausted, she thought with a pang, as if he needed to be cared for. She dunked the pouf again, picking up more bubbles, and then squeezed it so the water and the suds cascaded over her breasts.

A low rumble came from his chest. "Hi, honey. I'm home."

She turned her head and smiled lazily at him, even as her body flushed with heat. "So you are. You have too many clothes on. Get naked. There's plenty of room for both of us in this tub."

His grin was all male, and it chased some of the tired from his face and most of the tension from his body. She loved the way Alex looked, with his spiky dark hair and clear hazel eyes that were now sparkling with lust.

He pushed himself away from the door and started a very personal strip show. She swallowed hard as he unbuttoned his shirt slowly, torturously, exposing a broad, muscled chest with just the right amount of crisp hair.

She scooped up some bubbles and painted them on her body, drawing one finger through the froth, circling the tip of each aching breast, pinching the already-hard nipples.

He pulled his shirt off. "Kids asleep?"

"Yes," she breathed, groaning aloud as she became more aroused.

"Thank God," he replied thickly, reaching behind him to lock the door. He never took his eyes off her, which was incredibly sexy. "I like what you're doing with those bubbles, but save that job for me." Working quickly, he removed his belt with his strong, sure fingers.

Fingers she wanted on her body, *in her body,* doing things

she'd only read about and fantasized about. Things she wasn't sure she could ever ask him to do. Things she worried he'd find disgusting, considering what he saw on the job. She shuddered, shoved the insidious thought away, and feasted her eyes on her husband's body, letting him feel the weight of her yearning as she visually caressed the bulge of his arousal.

"You keep looking at me like that," he said, his voice rough with desire, "and things are going to be over before they even start." He unzipped his khaki pants and shoved them down, stepping out of them, pulling his socks off at the same time. He tossed the wadded ball of clothes behind him, toward the hamper in the corner of the bathroom, not bothering to look and see if he'd made the shot.

He hadn't. Like she cared, though.

"You're still wearing too much," she said softly. Even though she loved the way her husband looked right now, clad only in a pair of skin-tight black boxer briefs that left nothing to the imagination, naked would be *so* much better.

"Workin' on it." He skimmed his briefs down his body, giving her a quick flash of his incredibly sexy ass. In less than a second, he sailed them through the air toward the rest of his clothes.

She loved that part of his body, loved being on her knees in front of him, digging her fingers into the tight muscles as she stroked his penis and sucked him until he couldn't stand it anymore. And she loved it when he lost his famous control, threading his fingers through her hair, holding her head as he drove into her mouth, faster and faster, until he came, flooding her mouth and her senses at the same time. The salty sweet taste, the musky smell, the contradiction of soft and rough textures—all of it was pure, undiluted Alex. She didn't feel guilty afterward, because when she loved him that way, she didn't need the fantasies from those books.

And it was the fantasies that were slowly driving her insane.

When Alex pulled into the garage after the shift from hell, all he'd been thinking about was sleep.

Not anymore.

Tired flew right out the window as he watched his sexy wife playing with the bubbles in the tub. Playing him. She was definitely in one of those turned-on, hell-on-wheels-in-bed moods tonight, but he didn't mind the game. Not at all. Light from those scented candles she loved so much flickered over her body in the otherwise dark room. Her red curls were piled high on her head in a messy knot, her cheeks flushed pink from the steam, and she had a come-hither look in her gorgeous green eyes.

That was one invitation he wouldn't refuse.

He stalked over to the tub and crouched next to it, dipping his hand into the water, circling the tip of Jess's breast, catching her nipple between his thumb and forefinger. He leaned forward and kissed her, and at the same time he pinched her nipple gently. She gasped and he slid his tongue in her mouth, feasting on the taste that was uniquely his Jessica's, with a twist. "Sneaking the kids' Easter candy again, babe?"

She flushed prettily. "Guilty."

He laughed, bumping noses with her. "You're not the only one. I stopped in the kitchen before I came upstairs. Ben's bunny is missing a little more of his ears now."

She flicked some water at him. "You're worse than I am. I only took some jellybeans."

He kissed Jess again. "Scoot up."

When she did, he slid into the tub behind her. He leaned

back against the tub's high walls with a heartfelt groan. The hot water felt great. He slipped his arms around her, tugging her back against his chest. *That* felt even better—her ass was pressed right against his aching erection. He nipped at her shoulder and cupped her full breasts, reveling in the weight of them, slowly rubbing his thumbs over her hard nipples. Her head dropped back against his shoulder, and she clutched at his arms.

"Want me to stop?" he murmured in her ear.

"I'll kill you if you do," she said, the breathy sound of the words adding to his arousal.

"Hmm. What if I do this instead?" He kept one hand working at her breasts, but he slid the other lower, skimming gently over her stomach to her curls, using one fingertip to nudge her clit before sliding that finger deep inside her body. She was so wet and swollen he knew it wouldn't take long for her to come tonight. He kept up a gentle pace, loving how it made her writhe, which rubbed her body back and forth against his hard, straining cock.

The warmth of the water, the heat and movement of Jess's body, the potent scent of the candles in the air—all of it put him on the razor's edge of climax. When she finally went over, he fought against his need to do the same. He cupped her head and pulled her into a deep kiss, covering her mouth with his, swallowing the sounds of her release, a long, sensual orgasm that left her limp against his body, sated, at least for now.

He, on the other hand, was nowhere near done. His heart galloped, his breathing ragged as he held Jess close while she came back to earth.

She kissed the back of his hand and then turned all the way around and settled between his thighs, facing him on her knees. Water sloshed over the edge of the tub, and small waves rippled in the water's depth, caressing his cock the way he wanted Jess to. He gritted his teeth, not wanting to go over, not yet.

"Hi, there." She leaned up to kiss him, coming half out of the water like a mermaid from the sea. Her long, curly hair had fallen out of its knot and now trailed over her shoulder and tumbled down her back.

He wrapped a finger in one of her curls and tugged lightly. "Hi, yourself. This is a nice surprise."

She tilted her head and reached out, splaying her hand across his chest. "For both of us. I thought you wouldn't be home until morning."

"Really? You were already pretty wet when I got here. Playing without me?" he teased, intrigued by the thought. Damned if it didn't send a lightning bolt of lust straight to his cock.

She flushed, and something uncomfortable skittered across her face. She ducked her head, hiding her eyes from him. "From the hot bath."

Not wanting to ruin the mood, he let it go. Talking about sex was always hard for Jess, but something told him there was more to her embarrassment than just him talking dirty. This wasn't the first time she had distanced herself from him during sex, and one of these days, he was going to have to figure out what was going on in her head, why she seemed so flustered lately, because it was driving him nuts.

"It doesn't matter either way, babe." He stifled the frustration that seemed to be his constant companion these days and ran his knuckles gently down Jess's cheek. "I'm just glad you're awake and I get to spend some quality time with my gorgeous wife."

He'd deal with the questions some other day, though, because now Jess had her hands on his thighs. She slid them forward until her fingers nestled in the crook of his legs, close to his cock and balls, but she didn't touch them. And oh, how he wanted that. His muscles bunched and flexed as she rubbed her thumbs closer and closer.

"Babe, you're killing me here." He closed his eyes and dropped his head back against the edge of the tub. "Touch me. Please."

"Touch you how?" Jess's voice was like velvet, her softly uttered words uncharacteristically bold. And totally at odds with the uneasiness he'd seen in her eyes just a minute earlier. "Tell me what you want me to do."

His eyes flew open, and in the dim light, he saw raw desire on his wife's face. Damned if that didn't turn him on, too. Whatever was going on with Jess, whatever she wouldn't—or felt she *couldn't*—share with him, it definitely added a spark to their sex life. He liked it. A lot. All except for the emotional distance, but he shoved that thought away for now.

He kept his eyes locked on hers as his heart threatened to gallop out of his chest. He had to clear his throat twice to get his voice to work. "Get your hand all soapy, and wrap it around my cock. I want to feel your fingers on me, stroking me, touching my balls."

Her eyes lit up. "Like this?"

Steam rose around them, but he wasn't sure if it was from the water or from the heat they generated together. Her slick, soapy hand stroked tightly up and down his erection, and she slid her thumb over the head each time she reached the tip. Her fingers cupping his balls were gentle, caressing that sensitive spot underneath them. She scraped there with her fingernail, and his body jerked in response.

It felt like hell, and it felt like heaven. "Stop," he groaned. "Or I'm going to come like this."

She didn't listen.

As she worked him with her tight fist, she slid her other hand under his balls, pressing against the tight hole there, sparking the nerve endings to life. She'd never done that to him before, but *damn,* it felt good. He wanted her to do it again. Later, when he had more control over his body. His balls drew up, and he knew he was going to lose it, right there, without being inside her, if he didn't do something fast. And he didn't want to come alone.

He tugged Jess up his body, draping her legs on either side of his, and urged her down onto his pulsing cock. As good as her warm, soapy hand had felt, it was *nothing* like the heat and tightness of her pussy. He held her hips steady, thrusting up until he was fully enveloped in her body.

"Alex," she cried out as he pressed deep, closing her eyes and biting her lip.

"Ride me." He didn't care how needy he sounded. He could feel the ripples inside her body, urging him toward release. He slid his hands into her hair, pulling her down for a kiss as she rocked back and forth on his body, her movements drawing him closer and closer to the fire.

She went over first, and he tightened his hands in her hair, deepening the kiss, swallowing the ragged sound she made as her orgasm flashed over. She shredded his restraint, and he followed her almost immediately, holding her close as wave after wave of pleasure overtook him.

They lay together in the tub, breathing heavily, and he stroked a hand up and down her smooth back. He didn't know how long they lay there like that, entwined, his softening cock still inside the grip of her body. This was the first time in a long while she seemed content to stay connected to him, to rest in their intimate embrace, and he felt even more tension leave his body.

"A husband could get used to coming home to this every night," he murmured in her ear, and he felt her smile against his neck.

"So could a wife," she said with a satisfied sigh.

Chapter Two

Jess shivered as Alex helped her from the tub. He grabbed a towel and wrapped it around her. After drying himself off, he drew her toward their bed, naked but for the wicked grin on his face.

Slowly, he unwrapped the towel, his gaze heating her skin as he bared her body. He towel-dried her arms and legs, but he dropped to his knees and used his tongue to catch the moisture between her thighs. The chill vanished, replaced with a warm flush that swept over her.

He stood and pressed a quick kiss to her lips. "I'm glad you're still up."

She cast her gaze at his semi-aroused penis. "I'm glad you're still up, too." With her best shot at a sexy smile, she turned and reached for the nightshirt she'd tossed onto her side of the bed.

He laughed and flicked the towel, catching her right across her bare backside.

At the quick sting against her flesh, Jess bit her lip to hold back the moan that wanted to escape. Before she could even process her reaction, Alex scooped her up and tossed her onto the bed. She laughed, but her mind was otherwise occupied by the locker-room towel flick.

He dropped onto the bed, settling himself between her legs. "Love you." He whispered the words in her ear, nipping her lobe lightly.

She shivered again, this time from arousal, and wound her arms around his neck.

"Want you again." He licked a path down her throat to her breast, tongued her nipple. He groaned as he entered her body.

So did she.

"Right now." He said the words, but he took his time, stroking her body slowly, pulling all the way out before sliding in again, one excruciating inch at a time.

She whimpered, thrashing her head against the pillow as her mind wandered into fantasy. *I'm bound to a chair in my Master's front hall, naked and gagged. Every guest who enters the house for his dinner party touches me. Some pinch my nipples while others strike me with a small suede flogger. I love it all, but I need more.*

She arched her back, trying to get Alex to move faster, but he kept his pace steady. A frustrated sound tore from her throat against her will.

"Easy, love. We've got all night."

Air dances over my bare skin as I stand on the balcony overlooking the moonlit city, my feet spread wide, my breasts resting on the railing as my Master commanded. He stands behind me, and with a twist of his hips, his erection breaches the entrance to my ass. I cry out, the sound carrying to a building across the street from us, where a man sits on his balcony, his hooded eyes locked with mine as he fists his cock.

When Alex rolled them so they were on their sides, facing each other, she had to close her eyes for fear he'd see inside her vivid imagination.

He kissed her as he stroked inside her, lifting her leg over his hip so he could fill her more deeply with each thrust. "Look at me, Jess."

She forced her eyes open and was stunned by the fierce need on Alex's face.

"You with me?" He punctuated his words with sharp thrusts.

Damn good question. Guilt prickled her skin, but she forced it back, threaded her fingers through his hair and pulled him closer for a tongue-dueling kiss.

He laughed roughly, and his voice was uneven. "I'll take that as a *yes.*"

He slipped a hand between them, rubbing her clit on every stroke, until nothing mattered but Alex and the orgasm that seemed just outside her reach. *My Master pulls the vibrator from my body just as I'm about to come. "Not until I say you can," he says sharply. He withholds his permission for a long, frustrating minute, and I want to scream. Finally he relents, blowing a whisper of air across my clit. "Now, slave."*

She came as if the release had been ripped from her against her will, her body straining and her heart hammering. Alex followed right behind her.

While Alex took the kids to Ben's baseball practice, Jess cleaned up the mess in the bathroom. She picked up his clothes, wadded up in a ball next to the hamper but not in it. He'd been in a bit of a hurry, not that she could blame him. She'd *wanted* him to hurry.

It had been an amazing night, especially since it had been a gift. She honestly hadn't thought she'd see him until the morning. But over breakfast, he told her they'd caught an unexpected break in the case.

As wonderful as the night had been, when Alex came

downstairs for coffee this morning, he'd had that wary look
in his eyes again, the one guaranteed to make her guilty feelings rise up and choke her. She hated this, really she did. What
she needed was a time machine, so she could go back to that
day at the bookstore. The day she let the perfect opening slide
by, all because she'd been afraid.

A couple of weeks after she picked up that first book, Jess
had found herself at the bookstore again, this time with Alex
and the kids. Kara went looking for the latest preteen vampire book, and Ben went with Alex to scour the kids' section
for anything about baseball.

Which gave Jess a few minutes to look for herself. She went
right to the same author, hoping she'd find something like the
last book. And, at the same time, hoping she wouldn't, because
she still felt guilty, unsure how Alex would feel about them.

She found another book that intrigued her. The cover
showed three people. A man, in tight jeans and nothing else,
stood behind a naked woman, holding her bound wrists in
one hand and a leather flogger in the other. Another man,
clad in black leather pants and an open white shirt, was putting a mask over her eyes. The photo had been taken through
a sheer curtain, but it was obvious both men were going to
dominate her.

It was just as obvious she was excited by it. And, like the
last book, this cover image set her imagination off on a wild
journey.

She was reading the first page when Alex came up behind
her, sliding his hands around her waist, nuzzling her neck. Lost
in her own fantasies, she jumped a mile, her heart thudding.

"Whoa, babe, it's just me. Whatcha got there?"

"N-nothing," she stammered. She pulled away, trying to

put the book back on the shelf, but he took it from her. She felt mortified and a little angry.

He stared at the cover for a long moment, locked eyes with her, then handed the book back. He had on what she always considered his inscrutable cop face. "Looks hot. We're ready to go whenever you are. Are you buying anything?" he asked in a quiet, emotionally distant voice.

She didn't know what to say, how to respond to his lack of reaction, so she mutely shook her head. As much as she wanted that book, she put it back on the shelf and they headed home.

He didn't say another word about it, and he even went to bed early, still unusually reserved. Sitting alone in the kitchen, her anger at him and her own embarrassment faded into something a lot more uncomfortable. For the first time in nearly fifteen years of marriage, it was as if a wall had come up between them, and she knew it was all her fault.

She went back to the store several times after that, but the memory of the look on Alex's face kept her from buying that specific book—until she took Kara there to get a birthday present for a friend and found herself in that very spot, looking at that very book. Before she could change her mind, she paid for it and put it in her bag.

When she got home, she felt so guilty about it she almost threw it away without reading it. She shoved it in her nightstand drawer, still in the bag, and left it there as she tried to decide what to do with it. It nagged at her and because of it she was short with Alex, picking at him for things she'd normally ignore. She was aware of her cranky attitude but couldn't seem to stop herself.

But it didn't stop her from turning to him in the night, curling into his hard body for heat to warm a chill no amount of blankets could help.

"I love you, you know," he whispered, drawing her against him, lifting her leg over his hip, nudging her entrance with his erection. "Tell me what's wrong, so I can fix it. You don't have to be the one in charge all the time."

At his words, tears filled her eyes. "I love you back."

He rolled her onto her back, twined his hands with hers, and entered her fully with one long, deep, hard thrust. She groaned at the power behind his penetration, of being held in place, and something clicked inside her brain and her heart and her soul.

That was the exact moment she'd realized what it was she truly desired—Alex in charge, not to fix something, but to take control in bed. She wanted him to hold back nothing, to take what he needed and he wanted. She wanted to offer him that trust, and in return, be offered the pleasure she'd glimpsed inside a world she'd just discovered. Light bondage. Spanking. Toys to torment her. *That* was what she hadn't been able to tell him, what had turned her into a crazy woman. How could she have explained it, when she'd only just figured it out herself?

And, weeks later, she *still* hadn't explained it to Alex.

With a disgusted sigh, Jess tossed the comforter on the floor, then yanked the sheets off the bed, holding them to her face, breathing deeply. They smelled like Alex, and like her, the smell that was uniquely theirs when they made love. She loved that smell.

Once the bed was remade, she carried the dirty pile downstairs, tossed the whole thing into the washer, and, frustrated with herself for all her waffling and her lack of a damn spine, slammed the laundry room door shut. She winced as the dishes on the counter rattled. She was rattled, too, pulled apart by what she wanted, what she needed, and what she thought Alex—and their marriage—could handle.

Back upstairs in their bedroom, she sat on the floor and pulled out her hoard of books, the ones that fueled her fantasies. Because they were erotic stories, she wasn't sure how Alex would take them. He liked the results of them, even though he didn't know the *why* of it. The nights she fantasized, their lovemaking was always supercharged.

She wasn't sure why she thought Alex would mind. Mostly, she figured he'd lump her erotic romances in with porn. But they weren't the same. The stories engaged her brain and her emotions as well as her libido.

But that wasn't the real reason she worried, was it? No, this was no longer only about fantasizing. She wanted to *try* some light bondage, like being tied up and blindfolded, and other things that made her blush but set her heart racing. Some stuff was too extreme for anything but fantasy, at least for her. Ménages were exciting and arousing to read about, but she couldn't see them in reality. And anyway, the only man she wanted was Alex.

But now she wanted more.

Only, how did you ask the man you've been married to for fifteen years for things like that? *Excuse me, honey. Would you tie me up and blindfold me? Oh, and whip me with this flogger, too, if you don't mind.*

Yeah, right.

If they'd experimented before they were married, it would be different. But they hadn't. Now, what if he thought the things she wanted to try were too kinky? Talk about taking a potential wrecking ball to your relationship. Her heart clenched at the thought.

They had two mostly happy, relatively well-adjusted kids, a small circle of good friends, decent jobs. They had a roof over their heads, food in the fridge, and a small safety net of savings in the bank. Things hadn't been perfect for them—two miscarriages and various everyday challenges had seen to that—but they'd survived what life had thrown at them. Together.

Like most married couples, their sex life often suffered from too much to do, too little time, and no energy to do much about it, but their marriage was rock solid. And she wanted to keep it that way, because when she'd said forever, she'd meant forever. She'd rather keep their sex life as it was and not risk damaging their relationship. It wasn't fair to ask Alex now for something she'd never asked for before. Not something like this.

Period.

So she stowed the books back in the box, shoved it all the way under the bed—all the while wishing she could do the same with the images and fantasies in her head—and went back downstairs to make lunch for her family.

"Hi, babe." Alex kissed Jess on the cheek. "Practice was muddy today. I sent Ben upstairs to get washed up. He's a mess. And Kara's in her room, sulking because I told her we think she's still too young to have a cell phone."

"Hi," she answered absently, turning back to the sandwiches she'd been making.

Alex stifled a sigh. He'd hoped whatever she'd been worried about last night would be gone today, but it wasn't. He still saw the shadow of *something* in her eyes, and his heart twisted. Jessica's silence on whatever was bugging her was scaring him, way down to the hidden part of him that had never believed he could have—*or keep*—a woman like her. She was everything to him. She and their kids were his life.

Something had changed in the past couple of months. At first, he'd thought it was for the better. God knows, it'd been a long time since their sex life had been so active. It hadn't been bad, but after fifteen years of marriage, it had become predictable. Now, however, it was different, more intense. Exciting again. He'd initially chalked it up to the kids being older and more self-sufficient, which freed up time for both him and Jess. But he'd noticed lately there was a furtive, almost desperate tone to it, as if Jess was using sex to chase some demon away.

The thought of what she might be hiding from him made him sick. The first time, about three months ago, he'd been shaken to his core. She'd made love to him with wild abandon, and then immediately afterward had curled up on her side, shaking. He'd tried to get her to talk, but she'd just withdrawn further. He'd spent the night wrapped around her, holding her, unable to sleep as he tried to figure out what might be wrong. But the next day, it had been almost as if nothing had happened.

She'd begun withdrawing emotionally from him when it came to sex, and only sex. The things going through his head were killing him, because the rest of their life was absolutely normal. The insecure husband worried she might've had an affair and was feeling guilty. The cop in him worried she might have been assaulted and was trying to drive away bad memories by creating new ones. Neither of those situations was palatable.

If he'd learned anything in their fifteen years of marriage, it was how stubborn Jess was, but she was going to have to open up. This had gone on too long, and as good as the sex was, he didn't want it if it came with this emotional detachment.

He tugged gently on her ponytail. "Hey, you," he teased, trying to cajole her into a better mood.

Jess turned back around, a *what the fuck do you want now* look on her face. "What?"

His temper spiked, and good intentions be damned. "You know what? Never mind. I'm going upstairs to take a shower." He stalked out of the kitchen, pointedly ignoring the sheen of tears in Jess's eyes.

By the time he'd washed the dirt of the ball field off and gotten out of the shower, he regretted the way he'd handled the situation. He was still pissed at Jess's attitude, but he needed to go downstairs and apologize to his wife. He came out of the bathroom with his towel wrapped around his waist only to see Jessica sitting cross-legged on their bed, hugging a pillow, her head bowed.

Any residual anger fled when she looked up, her face stained with tears.

He dropped onto the bed and pulled Jess into his arms. "Babe, please. I know something's been bothering you. It's eating at you. Can't you just tell me what's going on? I hate what I'm seeing in your eyes these days, and how you keep pulling away from me."

"I don't know if I can," she whispered, her voice not quite steady. "And I'm not sure if I should."

"You should, because whatever it is, it can't be nearly as bad as the things I'm imagining." He hoped his words would get through to Jess because, damn it, he wanted things back the way they had been before. He wanted his somewhat reserved yet easygoing wife back without those damned shadows in her eyes. And unless she opened up, that wouldn't happen.

After a long pause, Jess took a deep, shuddering breath, as if she'd come to some sort of decision. "Your parents called while you were at practice. They picked up the new RV they've been looking at. They want to take the kids camping tonight, if you're okay with it. They'll bring them home tomorrow night, after dinner."

He silently thanked them for their impeccable timing. "Perfect. Then we'll have the house to ourselves, and we can talk." He kissed her temple, picked up her hand, and held it in his. "Tell me one thing, Jessica. Do you still love me?" His voice cracked over the words he'd been afraid to utter.

Her head jerked up and her tears spilled over. "I love you more than I ever have."

Relief poured through him, making him dizzy. "I love you, too." He wiped her tears away with his thumb. "Whatever else is going on, we'll deal with it. Together. Okay?"

"Okay," she whispered, leaning into his touch.

Alex held his wife tightly, feeling her heart pounding against his, and hoped like hell he hadn't lied to her. Because honestly, even with his experience as a cop, he didn't have a single clue what was going to come out of her mouth.

Chapter Three

While Jess helped the kids pack for the camping trip with their grandparents, part of her head was focused on the kids, and the other part was stuck on repeat, taunting her, reminding her she wanted something more, something different in her sexual relationship with her husband.

As if she could forget.

She'd never wanted to be anything but Alex's equal, in life or in bed, but now that had changed. The thoughts of him tying her up and giving her no choice in what happened to her in the bedroom were making her crazy, leaving her in a constant state of wet and wanting. The thoughts of her restraining Alex for the same reason had the same result.

Ben's protest refocused her thoughts. "Mom, why does Kara get to go, too? I want to go by myself. You promised I could."

Jess smiled at her son. The kids hadn't been told about the big camping surprise yet. "I know I said you could each take a turn spending time with them alone. But Grandma and Grandpa want both of you to come over tonight. Who knows? Maybe they have something special planned."

It didn't take long to drive the kids over to Alex's parents' house in Walkersville. Alex didn't say much in the car on the way over. He'd been pretty quiet since they'd talked earlier, and she wondered if he was regretting pushing for answers. Answers she still wasn't sure she could give him.

After seeing everyone off on their adventure, they headed for home. Alex was nearly as silent on the way back as he'd been on the way there.

"Are you going to say anything? This silence is killing me."

Alex reached out and squeezed her hand. His voice was wry. "That's how I've felt these past few months, every time you shut me out."

Ouch. A direct hit, and it hurt. "I'm sorry. I didn't realize it was that obvious."

"You're kidding me, right?" he asked, turning toward her with wide eyes.

The look on his face was so disbelieving, her red hair got the better of her, and the defensiveness came out in the tone of her voice. "No, I'm not kidding."

"Man, do we need to talk."

Dread pooled in the pit of Jess's stomach. Alex was nothing if not tenacious. She looked at him from the corner of her eye, at his rigid posture and the scowl on his face, and wished to hell she'd kept her mouth shut, or at least been better at hiding her insecurities. She had a horrible feeling about this, but there was no stuffing the proverbial cat back into the bag now.

An interminable yet short five minutes later, Alex led Jessica into their living room. He'd been silent on the ride back, brooding over the things he couldn't stop imagining, and it was making him crazy. He'd felt Jess's unease in the car, but enough was enough. It was time to get things out into the open.

The woman he loved more than anyone else in the world stood by the fireplace, touching the family photos on the mantel. Her hand hesitated over their wedding photo but didn't touch it, and his stomach clenched. Did that mean something?

Frustration zinged through him as he paced around their living room, waiting for her to speak. But she said nothing, so he came to a dead stop in front of her. Come hell or high water, he *was* going to have his answers. He took a deep breath, forcing himself to voice the question that had been torturing his vivid imagination for weeks.

"Have you been unfaithful to me?" His words were blunt, his voice raw, and his body and heart and soul hovered on the edge of fight or flight.

Jessica flinched as if he'd raised his hand to strike her. Her face drained of color, and her eyes filled with those damned shadows he so often saw in them these days. Not a word came from her open mouth. Not a refusal, not an angry outburst demanding to know how he could ask her that, nothing but an indrawn gasp that seemed ripped from her chest. Instead of words, she simply dropped her gaze to the floor, and then looked back up at him, tears welling in her eyes.

He'd thought he'd guarded himself against whatever she might reveal, but he'd never been so wrong in his life. Horrified incredulity leached into his muscles and turned his body to stone. "Son of a bitch."

That seemed to startle a reaction out of her. "Alex, no!" she cried, dismay overlaying the guilt on her face. She started toward him, but he stepped back, away from her, putting out his hands out to ward her off.

"Don't touch me." The pain of betrayal shoved a knife

through his gut and made his voice a low growl. "Not right now."

Jesus, he needed to get out of here before he did something he'd regret. He grabbed the keys he'd tossed on the coffee table and stalked to the front door. The last thing he heard before he slammed the door behind him was the sound of his wife's tears as she begged him not to go.

He didn't drive far. As a state trooper, he'd seen enough accidents caused by emotional distress to know he was in no shape to be on the road. His phone vibrated against his waist every few minutes, but he ignored it. On autopilot, still hearing Jess's sobs and seeing the guilt on her face, he drove to the park where Ben played baseball. It was late afternoon, and the fields were empty now. He got out of his truck and headed toward the footbridge that ran over Carroll Creek.

His phone vibrated again. He looked down at the display, at Jess's smiling face in the picture next to her name, and wanted to hurl the damn thing into the creek. But he didn't, and instead forced himself to look at the missed call log. She'd called several times and left voice mail.

He wasn't interested. Not now, while he felt as raw as the spring wind that had kicked up. He needed to punch something. Or throw up.

His phone vibrated again, and he swore. Loudly, and graphically, words he rarely uttered around his family. He went to turn it off but found a text from Jessica instead. His hand nearly crushed the phone when he saw the first two words. *I'm sorry.* Another text. *It's not what u think.* They started coming faster, and he stared at her words in disbelief. *I'm not cheating.* And then, *I swear.*

His heart wanted to believe her, so badly it ached. But all

he could see was the guilt on her face, and the way she hadn't denied being unfaithful, and his stomach heaved.

Pls come home. I'll explain everything.

He sat on a boulder next to the creek and stared at the words on his phone. Had he jumped to the wrong conclusion?

I love u, Alex. Pls.

He closed his eyes and swallowed down the bile burning his throat. He hit Reply on his phone, and typed his own message back. *Can't talk 2 u right now. Need time 2 calm down.* He hit Send, then added one more line. *Don't know what 2 believe.* He hit Send again, and turned the phone off. He shivered, but for the life of him, he couldn't tell if it was from the chill in the air or the chill in his soul.

If ever there was time for introspection, this was it. Earlier that morning, he'd told Jess that whatever was bothering her, they'd deal with it together. But he hadn't expected this. Well, maybe he had. His insecure self—the one he tried to shove back into the deep recesses of his mind whenever it escaped—worried she might have had an affair and been trying to atone for it with sex, but he hadn't truly believed it was possible. His wife was not the cheating kind. But, then again, he'd been a cop long enough to understand people had secrets and sometimes did things they normally wouldn't.

He stared at the creek for a while, then walked around the park in the cool spring afternoon, trying to burn off the vicious energy filling his muscles and his soul. After an hour, he still didn't know whether or not to believe Jessica's words, but he did know one thing. It had been completely unfair of him—and completely unlike him—to walk out without listening, without hearing all the facts first. Much of that anger roiling through him was directed at himself. He owed Jess the chance to explain.

He'd accused her of cheating and not even waited for her to answer with words. Maybe her tears had been ones of disbelief. If she was telling the truth, he owed her a hell of a lot more than a mere apology.

And if she *wasn't* telling the truth, he knew this—an affair was not something their fifteen-year marriage could survive. He could forgive much, but not infidelity.

Honesty compelled him to admit one more thing to himself. If Jessica *was* telling the truth, he wasn't sure he could forgive himself for the way he'd hurled that accusation at her. And he wouldn't be surprised if she told him to go to hell.

Jessica's emotions raced between frantic worry for Alex's state of mind, guilt for giving him reason to think she might be cheating on him, and fury at him for walking out on her after assuming the worst. After more than an hour of crying her eyes out, fury was in the lead. So when she heard his truck in the driveway—*thank God*—she was fired up and ready to go.

Alex came into the room looking ragged. His hair was standing up as if he'd run his hands through it over and over again. His face was pale, his hazel eyes bloodshot and rimmed in red. He looked as miserable as she felt, and the evil part of her thought, *Good.*

Jess didn't get up from where she'd tucked herself into the corner of the couch, her knees drawn up, their fat orange tabby curled up on her feet. She didn't hide the tissues or try to stop the tears that were flowing again.

Alex stood stiffly near the fireplace, looking at their wedding picture. She'd looked at it, too, earlier, when she'd tried to figure out how to talk to him about her fantasies.

They both began talking at the same time. "Go ahead," Jessica said as she braced herself for more accusations.

"I shouldn't have walked out without listening." His voice was unsteady and gruff, but not really apologetic, and that ticked her off even more.

"No, you shouldn't have," Jess agreed flatly. "Jesus, Alex. You didn't even give me the chance to answer. You just jumped right to an assumption. A wrong assumption. After fifteen years together, do you trust me that little? What does that say about our marriage?"

Her inner voice was rolling on the floor of her mind, laughing its ass off. Like she had *any* room at all to complain about lack of trust? She shushed her conscience and glared at him, wiping the damned tears away.

"How about how you didn't answer me? Did you want me to believe you'd been unfaithful? Was it that hard to say the words, *No, Alex, I'd never cheat on you?*" He raked his hands through his hair in exasperation. "Do you want to know why I made that leap? Because you're hiding something from me. I've known it for months. The worst part is how you always do an emotional retreat after we make love. What's changed these past few months, Jessica? I don't understand it. After sex—after some of the wildest sex we've ever had—why do you always look so…" he paused, frowned, as if the words coming out left a bad taste in his mouth, "…guilty?"

Bingo. It was hard to look Alex in the eye, but she did, because he'd just been more honest with her in the past three minutes than she'd been with him for the past three months. Her anger over his walking out fled in the face of his genuine confusion.

"Because I *feel* guilty," she said softly, twisting a tissue to shreds in her hands.

"For what?" His eyes went wide. "Having great sex with your husband? I don't get it. It doesn't make any sense. We're married. We're *allowed* to have great sex." He stared at her a long time, and she began to squirm under his scrutiny. "See? There you go. You have that damned look on your face again. You wanted a chance to explain. Well, explain." He crossed his arms and waited, his body language shouting he wasn't going anywhere without an answer.

"God, this is going to sound so stupid now." She muttered the words under her breath, but he heard her anyway.

With a curse and a heavy sigh, Alex sat down next to her on the sofa, hesitating briefly before reaching out for her hand. That hesitation twisted her insides, as did the pleading tone of his voice. She'd never heard him so unsure of himself, of their relationship, and she was to blame for that.

"Something's obviously bothering you, and it's definitely bothering me. Tell me what's been on your mind. Please, Jess."

She grabbed his hand as if it were a lifeline. And really, it was. She drew in a deep breath, trying to work up the courage to explain her convoluted thoughts and feelings to the man who owned her heart and deserved her honesty. She should have told him months ago, should never have let it get this far, regardless of the consequences. She sucked in a deep, shuddering breath and gathered her courage.

"What's on my mind? Forbidden fantasies," she admitted. She stood, still holding his hand, and pulled him toward the stairs. "Come with me, and I'll show you."

Chapter Four

Alex blinked as he followed Jess up the stairs toward their bedroom. The past few hours of his life had been a jumble of emotions, and he knew he was off kilter, but her softly uttered words made no sense. "Forbidden fantasies? What the hell is that supposed to mean?"

She stopped dead on the stairs and turned to look at him. Her face flushed a deep red, and Alex realized she was embarrassed. "It means I've been fantasizing while we make love."

But he was still lost. "And?"

She frowned and, even swollen from the tears that still stained her cheeks, her eyes glittered with shock. "That doesn't bother you?"

"Uh, no. Should it?"

She didn't seem to believe him, though. She shook her head and started up again. He almost smiled at her attitude—*almost*—but he was still damn confused, and several months' worth of worried. And now, on top of it all, guilty for having assumed the worst of his wife, when he should've known better.

She drew him into their bedroom and pointed at the bed. "You. Sit there."

He blinked again, this time at her tone, but he sat. "Yes, ma'am. Whatever you say."

A small, secret smile tilted the corner of Jess's lips and made its way to her eyes. It was sexy as hell and it stirred his blood. *Confused, worried, ticked off,* he reminded himself, but his body didn't seem to listen.

As Alex tried to work this whole fucked-up day out in his head, Jess sat on the floor, reached under their bed, and pulled out a large black plastic storage box with a snap-on lid.

"What's in there?" he asked warily. He didn't remember ever having seen it before, and had no idea there was even anything under their bed.

She leaned her back against the closet door and drew her knees up, facing him. Her eyes were wide and solemn. "My fantasies." With a shuddery sigh, she opened the box.

It was full of books.

Books?

She held one up. "This was the first one." She traced her fingers over the image on the cover, almost caressing it, then turned it toward him.

The cover showed a picture of a bed with neckties around the four bed posts, and a blindfold on the white comforter. Alex could easily imagine what had gone on in that bed, and to his surprise, his cock jerked in response, swelling against the tightness of his jeans. Painfully, but it was a welcome kind of pain. Or would be, if he weren't in the middle of trying to pry his wife's big secret from her.

She sat there, biting her lip, and he couldn't figure out how to make this easier for her.

"Talk to me, babe." When she didn't speak, he swore under

his breath. He came down off the bed, and sat on the floor next to her, nudging her with his shoulder. "Come on, Jess. Spill. No more hiding and no more waiting."

She kept her eyes squeezed shut as she started to talk. "Do you remember that night Ben was camping with his scout troop, and Kara was over at Kenzie's house? We were supposed to go on a date, but you wound up working a double shift."

Hell, yes. "I remember. That was the first night you scared the shit out of me. Nothing I said or did seemed to help. First, you were fine. Better than fine. You were a wild woman in bed, and I loved it. But then you closed up, shut me out. And I couldn't figure out what I'd done wrong. I was awake almost that whole night, trying to work it out. What happened, Jess?"

"*You* didn't do anything wrong. The book happened."

"Still confused here, honey. What does the book have to do with anything?"

She flicked a quick glance at him before looking down at the floor. "I'd never read anything like it before. It was erotic as hell, and it put some really, er, vivid pictures in my head. When you came home, I was so turned on, I practically jumped you."

"And I loved every second of it, like I said. But I still don't understand why it's a problem."

She flushed, and he heard her swallow. "While we were making love, I was imagining myself in some of the scenes from the book."

"Babe, everyone fantasizes. It's human nature. So, you pictured us doing something from the book." He shrugged. Hell, if it helped rev her engines and made her want to make love more often, then he was all for it. "Big deal."

She flushed even darker red. "I wasn't fantasizing about us, exactly." Her words came out low but fast, as if she had to get them out before she lost her nerve. "I was fantasizing about me. Tied to that bed, blindfolded. There were two men, doing all kinds of wicked things to my body, playing with me. Touching me, sucking my nipples. And you were there, too." Her voice cracked but she continued. "You were kneeling on the bed, stroking your penis, watching. Directing them. Telling them what to do to me. Just like the main character in the book had done with his girlfriend." She shuddered, hugged her knees, and put her chin down on them. "I felt like I was cheating on you. There weren't just two of us in bed that night. There were four of us."

Son of a bitch. That explained the whole hesitation thing when Jess hadn't answered when he'd accused her of being unfaithful. Considering her upbringing, he could see how she might consider that a betrayal. Shame slammed into him for his thoughtless words and his lack of trust. He had some serious apologizing to do. But not right now, while she sat here, staring at him through wounded eyes, waiting for him to condemn her for her fantasies.

Condemnation was the last thing on his mind, though. The image of what she described—and the fact that those erotic words were coming out of his usually modest wife's mouth—was enough to give him the hard-on from hell, and his heart rate jumped through the roof. "Honey, I'm so turned on right now, just listening to you talk, I could pound a nail into a cinderblock with my cock. Tell me more."

"Really?" she asked, almost timidly.

"Really." He took her hand and covered his straining erection with it, then leaned closer, and whispered in her ear. "This is what your imagination is doing to me. I've never seen this side of you before, but I like it. Tell me more about these forbidden fantasies of yours."

Jessica checked his face carefully. He didn't look bothered by her confession at all. And from the hard heat below her hand, she *knew* he was aroused. But she still hadn't told him everything.

Fantasies were one thing. Her rational mind knew that. But she'd been very sheltered as a child, and her parents had been almost puritanical. Their extreme modesty had influenced her so much that it had taken her years to get comfortable with her nudity around Alex, and they'd already been married. And forget about sex. Her mother had never given her *the talk,* and the little Jess knew about sex had come from embarrassed questions to her friends. It had taken nearly as long for her to understand that there was more to making love than wham, bam, thank you ma'am in the missionary position. But Alex had always been patient.

It was just as obvious he was trying hard to be patient now. She should have told him. She should have trusted that he'd understand about the fantasies.

But would he understand the rest?

Alex's face was still drawn, and he looked exhausted, stressed out, and upset. Between his long shift the day before, staying up making love with her, and getting up early to coach Ben's baseball team, he was working on not much sleep. She hated that she'd added to any of his stress with her inability to tell him—*the one person on earth she should be able to tell anything*—about what was going on in her screwed-up mind. It wasn't easy to let go of the absolute disbelief she'd felt when he'd walked out on her, but instead of thinking things to death, she took him at his word.

With a deep breath, she pulled out the next book. "This was the second book that got me going." She showed him the picture of a vampire standing behind a woman, with his fangs sunk into her neck. The woman was moaning in ecstasy, her head thrown back and her mouth wide open. The story had been dark, yet provocative and sensual.

She reached back in the box again and prayed she wasn't making another huge mistake. Hesitantly, she pulled out the book Alex had interrupted her reading at the bookstore. The cover left little to the imagination. It was obviously a ménage, although the idea was no more extreme than what she'd already shared with Alex about the first book.

But this book had been different. She'd purposely kept it hidden from him, had bought it when she'd told him she hadn't wanted it. Other than birthday or Christmas gifts—and the huge secret she was only now sharing—she'd never deliberately kept anything hidden from her husband, not like this. She handed him the book and watched his face, biting her lip with some trepidation. "And this was the third."

He looked at the cover and his eyes widened in recognition. The strong muscles of his neck worked as he swallowed, and his jaw cranked tight. "You lied to me."

Four little words. Her stomach clenched, but what was done was done. "Yes."

"For God's sake, why? If you wanted it, why didn't you just buy it then?" There was heat to his words, but it was overshadowed by exasperation and confusion. And anger lit his eyes, but something else was there as well.

Hurt, she realized. Her chest tight with emotion, she sucked in a shuddery breath. "When you saw me with that book, your face went totally blank, and it was obvious you weren't thrilled with me for reading it. So I didn't buy it then. I was right, too, because you were really quiet the rest of the night." She reached out to take the book from him.

He stopped her with a quelling look. "So, instead of telling me you wanted it, you waited until you went to the bookstore alone, and you bought it anyway?"

She shifted uncomfortably. It sounded cold and calculating the way he said it. And it hadn't been like that, not really. "It wasn't deliberate, but…yeah. That's about the size of it."

He blew out a long breath. "I really hate that you lied to me, Jess. And about something so stupid. Something you had the wrong idea about in the first place."

Startled, her eyes flew to his. "What do you mean?"

His voice was hard, a tone she rarely heard from him. "I wasn't angry. Shocked down to my toes, yes, because the book looked unlike anything I'd ever seen you read. And you were so flustered by me seeing you with it I didn't know how to react. But angry? No." He shook his head. "I'm not sure about the quiet part, but I think that's when I was getting sick. It didn't have anything to do with the book."

She'd forgotten about how the next day he'd come down with a nasty bug that had kept him off work for three days. How had she become so caught up in her own insecurities she'd not remembered that? She didn't like what that said about her.

She reached out to touch his arm, but he pulled away, and she cringed. She'd really screwed things up.

Chapter Five

Alex surged to his feet and stomped over to their bed, leaning against it, his feet crossed at the ankles. He knew he looked defensive, but he didn't really care. Two big things, and his wife had lied to him. He was angry again, too, but more than that, he felt like someone had shoved a stake through his heart. "What gets me is that you don't seem to trust me. We've been married fifteen years, and you felt like you had to hide a damn *book* from me? What did you think I'd do? Or say?"

Jess bit her lip again, looking miserable, but he refused to feel too badly about it. Shit, after fifteen years, she should be able to talk to him about anything. He didn't keep secrets from her. He didn't want to, and it wasn't worth the hassle.

"I don't know."

Her voice was soft, small. Confused, even. But he waited, let her think about it, didn't give her an easy out. This was too important to both of them, to their marriage.

"I think I was afraid."

That snapped his spine straight, sent his blood pressure into the stratosphere. "Afraid of *me?*"

She shook her head. "No, more afraid of what you'd think of *me*."

Ah. This he understood, and he let out a long, slow breath and settled back against the bed again. Her parents were incredibly uptight about sex, and they'd passed their extreme inhibitions on to their only child. Jessica had been a virgin on their wedding night. Not that he'd complained about it. His inner caveman had loved that she was his, and only his. He still loved that fact. But it had taken almost a year of marriage before she'd started loosening up. So he understood how her mind worked.

Sort of.

He kept this in mind as he figured out how to ease her worries—but also let her know that he didn't ever want to be lied to again. "They're fantasies, Jessica. Not real. Let me ask you this. Do you think I don't fantasize?"

"I've never really thought about it," she said, shrugging one shoulder.

"I'm telling you right now, I do." His grin was half real, half forced. "Maybe I don't add other people into the equation, but I fantasize. While we're making love. While I watch you sleep. While you're making dinner and you don't know I'm watching you. Sometimes even when I'm stuck in court, waiting for my turn on a case."

Her eyes widened, and he shook his head, snorted.

"I'm a guy, babe. And maybe if you'd said something to me about those fantasies of yours, you'd have known about mine before now. Before things got so screwed up." He tossed the barb out, but felt small and petty when she flinched.

He stepped over to where she still sat against the closet door, and reached out his hand. She put her hand in his, and he pulled her up so they were standing toe to toe. He used his other hand to cup her jaw, one thumb stroking her soft cheek.

She leaned into his touch as fat tears cascaded down her cheeks. "I really do love you, Alex."

He pulled her into a tight embrace, resting his chin on her head. "I love you, too, Jess. You don't need to keep things like that from me. And no more lies. Please."

Jess lay in bed with Alex curled around her, wearing nothing but his tight embrace. His words from last night echoed in her head over and over again, as if they were on a loop tape. *No more lies. No more lies. No more lies.*

Was not disclosing *everything* considered a lie?

Oh, yeah. Alex would definitely feel that way. Especially after yesterday's blowup and last night's talk. And doubly so after last night's lovemaking. It had been sweet, and sexy, and emotionally intense. She hadn't felt this close to him in months, and she didn't want to break their fragile, renewed bond of trust. So she was going to come clean with him, the rest of the way. He deserved it.

And so did she.

She'd been awake for nearly an hour, but she hadn't wanted to move. She loved resting in the cocoon of Alex's arms, safe and protected. As she lay there, listening to him breathe, feeling his heart beat in time with hers, she had plenty of time to think. And the more she thought about it, the more she realized she was cheating both of them.

He hadn't had any real problem with her fantasies, or her choice of reading material, except that she'd kept him in the dark about both. So, she figured, he might be open to her desire to try out some of her fantasies.

And maybe even some of his.

Alex stirred behind her, wrapping his arms around her, tugging her closer. The silken steel of his morning erection slid between her legs, nudging the entrance to her body. She was already slick with desire, wet and swollen and wanting. She'd been tucked up against Alex's warm, hard, naked body for the past hour. Imagining talking with him about her fantasies and asking him to make some of them come true had made her hungry for him.

Still asleep, Alex shifted, drawing her closer yet, and as he cupped her breast with his large calloused hand, he thrust his hips forward, sliding deep into her waiting body.

Jess shivered, clenching around him. Making love in the morning, when Alex slid into her from behind before she was even awake, was something she loved. She loved this even more. The knowledge that he was seeking her out, while *he* still slept, was an aphrodisiac that ramped up her desire.

A delicious tension spread through her body as he tightened his grip on her breast and continued to thrust, slowly, his pace so leisurely it was driving her mad. She couldn't hold back her moan of frustrated pleasure. It felt so *good,* hanging on the edge so close to orgasm she could taste it. For the first time in a very long time, she felt free of the guilt that had been weighing her down, casting a shadow over their lovemaking.

She closed her eyes and let the images in her mind loose. The fingers tugging at her breast became a nipple clamp, and the leg draped over her legs became ropes binding her to the bed, partly on her stomach and partly on her side. Her breath came in short pants as she clutched the sheets with hands she refused to lift off the bed, almost as if Alex had ordered her not to move.

The sound of his wife's plaintive cries and the feel of the tight fist of her pussy squeezing his cock woke Alex from the intense dream he'd been having. His voice was sleep-drugged, but his body was wide awake.

"God, you feel good," he growled, using his thumb and forefinger to tease her nipple, to twist it as he stroked in and out of her body, pumping his hips harder and faster. Suddenly, he realized Jess was practically pinned beneath him, and he started to move so he wouldn't crush her.

"No, don't." She grabbed his leg and held it tightly to her body. "Like this. Please."

The begging tone of her voice ripped something free inside him. He was already on the edge of coming, but he didn't want to leave her behind. He thought back to the dream that had gotten him hard, a dream based on the cover of that vampire book Jess had shown him. He'd been the vampire, she'd been the seduced innocent, and she'd loved it when he feasted on her neck. He gritted his teeth, holding back the impending explosion while Jess caught up with him. He wasn't gentle with her, but something told him she didn't want gentle right now. Each pinch of her nipples brought a moan, each time he drove into her heat and pushed her deeper into the mattress, she gasped. Soon, she was on the edge, right there with him.

He slid his hand over her hip and delved into her curls, finding that sweet spot, stroking her clit with her own slick fluids, and she started to come on a keening wail. Without thinking too much about it, he bit down on the sensitive skin in the curve between her neck and her shoulder. It sent her over the edge.

"Oh, God, Alex!" She came almost violently, her internal muscles milking him until he couldn't hold himself back anymore.

He thrust harder, nearly mindless with the need to come, grunting as he finally found his own release. His body shook with the force of his orgasm, his breathing ragged. He lay half on top of her, his chest pressed against her back, trembling, holding her now sated body close to his. Her body still gripped his cock, small spasms that drew out the pleasure for both of them.

"Mmm," she said softly a few minutes later, turning onto her back, breaking their intimate connection. She snuggled closer, resting her head on his arm. "Good morning."

Her face was still flushed with the aftereffects of their shared orgasm, her eyes a bit unfocused. He draped one arm across her stomach, absently cupping her breast, rubbing his thumb over a still-hard nipple.

"Good morning to you, too, love." He leaned down and captured her lips with his. This was so much better than it had been just a few days ago. The sex had been great, but, as unmanly as it sounded, he'd missed the closeness of *after*.

She kissed him back softly at first, then hungrily, and before he even knew what was happening, he was flat on his back, and she was straddling him. Gloriously naked, looking like a wild and wanton woman, she reached up and pulled her hair out of the ponytail she usually slept in. She shook it loose, arching her back so her generous breasts thrust forward.

His hands drifted up from his sides to touch her, but Jess shook her head. She grabbed them, pushed them over his head, her breasts just inches from his mouth. He strained to catch one with his mouth, but again she shook her head. "No touching unless I say so. Put your hands behind your head and leave them there until I tell you you can move."

His heart kicked up a notch. *This* was a side of his wife he'd never seen. He didn't know what game she was playing, but man, his body liked it. Liked it a lot. "You're in charge."

"Yes, I am." Her eyes danced with sensual delight. "You do only what I tell you to do."

His cock jumped at her order, and he swallowed hard. "Yes, ma'am." The words came out huskier than he'd expected. He reached out, grabbed a pillow, and shoved it behind him, then laced his fingers behind his head.

That secret smile lit her face, that same smile he'd seen a flash of last night when she was showing him the books she'd hidden. She leaned over, nibbling the side of his jaw, running her fingers through his chest hair. He squirmed when she moved her mouth lower, running her tongue over each of his nipples. Then she bit one, hard enough to sting, and he nearly came off the bed. His cock surged to life.

"Oh, God." He panted as she used one hand to hold him down on the bed. He could move if he really wanted to break free, but damn, he wanted to see where she was going with this. They'd just finished making love, and he was ready to go again. Right now. "Do that again."

"Maybe later." She climbed off him, but grasped his cock in her hand. "I've got other plans for you now."

God, he hoped so.

"Open your legs." His heart pounded triple time at the demand in her voice. She wasn't moving her hand, just holding him, as if she were leashing a beast and calling it to heel. "And bend your knees."

He shifted on the bed, his blood pumping as he did what Jess requested. He was more than willing to play along, even though it made him feel oddly vulnerable.

She knelt in between his legs, never letting go of his cock, staring directly into his eyes. "I'm wet. And I want you again. But first, I'm going to do what I've been dying to do all night." She licked her lips, staring at his cock, and started to lower her head.

He blinked. He'd been inside her several times over the night, and he wasn't exactly clean. "Babe, I'd love for you to do that, but let me wash up first."

She shook her head. "No way," she murmured. "I want to taste you. I want to taste you and me together."

Shit, that was hot. His breath strangled in his chest as she swirled her tongue around the tip of his cock, then sucked it into her hot, moist mouth. Her hand slipped down until she was circling just the base of his cock with two fingers. With her other hand, she cupped his balls. Her ring finger slid back and forth toward the crease of his ass, occasionally rubbing across his tight rear entrance.

Without thinking about it, he moved a hand to tangle his fingers in her hair. "Christ, that feels so good."

Immediately she stopped, sitting back on her heels, settling her hands on her thighs.

"No, don't stop," he growled deep in his chest.

"Then put your hand back under your head."

Damn it, he didn't want to. He wanted to touch her. He did it, because he'd told her he'd leave them there, but it wasn't easy.

"You need to understand who's in charge here. Now, what's the rule?" She stroked his cock lightly, flicking the slit with her fingernail, then licked the head.

"I do only what you tell me to do." Sweat popped out across his brow as he forced the words out, and his muscles trembled with the effort of keeping his arms up and his hands under his head. He dug his heels into the bed, struggling to keep his legs open and his knees up.

She nodded and gripped his balls tightly, almost to the

point of pain, but not quite. The look on her face was part his sweet Jessica, and part sultry dominatrix. "And you come only when I tell you to come."

Jesus. He was going to come right now, all over her hand. But he forced it back, swallowing convulsively. "Yes, ma'am."

"I'm so glad we have that settled," she murmured, dipping her head once again.

So was he. Good God, her mouth was a lethal weapon. And when she sucked his balls into her mouth, swirling them around on her tongue, he came unglued. "Please, Jessica, have mercy. I'm going to come."

"No, not yet," she said almost absently. "I'm not done playing. But soon. Let me help you with that." She reached over to the nightstand and picked up the small elastic band she'd used for putting her hair in a ponytail.

No. She couldn't be doing what he thought she was. Could she? She was. Dear God, she slid it onto his erection as if she was putting on a rubber, and then she rolled it all the way to the base of his cock. It was fairly loose, until she slipped a pinkie under it, and twisted it once.

His back arched off the bed, and he gritted his teeth. His body stayed on the razor's edge of climax but he didn't go over.

"Jesus, Jess." He moaned as she took his cock in her mouth again and sucked hard, deep, swallowing him. The back of her throat worked against the head, over and over again as she swallowed, her tongue lashing against his length. The pain of arousal was almost unbearable, and he thought he might die from the burning need to come.

But what a way to go.

He let out a disbelieving groan as Jess sat back again on her heels, her finger still twisted in the elastic band. His cock was glistening wet, and about as engorged as he'd ever seen it. A steady stream of fluid leaked from the slit, but there was no relief. He didn't think he'd ever been this turned on before, and didn't think he could string two sentences together if he had to.

"Would you like me to let you come now?" she asked softly, cupping his balls again.

"Oh, God, yes. Please. I'm begging."

"Begging is good," she breathed, gasping as she slipped her hand between her legs, dipping her fingers inside her pussy. God, he wanted to be there, where she was touching. He wanted his cock there, or his mouth. But she shook her head again when he rolled his hips toward her. "No."

When she removed her fingers, they were covered in her slick fluids, dripping with her desire. She held them up so he could see, and he swallowed hard. "Let me taste."

"No. I want you to close your eyes. No looking, no touching, or I stop what I'm doing."

His eyes drifted shut without his permission. She'd commanded it, he'd done it.

She rubbed her wet hand up and down his cock, and all over his balls, pressing against the tight hole of his ass with a wet finger. Then her hand disappeared, and when it came back, it was even wetter. She circled the hole, stroking lightly over it. The feelings were incredibly hot, wildly arousing, but not something he was used to.

"What are you—?" he asked, but she cut him off before he could blurt out his panic.

"Shh. Don't think. Just feel." She pushed harder, and his body started to open to her questing finger. As she probed gently with her finger, she took his cock back into her mouth.

He was coming apart at the seams, and she must have

known it. "When I count to three, I want you to come for me, Alex. One." She buried her finger deep in his ass, plunging it in and out as if she was fucking him there. "Two." She loosened her grip on the elastic band and eased the constriction. "Three," she finished, sucking him so hard he slid deep into her throat.

He came with a roar, shouting out his release. His hands came down, and he grabbed her hair tightly, pumping his hips, plunging into her mouth. Over and over and over again, until he was finished coming.

Or thought he was. He fell back against the pillow and forced his eyes open. There was a wild look on Jess's face as she pumped her fingers in and out of her pussy, across her clit, rubbing furiously. Moving faster than he thought he could, he flipped her onto her back, and drove into her, his cock still hard and throbbing from his release. He grabbed her hands, pulled them over her head and held them in one of his.

He stroked in and out, furiously, madly, wanting her to come as hard as he had.

She did, with a loud shout that echoed in their bedroom. She wrapped her legs around his hips and held on, holding them locked together. As she contracted around his cock, he came again, once more, draining him dry.

He knew he was too heavy, but damned if he could move. He lay on top of her, buried deep inside her, boneless and exhausted. "Where the *hell* did you learn that trick with the hair band?" Still breathing hard from the force of the best orgasm he'd ever had, he rolled onto his back, pulling her with him so she was lying on top of him.

"Where do you think?" Her voice was both shaky and seductive at the same time. She kissed him tenderly, then lay her head on his chest. "I read it in a book."

Chapter Six

The rest of the morning was surreal, and Jessica felt as though she'd fallen into an alternate universe. They lounged in bed for about another twenty minutes, then went downstairs to make breakfast. She wore nothing but a robe, and Alex wore his birthday suit. She whipped up some eggs, microwaved some bacon, and had just popped the toast in the toaster when Alex backed her up against the counter, shoved the robe wide open and dropped to his knees in front of her. By the time he was done pleasuring her with his mouth and his hands, she was as limp as spaghetti.

And breakfast was cold.

They warmed everything back up in the microwave, took their plates back to their room, and had a naked picnic on their bed.

"Will you show me the rest of the books?" Alex asked, out of the blue.

Jessica was finishing up the last of her toast and nearly choked on the piece in her mouth. "What?"

"The books you have hidden in that box. I want to know

what turned you on about them." He cocked his head and gave her a measured look. "Are there things in them you'd like to try?"

Gulp. Plenty of them. Maybe sharing those with Alex would be easier now since he'd asked the question. Which meant he was interested in trying new things, too. Right?

She hoped that was the case, but first, she wanted to be certain he knew what he was asking. "Are you sure you want to know? Yesterday morning, while you were all at baseball practice, I decided I'd rather have our sex life, and our marriage, just the way it is, and not take the chance of messing things up by making you uncomfortable. Or unhappy."

"I'm sure." He took her plate and put it on the nightstand with his, then clasped her hand, lacing his fingers through hers. "Honey, I love you. The thing that makes me unhappy is you hiding things from me. As for uncomfortable, I won't know until you tell me what you want. Like this morning, when you took control. That's something you wanted to try, wasn't it?"

Thank God, he'd started with a relatively easy one, although she felt a blush warm her face. "Yes. I really wanted you tied to the bed but this was good, too."

"*Damn,* babe. Did you think I wouldn't like being at your mercy? Sweetheart, that was, bar none, the best orgasm I've ever had." Spots of color rose in his cheeks, making them a matched set. "Never in a million years did I think a finger up my ass would make me come, but between that and you swallowing my cock, it felt damn good. I'm not so sure about being tied up, but I'm willing to give it a try. Especially if it means another five-star orgasm."

He blew out a long breath, then laughed self-consciously, waving a hand in the general direction of his semi-erect penis.

"Jesus, I'm already getting turned on. Again. I'm thirty-six years old, and I've been hard more times in one day than I was as a teenager. And you're afraid to share this kind of stuff with me." He smiled wryly. "Hell, no. Bring it on." He lifted her hand and placed a lingering kiss on her palm. "What else have you been imagining?"

The fire in his eyes seared her, and his voice, raw with need, gave her the courage to continue. Rather than answering, she climbed onto her knees and straddled him, rubbing her mound against his erection, wetting him with her arousal. She leaned forward and kissed him, openmouthed, loving the taste of him. He kissed her back, tangling his tongue with hers. But when he grabbed her hips and held her down against his body, she twisted out of his grasp and climbed off his lap.

"Hey," he complained. "Where are you going?"

She grinned over her shoulder at him. "I just needed to get to this side of the bed. To the books."

"Tease." He gave her a mock scowl but the light in his eyes gave him away. "I ought to punish you for that."

"Promise?" She kept a close eye on his reaction as she forced herself to respond. This was one of the more extreme—and therefore harder—things to share with him. "That's something I want you to do to me. I want you to tie me up, and I want you to spank me."

The look on his face was priceless, and she seemed to have rendered him speechless.

"Alex?" She turned back to face him fully. "Aren't you going to say anything?"

It took as long for him to answer as it did for him to move to the edge of the bed and plant his feet solidly on the floor, less than a foot away from her. "Once my heart starts beating again, yeah." He scrubbed a hand over his jaw, frowned. "I don't know if I can hit you, sweetheart. Are you sure?"

His concern seemed to be about her welfare, not about how kinky the request was, and that was a relief. "Sure I want to try it? Yes. Sure I'll like it and want to do it again? No." She shrugged. "It's not like I want to be whipped with a belt. I'm talking about using your hand, or a soft flogger. It's not abuse, Alex. It's foreplay."

"I know I keep saying this, but *damn*." He shook his head, looking a little dazed. "Is this something you fantasized about?"

"Yeah." She dropped to her knees, pulled the box out from under the bed and found the book she'd bought online. The cover was wild, with a woman on her knees, her hands bound behind her back. The man behind her was holding a leather flogger. The woman's ass was pink, as if it had just been kissed by the flogger's tails.

She handed it to him, staying on her knees in front of him. Striking a submissive pose, she clasped her hands behind her back, spread her knees, lowered her gaze—although she could still see Alex's face—and waited. Just like the woman on the cover. He'd understand the significance of it, if he looked at the book.

He read the back cover, then flipped it over, staring at the photograph. Then he looked at her, his eyes wide. "Babe," he said softly.

She lifted her eyes to his. "I want to submit to you. In the bedroom only, and maybe only once, but I want to try. I want you to do whatever you want to me. Whatever you think will make my pleasure greater, whatever you think I can handle. I want to put myself completely in your hands. That's what this book is all about. He's a dominant, looking for a new submissive. She's never tried it before, but she's wondered and fantasized and hoped to find someone open enough to help her find out if that's what she wants. It's all mutual. He takes his pleasure from hers. He doesn't want to hurt her, except in ways that will increase her pleasure. Like flogging, or tying her up. He wants her mindless with need, but he wants to make her beg to be allowed to come."

Alex gaped at her. "Like you did with me this morning. You wanted to play the dominant, and now you want to try the submissive role?"

Jessica nodded, but then frowned. "And don't ask me—I don't know why I want it. Part of me thinks it's sick and twisted."

He started to interrupt, but she cut him off.

"The other part of me says screw it. I don't know why it turns me on, why I want it, but I don't care. The fantasies of submission are driving me mad." She laughed self-consciously. "I'm so drenched right now, I'm going to leave a puddle on the floor."

Yeah, join the club, Alex thought. Jesus Christ. Who was this wild woman on the floor—on her fucking knees in front of him—and what had she done with his reserved, sweet wife? He could barely wrap his head around it. The mere *thought* of dominating Jess in the bedroom—tying her up, making her beg, hell, even spanking her sexy ass—made him want to get started. Right now.

Truth be told, their sex life had become more routine, less spontaneous in these past few years. He hadn't thought about it, hadn't realized he needed more until she'd started with the insatiable routine three months ago.

He cleared his throat, willed his cock to behave until they got through with this whole un-fucking-believable conversation. "What else is in that box?" he asked thickly, putting the book she'd handed him under his pillow. Tonight, he was reading. Cover to cover research.

Still on her knees, she pulled another one out and handed it to him. It was the damn book she'd hidden from him. He examined the cover, taking in every nuance of the photograph, and then flipped it over. He skimmed the back, then opened to a random page. Or maybe not quite random, he thought, noticing the book opened easily to this page. He cast a glance at Jess, who looked a little embarrassed.

"Your favorite scene, maybe?" he murmured. "Let's see what happens here."

He read the page slowly, his mouth drying up faster than the desert in summer. It was a threesome. One man was fucking the woman in her pussy, and the other had his cock up her ass. The words painted a picture so vivid, he felt like he was right there, watching it live. But he could understand why Jess felt guilty fantasizing about it. For a woman who'd been raised in such a puritanical house, this was inconceivable.

He'd always been more open about sex, and he was willing to try almost anything, but the idea of a threesome left him cold. No way was anyone but him touching his Jessica. No. Fucking. Way.

He must have made some kind of negative sound, because when he looked up from the book, Jess's eyes were glued to the floor, and her body was rigid. He swore. "Jessica, look at me."

She looked up, her eyes panicked. "I never should've let you see that."

"Why?" he asked bluntly.

"Because you're disgusted by it."

He shook his head. "No, I'm not. Quit assuming you know how I feel. But I want an honest answer from you. Do you *want* to have a threesome? No lies, Jess. Is this one of those fantasies you want to try?"

He waited, not sure what would come out of his wife's mouth. And not sure what he would do if she said yes. That was one boundary he didn't think he could cross.

"No," she said vehemently. "I don't want any other man but you."

He let out breath he didn't know he'd been holding, relieved. "Thank God. Call me a caveman, but I'd want to kill any other man who touched you. I don't even like it when they look at you." He held out his hand and, when she took it, he tugged her to her feet. He anchored his heels on the bed frame and pulled her between his knees, settling his hands on her hips. His cock bobbed, bumping against Jess's stomach, leaving a sticky, wet trail of his arousal against her skin. It was sexy as hell, and he wanted inside her. "But was I turned off by it? No. It's incredibly arousing to read. I guess there are couples who could really pull that off, but I don't think we're one of them. You're *mine,* and I don't like to share."

She shuddered, from both relief and the possessive tone of Alex's voice. Once again, she should've trusted him.

"How would you feel about making it reality, without anyone else involved?" She rubbed her belly against his erection. Talking about this, thinking about it, aroused her as much as reading about it. "How do you feel about, er…" she cleared her throat, forced the word out, "…toys?"

His eyes lit up and a quick, startled grin landed on his face. "What kind of toys do you have in mind? And what do you want to do with them?"

The minute the words came out of his mouth, though, she saw the light bulb flash over his head.

"Babe. You want to…" Looking dazed, he paused, started

again. "You want me to…" He cleared his throat. "Jesus, Jess. You're really trying to kill me today, aren't you?"

She felt the blush work its way from the tip of her toes to the top of her head. Of all the things she wanted to try, this was the hardest to ask for. Even harder than the submissive thing, or the flogger. If anything was going to turn the tide for him from arousal to revulsion, she thought, this one thing was it. "Is that gross?"

Before he could answer—an answer she desperately needed—a voice called out from downstairs. "Jess? Alex? Are you home?"

Jessica yelped and stared at Alex in horror. "Your mother!"

He grimaced, ran a hand through his hair and reached for a pair of sweatpants and a T-shirt. "I'll see what she needs." He dragged the clothes on and started for the door, hesitating briefly. "We'll get back to our talk later." The look he gave her before he left the room was indecipherable.

Still naked, she sank onto their bed, her arms wrapped around her stomach. It ached, maybe almost as much as her heart. Alex's face had gone straight from shocked at her words to disbelief at his mother's untimely appearance, without any clue as to what he was really feeling. So of course, here she was again, being an idiot and thinking the worst. She covered her face with her hands and sucked in a deep breath. "Backbone," she muttered, squaring her shoulders as she stood. "Grow one."

Disgusted with herself, she threw on some yoga pants and a cami, then started downstairs to see what was going on.

In the family room her mother-in-law sat next to a sad-looking Ben, whose face was pale except for two bright red, feverish spots of color. His eyes were glassy, and tears streaked his cheeks. Alex was just coming in from the kitchen, holding a wet washcloth and what they all referred to as the throw-up bucket.

"Oh, Ben, what happened?" Jess crouched in front of her son, pushed his hair back and felt his forehead. "Not feeling so well?"

He shook his head. "I threw up all over the camper," he whispered. "I tried not to."

"Don't worry about it, kiddo. I did worse in their house when I was your age," Alex said with a small grin. "Grandma is used to cleaning up boy messes."

Jess stood and gave Alex's mom a quick hug. "Where's Kara?"

"Still with Robert up at Cunningham Falls. They're fishing. We'll take her to school tomorrow," Adele Meyers said. "That way you can focus on Ben, especially if he's up all night."

"Thanks," she said with feeling. Kara loved to fish with her grandfather, and Adele was right. Like Alex, Ben was a really cranky patient. She took the bucket from Alex. "Come on, honey. Let's get you upstairs to bed."

As they went upstairs, Adele's concerned words drifted up after her. "I'm sorry we had to interrupt your time alone, but Ben will be more comfortable in his own bed." She paused. "Things seemed a little off between you and Jessica yesterday. Is everything okay, honey?" she asked, the worry obvious in her voice.

Jess hesitated on the stairs, her body tense.

Alex sighed, and she pictured him tugging his fingers through his hair, as he always did when he was frustrated. "Yeah," he said finally.

She didn't hear the rest of his answer, because Ben started making panicked noises like he was about to vomit again. She hurried him into the bathroom and then, when he was done, helped him into his pajamas and into bed.

A little while later, Alex came in and checked on Ben, who was dozing fitfully.

"Your mom gone?" she asked softly from her spot on the end of the bed, trying not to wake Ben. And, surreptitiously, trying to gauge her husband's mood.

"She just left," he murmured, his face neutral. "We talked for a while."

"Oh." What else was there to say?

"She took a change of clothes for Kara, and her book bag for school tomorrow. I'm going to grab a shower. Then I'll trade places with you so you can get one, too." He hesitated, so slightly she might have missed it if she hadn't been watching him, then leaned over and kissed her forehead. "Okay?"

"Thanks." She dropped her chin to her knees. The closeness they'd shared earlier this morning was gone, and things felt nearly as stilted as they had before their blowup. Her eyes burned, and she forced the tears away with nothing but sheer willpower. Was it just the fact they'd been interrupted? Or was it more than that?

She didn't get much chance to think, because moments later, Ben woke up and got sick, completely missing the bucket. With an ease born of years of practice, she helped him to the bathroom, then changed his sheets and got him settled back in bed. Exhausted, he drifted back to sleep almost immediately.

She left his bedroom door open and carried the sodden, stinky mess downstairs to the laundry room. The phone rang once, but it stopped before she could get it. Shrugging, she tossed the pile into the wash and headed back upstairs.

Alex stood in Ben's doorway, watching his son sleep. He turned his head as she came up the steps. "What happened?"

"Missed the bucket."

Alex winced. "Sorry. You ready to grab your shower?" he asked as they walked to their bedroom, where she realized Alex wasn't in his usual weekend attire of jeans and sneakers. He had on a button-down shirt and khakis, and held a tie in his hand. Work clothes.

She frowned and leaned against the door as he picked up his badge and unlocked his gun from the cabinet in their closet. "I thought you didn't have to go in until six."

"The whole squad just got called in." His brow creased with barely suppressed fury. "Details are sketchy, but there was a multiple homicide that includes children. There's some question of whether it's murder–suicide, or if the killer is still out there somewhere."

Jess's heart clenched, as it always did when he caught cases like this. The ones with kids were the hardest on him. "Go. We're fine here." She took his tie and looped it around his neck, tucking it under the collar of his shirt. When it was tight enough, she used it to tug him toward her as if it were a leash. She pressed a soft kiss to his lips, then rested her forehead against his. "Be careful. I love you, Alex. Always and forever."

He cupped the back of her head and deepened the kiss until her knees went weak, then broke away with a jerk and a sharp indrawn breath. "I love you, too, Jess. No matter what, don't ever doubt that. Call me if Ben gets worse." His voice was low, sexy, but she could tell he was already thinking ahead to the case.

With one last glance over his shoulder, he was gone.

Chapter Seven

Alex stepped into his bedroom as quietly as possible, trying not to wake Jessica. He locked his weapon away and stripped down to his boxer-briefs. His wife lay curled up in their bed on her side, one rosy-tipped breast peeking out from the edge of her nightgown. His body stirred, and he wished he had the energy to wake her and make love, but damn, he was bone tired. And he felt like a shit of a husband and father anyway.

Kara had caught Ben's stomach bug, so it had been a long week for Jess, too. She'd had to handle the kids herself. Even if they'd wanted to continue their mind-blowing conversation from last Sunday, there hadn't been a moment alone they could. All week he'd seen the wounded, worried look in Jess's eyes when she didn't think he was watching, but after dealing with two dead kids under the age of ten, the last thing on his mind had been talking about their sex life.

But finally, with long hours and some pretty damned fine police work from their squad, they'd captured the son of a bitch who'd done the deed. Now he could put those children and their mother to rest, and focus on his own family.

His kids were healthy again, he had four days off, and tomorrow, he and his wife were going on a grownup sleepover. He couldn't wait to tell her about it. He all but fell into bed, pulling Jessica into his arms. She never moved, and minutes later, he was out cold.

"A date?" Jess stared at Alex, who looked like he was holding a secret and was dying to tell about it. After the week they'd had, one where she'd been second—and third, and fourth—guessing herself, it was kind of hard to wrap her head around his words. "A real, honest-to-goodness date? Where?"

He shook his head as he practically bounced in his chair at the table. "Nope. Not telling. It's a surprise."

"But the kids…"

"Are both feeling better, but just in case, Mom and Dad are coming over here to spend the night." He got a serious look on his face, but the amusement in his eyes didn't fade. "All you need to do is pack."

She blinked. "I don't understand. Pack what? Why?"

"Okay, I'll tell you this much. We're staying at a bed and breakfast in Lovettsville. You'll need clothes for tomorrow."

"Just you and me?" A smile escaped. "Really?"

He came around the table and backed her up against the kitchen counter. "Really," he murmured, whispering in her ear. "Just us. You game?"

Her heart sped up as he pressed his hard body against hers and nipped at her neck. "Oh, yeah," she said, but it came out as a sigh.

Alex just laughed.

"Welcome, Mr. and Mrs. Meyers." The inn's owner, an attractive man Jess guessed was in his late forties, handed Alex an old-fashioned key. "This is for your room. I'll take your bags up, if you'd like."

"Thank you. Have you made the arrangements I asked about when I made the reservation?" Alex asked.

Jess slid a look at Alex. *Arrangements?*

The man nodded and smiled broadly. "Yes, sir. I hope everything is to your satisfaction."

"I'm sure it will be." Alex pocketed the key and handed over their bags. "Come on, sweetheart. I'm starving."

She wanted to know more about the mysterious arrangements, but her stomach rumbled, and they laughed. "I guess I am, too."

Dinner was at a quaint Italian restaurant connected to the bed and breakfast by a vine-covered pergola over a brick walkway. Inside, it smelled heavenly, the aromas of fresh bread, tomatoes and basil wafting through the air. The lighting was soft and muted, the tables intimate. Jessica fell in love with it even before tasting the food.

"This way, *signore e signora*." They were led to a table in a dim, quiet corner near the stone fireplace, by an older gentleman who bowed after he placed their napkins in their laps. "Enjoy your meal."

After a waiter brought over a basket of bread and a plate of olive oil, Alex slid his chair closer to hers and looped an arm around her shoulders. He dipped a piece of bread in the oil and brought it to her lips. "Open," he said, his voice husky.

Her eyes widened at the roughly uttered command, but she opened her mouth and took a bite. And proceeded to moan at the taste of warm bread and rich, tangy oil. "Oh, that's good."

"Let me taste." Instead of picking up a slice of bread for himself, Alex leaned forward and kissed her. "Delicious." He smiled and sat back in his chair, picking up his menu.

It took Jess a minute to recover from that innocent yet devastating kiss. Her pulse fluttered wildly, and every coherent thought but one flew out of her head. She wanted her husband, and she wanted him now. But, she thought wryly as her stomach rumbled again, she needed food first.

Every bite of the dinner tasted as good as the one before it. They lingered over their meal, talking about everything under the sun—everything except Alex's job and last weekend's emotional rollercoaster. When she said she couldn't eat another bite, Alex put down his fork and held out his hand.

"Dance with me."

Once again, he wasn't asking, but she wasn't arguing. It wasn't often Alex liked to dance, and she wasn't passing up this opportunity. Several couples were dancing to romantic Italian music, but there was plenty of room left for the two of them. She took his hand and let him pull her close.

"You smell good." She tucked her head close to his. "And you look sexy as sin in this suit."

His laugh rumbled in his chest. "That's what I was going to say. Well, except the part about the suit. Where the hell did you get that dress? I'm not even sure it's legal."

He danced her to a dark corner, then slid his hands over her ass, playing with the hem of the short silky black dress. Jessica shivered as the material slid against her skin. The heat from his hands made her inch closer to him, practically begging him to touch. Her fantasies took over, making her wish he'd slip his hand underneath the edge of her dress. She wanted him to find her surprise.

Which he did. "Jesus, Jess. Are those garters?"

"Mmm-hmm. You like?" she murmured, nuzzling his neck.

"I love." Fiddling with the edge of her thigh-high stockings, his hands dipped lower, and he stopped dead as his fingers came into contact with her core, barely covered by a lacy pair of crotchless panties.

He pulled his head back to look her in the face, and this put his groin flush up against her. There was not a shred of doubt in her mind that he was heavily aroused. But he was also stunned, if the comical look on his face was anything to go by.

"Someone's been shopping."

"Yup."

Alex laughed then, wicked and low. "God, I love you." He pulled her close, and they danced together for several songs, moving around the small wooden floor until they were back near their table.

Alex held her chair out for her. "Ready for dessert?"

"Not sure I can eat another bite, but I'll have some coffee."

After the waiter brought his chocolate mousse and her coffee, they sat close together, watching the dancing and listening to the music. Alex seemed content, calmer, and happier than she'd seen him in a long time. She relaxed against him, and he held her tightly, an indulgent smile on his face as they watched a couple in their eighties dancing close together.

A movement at the table across from them caught her attention, and she turned her head. She blinked twice to clear her vision, but the scene stayed the same. The table was isolated, tucked into an alcove where the occupants wouldn't be disturbed, and lit only by candlelight. She watched for a few minutes, her heart speeding up and her breath beginning to hitch.

"Oh," she sighed, but it was enough to catch Alex's notice.

He bent his head toward her. "You okay, babe?"

"Look," she said softly, inclining her head just slightly.

Alex's eyes followed her direction, and she felt him jerk in surprise. "Christ."

She'd never been a voyeur to anyone's sexual encounter

before, and she was shocked at how arousing it was. It wasn't just any encounter, though. It seemed brought to life by her fantasies. Most of it was out of her view, hidden by the long white tablecloth that covered the round table, but there wasn't a damn thing wrong with her imagination. Or her eyesight, even in the dim candlelight.

There were three occupants of the table, two men and a woman. She sat between them, and each of them had his mouth on her in some way. The man on her left was kissing her mouth, and the one on the right had his lips at her bare shoulder.

A flood of moisture pooled between Jess's thighs when the men pulled back, switching tasks. Now the man on her right was kissing her mouth, and the man on the left was— *Oh, my.* He slid the thin strap of her dress low, baring the top of one creamy breast.

"Jesus." Alex shifted in his chair. "I don't know if we should keep watching or if I should arrest them." But instead of turning his gaze away, he slipped the fingers of one hand off her shoulder onto her back, and then inside the straps of her dress, letting his fingers graze the side of her breast.

Damn, that felt good. When she didn't stop him, he moved his hand again and ran his fingers over her already-aroused nipple. Jess nearly choked. With the way they were seated, no one could see what Alex was doing. No one, except for the table they were watching.

The men at the other table lifted their heads and Alex hesitated, his fingers squeezing Jess's breast reflexively. The guy on the left raised his wineglass as if in toast. The guy on the right whispered in the woman's ear, and her eyes widened in panic as she looked over at their table.

Alex was torn. Part of him wanted to intervene on her behalf, but he didn't. Instead, in a move he'd never have imagined himself making, he raised his wineglass back.

One guy slid his hand around the woman's shoulders from behind, slipping his fingers under the wide band of silver she wore around her neck, holding her possessively. The other played with the charm that dangled from the necklace and nestled against her throat. The woman's eyes fluttered shut, a bright pink suffusing her cheeks. Like his wife, Alex was sucked in by the exhibitionism in front of him. He wished like hell he knew what the one guy had said to put that dazed look on the woman's face. One thing was obvious, though. She was a more-than-willing participant. He'd stake his badge on it.

Alex glanced at Jessica, whose color was nearly as high as the woman across from them. Her breathing was ragged, and her eyes stayed glued to the scene she was witnessing. He slid a finger across her nipple, and she gasped. Damn, but he wished he could bury himself inside her, right here, right now. But there was a limit to what he'd do in public, and he was already standing right at that line. Maybe even over it.

"I wish I knew what they were doing," Jess whispered, finally turning her head to look at Alex. "Is that wrong?" Worry shaded her eyes, and Alex moved to reassure her.

"So do I," he admitted softly, stroking her nipple again. He leaned his head close and murmured in her ear. "But I can imagine, and I'll bet you can, too. Put your hand on my cock, Jess."

She pulled back, and her wide eyes flew to his. "What?"

"Do you see her hands? I don't. I bet she has her hands on their dicks right now. No one can see behind that tablecloth. No one can see behind ours. Give me your hand, Jess." He made it an order, loving the thrill that came from telling her what to do.

She did, slowly, and when he took her hand and pressed it against his aching erection, her breath caught. So did his, when she closed her fingers over his length. Through his trousers, sure, because the last thing he wanted to be was a cop caught with his pants down—*literally*—in public. But it still felt damn good. He didn't think it could get any better, but then Jess opened her mouth.

Her voice was soft, her breath whispering against his ear as they both continued to watch the threesome. "Maybe you don't see her hands because they're bound in her lap, or behind her back. Maybe that silver necklace is a collar, and she's their submissive."

Alex heard the wistfulness in Jess's voice, and decided he'd made the right choice for this weekend. He slid his hand from her breast and set it on her thigh. He couldn't believe he was doing this in public, but he had to touch her again. Making sure she was covered by the tablecloth, he inched his hand back under the bottom of her dress, fingering the lacy garters and the edge of those fuck-me panties.

They were drenched, and Alex's dick throbbed in response. He slid his fingers through her slick curls, his eyes still on the trio at the other table. Jess's hand clamped down on his erection when he slid a finger over her clit, but she didn't take her eyes from their own private show either. Alex had to grit his teeth to keep from groaning out loud.

The men sat back, straightening the woman's clothes just before the waiter came to take their orders. After the waiter left the table, the man on the left murmured in the woman's ear. Her eyes flew open, and Alex saw the tablecloth rustle. When it settled, he could just see the woman's feet spread wide, intertwined with each man's closest foot. Her palms lay flat on the table.

He nudged Jess's clit again and leaned closer so he could whisper in her ear. "See her shoes? They're holding her legs apart. Do you think one of them, or both of them, are doing this to her?" With those words, he slid two fingers inside Jess's warmth. Before she could cry out, he captured her lips in a kiss. It backfired on him, though, because her taste was as heady as the wine she'd had with dinner.

Jess's thighs clamped over his hand as he stroked in and out, teasing her. Her hands dropped to her side, grabbing the chair as if it were a lifeline. A small noise from the other table made them break their kiss and look over. The woman was trembling, her lip caught between her teeth as she teetered on the edge of completion.

Jess was close, too, but Alex made a rash decision that was echoed by the men across the floor. He withdrew his fingers before she could come, and her eyes flew to his.

Blushing furiously, Jess grabbed his tie and pulled him close. "Why did you stop?" she growled, her voice trembling with pure need. "I was almost there."

"I know." He stroked her cheek with a knuckle. "But I'm a jealous man, and I told you last week that I don't want to share. No one gets to see you orgasm but me. Those men obviously feel the same about their woman. Look."

Flabbergasted was the only word he could use to describe Jessica's face as she took in the same frustration on the other woman's face. And he would've laughed, if he wasn't in agony and on the verge of blue balls. Instead, he calmly called for the check. And hoped like hell they'd hurry with it, so he could take his wife back to their room and finish what they'd started.

A few minutes later, with nothing more than a nodding goodbye to his partners in sensual crime, he and Jessica left the restaurant.

Chapter Eight

The cool air felt good on Jess's hot skin as she and Alex walked back to the inn, hand in hand. Her heart still pounded, and her mind wouldn't stop playing that scene over and over again. Before they reached the wide front steps of the bed and breakfast, she pulled Alex to a stop. "Did that really just happen?"

He laughed softly. "Yeah, I think so. You okay with it?"

She thought for a moment. "It was sexy as hell."

"Which part?" Alex asked, a rakish grin on his face. "Watching a threesome in action? Or me fucking you with my fingers in public?"

His words prickled her skin and sent a rush of heat to her core.

"Both," she admitted. Her voice sounded husky even to her own ears. She bit her lip. "Do you think there's something wrong with me, that I was turned on by watching a threesome, and that I almost came in the middle of a restaurant filled with people?" Without any warning, her deepest, darkest fear bubbled up and burst from her mouth. "You never answered me last week, Alex. Is what I want disgusting?"

He frowned. "Babe, there's not a damned thing wrong with you or what you want." He lifted her hand and kissed her palm. "And I'm going to prove it to you this weekend." One tug by his hand had them at the foot of the inn's stairs. "Come on. Let's go check out our room."

On the left side of the inn's foyer there was a large yet intimate sitting room the owner had said was for guest use. Comfortable chairs were grouped around small tables, bookcases lined one wall, and leather sofas sat directly across from each of the two fireplaces. On the right side was a dining room.

"Can we look around for a minute?" Jess asked. She knew Alex was ready to go upstairs and finish what they'd started at the restaurant, and so was she, but she also wanted to slow things down a bit so she could savor every moment, big and small.

Alex put his hand on her back and guided her forward. "Your wish is my command, sweets." If he was frustrated by her request, he hid it well.

There was another couple at the far end of the dimly lit room, seated on the sofa. They were engrossed in each other, so Jess didn't interrupt by saying hello. Instead, she turned her attention to the large bookcases, which looked like they contained antique books.

"This room is gorgeous," she whispered, feeling like she had to be quiet. Some of the shelves held small pieces of framed pen-and-ink drawings. She bent to look at them, then gasped.

"What?" Alex asked, looking up from the book he'd picked up.

"Look at this," she hissed. She held out one that depicted a nude woman bound hand and foot, and waited for him to say something. Anything.

He smiled wickedly. "Interesting choice of artwork." He held out the book. "And reading material."

"The *Kama Sutra?*" Seemed like an odd choice to have out for guests to see in a bed and breakfast, but, then again, what did she know?

Shrugging it off, she continued around the room, looking at the different art objects. Some were suggestive, or maybe it was just her brain that was all wrapped up in sex.

"Excuse me," she murmured as they walked past the seated couple, but she nearly tripped over her own feet as she caught sight of the woman, her shirt open, her breasts bound by rope. The man sitting near her held a small flogger.

Alex steadied her and whispered nearly silently in her ear from behind. "Keep going. Let's not interrupt them."

He kept her moving, straight out of the room. As he propelled her forward, she glanced back over her shoulder, catching a long enough glimpse to see the woman's mouth open in a silent, wide O as the man teased her nipples with the fringed ends of the flogger. Alex guided her up the stairs, not stopping until they were in their room.

She whirled around the second they were inside with the door closed. "Alex, what the hell is—" She was cut off by his mouth on hers.

He pushed her back against the door, his body pressed hard against hers. His mouth devoured hers, nipping the corners of her lips, stroking her tongue with his. She whimpered at the dominance of it, loving the way he took control. When he slid his fingers through her hair and angled her head the way he wanted it, she whimpered again, drowning in sensation. The kiss went on forever, but was over far too soon.

When he pulled back, they were both breathing hard, and Alex's eyes were diamond bright. "What the hell is this?" he repeated raggedly. "*This* is proof for you that there's not a damn thing wrong with what you want."

Her own voice was none too steady. "What?"

He grabbed her hand and led her toward the bed. He clicked on a small lamp on the bedside table, and she gasped at what the soft light revealed.

"Oh. My. God," she whispered, bumping backward into him. It was the first book's cover come to life. A wrought iron four-poster bed, with thick white bed linens. A silky black scarf, tied like a blindfold, at the foot of the bed. One of Alex's ties looped around each of the four bed posts.

She shivered, and her hands shook as he lowered the zipper of her dress, sliding his hands inside the open material to cup her breasts. He nuzzled her neck, then licked a path down her spine, stopping where the zipper ended, just above her ass.

Then he stepped back. "Turn around."

She looked over her shoulder first and was nearly bowled over by the hard look of need on his face. She turned slowly, never taking her eyes from his face.

He smiled then, rakish and sexy and sweet all at once. "Take off that dress."

Her heart stuttered as she slid the strap off one shoulder, then another. It dropped past her hips, pooling on the floor in a puddle of black material. For a quick moment, she worried about her body. Here she stood in front of her husband in nothing but a sheer bra, a pair of lacy crotchless panties, a garter and stockings, and heels. Her body wasn't perfect, and she wasn't twenty anymore. She'd had two kids, she had the hips to show for it, and she probably looked ridiculous.

But when she lifted her gaze from the floor, she saw nothing but raw desire on Alex's face. High color lit his cheeks, and his breathing was rough. He was as aroused by this as she was.

"My God, you're gorgeous." His eyes met hers, and then his face got serious. "Turn around. And put your hands behind your back."

Oh, sweet Jesus. Jess's heart nearly stopped as he picked up the scarf from the foot of the bed. But instead of using it on her eyes, he used it to tie her hands together. They rested just above the edge of her panties, and the ends of the scarf trailed teasingly between her thighs.

There was a rustle of clothing being removed, and then Alex crowded her from behind until the front of her legs pressed up against the bed. "Spread your legs and bend over," he said thickly. One large, hot hand pressed between her shoulders, pushing her forward. "Now."

Her heart pounded, and the thrill that ran through her at the dark demand in his voice made her lightheaded as she did what he ordered.

Alex's lips coasted along her spine, his tongue trailing moist and warm along the same path. "I do like these naughty panties. Sexy as hell."

His hands slid to her hips, cupping her ass as he used his thumbs to open her cheeks and bare her most intimate parts to his eyes. He dipped his fingers into her swollen, drenched sheath, stroking her, preparing her body.

"Is *this* where you want me, Jess?" he asked darkly, pressing a wet thumb against her anus. "Is this what you're worried I'll find disgusting?"

She whimpered, drowning in the incredible sensations of nerve endings sparked to life. "Yes."

He pressed harder with his thumb, and she whimpered again.

"You're tight, love. Have you ever played with yourself

there?" His voice was low, demanding, in control. Dominant. Sexy as all get out. "Answer me. And I want the honest truth."

A thrill chased through her, even as she balked at answering. "Or what?"

"Or else I'll stop." He laughed knowingly and lightened the pressure of his thumb.

No. She didn't want that, so she pressed back against him, trying to force his finger deeper, but he kept his pressure light. Desperation won out over embarrassment. "I tried once," she panted. "It made me come, but I felt dirty after, like I shouldn't have done it."

"You don't want me to stop." He growled the words, pushed his thumb deep inside her ass. "Whether you think it's dirty or not, you want this."

She moaned in pure pleasure. "Oh, God, yes," she cried. "I don't care. More, please."

"So much time." He stroked in and out with his thumb, steadily, driving her insane. "We've still got so much time tonight to do all the things you want to do. You want me to fill your ass with my cock, don't you?"

"Now," she begged. When he slid his thumb out, she tossed her head back and forth, crying out at the loss of sensation.

His voice deepened even more. "God, babe. I love it when you beg. But I'm too primed right now to go easy, so I'm going to fuck your pussy instead, and you're going to take it hard and fast, aren't you?"

Without any further warning, he slid his penis into her, his balls slapping against her clit. His hold on her hips was tight, and it was intoxicating. He pulled out, all the way, and dipped his fingers inside her, then plunged his penis in again. The heat of one of Alex's hands warmed her back, made her feel like she was under his control, and the next time he stroked in and out, he slid his thumb back in her ass. Then he slammed into her again, and again, filling her in both holes.

"More," she begged, nearly mindless with the need to come. The sensation of being filled in both places was like nothing she'd ever felt before. Goosebumps raised on her sweat-slickened body. She came with a keening cry, arching her back, nearly coming off the bed as her body spasmed. Having her arms bound behind her only added to the unbelievable experience. Her orgasm went on, and on, and on, turning her muscles to jelly.

Alex panted with need as he slid his thumb free, swallowing at the way her ass grabbed at it, as if it didn't want to let the sensations go. God, it would be so easy to slide his cock in her ass now, to take her like she wanted. Like he'd wanted to for years, but hadn't ever tried, because he'd always worried she'd find it perverted. Later, though, when he wasn't as worked up as he was right now. When he could be gentle with her for her first time.

Later, tonight.

Right now, though, he needed to finish making love to his wife. He untied her hands, stripped off those fuck-me panties, turned her onto her back, and slid in deep. "Wrap your legs around me," he muttered, all the while stroking in and out of her pussy, slowly at first, then faster. Finesse flew out the window, but he didn't care, couldn't think of anything but making Jess come again. And making himself come with her.

"Look at me, Jessica," he demanded. Jesus, being given free rein to take control was an aphrodisiac like no other. "I want to see your eyes when you come again." He found her clit, and rubbed it while he fucked her. The sounds were lush, earthy, tantalizing in the extreme.

"I can't." She writhed on the bed, tossing her head wildly. "Not again."

"You can." He leaned over her to suck her nipples. "You will." And to make sure of it, he bit lightly on one, tugging it with his teeth.

"Alex!" she cried, flying apart at the seams, taking him to heaven with her.

Moments later, they were sprawled on the bed, gasping for air, both of them covered in sweat, trembling.

"You okay?" Alex asked the question softly, pulling Jess tight against him. "I didn't hurt you?"

"Not in a bad way." Her words were soft puffs of air against his skin. "That was amazing."

"Good." He tucked her head under his chin and wrapped his arms around her. The only noise in the room for the next few minutes was their uneven breathing.

Until Jess spoke, looking up at him with eyes that begged him to tell the truth. "There's nothing wrong with what I want?"

"Not a damn thing." Alex stroked her cheek. "Remember Marcus, the paramedic friend I told you about? He told me about this place. It's not your average B&B."

She laughed lightly, her cheeks pink. "Yeah, I figured that part out when I saw the half-naked woman in the sitting room."

"The owner advertises by word of mouth only. Did you notice there was no sign out front? Nothing to advertise it's an inn?"

She frowned. "I didn't catch that."

He tweaked her nose and grinned. "Some detective you'd make." When she swatted him, he told her the rest. "It's a

B&B that caters to people who prefer a bit of *extreme* in their sexual encounters. The owner calls it Bondage and Breakfast."

Jessica sat up so fast, she elbowed him in the nose. "Are you serious?"

"Babe," he drawled. "Naked lady, bound breasts in the parlor. Erotic art and books on the shelves. Threesome in the attached restaurant. Hello?"

Her face flushed bright red. "Oh. My. God." Then her eyes widened. "And you told Marcus you wanted to bring your wife here? Oh. My. God." She buried her face in her hands.

"Not exactly, but he probably figured it out." Shrugging, he sat up, cupped her chin in his hand. "I wanted to bring you somewhere where you can see that normal people like kinky sex. There's not one single thing wrong with you, Jessica Meyers. Nothing." He punctuated the sentence and sentiment with a hard kiss. "No more worries, no more hiding desires from me. You want to try, you ask. If I'm uncomfortable with something, I'll tell you. Otherwise, we give it a try. Deal?"

Her eyes filled with tears and spilled over. "Deal. I'm so sorry for the last few months, Alex. I was like psycho woman, I know. And I'm sorry I made you think I was having an affair. But when you asked me if I was unfaithful, that's how it felt to me. So I didn't know how to answer."

"I know, honey. I figured that out once you told me about the fantasies. And it wasn't all your fault. I'm so sorry I doubted you. Can you forgive me?"

Jess wiped the tears from her cheeks. "Oh, Alex. There's nothing to forgive. We both made mistakes." She shook her head, sniffed, and turned wide eyes on him. "A sex hotel? Really?"

"If you like, we could join a group session," Alex teased,

Chapter Nine

Jessica's heart nearly stopped, and she felt the flush of red move from her toes to her face.

"Then again, maybe not," he murmured, pulling her so close she saw the flecks of green in his eyes. Eyes that turned even greener as she went with the motion, enjoying the slight pain of the tug. She liked it, and thanks to Alex, she decided to believe there was nothing wrong with her desires.

"Maybe next time," she countered with a smile meant to tease.

"Jessica Marie Meyers, I am shocked." No, Alex didn't look shocked at all. Aroused. Intrigued. Charmed. But definitely *not* shocked. "You should be punished for your wicked, wicked thoughts."

Her inner wanton broke free. "Oh, I hope so."

Alex's eyes burned with amusement and lust. "Later. Right now, I have other plans for you. C'mere." He stood and held out his hand, drawing her to her feet. "How does a hot shower sound?"

Jess swallowed the slight pang of disappointment his words

brought. "Good," she answered, hiding her feelings as best she could. Obviously, it didn't work.

"Liar." He laughed softly. "But trust me. You *won't* be disappointed, if it's as extravagant as Marcus said." He whistled as he stepped into the large bathroom. "Jesus."

"Oh, wow," Jess whispered as she got an eyeful of a glass-enclosed shower stall with eight shower heads at various levels, a spa tub and marble countertops and floors. Live green plants intermixed with white candles on every flat surface. The whole thing combined to create a sensual retreat. "Can we do this to our bathroom? Please?"

Alex snorted. "On a cop's salary? I don't think so, sweetheart. Not unless I go on the take. Would be nice, though." His eyes roamed the room and came back to her. "Now," he said, the huskiness in his voice making a liar out of the stern look on his face. "About that punishment."

Her heart skipped a beat. Or ten.

He turned her so she faced the counter, and met her eyes in the mirror. "Stand with your feet shoulder width apart. Bend over and put your hands flat against the counter. I want to see that pretty ass waiting for my touch. But whatever you do, don't take your eyes off mine."

Jess shivered at Alex's words. Dear God, this was really going to happen. Without breaking their eye contact, she spread her legs, leaned forward and put her hands on the cold marble. The position made her feel vulnerable, and she loved it.

Alex broke eye contact for a minute and sucked in a harsh breath. "Shit, Jess. Do you have any idea what it does to me, watching you do what I tell you to do? Seeing how wet you are, just waiting for my next move? I'll tell you what it does. It makes my cock hard as steel."

Jess's eyes broke from Alex's as she tried to see what he described. He stroked his cock once, twice, and Jess wished it was her hand. Then she remembered the rules, but before she could shift her eyes back, Alex's hand landed on her bare bottom with a loud *thwack*. She gasped at the sting, but didn't get a chance to process it before Alex spanked her again, this time on the other cheek. By the time he hit her for the third time, the slight pain turned to raw pleasure that made her senses reel. She locked eyes with him again and began to beg, not caring how it sounded. "Oh, God. Do that again."

Alex's eyes flared brightly and he spanked her four times in rapid succession.

Her knees nearly buckled under her. "It feels so good," she moaned. "Whenever I read a scene where the man spanks the woman, I wondered how it felt. When we made love and you came into me from behind, and your body hit mine, I fantasized you were spanking me. But I never imagined it would feel *this* good for real."

He turned her around quickly and devoured her mouth, swallowing her cries as her now-sensitive skin made contact with the cold marble. "Jesus, Jess. I want you so bad, it hurts. But I'm not done with your punishment yet. You broke eye contact with me when I told you not to. So now, you need to wait. First, we'll get that shower we both need."

Jess wanted to scream in frustration, but she was the one who'd asked him to play this game. When he stepped away from her to turn on the shower, she dropped to her knees and bowed her head. "Yes, sir."

He whirled back around and cursed. "You're going to kill me, I swear." He fisted a hand in her hair and drew her head back. "Open," he demanded, guiding his penis to her lips.

"Take all of me. Keep your hands behind your back and lean on your heels so you can feel the burn from my hand."

Oh, Jess loved this part, she did. She opened wide, using her tongue to lick his length before taking him inside. She sat back on her heels, gasping as they pushed against her tender rear. Alex took that opportunity to plunge inside her mouth, deeper than he ever had before. He'd always held part of himself back, but not tonight. She gagged once, but he changed the angle and slid deep. It didn't take long before she felt him harden even more, as he always did before he came. Instead of finishing in her mouth, though, he withdrew, covering her breasts with his come.

Alex's body was still shaking with release when rebellion rose in Jessica's eyes, and she brought her hands forward to her lap. Oh, she wasn't getting off *that* easy.

"No way, naughty girl. Into the shower with you," he ordered, his voice still uneven. He held out his hand and helped her to her feet. When they got into the shower, Alex noticed handles hanging from the ceiling. *Sweet.* "Grab hold of those, and don't move."

Jess's eyes darted upward and widened. "Unbelievable," she muttered, but she did as he told her to.

She still had enough slack that her elbows were bent, and Alex thought for a moment. He put his hands on her waist to steady her, and kicked her feet wide, as if he were frisking a suspect. Sometimes, cop know-how came in really handy. He looked at her arms again, and nodded. "Perfect. Now, don't move. And no talking unless I ask you a question." He smiled at Jess's raised eyebrow. "Hey. You're the one who put me in charge."

She rolled her eyes, but she was as into this as he was. Her chest rose and fell with each raspy breath she took.

He picked up the hand-held showerhead and got Jess wet, letting a gentle stream of water trail down her belly and between her legs. Enough to torture, not enough to give her the release she so obviously wanted. She moaned, but didn't speak. He filled his hand with liquid soap, and rinsed every square inch of Jess's delectable body, paying special attention to her tight nipples. He pinched them, and she moaned again. "Oh, you like that, don't you?"

"God, yes," she panted. "More."

He pinched harder, then slid his soapy hands from her breasts and over her stomach, skipping the curls covering the sweetest part of her body. He washed her legs, and then moved behind her and washed her back.

Just thinking about what he was going to do made his cock jerk. He took some more soap, lathered his hands and sank to his knees. "No moving," he reminded her as he rubbed large circles over her still-red ass cheeks. He'd never thought he'd get off on hitting a woman, but Jess had been right. She'd been so aroused by it that he'd been aroused, too. To hear his wife beg for more, and to tell him how she'd fantasized? God. He'd nearly come then and there.

He cupped one hand over her mound from behind, and slid his hand and fingers through slick heat that nearly scorched him. When he pushed two fingers in her pussy, she moaned again. Her body trembled, obviously on the edge of coming. But he didn't want her to come yet, so he stopped.

Jess's head fell forward, and she growled. But that growl turned into a long, needy moan when Alex slid his soap-covered finger down the crack of her ass, playing with the tight bud of her hole. His finger slid easily past the muscle, in and out, and moments later he added another. Jess breathed hard, and her legs trembled, but she didn't protest, and she didn't cry out in pain.

Alex's pulse thundered through his body, but his head was clear. He was aroused but in control. He could take his time and make it good for her. It was time for Jess's biggest fantasy to come true. He slid his fingers free, kissing her hip as she cried out in dismay.

"Shh," he murmured. "We're not done yet. But let's move this to the bedroom."

She was quiet as he toweled her off, and he worried he'd overstepped the boundaries, until he realized she was still following his orders. That was a heady thought, and it punched his gut with satisfaction. He hung up the towel, took her hand, and led her back to the bedroom.

Jessica was one giant bundle of need wrapped up in sensitive nerve endings that covered her entire body. Even her hair seemed sensitized. If Alex didn't let her come soon, she was going to take the reins back, tie him to the bed, and take care of things herself.

Alex drew her to the bed and pulled back the covers. "Lie down on your side, facing the mirror." He placed a fat pillow under her head. "And keep your eyes open."

The bed was angled so she could she could see everything, including the wetness coating her thighs, moisture that came not from the shower but from Alex's dominant words and actions. He climbed into bed behind her, gripped her hips and drew her back, until her body enveloped his erection. This was good—really good—but she wanted so much more tonight. God, she wanted more.

Her brain prodded her with Alex's words from earlier that evening, and she took them to heart. In spite of the fact that she was breaking the no-talking rule, the words tumbled from her mouth. "Please, Alex. This isn't what I want."

He froze, as if he weren't sure what she meant, and withdrew. In the mirror, she saw the confusion on his face ease. "I know, love. You don't want me in your pussy. You want me to fuck your ass." She jerked at the bald words, and again when he leaned up and lightly nipped her shoulder. "I'll let you slide on the no-talking rule for this one. In fact, I'm changing the rules. Talk all you want. I want to hear every thought in your head, every fantasy you've ever had."

Jess met his eyes in the mirror, saw the truth in them. He did want that. Could she possibly love Alex any more right this minute? She didn't think so. She laid her head down on her arm, swallowing the lump in her throat.

She heard a small click and smelled the scent of strawberries. Then she felt Alex's hand between her legs, probing at her anus. She relaxed, pushing against his hand until his finger eased inside. It burned, but oh, it felt good.

"So full, and warm," she whispered. "Give me more." He lifted her leg, bending her knee, giving him greater access to her body, replacing one slick finger with two. "It feels different, but so good." She moved back against his hand. When he twisted his fingers, she gasped. "Oh."

He played with her that way for a while, gently, slowly, allowing her body the chance to adjust. But she was greedy, and she wanted more. "Now, Alex. I'm ready."

"Tell me what you want. Tell me what you're thinking." He moved his hand faster, deeper, and she moaned at the increased sensations flooding her body and muddling her head.

"I *can't* think when you do that," she admitted, her voice shaking and her body trembling on the edge of something new. "But I want your cock in my ass." The words felt awkward on her tongue, but freeing, too, so she said it again, her voice stronger this time. "Fuck my ass, Alex. Please."

He rubbed his cock, already slick with lube, against the ring of muscle he'd loosened with his fingers. She panicked, her heart threatening to explode in her chest. *What the hell was I thinking?* He was big, much bigger than his fingers. He pushed, the head of his cock stretching her, wider than she'd ever been stretched. It hurt, and she whimpered, squeezing her eyes shut.

Alex froze. "You okay?" he asked, his voice tight with tension. "Jesus, you're so tight. It feels like heaven."

"Just go slow," she said shakily. "But please, don't stop."

His fingers tightened on her leg, and he moved in small thrusts, giving her a chance to get used to the feeling. She was sweating, but the pain of this first time was easing. She'd never felt so full before, and she nearly wept with relief. But, God, she needed more. "Come inside me all the way," she begged.

He swore, and then with one long, steady thrust, she felt him sink deep. "Oh," she cried, unable to hold back the tears. "So good. So good."

Alex wrapped his hand around her leg and drew it up. "Look," he ordered, his voice thick with emotion. "Look at us. I'm buried balls deep in your ass, Jessica. You're so hot, so tight, I could come from this alone."

Jess forced her eyes open and nearly came herself from the look of pure bliss on Alex's face as he stared at the way they were joined. Her mind was a jumble of thoughts, but that one stood out over all of them. Right now, at this time, there wasn't a single way he could be faking how he felt about what they were doing. He really was okay with it.

Then he moved, and all thoughts fled.

Nothing was left but feeling as Alex stroked in and nearly

all the way out, slowly, as if he had the rest of his life to do nothing but please her. His harsh breathing puffed against her ear, sending a shiver down her spine, making her toes curl. He slid the hand that held her knee to the juncture of her thighs, and when he rubbed her clit, she couldn't hold back the moan.

"Oh, Alex."

He laughed, but there was a rough, aroused edge to it. "Feel good?"

"Feels great," she breathed.

"Let's see if this feels even better." He dropped her leg and guided her onto her knees, never breaking contact with her body.

Jess grabbed the pillow and tucked it under her chest, resting her head on her arms. She watched in the mirror as Alex slid out of her body, his cock glistening with lube. When he leaned over her back and pressed kisses down her spine, she shivered again. Alex was watching in the mirror, too, and she winked then, giving him a saucy, if shaky, smile.

"What are you waiting for?" she baited him, loving the way his eyes darkened.

It was his turn to grin when he grasped her hips—hard enough to make her bite her lip, but oh, so good—and thrust into her, much deeper than he'd been able to when they lay on their sides.

"Oh, Alex," she cried, her eyes fluttering closed. "Do that again."

He did, either ten times or a hundred or maybe even a thousand. She lost count, drowning in the amazing sensation of his balls slapping against her clit while his cock slid deep into her ass. It was just the added friction she needed, and she came with a long, drawn-out shudder of release. Her heart pounded and her mind went blank.

God. He'd never felt anything quite like this. As Jess came, her muscles contracted around his cock, drawing him to the edge and hurling him over the cliff. His body tensed, and then his cock jerked. He grabbed Jess's hips and held himself tightly against her as he came. Bowed over her back, breathing hard and pulse racing, he wrapped his arm around her waist and pulled them both to their sides, his cock still buried in her ass.

In the mirror, Jess's whole body was flushed red, and her hair was a mess. His face was slick with sweat, and they were both shaking. Shit, they needed another shower, but he didn't want to let her go. His body had other ideas, however, and his softened cock slid from inside her, and she gasped.

"You okay, babe?"

She laughed shakily. "Define *okay.*"

For a second he panicked, but then he caught her gaze in the mirror, and he relaxed.

"I'm better than okay. That was…" She paused, blinked twice. "Amazing. Incredible. And I can't think of any other words right now because my brain is mush." She frowned slightly. "You?"

He swept some of her hair back and kissed her neck. "Another five-star orgasm. I'm going to have to take vitamins if we keep up with this."

She snorted, and he smiled, resting his head against hers. He kissed her nose and settled her closer in his arms. They needed that shower, but damn, he didn't want to let his incredible wife out of his arms. Besides, he still needed to clear up one point with her.

"I have a confession to make," he said. He owed her this much. She'd opened up to him in ways he'd never expected, had given their sedate sex life a welcome jolt.

"What's that?"

"You know the question you almost asked me before we were interrupted last week? Am I disgusted by the thought of anal sex? You have to know by now the answer is no. And honestly? I've wanted to do that for years," he admitted. "I never said anything, because I figured you'd think it was sick, and I didn't want to wreck what we had. I decided I could live without it."

She lifted her head, looked at him with wide, shocked eyes. "Really?"

He gave her a sheepish grin. "Sound familiar?"

She nodded, then laid her head back down against his chest.

Alex rubbed gentle circles on Jess's back. "I'll tell you this. Now that I know the kinds of things you want to try? Try keeping me away. Part of me feels like we've wasted years."

"It wasn't time," Jess countered, realizing just how true her words were. "I needed to think about them by myself, first. I wouldn't have been ready before, but I'm ready now. I'm glad you know how I feel. I don't think I could've kept this hidden much longer. I love you, Alex."

Alex's voice rumbled under her ear. "Me, too. I love you, Jessica." He was starting to sound sleepy. "One of these days, maybe we can try my fantasies. I have this one about the Old West, where I'm the only law in town, and you're the loose woman trying to seduce me into letting her go free after being arrested for being a horse thief."

"Definitely." She caressed the side of his face, listening to the comforting beat of his heart under her ear. It was steady and strong, just like the man himself. God, she loved him. In all the ways she'd imagined this playing out over the past three months, never once had she imagined Alex wholeheartedly jumping into her forbidden fantasies with both feet.

His breathing evened out, and she could tell he'd fallen

asleep. She was exhausted, too, not just from their evening, but from the strain of the past several months.

She'd been worried about how he'd react, but she'd been so wrong. Instead of making her feel perverted, he made her feel sexy for wanting to act out her fantasies. Instead of living with unspoken desires, they'd opened a whole new, exciting chapter in their lives. Instead of ruining their marriage, they'd made it stronger. Jess closed her eyes and settled deeper against her husband, drifting toward sleep.

She couldn't wait to see what tomorrow would bring.

★ ★ ★ ★ ★

Welcome to Mavericks. Live out your wildest fantasies
in the place where anything goes. Treat yourself
to a return trip to the carnal club with the rest of the
titles in Christine d'Abo's Long Shots series,
available now!

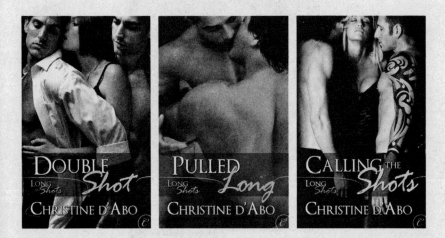

Connect with us for info on our weekly new releases,
access to exclusive offers and much more!

Visit **CarinaPress.com**

We like you—why not like us?
Facebook.com/CarinaPress

Follow us on Twitter: **Twitter.com/CarinaPress**

CPDABO1112TR

In the mood for more Bondage & Breakfast?
Indulge yourself with the next installment in the sexy
series, where a five-alarm hot firefighter submits
to a sexy-as-sin librarian!

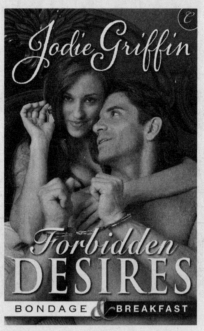

Available November 19, 2012

Connect with us for info on our weekly new releases,
access to exclusive offers and much more!

Visit **CarinaPress.com**

We like you—why not like us?
Facebook.com/CarinaPress

Follow us on Twitter: **Twitter.com/CarinaPress**

CPBB1112TR

Introducing a brand-new,
highly acclaimed trilogy from

TIFFANY REISZ

Nora Sutherlin is an erotica writer by day and a
Dominatrix by night. With a nymphomaniac Frenchman
for a boss, a stuffy Englishman for an editor and an
all-American college boy for a roommate, the only thing
wilder than Nora's fiction is the truth. And don't even ask
who she's sleeping with....

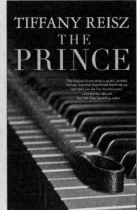

Available Now.   Available Now.   Available Nov. 20, 2012.

www.Harlequin.com

MTRTRII1212TR

THE BESTSELLING AUTHOR OF *DIRTY* AND *TEMPTED*

MEGAN HART

Tesla Martin is drifting pleasantly through life, slinging lattes at Morningstar Mocha, happily devoted to her cadre of regulars. But none of the bottomless-cup crowd compares with Meredith, an irresistible, charismatic force of nature.

Caught in Meredith's sensual orbit, inexpressibly flattered by her intoxicating attention, Tesla holds nothing back. Nothing Meredith proposes seems impossible—not even sleeping with her husband, Charlie, while she looks on.

In a heartbeat, vulnerable Tesla is swept into a willing and spectacular love triangle. Gentle, grounded Charlie and sparkling, maddening Meredith are everything Tesla has ever needed, wanted or even dreamed of, even if no one else on earth understands.

But soon one of the vertices begins pulling away until only two points remain—and the space between them gapes with confusion, with grief and with possibility…

Available wherever
books are sold.

www.Harlequin.com

MMH1308TRR